THE RUSSIAN RUN

Volume 3
PLANETS SHAKEN

Lee W. Brainard

Soothkeep Press

This book is a work of fiction. Apart from several mere mentions of actual people, the characters are fictitious. Any resemblance to people living or dead is purely coincidental.

If perchance my conception of events—geopolitical, political, astronomical, or prophetic—proves to be uncannily close to what actually transpires, let it be known beforehand that I do not have access to inside information, nor do I have the ability and wherewithal to hack into computers storing classified information, nor am I a prophet who enjoys special communication from God. The scenario portrayed is just an educated guess based on various factors: biblical prophecy, geopolitical trends, historical precedent, ancient history, ancient cosmology, electric universe cosmology, and a fertile imagination.

© 2021 by Lee W. Brainard
Soothkeep Press

Cover design: Bespoke Book Covers, Bedfordshire, UK
Formatting: Polgarus Studio

1

FEMA 286, Syracuse, NY
Tuesday, October 22, 2019

Jack was shivering. Though he had only been in the sewer for sixteen minutes, the chill had already gone bone-deep. *Gonna have to wear an extra layer next time.* He considered crawling faster so he could warm himself, but he resisted the temptation. *Pace yourself. Don't break a sweat. One mile per hour is the plan ... about four minutes per football field.*

When he reached the tee that he had expected to find, the stench almost took his breath away. *Lovely. The entire southern business park must flow through here.* He steeled himself and pushed around the corner to his right, only to face an even worse obstacle. The fetid water was four inches deeper than it had been in the line he had just exited. *Bugger! Gonna have to shorten my gate, or this slop is gonna go down my gloves.*

Several dozen yards down the line, when he was just getting into a new rhythm, an out-of-place sound raised the hair on the back of his neck. He froze and cocked his ear. Something was moving in front of him, splashing and scratching on the concrete. Something way too big to be a rat. Despite his jitters, he continued forward. He couldn't afford to lose any precious time.

Twenty feet in front of him, two gleaming orbs of green appeared, followed by a snarl. His pulse spiked. A confused raccoon, startled by his lantern, turned away from him, then turned back again and began slogging its way toward him, growling and hissing, only its head and back out of the water.

Jack pinned himself against the right side of the sewer line as the terrified creature lumbered past him on his left, brushing his side. A wave of relief washed over him, and he chuckled at the absurdity. *A stinkin' raccoon in the sewer. Nobody's gonna believe me.*

When his pounding pulse slowed, he continued plodding forward. After what seemed like an eternity, he stopped to rest his knees, which were throbbing with pain. He checked his watch. *Forty-six minutes so far on this stretch plus the original twenty-one ... comes to sixty-seven minutes. Nuts! Only three minutes left till I have to turn around.* With a sigh, he pushed forward on his wretched journey.

Nine minutes later, well past his turn-around time, with his heart as heavy as lead, Jack resigned himself to failure. With a huff he whirled around, banged his head against the wall, and knocked his headlamp off, plunging himself into blackness. Cautiously, he turned back, groping in the sewage for his light. A faint glimmer caught his attention out of the corner of his eye. Craning his neck sideways, he peered down the dark tunnel. It was the exit. A rush of relief flooded his soul. *Thank you, Lord!*

As he turned around to face the opening, his hand brushed against his headlamp. He fished it out of the sewage, wiped the slime off the lense with a paper towel, and placed it back on his head. Then he turned the lamp off and continued his crawl. He didn't want to give himself away in the unlikely event that someone was near the exit. One mistake like that, and their escape plans were toast.

It took him a few minutes to adapt to the darkness. The sewer had been creepy enough, but negotiating it without light took the eeriness to a whole new level. He had no idea what was in front of him or where he was placing his hands and knees.

Gradually the glimmer loomed larger until he was able to discern the individual bars of the grate. Two minutes later, he placed his hands on the rusty cover and stared longingly at the world outside. It was a bittersweet moment, granting him both a taste of freedom and a reminder that he was a convict—though he had never been convicted of any real crime.

The surroundings were as he had anticipated. Thick trees and shrubs ringed the pond. He couldn't see the fence which surrounded the pond nor the gate at the end of the access road, both of which were visible from his spy loft in the north warehouse. But he knew they were off to his left. When he and Sally would make their getaway, they would climb over the gate and follow the access road to the highway. He estimated it was about a hundred and fifty yards from the pond to the highway. From there they would make their way to the storage yard of Sonny's Salvage and

Recycling, then continue across the field to Jiffy.

He turned his attention downward and stared numbly at the drop to the pond. He guessed it was six feet. *Sally's not gonna like that. A nasty drop into ice-cold water in the winter.*

The grate was even more discouraging than the drop. It was a heavy beast, three-quarters of an inch thick, with ten vertical bars and eight horizontal. Each needed to be cut on both ends, so there were thirty-six cuts between him and freedom. That was doable, but it would be tedious and exhausting. All he had was a mini hacksaw.

He didn't hear any human sounds—not traffic, not industry, not voices. That was a good thing. All he could hear were dogs barking in the distance, the breeze in the trees, and the sewage tumbling from the pipe into the pond. He closed his eyes and visualized himself in the wilderness, sitting around a campfire. The barking dogs became, for a moment, howling coyotes. The splash of sewage became a stream tumbling down a steep valley.

His wandering thoughts were interrupted by a deep, reverberating chugging sound, which sent a shot of adrenaline coursing through his body. He considered the potential sources and relaxed. *Probably just the pump that moves the sewage to the treatment system.*

The last item on his mental checklist was the time factor. This too was frustrating. It had taken him eighty-two minutes to crawl from the manhole to the grate. That meant the round trip would take two hours and forty-five minutes. Plus, he figured he would need a half hour at minimum for making his cuts. That came to three and a quarter hours total. Plus, he needed a hot shower when he came out. *Gonna have to start earlier, crawl faster, and work harder.*

His mission accomplished, Jack turned his weary, chilled body around and began the long slog back to a hot shower and hot coffee. As his mind wandered in day-dreamy anticipations of a steaming mug of heaven's elixir, he recalled the bitter-cold nights he had endured in the Safed Koh range in Afghanistan, nursing canteen cups of piping-hot instant coffee. A feeble smile spread across his face. It's amazing how good crap tastes when you're cold and desperate for a cup of joe.

At the intersection, hampered by the fog of exhaustion and a cold-numbed brain, he struggled to remember which direction he was supposed to turn. He replayed his inbound trip several times before it dawned on him that straight couldn't be right because he had turned on the way in. Left had to be right. Fighting waves of panic—which threatened to resist the omnipotence of logic—he forced his tired, aching body to turn left. *The only battle now is to keep moving.*

Twenty-five minutes later, he placed his cold, stiff hands on the ladder, but he couldn't grip the rungs. His fingers only half curled. Ignoring the hindrance, he pulled himself up rung by rung with a herculean effort, until both of his quivering legs were on the bottom rung. Then he began a painful climb, his frigid limbs complaining every step of the way.

When he finally appeared on the ladder in the manhole, Sally broke into tears, grabbed the shivering man, and helped him climb out of the hole. "I was worried sick when you didn't show up on schedule. I thought you had suffered a heart attack or something. You were down there for two hours and fifty-seven minutes, which is thirty-seven minutes beyond your stated return time. I had decided that if you weren't back in three hours, I was going to notify the camp director. You showed up with three minutes to spare."

Jack looked at her blankly as if he couldn't believe what he was hearing.

"What!" she said defiantly. "I couldn't just leave you down there. Better to go to jail with you alive than go to jail with you dead."

The weary man eked out a weak smile. "Can we blubber later? I need to get out of these wet clothes and into a hot shower."

"Sure," Sally replied, laughing at his dry humor and handing him a hot mug of coffee. "Did you see any dragons or alligators?"

"No," he answered as he hobbled around the corner of the wall of pallets to change his clothes. "But I did see a raccoon."

"I saw him too," Sally bantered back, thinking he was jesting. "He climbed up the ladder, said *bonjour*, and asked for directions to the nearest exit."

"No. I'm serious," he replied. "I don't know how he got down there, but I startled him, and he scurried past me and disappeared into the darkness."

Sally rolled her eyeballs.

When Jack returned, wearing sweat pants and a sweatshirt,

he was shivering miserably. Sally grabbed his bag of sewer clothes, took him by the arm, and led the weary warrior to the emergency shower in the maintenance area. They had decided to use it instead of the shower room so they wouldn't draw attention to their escape efforts. She was chattering about something, but Jack's mind was elsewhere—trying to sip his piping hot coffee while walking in a cold-stiffened body.

When they reached the small shower room in the corner of the shop, Sally opened the door, pushed him in, and set his towel and dry clothes on the bench. "You take your shower. I'll put your sewer clothes in the washer. Don't dally. We're cutting it close for curfew." She closed the door, and her footsteps shuffled away.

Jack kicked off his slippers, tossed his sweats next to his towel and clothes, stepped into the stall, and turned the water on as hot as he could handle it.

As the soothing streams warmed his body, he contemplated their situation. What had happened to America? How could astronomers like Sally and NASA employees like himself wind up in a FEMA camp simply for being aware of a danger that threatened the world? That was the million-dollar question. He knew the simple answer. The government didn't want chaos to break out when everyone began frantically preparing for the apocalypse. But he wanted to understand it on a deeper level. Why had they chosen a cover-up instead of a controlled release? Why not level with the public but control the flow of goods and encourage industry to boost the production of stuff that everyone would need?

He shook his head and sighed in frustration. Somewhere along the line, Washington had lost its way. Right rarely meant morally right anymore. It usually meant the path of profit or expediency. In this instance, the government had taken an expedient path. It was much easier for them to look out for the welfare of a select group than the entire population.

At least he and Sally had a reasonable hope of escape from 286. The effort would cost him twelve more trips into the sewer to cut the bars, where he would have to deal with the bone-chilling cold and the aching joints and muscles. But that was a small price to pay for freedom. If everything came together as planned, they would be leaving this rat hole in December or January.

2

the Compound
Tuesday, October 22, 2019

Irina hammered the heavy bag with a flurry of punches and kicks, imagining that she was giving Dr. Goldblum his comeuppance. After two minutes of intense action, she embraced the bag and leaned on it, breathing hard, sweat pouring off her forehead and stinging her eyes. Andy smiled and gave her a thumbs up. She walked over to her chair, yanked her towel off the back, mopped the sweat off her brow, and slumped into the chair, exhausted but jubilant.

The boys had been skeptical that she could handle special-ops fitness and martial arts training. Yet here she was. Contrary to their anticipations, she had proven to be such a natural—intuitive and quick, with a surprising force in her kicks and punches—that they had nicknamed her Nikita after the female assassin in the television series. But the impressive ground she had made over the past three weeks was only possible because she had diligently maintained her ballet regimen over the years. The fitness, nimbleness, and balance that she had developed while pursuing her passion carried over well into Krav Maga and Systema Spetsnaz training.

As she chugged a half bottle of sports drink, her mind drifted back to where this had all started three weeks earlier. She and Ariele had been sitting on the corral fence near the barn, gazing at the starry skies over the pasture and reminiscing about their days at Caltech—before the Rogue, the Minoa cover-up, and their troubles with the feds. After chattering for fifteen minutes, Irina had confided that she was hurt that she hadn't been selected to be part of the Russia team. Ariele had encouraged her to be assertive, step out of her comfort zone, and pursue being on the team if that's what she wanted. She had talked to the boys that very night. To her surprise, they had admitted that her skills in the culture and language would be a huge help. And they had agreed to give her a shot. But they would only go to bat for her if she trained hard and proved up to the challenge.

"Back to work, slacker," Tony razzed. "Hit the heavy bag for another five minutes, practicing your punches and kicks. Then we'll work on your form for blocks and throws."

Irina snapped out of her daydreamy drift into the past, gave him one of her I-wanna-kill-you looks, tossed her towel onto the back of the chair, and stalked over to the bag. Now she was going to take out her aggression on Tony.

3

the Compound
Tuesday, October 22, 2019

Ariele poked at her biscuits and gravy. She should have been in the garden already. Her partner, Joby, had left ten minutes earlier. But she didn't feel like going to work. She wanted to go back to bed and hide from the world.

Betsy, who had made a Southern breakfast for the lodge crew, interrupted her brooding. "What's up, hon'? You'd think the sun just set for the last time."

A faint smile creased Ariele's face. She appreciated the Southern belle. Her arsenal of one-liners, delivered with a mild Southern accent, was a frequent source of wisdom and motivation. As usual, her analysis was spot on. She probably was blowing her problem out of proportion.

"It's a guy thing," Betsy prodded. "Isn't it?"

The younger woman nodded. "I'm not sure what I should do. Irina gave me some good advice several weeks ago, but I haven't found the right time to follow up on it."

"Fear never sees the right time or opportunity. As Proverbs says, 'there's a lion in the streets.'"

Ariele nodded again. The observation was not lost on her. It was hitting a little too close to home.

"Advice doesn't do any good if you don't implement it. What did she tell you to do?"

"She told me to ask him if he would study the Bible with me."

"So what are you waiting for? Go ask him. You can't lose. If he's interested, you gain a relationship. If he isn't, you still gain clarity."

A few minutes later, Joby leaned on his digging fork and watched the cute redhead approach. Her trepidation evaporated when she saw his broad grin. He bent over, picked up a whopping spud about eight inches long, and hoisted it for her to see.

"Wow!" she exclaimed. "I've never seen a potato that big."

"Yeah," he replied. "Potatoes can get way bigger than the ones you buy at the supermarket. The commercial operations sort out the undersized and oversized potatoes before they sell for table stock." He went back to work, forked up another hill, and put his finds in a garden cart. On his advice, they had left the potatoes in the ground for a month after die-off to harden them up for winter storage. Today, was the first day of harvest for the russets. Later in the week, they would dig up the whites and reds.

Ariele stopped at the gate and watched Joby work. When he realized that he was being observed, he turned his head, their eyes met, and his circuits overloaded. He was captivated by her emerald-green eyes, her strawberry-blonde locks, her perky personality, her laugh, her smile, her everything. The power she had over him reminded him of a verse in Proverbs, 'Three things are too amazing for me, the way of an eagle in the sky, the way of a ship at sea, and the way the way of a man with a maiden.'

She pushed the gate open and strode over to him, determined to take their relationship to the next level. "Say, Joby," she said as she approached him. "You've been reading the New Testament and the Tanakh a lot lately. What do you think about the idea that Yeshua is the Mashiach?"

Heart in his throat, he replied, "There's not a doubt in my mind that Yeshua is the promised Mashiach. The evidence in the Tanakh is so vast that it's mind-boggling. Over a hundred prophecies were fulfilled in his life from his birth to his death on the cross."

Her eyes widened in amazement. "So, when did you first believe on Yeshua?"

"I started pondering him this past summer, but I didn't surrender to him with my whole heart until after the Backstrom boys and I had broken Irina out of FEMA 286. That experience changed me. I prayed more in those days than I did the rest of my prior life."

"So, what kind of evidence in the Tanakh points to Yeshua?"

He leaned on his digging fork. "One of my favorite passages is Isaiah 53:3-6, 'He is despised and rejected by men. A man of sorrows and acquainted with grief. We hid our faces from him. He was despised, and we did not esteem him. Surely, he has borne our griefs and carried our sorrows.

Yet we esteemed him stricken, smitten by God, and afflicted. But he was wounded for our transgressions and bruised for our iniquities. The chastisement for our peace was laid upon him. And by his stripes we are healed. All we like sheep have gone astray. We have turned everyone to his own way. And the Lord has laid on Him the iniquity of us all.' This passage is not a description of the nation of Israel suffering for the world as many of the rabbis like to say. It's a description of a lone man suffering for God's people that they might have their sins and iniquities forgiven."

The passage rattled Ariele. The idea that Mashiach had died and the idea that mankind needed someone to die for them were both hard to digest. "I thought Mashiach would deliver us," she replied, "not die as some sort of pacifist. And … are we … I mean, all of mankind … really that bad?"

"Mashiach will certainly deliver Israel in the last days from all of her enemies. That's clearly stated in many prophecies, and Scripture cannot be broken. But his first concern is delivering us from our wrongdoings. And, yes, we really are that bad. Isaiah the prophet says that our righteous deeds are like used tampons in God's eyes."

She bristled at this inditement of her character, yet something in the challenging message beckoned her. "I guess I need to look into these things myself, get to the bottom of this whole Mashiach issue. But I don't know where to start. I was raised a secular Jew, but lately, I've had a growing desire to know the God of Abraham, Issac, and Jacob."

"Good for you," he replied. "Jesus is not the end of

Judaism in the sense of throwing it away. He is the end of Judaism in the sense of its goal. The law, the prophets, and the writings all point to him, and they are all fulfilled in him."

She stepped a little closer to him, pushing the boundaries of his personal space. "I was wondering if you would study the Bible with me?"

His heart began to race. "I'd love to. When would you like to get together?"

"I don't know. Saturday evening, maybe?"

"That'll work for me. How about seven o'clock in the Hallelujah Tavern? We can use the material from my online rabbinical course. Maybe we could start with *Yeshua the Mashiach*."

"Sounds good to me. Bring your guitar too."

Joby grinned. "Will do."

Ariele decided to retreat before she melted down. She grabbed a garden fork from the small shed by the gate, turned her back to him, stepped the tines into the soil, pried the soil up, exposed a half dozen spuds, and stepped her fork down again.

Joby watched the mesmerizing female, her locks bobbing around her shoulders as she worked, feeling like he had won the lottery. His mother believed in soul mates. Maybe she was right after all.

4

the Compound
Tuesday, October 22, 2019

"All right then," Jordy declared. "Let's move on to the telescope project. Does anyone have any leads on sensors in Russia?" He looked at Woody. The grizzled veteran shook his head. He turned his gaze to Andrius, and the young man hung his head in shame. Admitting to failure was more painful for him than death. Without looking up, he replied in a halting manner, "I'm sorry. My efforts on the dark web have flatlined. I'm an unknown entity to them. They don't trust me. Honestly, I'm beginning to suspect that I don't have the ability to pull off the acting that would be necessary for me to gain credibility.

"On top of that, the more I poke around, the more it seems like the rooms I'm trying to make connections in are a poor fit for our mission. They're hangouts for small players trafficking in small amounts of regional-strain marijuana, foreign-sourced prescription drugs, and stolen consumer items like phones and laptops. There doesn't appear to be any higher-tier activity like banned technology or gun-running. So even if I do somehow gain a connection, it would still be a longshot that they would be able to help us obtain the sensors."

"No worries, Andrius," Jordy consoled him. "Thanks for the effort." He turned to his boys.

Andy frowned. "Our contacts in Russia have also proven to be a dead-end. Despite their big talk and their help in the past in procuring Russian equipment that we needed, it turns out that they're just small-time players who deal in small quantities of military equipment. They suggested that we contact one of the major syndicates—like Solntsevskaya Bratva in Moscow—which dominate the markets for military arms and banned technology.

"When I asked them to contact the Solntsevskaya family for us, they declined. They avoid the big syndicates. It's way too easy to get on their wrong side and disappear."

"Sounds risky to me," Jordy stated.

"It is risky. But if we can find a way to connect with them, bring hard cold cash to the table, and avoid doing anything stupid, they'll do business with us. But making contact with them ... well, that's the rub. They won't deal with anyone they don't trust. That means we need a contact who already has their confidence."

"Looks like we're back to the drawing board," Red declared.

"Definitely a belly flop," Jordy agreed. "Maybe we need to rethink the Russian connection. It's a dangerous idea, and I've been uncomfortable with it from the very beginning. Maybe we can find another source that involves less risk."

Tony, who had been silent up to this point, interjected. "There really isn't another way. Several weeks of pursuing connections on both sides of the Atlantic point to Russia as our only real option. If we want the mirror, we need to deal with the Russian mafia and have them help us with the logistics. While we could conceivably have them import the sensors for us—for a price—the only way to get the mirror is to have it shipped to an address in Russia and try to smuggle it back ourselves. There isn't one chance in a million that we could pull off a scheme to have the mirror shipped to us in the states. Only registered astronomical organizations are allowed to have mirrors larger than hobby size shipped to the US."

"Finding yourself on the wrong side of the mafia isn't the only risk involved," Woody countered. "You would also be risking prison time in Russia for illegal entry and black-market activity. Need I tell you that the accommodations in Federal Penitentiary Service prisons make our federal prisons look tame. And the mafia does what it wants in them with impunity.

"On top of that, if you managed to make it out of Russia with the goods, you'd still be facing federal charges here if you were caught with the mirror and sensors. You'd be charged as terrorists under the Homeland Security Act and shipped to a FEMA camp.

"In either scenario, you could wind up spending the rest of your life in an ugly hole."

Andy jumped back into the fray. "We are fully aware of the risks. But we aren't worried. This mission needs to be done, and we are prepared to carry it out. We've been on dangerous missions before, including a couple in Russia. This one is manageable provided we bring plenty of baksheesh to the table, have the right tools, and put some serious effort into the terminology and slang we need to know."

Woody looked at Jordy, and the two of them looked at Red. After a round of shoulder shrugging, Jordy skirted the subject. "Well, we can revisit black-market connections in Russia at a later time. For now, let's talk about our plans for ordering the mirror and getting that massive unit out of Russia. Anyone come up with any good ideas?"

Ariele noticed Andrius biting his lip, which implied that he had something that he wanted to say. She jabbed her elbow into his side. "Speak up, dude!"

He cleared his throat. "We need to set up a cover company in Moscow with a landline and a professional secretary. The company will also need a website presence, a funded bank account, and a cover story, like an observatory project in Siberia. Irina should have a secure phone dedicated to the company. And she should have proficiency in Russian astronomy and business terminology so she sounds like a consummate professional.

"Not to mention, we should order the mirror as soon as possible, because it might take months for the order to be filled. We might even want to consider ponying up for a rush order."

Jordy was curious. "So, how do we go about setting up a business in Russia?"

"That won't be hard at all," Tony noted, "if we actually

make contact with the Russian mafia. They have decades of experience with setting up business fronts."

Woody wasn't satisfied. "We're not merely setting up a phony office. We need access to a dock where the mirror can be shipped and, if necessary, stored for a while."

"True," Tony replied. "But if we can't obtain an office location in a building with a loading dock, then all we have to do is connect with a shipping company in Moscow that will receive the mirror for us."

"That might work," Jordy responded. "But what's your plan for getting it from the loading dock back to the States?"

"Load it on a box truck or a military surplus truck, drive across Russia on the Trans Siberian Highway to Skovorodino, then go north on the Lena Highway to Yakutsk, then take the Kolyma Highway east to Magadan on the Sea of Okhost."

"What if it's winter?"

"It probably will be winter. We'll just have to deal with it. At least we won't have to fight mud and mosquitoes."

"How long do you think the drive will take?"

"I'm guessing a month. We'll be facing winter road conditions, and we'll likely have to hole up a few times for bad weather."

"What's your plan once you get to Magadan?"

"Hire a fishing boat to take us to a rendezvous location on the Maritime Boundary Line somewhere north of the Donut Hole, where we'll connect with an American fishing boat and transfer the mirror."

Woody raised his eyebrows. "So, where are you going to

find a fishing boat captain willing to risk his livelihood and freedom for a piece of glass?"

Tony smiled. "Andy and I have an old friend who lives in Alaska and fishes pollack in the Bering Sea."

"And he'd be willing to help with the project?"

"Not a doubt in my mind. He's a prepper who has long believed that we're going to face serious problems in the future from both the heavens and our government. The last time I talked to him, he was furious over the Rogue cover-up."

"So you've had recent contact with him?"

"Yes. He called a few weeks back and vented on the subject, unaware that we were already aware."

"Okay. So what's your plan after the rendezvous in the Bering Sea?"

"Our friend will take us back to Alaska, then down the Inside Passage to Puget Sound where he'll unload us and the mirror at some secluded location. At that point, we requisition a box truck and make the two-day drive back to the Compound."

Woody nodded. "Okay. You've sold me. That's a workable plan. Good enough, at any rate, to get the ball rolling."

Everyone started talking at once, asking questions and offering suggestions. Jordy grabbed a small bronze bronco from the mantel and used it as a gavel to rap his podium. Silence fell upon the room. "Raise your hand if you're in favor of adopting the plan Tony outlined as our operational plan." Everyone's hand went up. "Then the plan is officially adopted." He turned to his sons. "You two do whatever is necessary to make this happen—mafia contacts, travel, purchases."

"I'll cover the expenses," Red volunteered.

"Now that we got that settled," Jordy suggested, "let's move on to the Louisiana trip."

"Not so fast!" A voice insisted. All eyes turned to Andy.

"There's still one item of business regarding the Russia trip that we need to address."

His father looked at him, puzzled. "What's that?"

"Tony and I think Irina belongs on the Russia team. Her expertise in the language and culture is essential if we want the mission to have the highest possible odds of success."

Jordy glanced around the room, fishing for moral support from the other men. Red, Woody, and Blake shook their heads slightly, encouraging him to stick to his guns. He turned back to Andy. "There's no doubt that her language skills would be useful, but we already considered this matter at length, and we vetoed her inclusion. She doesn't have the toughness or skill set needed for the mission."

Tony spoke up. "There's a long history of females in such elite organizations as Russia's SVR and Israel's Mossad who have faced danger and hardship."

"We're aware that Russia and Israel have employed female agents in their foreign intelligence services," Woody retorted. "But we're skeptical that Irina has what it takes to follow in their footsteps."

"We were too," Tony spat back. "But we changed our minds."

All eyes in the room were fixed on him.

"We have been training her, and she has surprised us. She's in way better shape than we anticipated—chalk that up to years of ballet. All that fancy-pants ballet stuff—balancing, skipping, kicking, and spinning—gave her a great head start for martial arts. She has amazing speed and coordination."

Jordy met Irina's eyes. She spoke quietly but firmly. "I really want to go. I can be an asset to the team. I've been training hard, and I'm willing to do whatever I have to."

Uncertain what to say, Jordy turned to Woody. "What do you think?"

The former Green Beret hesitated. He didn't like the idea of encouraging her to endanger her life. But he disliked saddling her with an artificial restraint even more. He eyed the boys. Their subtle nods and steady gaze indicated that they were firmly in her camp. He turned to Irina. Her eyes were filled with resolve. He exhaled. This was as much a turning point for him as it was for her.

He turned back to Jordy. "I think she should be allowed to go," he replied in her defense, "provided that Andy and Tony are satisfied when mission time comes that she's able to do her job competently."

Jordy relented. "All right, then. If you special operations vets are comfortable with this, I can go along with it." Scanning the entire group, he asked, "Does anyone have any objections?" Nobody spoke up. "So be it. Irina, tentatively speaking, is part of the Russia Team."

Tony winked at Irina, and tears of joy welled up in the corners of her eyes.

Jordy moved the meeting along. "Let's move on to the Louisiana mission. Does anyone have any updates?"

"I've been in contact with Lobo, the cowboy I met on the train, who has contact with Burt," Woody replied. "He says that if we want the two sensors that Burt has in his possession down in Atchafalaya Swamp, we had better get on it right away. They're first-come, first-served. He's not gonna hold them for anyone. Not even for an old friend.

"He also warned that whoever goes down there needs to exercise caution. Federal agents and mysterious men in plainclothes have been prowling the communities on the edge of the swamp, asking folks if they have seen any suspicious figures or activity and offering rewards for information that leads to the arrest of Homeland Security fugitives or the locals who are assisting them. Thankfully, the folks in the rural areas don't trust the government and generally give the agents and the plainclothesmen a cold shoulder.

"When I told Lobo that we planned on sending a team down to get the sensors, he asked me to hold off for a few weeks. He won't be available to guide them into the swamp until late November. After he guides his last elk-hunting party into the Beartooth Wilderness and makes his annual snowshoe trip to Rock Island Lake with his boss for some ice fishing, he'll hop the train and head south for the winter.

"Contrary to Lobo's expectations, Burt agreed to meet the girls in person. This was partly in deference to our long friendship, partly because he looked forward to talking shop with a fellow astronomer, and partly because he wanted to meet one of the astronomers involved in the discovery of the Rogue."

Sam interrupted. "How are the logistics going to work?"

"The plan is for the girls to call Lobo around noon on Thursday, November 21 from Effie, which is about halfway down Louisiana. At that time he'll give them further directions, including where they'll spend the night, and where and when they'll rendezvous the next morning. Once they meet up, he'll drive them to a private cabin with swamp access, get them situated with a canoe, and guide them to an isolated platform deep in the swamp. There he'll leave them to wait for Rat, who will be their guide the rest of the way."

Sam interrupted. "Why doesn't Mr. Secret Agent Cowboy just send us the directions to Burt's place?"

"Because he doesn't know how to get there. He has never been there."

"Okay. So why not have him give us directions to the platform?"

"Two reasons. First of all, you would never find it on your own. You would get lost in the swamp. Secondly, he has the wendigo that you need to meet with Rat. No wendigo, no Rat. And if you don't meet with Rat, you don't meet with Burt."

"What in the world is a wendigo?" Ariele asked.

"I've got no idea," Woody replied, shrugging his shoulders. "When I asked Lobo about it, he just laughed and said that they'll have to see it to understand. All I know is that it's a secret sign. If Rat doesn't see Lobo's wendigo in its perch in the tree, he won't meet up with the Louisiana team and take them to Burt."

After several more minutes of discussion on the girls' rendezvous and canoe trip into the swamp with Lobo, Jordy moved on.

"The next item on the agenda tonight is specialized equipment. I'll start with the new phones." He held up a sleek-looking black unit. Red picked up a dozen of these Solarin secure phones—the most secure phones on the planet. Made in Israel. Military-grade security. NSA proof. Work anywhere on the planet. Starting immediately, these are our new commo units. If you were issued a Blackphone, turn it in after the meeting and pick up your new phone.

"I have also made arrangements with an optometrist in the Rogue Underground who can source sunglasses for us that hinder facial-recognition technology. Those of you going on missions need to get your prescriptions to me. If you don't wear glasses, you'll receive plain versions. Get this info to me as soon as possible. You can't leave here without this technology.

"Any questions on anything we covered tonight?" He scanned the room. "No? Then we'll move on to the final order of business. Donuts and hot chocolate are in the kitchen."

5

the Compound
Tuesday, October 22, 2019

Woody woke up startled, and sat up in his bed, adrenalin flowing and his heart racing, but uncertain why. After ten seconds of daze, his dream came back to him with a jolt. It had been about Ghost, the stone-cold transporter who had picked him up deep in the Sierras and dropped him off at Truckee so he could hop the train.

In his dream he had met Ghost at the pier which was shrouded in a mysterious bank of fog and gloom, and the transporter had insisted that they take a walk together. In the mysterious way that dreams work, the pier morphed into an unknown neighborhood and then morphed again into Red Square. Woody was having a hard time keeping up with Ghost, and his fears were growing every minute. He hustled after him through the crowds, trying not to attract the attention of the Federal Security Service agents that were everywhere. When he finally caught up to him, the transporter was talking to a member of the mafia in front of St. Basil's Cathedral. The man fixed Woody with a cold stare, reached into his coat, and retrieved a package, exposing what appeared to be an SR-1 Vector, a particularly deadly handgun with armor-piercing capabilities. As Woody reached out his hand, the man glared at him, drew back the package, and stuck out his other hand, palm up, apparently demanding payment. That was the end of the dream, or at least as much as he could remember.

He laid his head back down on his pillow, his heart still racing, and turned the scenes over in his mind. Why did he dream about Ghost and meeting someone in Red Square for a package? Was this merely his subconscious mind playing on his fears? Or was this a hint from God that Ghost was their way out of their dilemma? He decided the matter could wait till morning. He picked up the notebook that he kept by his bedstand, jotted down his dream, checked the clock—it was 2:27—and laid his head back on his pillow.

But after spending the next hour tossing and turning, and trying various tricks to fall asleep like counting sheep and rolling his eyes backward in his head, he tossed his blankets aside in frustration and hopped out of bed. *Nuts. Not gonna happen.* There was no going back to sleep. His mind was fixated on Ghost and the potential for contacts in the Russian mafia who may be able to help them.

He stepped into his moosehide slippers, pulled on his Woolrich bathrobe, wandered out to the kitchen, and made himself a peanut butter and banana sandwich, which he wolfed down with a glass of milk. Then he settled into his favorite chair, a brown leather recliner near the fireplace, and picked up the latest edition of *Fly Fisherman* magazine. The second article was a story on fly fishing for grayling in Siberia. *Russia again? Seems like an unusual coincidence.* He was fascinated to discover that there were seven species of grayling in that vast wilderness—one with razor-sharp teeth. That was enough to make any fly fisherman drool. He devoured the article, then flipped through the rest of the magazine. After sifting through the magazines and books on the end table, he settled on his next read, a boring tome that Jordy had recommended on the religious, ethnic, and political complexities of the Middle East. Halfway through the first chapter, his eyes got droopy. Then he was out.

***

Woody was awakened the next morning at 6:35 by rustling in the kitchen. He heard the distinct sound of a cast iron fry pan getting set down vigorously on the stovetop. *Must be the A-team.* He rose from his chair, stretched his stiff back, cracked his neck, and made a beeline for his room to fetch his clothes and shaving kit. As he passed the kitchen entry, he saw, as he had expected, Ariele and Andrius bustling about, preparing breakfast.

"You're dressed to the nines, Old Timer!" the perky gal quipped. "Are you going to the opera?"

He cracked a wry grin as he lumbered past.

As he dragged his razor across his face, he pondered his dream and warmed to the idea that Ghost might be able to help them make a connection with the Russian mafia. While lounging in the shower, the conviction gelled that he should pursue the Ghost avenue without delay. He snapped the water off and hastily dressed.

"Add six to the breakfast plans," he instructed as he burst into the kitchen.

Ariele furrowed her eyebrows. "You're not serious, are you?"

"Dead serious," he called over his shoulder as he strode to the old-school phone that hung on the wall between the dining room and the great room. "Got an idea for the sensors. We need to have an urgent planning meeting over breakfast." He picked up the handset and dialed Jordy.

The pastor answered on the eighth ring.

"Hey, Jordy! Can you and Beth join us for breakfast at the lodge? I've got a plan for contacting the Russian mafia, and I want to run it past you, Red, and the boys."

"Yea. No problem. We'll be there in half an hour."

He started to dial the Backstrom boys and hung the handset back up. *Bet they're on a run.* He pulled out his new secure phone and called Andy. The young buck answered, breathing hard. "We're in the middle of a run, bud. Can I call you back?"

"Nope. You two cut your run short, get a quick shower, and hustle over to the lodge for a 7:30 breakfast."

"Okey dokey, Top. We'll be there."

He holstered his phone, picked up the handset again, and dialed Red. Betsy answered.

"Hey, Bets. Is Red handy?"

"He's just sitting down for toast and cereal."

"Tell him not to bother. You two need to join us at the lodge. I have an idea for getting sensors that we need to discuss ASAP."

"I'll let him know, Woody."

Over eggs, hashbrowns, and bacon, Woody told the assembled crew about his dream and his plan for contacting the transporter.

Red grinned mischievously. "Contacting Ghost again? Are you sure you want to do that? As I recall, you said you never wanted to have anything to do with him again. Or any part of the underworld for that matter."

"I did say that. And I still feel the same way. But necessity trumps feelings. We need sensors, and we need a way to order and receive a mirror. That means we need to somehow gain a connection in the Russian underground. There's a half-decent chance that Ghost can provide us with that. That means that I ought to call him again—though the thought is as distasteful as spoiled spam."

"Score another one," Red teased, "for the old adage that we should never say never."

"No doubt," Woody chuckled. "I've learned that a dozen times over and still haven't learned."

"Do you still have his number?"

"Yeah. I never deleted it."

Jordy interrupted. "Why do you think that he might be able to help?"

"Because he's an independent contractor who transports illegal goods like drugs and guns. That implies that he probably has a pretty broad network of underworld clients."

Tony spoke up. "I agree with Woody's assessment. The Ghost option is definitely worth following up. Based on intel we were privy to when working with the DEA and the CIA, the Russians have significantly expanded their West Coast operations over the past five years. They're heavily involved in drug running and arms trafficking. So the odds are pretty good, if Ghost has been in the transporting business for a while, that he either has connections in the Russian underworld, or he has business associates that do."

"The plan sounds good in theory," Jordy replied. "But what if the feds have flipped him? That would be the end for you."

Woody nodded. "I understand your concern, but I'm not worried."

"Why not?"

"Because the feds have bigger fish to fry than small-time players in the underworld. Right now, they're focused on the Rogue-aware folks they accuse of the soft-terrorism malarkey."

"I know that's largely the case, but what if law enforcement for some reason or another is stepping on him?"

"The job needs to be done. I'm willing to do it. And I'm not gonna worry about low-probability contingencies."

Jordy relented. "Okay. Count me in. If you're willing to take the risk, the potential upside is significant."

Later that morning, Woody climbed the hill behind the lodge, took a seat on a log underneath a chattering squirrel, and called Ghost. He was forwarded to voice mail, which he had expected, and read his prepared message. "This is Tenkara. You picked me up in the Sierras last June and dropped me off near Truckee. I need a connection in the Russian underground who can procure banned infrared technology and provide a business front in Moscow. This job pays twenty-five thousand in cash—half upfront for a name and number and the other half if the connection proves legit. I'm not ponying up for mere talk. I need results. Call me back within forty-eight hours if you're interested."

As he hung up, a wave of foreboding challenged the wisdom of the course. He shrugged his shoulders. What could he do? There was almost always inner conflict in the line of duty. He stood up, rubbed his aching hip, which hadn't yet fully recovered from his ordeal in June, and headed back down. Almost immediately, a magpie intersected his path and flew in front of him. Though he didn't believe the old superstition that seeing a lone specimen meant bad luck or misfortune, he still shuddered.

***

The next afternoon shortly after two, while Woody was perched on a ladder helping Red install a window on Jordy's new home, his secure phone rang, startling him. Balancing the slider with one hand, he fished his phone out of his sweatshirt pocket with the other. Then he made several awkward swipes with his thumb before he managed to answer.

"Tenkara."

"Hi, Tinker. I might be interested in the job. What kind of tech and what kind of business front are you looking for?"

"We need several sensors for an infrared telescope. And we need a real office space in Moscow with an actual secretary, a loading dock, and a storage cage."

"I'll make a few phone calls. But they'll cost you five grand even if I'm unsuccessful. I hate dealing with the Bratva."

"Understood."

"I'll call you to set a date, time, and place for the transfer. You bring the cash. I'll bring the information … or maybe not."

"Okay—" Woody started to reply, but a beep informed him that the transporter had once again hung up abruptly.

***

Sunday afternoon under an overcast sky, Woody was drifting an emerging-Baetis pattern on the woodsy stretch of Sweet Grass Creek on the ranch property, the only stretch he dared to fish because it gave him ready access to the woods if he heard aircraft or drones overhead. The browns were cooperating as they often do in the late fall. He had already netted three, including a fat nineteen incher. As he moved upstream to position himself for the next pool, his burner vibrated. He headed for the tree line while reaching for his phone.

"Tenkara."

"Hi, Tinker. A contact put me in touch with a brigadier in Atlanta. He assured me that his boss knows the operation in Moscow and that the Moscow pakhan will be able to meet all of your requirements. He owns a suitable building with a loading dock and storage cages. He has connections that can obtain the infrared sensors. And he has ladies available with secretarial skills."

"Good. Can we meet this week?"

"Thursday. Same pier. Be on-site an hour before sunrise. Stand where you stood before except this time you'll be fishing. I'll walk up, set my tackle box down next to yours, lean over the rail like we're making small talk, and ask to borrow a smoke. After a few minutes, I'll pick up your tackle box and go my merry way. In my tackle box you'll find a pill bottle containing a folded note with the contact info. There will be twenty-five thousand in your tackle box."

"Twenty-five? I was expecting seventeen thousand five hundred."

"I'm not gouging you, Tinker. On top of the fifty percent down and the upfront fee for dealing with the Bratva, other expenses came up. The Atlanta contact charged me five thousand for the information, and the nosy Russian agent looking over his shoulder demanded hush money. Just so you know, the SVR takes a cut from all Bratva activity in America. Every deal comes with a premium."

"No problem," Woody replied. "It is what it is. Guess you got to feed the hungry dogs."

A muffled snorty laugh erupted on the other end of the line, but it was quickly squelched. "Especially the big dogs," Ghost noted. He segued into his instructions. "The money will be in twenties, banded in stacks of fifty. The twenty-five stacks will be in a zippered nylon or cloth bag."

"No problem."

"The tacklebox will be a Plano 5300 3-Tray. The zipper bag will be in the bottom."

"Gotcha."

"Same conditions as last time. You must come alone. No friends. No dogs. If I don't like what I see, I don't show my face."

"Can I come with a driver?"

"Nope. No new faces. The more people involved, the messier things get. I hate messy. Messy means trouble."

Woody wasn't sure how to respond. *Gonna have to push my luck.* "I need a driver. I won't go into the details, but I prefer to keep my face off traffic or security cameras."

Ghost snorted. "Looking for illegal tech and avoiding cameras. Are you one of the fugitive terrorists that the feds are looking for? There's some big money in that market. How do you know I won't turn you in for a big reward?"

Woody's heart skipped a beat, but he figured that the transporter's remark was probably dry humor with a dose of intimidation. "Not one chance in a million," he cooly replied.

"What makes you so certain?" the young man challenged.

"In the big picture, a federal reward is small potatoes compared to the cash flow from your business. You wouldn't risk that income stream for a one-time whistleblowing transaction that your business associates would regard as a serious breach of trust."

"What if I didn't care anymore because I was getting out of the business and retiring in someplace like Bermuda?" Ghost threatened.

"Your old associates would still care. They wouldn't overlook it. Honor is honor, and a breach of honor is a breach of honor."

"Hmm," Ghost replied in a tone suggesting respect. "Okay. Your friend can come. But he must park with the nose of the vehicle away from both the pier and the entryway, and he must not get out of his vehicle. I don't want him to see me or my car."

"Done."

"What kind of vehicle will you come in?"

"Does it matter?"

"Not really."

"I'll be there."

Like usual, Ghost just disappeared.

As he slogged back to the lodge in his waders, the cold drizzle starting to drip off the pines and Douglas fir, Woody brooded over the impending trip. Dealing with Ghost again didn't stress him as much as he had feared it would. But the thought of going on an extended trip to a progressive part of the country did rattle him. Getting caught meant detainment in a FEMA camp. While he wasn't worried about spending time in one himself, the fact that he was putting his friends at risk, Blake for certain and possibly the entire crew, was a crushing load. *I'm gonna need your help on this one God. This is way beyond my pay grade.*

6

the Compound
Wednesday, October 23, 2019

Jordy scanned the array of computers, monitors, servers, and routers that lined the small room, shaking his head in wonder. "This gives off an aura like the operations center at Langley." He turned to Andrius. "Thanks! I couldn't have done this myself. Computer stuff is beyond me."

"You're welcome, pastor," the young man replied. "Glad to help. But hardware and networking aren't really that difficult. You just need to connect the right wires to the right equipment."

Jordy chuckled. "Oh, it's definitely easy. There are only a few dozen pieces of equipment, a hundred wires, and tons of connections. I could have done it with my eyes closed, but I wanted to throw you a bone."

Andrius smiled sheepishly. He knew hardware and networking were intimidating to most people, and he liked being the smartest guy in the room.

Jordy reached out and touched the heavy-gauge wire mesh that lined the entire room. "Why is the room set up like a big cage?"

"Because it is a big cage—a Faraday cage. It shields electrical equipment from electromagnetic pulses, which are usually referred to as EMPs."

"Like bursts from the sun?"

"Exactly. Coronal mass ejections from the sun, CMEs for short, are the most dangerous source. That's why they're a common theme in apocalyptic films. But they're not the only source."

"What are some other sources that we could conceivably face?"

"A lightning strike. An electrostatic discharge on the electrical grid. A nuclear warhead detonated in the atmosphere. A non-nuclear weapon designed to disrupt or destroy electronic communication."

"How likely are we to face one of these discharge events?"

"I'd say close to a hundred percent over the next decade."

"Which of these threats are you most worried about?"

"If you're talking about the extent of damage, my biggest worries are coronal mass ejections and nuclear weapons detonated in the atmosphere. Either one could wipe out one-third of the country. But if you're talking about the likelihood of damage, my big concern is nonnuclear EMP weapons like microwave bombs, whether wielded by terrorists or by our own government."

"That's a scary thought. The government employing microwave weaponry against their own citizens."

"Sure is. And it's already happening according to insiders who have blown the whistle on the FBI. Federal agents have begun using microwave drones when they raid properties of interest in Security Act matters. They detonate a drone over the property in the cover of night, which destroys all electronic equipment in the vicinity, and then cordon the area off."

Jordy caught the drift. "So no one can see or record what is going on."

"Exactly. They're free to put any spin they want on the raid."

"Well, this is a fascinating subject, and I want to pursue it further, but let's wrap up this tour. I need to meet Red in a few minutes to discuss plumbing and wiring issues in the new house." He pointed to the bank of servers. "I assume that everything that comes into and leaves this room is hidden from prying eyes?"

"Absolutely. All incoming and outgoing traffic is encrypted with TOR. On top of that, it's routed through a deep-web VPN host in Moscow, the same one that Krake used when he set up the *Rogue Underground* platform on Buster."

"Do we have a backup plan?"

"Yes. I set up a mirror-image backup on two deep-web servers in case Buster goes down. The entire system, even your bookmarked websites and study notes, backs up every four hours. If the need arises, you can access a backup system by clicking the system-2 or system-3 icon on your desktop, and within a minute you'll be up and running again.

"On top of that, I set up two backup-VPN-host options that will kick in hierarchically if our main host goes down. So you can rest assured that you're protected against accidents, power outages, system failures, government interference, and hackers."

"How do you plan to mask the traffic from this room?"

"You mean the amount of traffic?"

"Yeah."

"It's already done. I'm hiding it with Red's investing business. Using a few tricks of the trade, I set it up so that this room has the same IP address as his investment office in his home."

"Does he generate enough traffic?"

"He has so much data coming in and going out that the NSA is unlikely to notice anything unusual in his traffic no matter how much information you download or send. I would guess that your traffic will be less than two percent of his overall traffic. So even if the NSA grabbed a dozen random samples, the odds are low that they would notice that some of the traffic is encrypted and routed through Buster, or a VPN, or both."

"I didn't realize he generated that much traffic."

"He has subscriptions to data, research, and news services in the US, Canada, Australia, and Europe so he can monitor the markets. On top of that, he participates in a dark pool for mining and petroleum stocks on the Amex, the Pink Sheets, the London Stock Exchange, the Canadian and Australian exchanges, and a few others. The dark pool gets a lot of traffic from hedge funds and other large institutions."

"Sounds good to me. So what do I need to do to make sure that I follow the security protocols?"

"Nothing. Just point and shoot. Everything you do—both inside and outside the *Rogue Underground* platform—

is encrypted, onion routed with TOR, and routed through the VPN in Moscow."

"So we're secure all the time, not just when logged in to the *Rogue Underground*?"

"Correct."

"That's a relief. This techno-geek stuff goes over my head." He pointed to the left wall. "Tell me about this insane setup with six monitors."

"That's your workstation. The two monitors in the middle on the bottom are for communication, writing, and studying. You can set the others up to display news and prophecy websites."

Jordy pointed again. "What about the two stations on the right wall that each have two monitors?"

"The farthest station is mine. That's where I'll work on back-end stuff, security stuff, and my deep-web and dark-web research. The nearest one is for anyone else who wants to use the internet or access the *Rogue Underground* site."

Jordy nodded approvingly. Andrius had a question of his own. "So what's the latest on the *Down the Rabbit Hole* program?"

"Big speed bump. I finally heard back from Nicholas Flieger, the former producer of the program. The day after the boys broke Irina out of 286, he was visited by FBI agents who questioned him about his friendship with Burrage Krakenhavn and his relationship with the program. He was forced to lay low for the past five weeks. Though it was risky, he borrowed a burner phone and texted me, informing me that he was a liability to the cause. He tendered his resignation, requested that we purge him from the Rogue Runners membership roll, and wished us the best of luck."

"So what are you going to do?"

"Woody and I put up a post on the *Rogue Runners* bulletin board, the *Rogue Underground* website, and the *Down the Rabbit Hole* website, seeking someone to take over production and hosting. We had three requirements. They have to be a real follower of Jesus. They have to speak excellent English. And they have to live in a country that doesn't have close ties with the US."

"Sounds like a plan to me. What's your plan for disseminating the program?"

"Post the video on YouTube and post the link on the *Rogue Underground* website and the *Down the Rabbit Hole* website."

"You're gonna need a better plan than that."

"Do you got a better one?"

"Yeah. Post the link on a series of dark bulletin boards and have Underground volunteers repost it on dozens of video and social media sites. If you do this, they can put up new links and start new channels when existing ones are removed. This will make it nearly impossible to stamp out the *Down the Rabbit Hole* testimony."

"That's a great idea," Jordy said as he checked his watch. "Hey, I gotta run." He shot out his arm and gripped Andrius's hand. "Thanks again for your help. I would have been at sea without you."

"You're welcome. But honestly, I'm just thankful I get to be part of a ministry whose purpose is to share the three most important messages of the hour: Jesus, Bible prophecy, and the Rogue."

"I feel the same way," Jordy replied as he headed for the door.

7

FEMA 286, Syracuse, NY
Saturday, October 26, 2019

As Jack crawled out of the cabinet cart, a jolt surged up and down his back. He winced and shot out his hand to steady himself. While waiting for the searing pain to abate, he massaged his tender hips and knees. Despite several days of rest, his joints and back still ached from the first foray into the sewer.

A melancholy funk barged its way into the citadel of his heart, and he recoiled at the thought of going down again. Not only did he have to repeat the arduous crawl down and back, he also had to cut through three bars on the grate. But as he had done hundreds of times in his life, both in the SEALs and in the civilian world, he gave his feelings the boot and focused on duty. If they wanted to escape FEMA 286, he had to make another sewer run today and many more after that.

He gingerly stretched his arms, legs, and back, punctuating his efforts with grumblings and groans. Sally teased him. "I recall hearing a tough Navy SEAL guy tell me once how pain was all in the head." He flashed a pretend scowly face, turned away to hide the grin that was spreading across his face, and grabbed his bags of sewer clothes.

"Hey, Jack. Before you disappear around the corner to change into your waders, can you help me unload the cart? This stuff is too heavy for me to get them down by myself."

"Sorry. Completely spaced it. Guess my mind is on the mission."

As he helped her unload a coffee table and two end tables, he retaliated with his own barb. "I gotta hand it to you, Sally. Using a refinishing shop as a cover was a brilliant plan. It smells so bad down here that nobody would want to come within a mile of this place."

She grinned. "I kind of like the smell myself. And the idea was a win-win. You get to do your sewer escape thing, and I get to indulge in a hobby. But I do feel a little conflicted sometimes that my passion is being used as a cover for criminal activity."

"The real guilt lies with the government, not you. They wrongly regarded your noble efforts as criminal activity, and they wrongfully detained you in a FEMA camp." He fell silent for a moment, shook his head, and muttered, "The whole stinkin' country is fouled up beyond repair."

Ten minutes later, Jack descended the ladder into the darkness below. His legs wobbled like jello on the rungs. Not a good start to a demanding journey. The complaints from his battered body intensified when he began his crawl on the concrete. Shockwaves of fire exploded from his knees with every move forward. Then his back, shoulders, and neck knotted up, like burls on a gnarly pine.

Gotta block out the pain. He distracted himself by recalling his favorite memory—the camping trip in the Uintas with Woody, Kit, and Sam. Start to finish, he replayed the highlights, lingering on the scenes that involved the latter. The trick helped, but he was going to need more firepower than that.

He turned to God. *Lord ... strengthen me to press through the wall of pain and see this through to the end ... help Sally and me escape so we can expose the cover-up ... let me see Woody and the girls again.* The prayer seemed to help. Over the next few minutes, the pain slowly subsided into dull ache and numbness.

Several hundred feet past the intersection, something swimming or crawling in the fetid waters brushed against his left calf. Startled, he awkwardly sprang to his right. But whatever it was had a firm grip on his waders and yanked his momentum to a stop like a dog stopped by a leash. He threw his arm out to catch himself and smacked his elbow against the lower part of the wall.

Dazed and nervous, Jack looked back at his attacker but saw nothing ... except a rusty ladder. He slapped the water. *Nuts! I forgot about that.* Somewhere in the sewer's sordid past, the bottom rung of the ladder had partially broken off and twisted around so that it stuck out. Fuming, he crawled back to the snag, freed his wader, grabbed the offending piece of metal, gave it an angry yank toward himself, then bent it back again. He repeated this action several times until it snapped off. Then he hooked the rung on the backside of the ladder where it would be out of the way.

Frustrated at the delay, he hastened toward the grate, trying to make up for the lost time. But he was nagged by the impression that something was wrong. Soon the answer became apparent. Water was seeping into his left wader, and his left foot was soaked and cold. An examination revealed an inch and a half tear above the left ankle. There was nothing he could do about it. He had neither the time nor the means to patch it. *This day just went from ugly to ugly with a vengeance.*

After a few minutes of misery, he contemplated turning around. He wouldn't have blamed anyone else if they had done so under the circumstances. The situation was grave. Hypothermia—even death—was a possibility. And the thought of a hot shower sooner rather than later was tantalizing. But Jack spurned the idea of aborting. Losing even one day of cutting could cost them their escape window. He had to press on. The risks had to be embraced. Comfort could wait.

By the time he arrived at the bars, his foot was so numb that he couldn't feel his toes. With hands shaking and teeth chattering, he dug his mini hacksaw out of his belly pouch and went to work on one of the lower bars. But the blade kept skittering around, and he struggled to get a cut started. After a couple minutes of frustration, the blade finally found a groove. He sawed like a mad man in bursts of fifty strokes with a few seconds of rest between.

Twenty-seven minutes later, the blade burst out the backside of the third bar and his hand slammed into the grate, skinning yet another knuckle. He leaned his head against the grate, dropped his burned-out arms onto his quivering thighs, and prayed. *Thank you for giving me the strength.* He returned the saw to his pouch, retrieved the canister of filler wax that he had concocted—toilet bowl wax, carbon black from the boiler, and iron oxide—and packed the mixture into all three cuts. Then he wiped the excess off the bars with a paper towel and crawled backward a few steps to examine his handiwork. *Not too shabby. Don't think anyone's gonna notice unless they get real close.*

With slow and clumsy movements, Jack turned his stiff body around and began the long crawl back, both thankful for and worried about the numbness that had spread through his body. Before long, he was crawling in drone mode. Then his mind began to drift.

He was laying in the snow, cold and shivering, glassing a house a half mile away, waiting for a Serbian warlord and his men to show. When they did finally show, hours after their anticipated time, he could barely operate the radio because his hands were stiff, and he could barely pass the intel on to headquarters because his teeth were chattering so hard. After he stowed his gear, he crawled two hundred yards through the snow When he was certain that he had dropped far enough over the ridge that he was out of sight, he struggled to his feet and walked seven brutal miles back to his hooch, stumbling over and over again. He sat next to the oil stove, wrapped himself in a space blanket, and sipped hot coffee thickened with hot cocoa mix and sugar. It was an hour before he stopped shivering. His fingers and toes stung for days.

His mind wandered through other dreamy memories of being cold. The Alaskan Range and the Sierras with the SEALs. The mountains of Afghanistan with the CIA. The snow cave adventure in Vermont as a teenager. He was reliving the latter, shivering in wet clothes, draped in a wet sleeping bag, trying to light his stove with wet matches when he noticed a light shining on him. At first it startled him. Then it puzzled him. *Why is there a light in my path?* He hadn't passed a light on the way to the grate. His foggy mind struggled to process the information. He decided to keep moving. *Not gonna let anything keep me from getting back.*

"Jack!" a voice called out.

He stopped.

"Jack. You made it. I was getting worried."

A woman's voice was speaking to him, though it sounded distant, echoey, almost dreamlike. *Am I going crazy? Hallucinating?*

He craned his head upward toward the light and saw a woman's face, framed by a halo of light, looking down at him. Only a ladder stood between him and her. He was confused. *Is this Jacob's ladder? Am I dying? Why does the angel look familiar? Don't really care. Just gonna climb.*

He placed his stiff hands on the highest rung he could reach and—with all four limbs quivering—struggled to his feet. After resting for a moment, he lifted a shaky right leg to the first rung, crooked his left forearm over the next rung up, and began to climb out of the abyss.

Sally, tears streaming down her cheeks, watched the determined man ascend with awkward motions and missteps that resembled a drunk staggering down the street. The arduous process, which took two minutes, seemed like an hour to her. When his waist rose above floor level, he stopped climbing and looked around, trying to figure out his next move. He didn't dare move his feet higher because he had no handholds to balance himself. He stretched out his arms to catch himself and tumbled onto the floor.

Sally, energized with fear and adrenalin, grabbed him by the arms and dragged him out of the hole—a task beyond her unathletic 140-pound frame. Dropping to her knees, she flopped him onto his back, unhooked the suspenders on his waders, scrambled toward his feet, and halted. What should she do first? Cover the manhole or assist Jack? Her heart pleaded for Jack. Reason argued for the manhole. The pain cut a furrow in her heart. She knew Jack would put the mission first, replace the cover, and guard the escape route.

But she couldn't drop the crate yet, not when his feet were less than a foot from the manhole. They would get crushed. Miffed, she seized his right leg and spun him around. Then she frantically pumped the handle to raise the crate and cover combination, maneuvered the unit over the manhole, and dropped it with a clank. *Nuts!* One side of the crate was noticeably higher than the other. She bent down for a look. *Double nuts!* The cover was hanging over the lip by a half inch. Any observant person who walked into the room would notice that the tilted crate wasn't sitting flat on the floor, and that would expose the manhole.

Furious, knowing that she could screw it up three or four more times while Jack lay in a hypothermic state, she jacked the crate back up, jimmied it around, centered it, and squeezed the release handle. This time it clanged into place with a satisfying ring. Now she could attend to Jack and remove his waders.

Jack, still shivering violently, was sitting up and had managed to remove his gloves. But he was trapped in his partially removed jacket, his cold-stiffened arms pinned at his sides. Sally grabbed the sleeves and vigorously jerked them upward, freeing him from his yellow straightjacket. Then she started for his feet, paused, and tousled her hair as she often did when perplexed. Removing the waders while he was sitting down was going to be a bit more difficult. A smile creased her face. *Just like pealing tight rubber gloves off.* She rolled the top a few inches at a time until it reached his waist, yanked it under his backside, and worked it down past his knees. Then she pulled the waders off his feet with a hefty tug, and a cascade of foul-smelling water spilled onto the floor.

The moment he was loose, Jack attempted to stand up but a spasm in his back rebuffed him, leaving him hunched over like an old man crippled with arthritis. Sally rushed to his side, wrapped his arm over her shoulder, and helped him hobble to the maintenance department, a sopping-wet sock dangling off his left foot.

While he sat on an ancient office chair, cradling a mug of hot chocolate, she hunted down a short stepladder, leaned it against the wall of the corrugated steel shower stall so he could steady himself, and turned the water on. When it was hot enough for her taste, she snatched the cup from his hand, pushed him into the dressing room, and pulled the door shut.

He didn't bother to remove his clothes. He just stepped into the torrent, placed his hand on the ladder, and indulged the welcome heat. After fifteen minutes, Sally, who had been pacing like a caged tiger, cracked the door and unloaded on him, "Hurry and finish, Jack! We don't want to break the curfew. You're the one always harping on guarding the mission."

The water stopped. "Sorry, Sal" he called back. "I'm still a bit foggy."

He snarled as he struggled to remove his drenched garments, and as each piece finally came off, he hurled it to the floor, finding twisted delight at the distinctive thwack they made on the concrete floor. But his spirit picked up as he pulled his favorite sweater over his head, an olive-drab Army issue. He savored the musky scent of wool. *Gotta keep things in perspective. Things are gonna get easier. Tonight will likely prove to be the low point of the mission.*

***

The next evening, while Jack and Sally relaxed in his maintenance cage munching on a batch of Cajun-spiced popcorn, she kicked him in the leg. "What's on your mind, Jack? Something's bugging you."

"Just attending the funeral for dashed hopes."

She furrowed her eyebrows and squinted at him.

"I'd been hoping that I might be able to accelerate the timetable by either crawling down the line more often or cutting more bars when I'm down there, but after last night … well … let's just say that I've been forced to face the painful truth that I won't be able to work more than two nights a week or cut more than three bars at a crack."

"So the tough guy actually has his limits?"

He grinned. "My body is crazy sore. I definitely need a few days of rest in between trips. So I'm gonna stick with my original Tuesday and Saturday schedule." He picked up his calendar. "I'll go back down on Tuesday, October 29, on Saturday, November 2, and so forth until the project is finished. If everything goes according to plan, I'll be cutting the last bars on Tuesday, December 3. We can make our escape any time after that. Just need favorable weather."

"Is your body going to hold up?"

"I think so. It should slowly get used to the abuse, so I won't be as sore a month from now as I am today."

"Is there anything you can do differently?"

"Not much. I'm gonna add an extra layer of longjohns and eat more sugar before I go down."

She tucked her legs up on her chair, wrapped her arms around them, leaned her head on them, and smiled mischievously as if she had just won a friendly debate. "To be honest, I never did like the idea of you going down there more than twice a week. I cringed whenever you brought it up."

"Yeah. It was overly ambitious. But fifty-year-old men sometimes have a hard time being reconciled to the fact that they're not thirty anymore."

She laughed. "Yeah. Especially you military types."

He reached into his drawer and pulled out his mission notebook, a yellow legal pad, and flipped to the first open page.

Sally shook her head. "I don't want to talk mission tonight."

"What's up?"

"Now that escape looks like a reality and not merely a daydream, I'm having some sentimental thoughts about this place. I've made good friends here, and I want to spend as much time as possible with them before we vanish without saying goodbye."

"So you want to go to the cafeteria."

She smiled. "I do. I want to play Dutch Blitz, eat outdated cookies, and laugh till my guts hurt."

"Sounds like a *go* to me. But I'm gonna pass on the Dutch Blitz and double down on the cookies."

8

Redondo, CA
Thursday, October 31, 2019

Woody stood on the Redondo Municipal Pier, shivering, trying to skewer a piece of squid on an 0/3 hook. His lightweight jacket did little to protect him from the biting wind blowing in off the sea. He dropped his bait into the choppy waters and let it sink. When his line went slack, he reeled up until it was taut, then he reeled up a little more, leaving his bait a few feet off the bottom.

He wasn't really fishing, though, and he hoped that he wouldn't get a bite. Things were complicated enough already. He glanced at his watch. It was 6:09. *I'm on time. Where's Ghost?* He reached into his pocket—for the third time—to make sure that the open pack of Marlboros was still there. It felt out of place. At least the brand was right. He chuckled at Red's sentiment, expressed when informed of this meeting, "If I had to carry smokes, it would definitely be Marlboros."

A deep voice interrupted his thoughts. "Hey, brah. Can I borrow a smoke?" Ghost set a tackle box down next to his and turned to face him. Woody retrieved his pack of smokes and shook it as he had seen macho guys do, then held it out. The transporter snagged one of the protruding sticks and leaned forward for Woody to give him a light. The old soldier bristled at the demeaning gesture, but held his peace, reached for his lighter—*good thing Red convinced me to carry one*—and lit the cigarette dangling from the younger man's lips.

Ghost leaned on the rail, blew a couple smoke rings, and ignored the man he had come to deal with, who was standing a mere two feet from him. When the cigarette had burned halfway down, he snuffed it out on the railing and tossed the butt into the sea—a careless act which galled Woody. With neither a word nor a nod, he bent down, picked up Woody's tackle box, and walked away.

He watched the transporter fade into the darkness, wondering what mechanisms were at work in such dark souls. He had been just as aloof as before, though not so icy. *Maybe I have a little street cred now?* Thankfully, he wouldn't have to see him again. On Red's suggestion, he had placed the entire fee in the tackle box, not merely the first half. There was some risk in this, but they figured it was worth it. Woody reeled in his line, picked up Ghost's tackle box, and trudged up the pier. In the distance, headlights flashed on in the parking area, spun around, and darted away.

At the table in Blake's camper, Woody opened the tackle box. It was filled with gaudy lures and cheap equipment—perhaps a hundred bucks worth. He rifled through the packages, spools, stringers, pliers, and doodads crammed into the bottom. A glimmer of brown caught his eye. He snatched up the prescription bottle, popped the lid off, fished out the folded and rolled sheet of paper, and spread it out on the table. It wasn't much. A few scrawled lines.

> Contact brigadier Boris Sokolov in Atlanta. His cell is 499-627-5150. He will give you details on when and where to meet. If he feels comfortable, you will meet his pakhan. If the pakhan is satisfied, he will provide a connection in Moscow.

Welcome rays of relief dawned on Woody's soul. It looked like things might actually be going forward. Their pains and efforts had paid off. But fear nipped at the heels of hope. This opportunity would send the boys and Irina into a den of wolves. He wished there were other options. But they didn't have any.

His hand trembling, he picked up his secure phone and called the Atlanta contact.

"Who is this?" a gruff voice answered with a Russian accent.

"Tenkara."

"Ah, yes. Ghost told me you that would be calling. Where did you come up with a stupid name like Tenkara?" The speaker waited for a moment like he expected an answer. When Woody didn't respond, he continued. "What can I do for you?"

"I'm looking for Boris?"

"This is Boris. Who else would answer Boris's phone?

Marilyn Monroe? Mickey Mouse?"

Woody ignored the cutting remark. "We're seeking a connection in Russia who can help us procure infrared sensors for a telescope and set up a business front in Moscow with a physical location and a loading dock so we can order a 60-inch mirror."

"My boss can help you with both … for the right price. But first things first. I took this job on Ghost's recommendation. He said you were from the clean side of the underworld and could be trusted."

"We aren't criminals."

"Of course not," he chuckled, with a throaty rumble. "Now, let me warn you. Don't cross us. We play nice with those who play nice in our sandbox. But if you cause problems, we fix those problems."

"We have no interest in causing trouble. We just want to get the things we need for a telescope."

"You keep saying, *we*. Ghost said nothing about *we* when he contacted me. He only mentioned *you*."

"I hired Ghost to find me a contact who can help with our project. We didn't talk about how few or how many people are associated with me in this project."

"It's a good thing we like Ghost and Ghost likes you. Normally, it's a dealbreaker if folks leave out critical information. But we'll let your mistake slide this time. Just make sure you avoid such mistakes in the future. We like openness, got it?"

"Got it."

"So tell me about your team."

"There are a dozen of us, but you only need to know about the three associates who'll be meeting your guys and taking care of the procurement."

"Before we can proceed, I'll need photos of them. I'll also need a photo of you."

Woody's nerves glowed hot with trepidation. Sending pictures entailed tremendous risk for Irina and the Backstrom boys. But he had no choice. He swallowed hard. "Not a problem. I'll send them to you within the hour."

"Text them to this same number."

"Will do."

The young folks were enjoying breakfast at the lodge, eggs and Betsy's blueberry scones, when Andy's secure phone vibrated in his pocket.

"It's a text from Woody," he announced. "His Bratva contact wants recent photos of all three members of the Russia team, or the deal is a no-go. Theoretically, the photos are only for identification, but Woody suspects that they would not hesitate to use them for blackmail or revenge if we cross them. What do you guys think?"

Tony shrugged his shoulders. "It's risky, but the truth is, we got no other options. I think we should do it."

"I agree," Irina replied. "If we have to send them our pictures to get our mirror and sensors, then we send them our pictures."

"Then it's unanimous," Andy said as he handed his phone to Ariele. She shook her head *no*, but when he continued to hold the phone out, she reluctantly took it from his hand and snapped headshots of all three.

A few minutes later, Andy sent a text to Woody with the photos and a note explaining that Irina might not look exactly like her picture because she would likely be wearing tinted contacts on the mission. Woody forwarded the photos to Boris along with one of himself.

Two hours later, while Blake and Woody were passing through Cajon Junction on US 15 on their way back to Montana, Woody's phone chirped. "This is Boris. The deal is on. Your associates will bring forty thousand dollars in cash: ten thousand for me, twenty-five thousand for the pakhan, and five thousand for the SVR agent. Three bundles. All Jacksons. They will meet my boyeviks Monday evening at 6:30 at the Walmart in Dunwoody on the north side of Atlanta. My men will be in a white utility van under a street light in the southeast corner of the parking lot. Your team will park nearby and join my men in the van. The van will bring them to a meeting with me. On the way my financier will count the cash. If it's all there, things will go well. If it's not all there, things won't go well. I will decide during our visit whether or not you get to see the pakhan."

"What happens to the money if you or the pakhan decides not to meet with us?"

"We'll cross that bridge if and when we get there."

"I don't like that way of doing business. But it's your sandbox."

"Glad you see it my way. Have a nice evening." Woody's phone beeped. The call was over. *The aloofness and coldness must be an underworld thing and not an idiosyncrasy with Ghost.*

He shrugged off the psychology questions and sent Andy an encrypted text, once again thankful for the fully loaded secure phones they were all carrying, courtesy of Red's deep pockets.

> Operator One. Atlanta trip is a go. Procure funds in twenties from the source. Three packages. Ten thousand for brigadier. Twenty-five thousand for pakhan. Five thousand for colluding SVR agent. Meet boyeviks Monday evening at 6:30 at Walmart in Dunwoody under street lamp in southeast corner. Join them in van. Transfer funds. Travel to unknown destination to meet brigadier. He may or may not take you to the pakhan. Keep your heads up. Dangerous situation. Godspeed. Tenkara.

Andy shouted to Irina and Tony who were sparring in the ring. "Hey, you two."

They stopped and looked at him.

"The Atlanta trip is a go. This is gonna be your dry run, Irina. It'll give us a chance to see how well you perform under stress."

She spit out her mouthguard. "Will I be graded go or no-go?"

"Yep."

"Fair enough," she replied. Then she put her mouthpiece back in, touched gloves with Tony, and the two started trading punches again.

Andy watched her smooth, snappy blows. She was

impressive. But he saw something that worried him. Overconfidence. That was not good. Overconfidence breeds carelessness. Carelessness makes mistakes. And mistakes can be costly.

9

Atlanta, Georgia
Monday, November 4, 2019

Andy had jubilantly pumped his arm and shouted "Yass!" when he had received the text from Woody informing him that the Atlanta trip was a go. Now, four and a half days later, his nerves were on edge beyond anything he had experienced during his Ranger and Delta days. On every one of his combat missions, he had enjoyed tactical advantage and superior firepower. Now he had neither.

The three members of the Russia team were in a modified Lexus van—seats along the sides instead of in rows—facing three armed and scowling boyeviks. They had been ordered to sit with their hands in their laps and make no sudden moves. While Andy hadn't expected a warm reception, this was bordering on hostile. And it could get worse. They were heading into the pakhan's lair.

He studied the men sitting across from him and noted that they held their handguns in sul position, ready for action. *Definitely not amateurs.* The scarface across from him cradled a Smith and Wesson 9 mm. The hulky goon across from Tony was armed with a Glock .40. The sadistic grin across from Irina kept massaging the trigger on his Russian Yarygin.

If things went south, they would be in a bleak situation. Nothing was to their advantage. Nor did he see any glaring weaknesses they might be able to exploit. Hopefully, the mafia boss wasn't playing them. Andy recoiled at the dark scenarios and pushed them out of his head. Worrying about the unlikely wasn't going to help the present reality. He needed to stay in the moment. They needed to keep calm, avoid doing anything rash, and let the whole thing play out by the Russians' rules. That was their best bet for coming out unscathed and for completing the mission that they had come to do.

Five minutes into their ride, Tony couldn't take the intimidation any longer and decided to test the Russians. While yawning, he slowly raised his arms and locked them behind his head. The muscular grunt across from him leveled his Glock at his chest, cussed him out in Russian, and yelled, "Hands down! Hands down!" Tony just smiled back—the impish grin that had often disarmed his mother when she had been angry at him.

The barrel-chested man leaped to his feet, took two quick, hunched-over steps, and slammed a massive fist into Tony's chest. The youngest of the Backstrom twins—by three minutes—absorbed the blow without flinching, uttering only a faint grunt, the whole time maintaining eye-lock with his protagonist, grinning like a crazy man. Irina watched his antics with dread. *Has he lost his marbles ... a screw or two come loose?*

The ugly mug in the passenger seat, who had been occupied with counting the money in the bags, turned around to see what the ruckus was all about. He warned the troublemaker, "I recommend that you put your hands back on your lap." Tony didn't comply and continued grinning.

Mr. Ugly tried to enlighten his stubborn passenger. "Gennady, the man you're irritating, is former Spetsnaz. He enjoys hurting people, and he's pretty good at it."

Tony calmly replied, "If he doesn't take his pistol out of my face, I will disarm him and break his arm."

"You're not afraid of getting shot?"

"You won't shoot me in city traffic and risk a run-in with the law."

Mr. Ugly glared at Tony, taken aback by his brashness.

Irina added her own fuel to the fire. She retrieved her lipstick and mirror from her purse and began touching up her lips.

"Hey!" Mr. Ugly barked at her.

She ignored him and blithely offered him some advice. "Tony has a fifth-degree black belt in Krav Maga and black belts in Systema Spetsnaz and Muay Thai. It would be a mistake for Gennady to mess with him." As she checked her lipstick job in her mirror, she noticed that the three goons were confused. *Guess none of them know much English.*

The veins on Gennady's neck started to protrude. He was red with rage. And his pistol was still pointed at Tony.

Mr. Ugly realized that a different tack was needed if he wanted to calm the situation. "Let him be, Gennady," he barked in Russian. "Boris wants him to show up in one piece."

The big man returned to his seat, fuming, played with his Glock for a few seconds, then pointed it at Tony's head and pretended to pull the trigger. Tony winked at him which caused his companions to erupt in laughter. Gennady stewed in humiliated but haughty silence.

Ten minutes later, the van turned down a dark alley and stopped. Tony tensed. The rear door swung open, and the driver motioned for his henchman to exit. Once they were out, he locked eyes with Tony, upping the ante on the psychological warfare. The seconds ticked by. A man in the doorway called out, "Bogdan! The brigadier is waiting!" But the brodyaga, intent on showing his clients who was in charge, ignored him.

He motioned for Andy to exit. When he stepped down, one of the goons took him by the arm and escorted him into the building. Tony watched in silent indignation, clenching and unclenching his fists. When Tony's turn came, Gennady, looking for revenge, grabbed him roughly by the arm, hustled him toward the building at a fast clip, and attempted to walk him into the doorjamb. But Tony—at the last second—turned toward his assailant and slammed his fist into his ribs. Ligaments, cartilage, and bones gave way, and the man bent over in pain. While his head was moving downward, Tony seized it and pulled it forcefully into his rising knee. "Welcome to Muay world," he deadpanned.

The thug crumpled to his knees and fell forward into the entry, and Tony found himself staring down the barrels of several pistols. Before he could respond, Bogdan hollered something in Russian. The men lowered their weapons, and two of them raised Gennady by his arms and led him away, leaving a trail of bloody prints on the floor.

"Hand over your phones," Bogdan ordered, his voice calm but icy. Reluctantly, they logged off of their secure phones and relinquished them. "Now your weapons!" Andy turned over his Sig Sauer P365 and combat knife. Irina dropped her pepper spray into his hand. Tony surrendered his own Sig and a karambit.

Fear placed its clammy hands on Irina. They were in a dimly lit room, surrounded by tough-looking characters, and weaponless. *God ... you need to come through as our shield and defender.*

"Pat them down, Ilya"

A young man stepped forward and motioned for Andy, who coolly spread his legs and held his arms up. The search found nothing. He then signaled for Tony, who barely spread himself. The searcher cleared his right leg and moved to his left leg. His hands stopped on the front side of his hip. Two brutes sprang to secure Tony's arms, and the searcher retrieved a low-profile, quick-draw holster with a Springfield XDM Compact and a micro knife, which he held up for his boss. Bogdan shook his head disapprovingly at Tony. He grinned back. He may have been outnumbered and outgunned, but he was winning the psychological battle.

Ilya nodded to Irina, and she moved forward. "Hands out to the side," he directed. Irina shook her head *no* and stood in determined defiance, eyeball to eyeball. "I want a woman to search me," she demanded. He reached out and tried to force her arms up. Thwack! A hard right on his cheek snapped his head back. The startled man rubbed his jaw and looked to his boss. Bogdan nodded to another grunt. "Bring Tatiana back here."

The young lady performed the patdown without further difficulty, though Irina's glare let her and everyone else know that she resented the intrusion. When her ordeal was finished, she spun around to face Bogdan, and spat, "When do we get our phones and weapons back?"

A smirk creased his face. "After your meeting with the pakhan. Now follow me." He turned and headed down the hallway with Pyotr on his heels. She and the boys obliged. Four or five boyeviks shuffled behind them.

The group turned down another hallway to the right and entered a small, brightly lit room. A shot of adrenalin amped Irina. She was face to face with a sinister character in a white lab coat standing next to a Casper unit and a polygraph. The table on his other side displayed an array of the tools of the interrogation trade—knives, nails, pliers, a blow torch, a car battery, and clamps. She looked away from his hollow stare to his moving hand. He was rolling a short nail between his thumb and forefinger. Dread danced a fiendish waltz in her heart.

Bogdan introduced the sinister character. "Meet Kiril, former instructor on interrogation with the Foreign Intelligence Service." He turned his icy stare upon the boys. They didn't flinch. Andy processed the new information. *Former? Bet he's still an SVR agent, making big bucks on the side collaborating with the Bratva.*

Bogdan pushed Tony toward the chair. He shot the

brodyaga a fierce look, sauntered across the room, and eased himself into place. Kiril strapped him down, connected the blood pressure cuff and the probes for the polygraph, and placed the Casper helmet on his head. Then he turned a few dials and hit a few switches and buttons, and the electronic wizardry hummed to life. Tony looked uneasy as the probes poked into his scalp. He clenched his teeth and gripped the armrests until his knuckles turned white.

Something's not right, Irina realized. She scanned the control panel and noticed that Kiril had set the Casper depth at 1.5 mm. *What a puke-eating monster!* She knew from her own experience that the usual depth setting was 0.6 mm.

What could she do? The team hadn't foreseen this, so they didn't have a plan. *Time to improvise.* She walked up to Tony, patted him on the hand like she was reassuring a child, and said, "It's okay. The nice man won't hurt you. Just tell him the truth, and you'll get a piece of candy when you're done." A pained grin appeared on his face. Andy joined in and did the see-no-evil, hear-no-evil, speak-no-evil mime. Tony's grin became a stifled laugh.

Bogdan fought the smile that was trying to erase his usual hard demeanor. He had seen chutzpah in Russian girls before. But this Ukrainian American was different—in a league of her own.

The boys understood Irina's message, and her counsel resonated with them. Tell the truth no matter what the question was. They would deal with the consequences later. They were caught between a rock and a hard place. To lie meant a painful beating, if not death. Telling the truth meant giving both the Solntsevskaya Bratva and the Russian government leverage against them. But it was too late to back out or change course. The only way out was giving two untrustworthy organizations ammunition that could be against them in the future.

Kiril started with fingerprints and a retinal scan, then went to work on his questioning. "What is your name?"

"Tony Patton Backstrom."

"Anthony?"

"Nope. Plain Tony."

"Where were you born?"

"Harlowton, Montana."

"Did you serve in the military?"

"Yes."

"What was your MOS and training?"

"18-Bravo, 3, Poppa, Victor, Whisky-3, PU."

What units did you serve with?"

"The 2nd Ranger Battalion, the 5th Special Forces, and Delta."

"Special Forces weapons specialist and sniper?"

"Yep."

"Impressive. The Special Forces are the equivalent of Russia's Spetsnaz."

"Nope."

Kiril eyed him in apparent disbelief, then moved on to a series of control questions about his upbringing, political views, education, and general military experience.

When he was satisfied that he had a good baseline, he moved an odd-looking machine over to Tony's right side.

Andy and Irina looked on, confused. The mad practitioner adjusted its arm to throat height, then he picked up a large knife from the table and sliced a piece of paper with it, demonstrating that its edge was razor sharp. With his eyes locked on the hapless young man strapped into the seat, grinning evilly, he locked the knife into a fitting on the end of the arm and maneuvered the unit until the blade touched Tony's throat just above his Adam's apple.

Irina felt light-headed. Andy tapped her lightly with one finger from his hand hanging at his side, attempting to reassure her. She turned to the only strength she had left. *God. Watch over him. Watch over us. Help us out of this mess.*

Kiril plugged a cable into Casper and then plugged the other end into the knife-wielding contraption. Facing Andy and Irina, he patted the machine. "This is our secret weapon. Technically it's known in intelligence as Guillotine 3, or G-3 for short. But we call him Slice. If Casper senses that you're lying, he relays the message to Slice, and Slice does what Slice is designed to do ... fast and efficient. You won't even have time to pray." He put his hands on Tony's shoulders and leaned over toward his ear.

"How long have you been working for the Volkovskaya gang?"

"I don't work for them. Never even heard of them."

"Does the name Yuri Morozov ring a bell."

"No. Never heard of the guy."

"Do you know any Russians or other Slavic peoples with a wolf tattoo on either one of their shoulders?"

"Nope."

"Have you ever done business with anyone who served you Volkov Light Vodka?"

"Nope. Prefer Grey Goose myself."

Disappointed that Tony was telling the truth, Kiril pulled the G-3 unit away from him and grilled him on the whats and whys of their unusual request for high-end telescope components. Tony grudgingly opened up on the Rogue and the Compound in Montana. When the agent was finished with him, he unfastened his restraints and nodded for him to exit the chair. Ignoring the young man's slow departure and glare, he turned to Andy and pointed to the chair.

Kiril subjected him to the same kind of introductory and control questions that he had plied his brother with. Then he wheeled Slice over and repeated his questions on the Volkovskaya gang. When it became obvious that Andy too had zero knowledge of the group, he removed the G-3 unit and asked him a few more questions about their survivalist group in Montana.

When Irina's turn came, her emotions reached the boiling point. Fury glowed on her face, and her hands were trembling. It reminded Andy of the time he had cornered a fox in their henhouse. At first the creature had cowered against the back wall, pacing restlessly, then it had launched itself at him, forcing him to dodge sideways, which gave the creature room to escape. Fight had conquered flight.

"Remove your contacts," the agent directed her as she sat in the chair. "The glare will hinder the retinal scan."

Her shaking hands complicated the effort. Twice she lost

her left contact under her eyelid before she managed to secure it. She gave her contacts to Tony and sat back. *Relax. Breathe. This is just a game.*

But it had become more than a game for Kiril. He cinched her waist, chest, legs, and arms tighter than usual. Then he wheeled Slice over, set it up, and turned it on. Irina trembled as the cold, thin edge of the blade touched her throat. Her pulse quickened. Tears welled in her eyes. Her palms were sweating. She was afraid to swallow, and she needed to. Spittle was building up in her mouth. *God. I'm more scared than I have ever been in my life. Give me strength. Please don't let me cough or choke.*

The boys watched in disbelief. What was the sadistic man up to? Why bring the G-3 unit into the picture for the control questions? When the agent extended the questions for establishing her baseline, Tony began to clench and unclench his fists. When Kiril tarried on the Volkovskaya gang, asking her half again more questions than he had asked the two boys together, Tony's fists were at full tension, like a trebuchet ready to launch its destruction.

When Kiril left the G-3 unit humming at Irina's throat after the Volkovskaya gang section was completed and began asking questions on the comet and the Compound, Tony couldn't take it any longer. He took a step toward the villain. Andy grabbed his arm with a vise-like grip and drew him back.

The agent questioned her extensively about the Compound, the comet, the part she played in the big picture, and their need for a large infrared telescope. He showed her a photograph of Woody and asked if it was Woodrow Lundstrom. He probed her on her education, her crimes against the U.S. government, and her escape from 286.

It had become obvious to the boys what the SVR agent was up to. It had infuriated him that he hadn't been able to intimidate them—inspiring fear was his fetish—so he was upping his efforts with Irina.

During questions on her escape from FEMA 286, Irina's elevated heart rate plummeted, her blood pressure plunged, and her face began to pale. The boys looked at each other and nodded. Kiril was gonna pay for his indiscretion. What he was doing was an unforgivable sin.

The agent, moving with a casual air which suggested that fainting episodes were not unfamiliar territory for him, loosened the straps, tied a length of tubing around her left arm, and gave her an injection. Then he disconnected her from the polygraph and Casper, picked up his clipboard, and jotted a few paragraphs of scribbled notes. When she revived a few minutes later, he released her straps, ending her ordeal.

The agitated female sprang to her feet, wobbled, and steadied herself on the G-3 cart. When the room quit spinning, she shoved the cart out of her way, smashing it into the polygraph cart. Kiril scowled at her. She tossed her hair and marched over to the boys.

Bogdan addressed the team, "You will meet Boris now," and exited the room. The two guards that had stayed with him the entire time filed out after him. Tony hurried right behind them and manned the door. When Kiril attempted to leave the room, he stepped in front of him and blocked his path. The agent stepped to his right, and the angry Backstrom mirrored him. He stepped back to the left, and Tony again mirrored him in a provocative dance.

"Out of my way, big talker," the Russian demanded as he tried to shove Tony out of the way.

Tony seized his arm, drew it down to waist level, pressed his wrist backward, twisted his arm, which spun the man around, pinned his hand behind his back, and smashed his face into the wall. "I'm a nonverbal communicator who prefers to do my talking with my hands." Then he slammed a fist into Kiril's left kidney. The agent grunted. "I think you enjoyed interrogating my associate a little too much."

An imposing figure with salt-and-pepper hair appeared with Bogdan at his side. He placed his massive hand on Tony's shoulder—overlooking the scene that was unfolding—and introduced himself. "I'm Boris. Boris Sokolov."

Tony released his grip on the fuming SVR agent and offered his hand to the gentleman. "I'm Tony. This is Andy. And this is Irina."

Did you enjoy your little ordeal?" he asked, his eyes twinkling and the corners of his mouth turning up slightly.

"Like a lard and cat food sandwich," Irina snarked.

"I can assure you that it wasn't any particular dislike for you three. All of our clients get vetted in more or less the same way before they get to meet any of the brigadiers or the pakhan."

"I have heard good things about you. Bogdan here, one of my brodyagas, informs me that you're exceptional partner material—compliant but unintimidated. Your interactions with his men suggest that this is not your first experience with the Bratva. You seem to know the ropes." He scanned the faces of the boys, looking to gauge their response. But none was forthcoming.

He extended his arms toward Tony and embraced him heartily. Then he pivoted toward Andy and greeted him in the same manner. The boys endured his forwardness. Boris turned his attention to Irina, raised her hand to his lips, and kissed it. "It's a pleasure to do business with you."

"The pleasure is ours," she responded, smiling sweetly, though inside she was recoiling at the syrupy charm that the brigadier was laying on. It seemed artificial and insincere. She recognized the ploy from the reading she had done on the history of the Bratva. *Act like a cultured gentleman while your goons act like barbarians.*

"What do you think of our associate, Kiril?"

"Personally," Tony panned. "I think he would look good with the mark of the Beast on his forehead."

Bogdan and Boris looked at each other, unsure what the American tough was referring to. "Do you mean the mark of the beast, like in the book of Revelation?" Boris asked, his gaze returning to Tony.

"Nope. The Beast I'm talking about leaves a different kind of mark."

Irina interpreted his cryptic answer. "The Beast is his nickname for his .50 caliber Desert Eagle."

Their eyes hovered on the vivacious brunette as if waiting for further explanation.

She ignored them and changed the subject. "Who is this

Yuri that we were all asked about with a knife to our throat?"

"The leader of a rival family that has killed twenty-two of my men, six in the past four months."

"What is law enforcement doing about this?"

"The police haven't been notified. That would be as bad for us as for them.

She cocked her head, looking for further elaboration.

"A friendly coroner signed off on heart attacks and other common causes of death." He offered Irina his arm and ushered the three to the supper club, where he chose a corner table in a back corner. A waiter was at the ready before Irina had sat down.

"Vodka and menus," Boris directed. When he returned, he set out four squat tumblers, dropped a sprig of spruce in each, opened a bottle of Moskovskaya Osobaya, and poured it straight. The brigadier lifted his glass for a toast. "To success." The three raised their glasses with him and echoed, "to success." Boris tipped his glass and drained it. The boys looked at Irina. She shook her head and set her glass back down. She had never drank in her life and wasn't about to start now. Andy and Tony followed suit, though they shifted in their seats, ill at ease. She wasn't sure if they were more worried about displeasing her or the brigadier.

Irina swirled her glass and watched the sprig spin. Its inability to resist the power of the alcohol reminded her of family members and friends who had succumbed to its wiles.

The brigadier watched the scene unfold with a puzzled look on his face. Then he furled his eyebrows and wagged his finger. "You three haven't touched your vodka. Drink up. Celebrate."

"We never drink while on mission," Andy offered in their defense. "Even a five percent impairment in reaction time or mental awareness can be fatal."

"Suit yourself." He drained his glass and poured himself another shot. "Vodka is the nectar of the gods."

"So when do we get to meet the pakhan?" Irina asked, trying to steer the conversation away from the awkward toast.

"Oh, maybe I won't be taking you to see him," Boris replied, a sly smile revealing his pleasure at tormenting his guests. "Or maybe you will get to see him. Time will tell."

Irina glared at him, infuriated at his doubletalk.

"Be patient, darling. Whether and when you get to see the pakhan are matters out of my hands. He alone will decide those questions."

Irina turned the words over in her mind. She suspected that the brigadier was toying with them, but it probably was true that he had little say over their visit with the pakhan.

The brigadier tossed back half of his glass, sat back in his chair, and crossed his arms. "How do I know that you're not working for the US government? Maybe you're agents with the BATF or the FBI. Or maybe you're internal agents with the SVR."

"You can't know for sure," Andy replied matter-of-factly. "But you've been in this business for a long time. If you had the slightest suspicion that we were American agents or rats, we would never have seen your face. The fact is, we wouldn't have made it past Slice."

The brigadier gave no indication as to what he thought of the answer. He picked up his glass, drained the rest of it, then continued the cat-and-mouse game for another half hour, plying Andy and Tony with questions on their experience with the military, federal agencies, and the mafia.

Irina began doodling on a napkin, hoping it would help her to fend off impatience and bite her tongue. Soon it was adorned with pixies that were struggling to harvest and transport strawberries. *Keep things in perspective. It's just part of the vetting process.* The brigadier and the pakhan were satisfied with their trustworthiness. Now they were grading them on their skill sets and experience. Did they have what they needed to do what they intended? If so, they were a lucrative opportunity for the mafia. If not, they were a risk for them.

While sketching two pixies loading a strawberry into a tiny cart, she was distracted by motion in her peripheral vision and looked up. A dashing, older gentleman in a tailored suit was approaching their table, flanked by two muscular bodyguards. Boris rose and spread his arms toward him. "Konstantin. Good to see you." Sleeve creep during their embrace revealed that the pakhan was wearing a Patek Philippe.

He turned to Irina, flashed a warm smile, and held out his hand, palm up. Her hand felt tiny in his. He raised it to his lips and kissed it softly. *The silver fox is even more refined than Boris.*

When the pakhan focused his attention on Tony, the young man shot out his right hand, trying to avoid another embrace. The older man, unfazed, placed his left hand on Tony's shoulder and with his right gripped Tony's hand as few men had. Tony squeezed back, far harder than his usual firm handshake, and looked the pakhan straight in the eyes. Irina's nerves stood on edge. *Wonder who's gonna flinch first?* The seconds dragged on. Konstantin, in a magnanimous display, released his grip, smiled, and took Tony firmly by the shoulders. "You'd make a good brodyaga."

The pakhan greeted Andy with the same, though brief and polite, shoulder grip and handshake, then gestured to the table. After seating Irina, he settled into the chair to her left.

The dinner featured roasted boar, caviar, and endless tales of hair-raising adventures—hunting trips in Siberia, two tours in Afghanistan as an officer with the Spetsnaz, and surviving an attack on his dacha by a rival family. While they were finishing their dessert—medovik, Konstantin finally got around to business. He retrieved a note from his jacket pocket and turned to Tony. "So you and your friends back in Montana are seeking three infrared sensors for a telescope, along with a business cover that includes a loading dock so you can take delivery of a large mirror for a telescope. Is this correct?"

"Yes," Irina replied emphatically.

"Oh," he said, turning back to face her. "So you really are in charge."

"I am," she replied with a hint of indignation.

"My apologies. Then I will deal directly with you."

"I would appreciate that."

He opened his portfolio. "I need to get some information from you so we can get this process rolling."

"Sounds good to me."

"What will your cover name be?"

"Aleksandra Aksakova."

"And what will the name of your company be?"

"Nebesa Smotret."

"Does the telescope project have a name?"

"Sibirskogo teleskopa."

"I'm assuming you'll need a bank account for your mirror purchase and other expenses?"

"Correct."

"What will your email address be?"

"I was thinking maybe Aleks.Aksakova@nebesasmotret.ru, so we need a live website too."

"That can be arranged. Do you have a preference for your cell phone number?"

"I would like a Moscow number."

"Would a 499 number be acceptable?"

"Yes."

"Since you're requesting a Moscow cell phone number, I assume that Moscow is your choice for your office?"

"Yes. We definitely prefer Moscow."

"What are the names of your associates"

"Dmitriy and Sergey Stepanychev. Tony is Dmitriy and Andy is Sergey."

"Do they have cover stories?"

"Only that they're bodyguards for me on a project in a part of Siberia which has a reputation for being lawless.

Make up something for their background that's suitable, like Spetsnaz and FSB. We'll run with whatever you provide."

"Ah, yes. Special forces experience. Now serving with the Federal Security Service. Good choice. I have connections. Where is your Siberian telescope project?"

"In the Kolyma Mountains in Magadan oblast. Our local office will be in Magadan itself."

"What infrared sensors are you seeking?"

"We need a 10-micron, a 4.75-micron, and a 2.2-micron."

"What other symbols or marks will be on the sensors that will help us to identify them?"

Irina pulled a pen from her purse and jotted the sizes and a list of symbols on a napkin. "The μm after the numbers is the Greek m and the English m. It's the symbol for a micrometer, commonly known as a micron. The letter combinations are the symbols of rare elements from the periodic table that are used in various combinations in the sensors. The most common are HgCdTe which is Mercury cadmium telluride, InSb which is Indium antimonide, InAs which is Indium arsenide, GaSb which is Gallium antimonide, GaAs which is Gallium arsenide, and InGaAs which is Indium gallium arsenide. But other combinations are used."

The pakhan patted her hand. "Thank you, dear. I have all the info I need for now. If you'll excuse me, I'll go make a few phone calls and, as you say here in America, get the ball rolling."

"Absolutely," she replied warmly. But as he walked away,

her conscience smote her. *No matter how likable the old gentleman is, he shouldn't be trusted.*

The trio endured the brigadier's humor and storytelling for forty long minutes. Though he attempted an air of refinement, the truth was, he was a coarse, uncultured braggart, given to exaggeration. They were relieved when the gentleman returned and silenced him with a wave of his hand. Irina marveled. *Wish my hand could work that kind of magic.*

"My associate in Moscow," Konstantin began, "has agreed to help with your request. One of his partners, a high-ranking general in the FSB will put you in the system as category 5 agents who are on a highly classified mission and not to be bothered. But this won't come cheap. The pakhan wants two hundred and fifty thousand dollars. The general, who will provide the background documentation for your cover, wants two hundred and fifty thousand dollars for himself. He will have to pay off a few fellow officers to make things happen."

Irina dissed the cost with a wave of her hand. "The cost isn't an issue. Speed and quality are our main concerns."

"Of course!" he agreed, handing her a business card with an email address and a phone number written on the back. Contact the email address, the pakhan's aide, tomorrow morning from a secure email account, and the two of you can make payment arrangements. Expect three initial charges: the pakhan's fee, the general's fee, and the funds that will be placed in your business account to cover the mirror and business expenses."

"Do you mean tomorrow morning American time or Moscow time?"

"American time."

"What happens after that?"

"Once the payments have cleared, the aide will send you your business address, your business phone number, your secretary's name and cell phone number, your business email address, and your cell phone number.

"Shortly afterward, you'll receive an application in your business email to set up your banking account. Within twenty-four hours of your response, you'll have an active account."

"Who do we contact once we arrive in Moscow?"

"Igor Federovsky, one of my associate's brigadiers. His phone number is on the back of the card. He will set a time and a place for meeting." He leaned closer to her. "Be prepared to pay for the meal."

"Thanks for the advice. How will we recognize him?"

"You won't need to. We already sent him your pictures. At the restaurant, Igor will approach you and say 'Cheap vodka tastes like rotten fish.' You will answer back, 'What do you suggest?' He will reply, 'Moskovskaya Osobaya is my favorite.'"

"So we get vetted before we meet your friend?"

"You won't meet my associate. And I hesitate to call him a friend. He's my brother and fellow pakhan in Solntsevskaya Bratva. Now, tell me about your plans for getting to Moscow."

"We haven't made any yet. We can't fly on commercial airlines or take a cruise ship because the federal government has warrants out for my arrest. We need to travel discreetly—fly under the radar."

Konstantin touched her arm. "Let me make another phone call, dear. I may have a solution."

While waiting, Irina picked at the tray of hors d'oeuvres while he was gone, taking a few green olives and pickled baby onions. She didn't appreciate the pickled fish, caviar, or the other oddities. *How do people even eat such nasty stuff?*

The pakhan returned ten minutes later with a twinkle in his eyes. "It's all set. An old friend—a senior officer from my Spetsnaz days—is vacationing in Palm Beach. He has agreed to take you with him on his yacht when he leaves for Sevastapol in a few weeks. Upon arrival, he'll arrange a ride for you to Moscow."

"A yacht? Irina replied with raised eyebrows.

The older man laughed. "Mikhail is an oil oligarch. He owns two mid-tier oil companies outright and holds a large stake in Gazprom. He spent more money last year than I'll make in my entire lifetime."

"Does he have a definite departure date?"

"Wednesday, November 20."

"How long will the trip take?"

"He says it usually takes him about three weeks to sail from Fort Lauderdale to Sevastapol. But this trip will be extended somewhat because he has business to attend to in Bermuda, Barbados, the Cape Verde Islands, and the Canary Islands.

"How extended?" she asked, grimacing slightly.

"Not long. Mikhail wants to spend a week of quiet in his

cabin in the northern hills of Crimea before his family arrives for Christmas."

Irina furrowed her eyebrows. "So we could be at sea for six weeks?"

"No. Just four. His wife Astrid is Swedish, so they celebrate Christmas western-style on December 25 and Russian-style on January 7."

Irina laughed. "I could handle two Christmases every year."

"Yes. The womenfolk seem especially attracted to the idea." He returned to the matter at hand. "So the departure time and arrival time will work for you?"

"I think we can make them work." She looked to Andy and Tony. "What do you guys think?" They shrugged their shoulders. She sensed that their response was more than indifference. *Probably not looking forward to spending four weeks with a man with mafia ties, even if it does come with a berth on a yacht.* She gave Tony the eye, forcing him to speak up.

He eyed her sullenly before he complied. "It doesn't really matter how we get there as long we get decent beds, decent food, and decent showers."

"So it's settled then," Konstantin announced with a toast. "You will meet Mikhail at his yacht, the *Ekaterina*, on the evening of the nineteenth of November. He'll be berthed at Bahia Mar Yachting Center in Fort Lauderdale, Florida. Bring two hundred and fifty thousand dollars in cash for the three of you."

Irina wrote the information on the back of the card that

the pakhan had given her. MIKHAIL, NOV 19, BAHIA MAR, 250 K.

"One last thing. You'll need to make a stop in Philadelphia for your Russian passports, driver's licenses, and FSB IDs. I made an appointment for you with Phantom at 1 p.m. on Wednesday. He may be strange, but he is the best in the business. My secretary will text you his address and directions late Wednesday morning." Konstantin surveyed the trio. "Do you have any questions about the plan or the arrangements?" They shook their heads. "Then, if you'll excuse me," he apologized as he rose, "I have another meeting tonight." He turned to his brigadier. "Have Bogdan escort our friends back to the Dunwoody Walmart. Make sure that that devious rascal returns their weapons." Then, he pulled the boys in for an embrace, kissed Irina's hand, and walked away.

Thirty-five minutes later, the team disembarked from the same white van that had picked them up. Exhausted, they decided to crash in the camper for a few hours before continuing their journey. Irina crawled up into the sleeper over the cab, Andy folded the table down, turning it into a bed, and Tony rolled out a sleeping pad on the floor. Within minutes, the boys were snoring. Irina, however, lay awake, her mind careening through a labyrinth of concerns and fears. *What if they take the money and run? What if our cover is blown? What if we end up in a Siberian gulag?* The what-if scenarios piled up like a multi-car accident on an icy freeway. She calmed herself. *Get a grip. It's just the sugar. You had two large pieces of medovik. Now you've got a case of paranoia. And you'll probably have nightmares ... like Russian robots gone rogue.*

10

Philadelphia, PA
Tuesday, Nov. 5 to Wednesday, Nov. 6, 2019

The boys dragged themselves out of their sleeping bags after four hours of rack time, choked down several of Irina's bagels, and hit the road. She ignored them and retreated deeper under her covers, trying to fall back asleep. But the continual stopping and starting in morning traffic prevented her efforts.

With a huff, she threw her bedding aside, jumped down from the sleeper over the cab, stumbled over to the kitchen counter, and started a pot of coffee. *Definitely need to prop my eyes open this morning.* When the dripping stopped, she poured herself a mug, and took a quaff of the dark nectar, savoring the earthy tang on her tongue. *Enough lollygagging. Time to get this day rolling.*

After transforming Andy's bed back into a table, she fired up her laptop, logged in to Buster, accessed her deadlybrunette@GASmail account, and zipped off an email to the Moscow pakhan's aide. *Send payment details for the Konstantin deal re the business cover in Moscow and sensors for an infrared telescope. Aleksandra.*

A half hour later, she received a reply with the requested details and transferred eight hundred and fifty thousand American dollars to the specified bank account: two hundred fifty thousand for himself, two hundred fifty thousand for the FSB general, and three hundred fifty thousand for funding the business account.

Two hours later, another email arrived from the aide verifying that the funds had cleared and giving her the address and phone number for Nebesa Smotret, the secretary's name and number, and her own email address and cell phone number. When she retrieved a secure phone from her purse which had been set aside for her Nebesa Smotret cover, she noticed that her hands were shaking. *This spy stuff has me on pins and needles.* She put on a favorite classical piece, her nerve-calming weapon of choice, and proceeded to set up the phone, happily distracted by Rachmaninoff's Piano Concerto No. 2.

When she finished, she opened yet another email from the aide, which contained a link for account applications with Gazprombank, and opened a checking account with that institution for Nebesa Smotret.

Her slate finally clean, she made herself a mug of hot chocolate with extra cream and sugar, drained it quickly, then crawled back into her sleeping bag. This time, sleep came easy.

Thirteen hours later, at a quarter past eight, the team checked into a seedy motel in a rough neighborhood in northeast Philadelphia. Andy took the first shower. Tony ordered pizza. Irina, weary of road food, moped. *So looking forward to the homestyle cooking back at the Compound.*

The pizza was a major-league disappointment. Too little cheese, too much tomato sauce, and way too much salt. Halfway through her second piece, she tossed it back into the box in disgust, brusquely stood up from the table, and snapped, "I'm gonna take my shower." But rather than finding relief in the shower, her frustrations reached a boiling point. *Low pressure and lukewarm water! What a lousy way to end a lousy day!* She hastily rinsed, snapped the shower off, and dried herself with frenzied fury. Then she crawled into bed, shivering. Tony was already snoring on the couch.

The next morning, Irina sat down at the table in the corner and prepared to make her call to Alluna Optics to order the mirror for the telescope. The room was abuzz, making it difficult to concentrate. The guys were joking and laughing about the Phantom, whom they were going to meet later that day for their counterfeit passports and driver's licenses. Tony launched into an impersonation of the creepy cobbler, imitating the one they had watched Joby perform, and Andy exploded with a raucous guffaw.

"Can you guys just grow up for five minutes?" Irina snarked. "I need some peace and quiet to make my phone call."

"Sorry, Nikita," Tony apologized, a sheepish look on his face. "Joking around is how we take the edge off."

Her conscience stabbed her. They really were just unwinding. "No worries," she half apologized. "Maybe you guys can go find us some breakfast."

"That's not a bad idea," Tony replied. "Maybe you

should do some ballet while we're gone. You need to unwind, too." He arched his hands over his head and tippy-toed in a circle.

She launched her empty travel mug at him, half mad and half trying not to laugh.

Tony deftly caught the mug, walked it back to her, and placed his hand on her shoulder. "I'll bring you back a good cup of joe, Nikkie, if I can find one."

Touched by his tenderness and embarrassed at her angry outburst, she reached her hand back and set it on top of his. That brought to mind counsel she had heard from her grandmother. *Sometimes a touch is a better apology than words.*

The Backstrom boys left on their errand, and the overwrought woman breathed a sigh of relief. When she heard the truck pull away, she fired up her Beethoven playlist, dropped into a butterfly, and lost herself in one of her ballet stretching routines. When the eight-minute routine was completed, she returned to the work at hand—refocused and refreshed—tuned in a Russian top-twenty radio station on the internet to play in the background, and reached for the phone.

She dialed Alluna Optics in Bobingen, Germany. The line rang three times.

"Hello," a pleasant female voice answered with a pronounced German accent. "Alluna Optics. My name is Gabriele Sommer. How can I help you?"

"Hi. I'm Aleksandra Aksakova," Irina answered with a flawless Russian accent. "I am the purchasing and acquisitions representative for Nebesa Smotret, a Moscow-based astronomical organization that specializes in installing telescopes in Siberia. I would like to place a rush order for a 60-inch Zerodur mirror with extremely low thermal expansion for our telescope project in Magadan oblast."

"I'm sorry, Ms. Aksakova. We no longer take rush orders. Recent German legislation forbids us from taking rush orders and requires us to process government and institutional orders in the order that they are received. It's part of an agreement that the German government has made with other governments and with agencies like the ESA, NASA, and Roscosmos."

"So how long of a wait am I looking at?"

"Twenty-six months."

"What! Over two years?"

"Yes. I'm sorry, Ms. Aksakova. Currently, orders are backlogged more than two years."

"That's crazy. I can't wait that long. How did you get so far behind on orders?"

"Despite our recent plant expansion which doubled capacity and enabled us to increase our mirror sizes to 84 inches, the big increase in orders the past few years from NEO projects in the US, Europe, and other parts of the world has vastly exceeded our capacity."

"Is there anything we can do to speed things up?"

"The only possible option is if you're willing to change your specifications."

"How much change are we talking about?"

"We have a 72-inch mirror that a company backed out

on a month ago that's identical to your desired specifications except that it's twelve inches larger in diameter. It is ninety percent completed and only requires finish polishing. If you're willing to take this project off our hands, we would return it to the processing queue, and we would let you have it for the discounted price of two hundred and fifty thousand euros."

"How long would it take for this mirror to be finished?"

"If we start next Monday, it would be done in six weeks. The shipping would take approximately two weeks from our location in Bobingen, Germany to Moscow. So eight weeks total."

"This sounds like a wonderful opportunity. But I need to discuss it with my engineering team and see if they can make this option work. Can I get back to you next Monday?"

"Next Monday will be fine. However, if I don't hear from you then, I won't be able to continue holding the mirror for you. I will be required to offer it to others."

"I understand. No worries. You'll hear from me on Monday, one way or the other."

11

Hebron, OH
Thursday evening, November 7, 2019

The Russia team was cruising west on U.S. 70 in Ohio, heading back to Montana. Irina was in the camper, staying out of sight. Tony and Andy were in the cab, reminiscing about the wild events of the past few days.

"No doubt about it," Tony agreed. "Meeting the Russian mafia was dicey. Kiril has a screw loose somewhere. And Slice literally made the hair on the back of my neck stand up. Never had that happen before. I always thought that was an urban legend. But the spookiest part of the past few days for me was the visit with Phantom. He made my skin crawl."

Andy chuckled. "I didn't think the Phantom was worse, but that was definitely a bizarre three hours. Guess I owe Joby an apology. When he told us about his visit with the cobbler, I thought he was exaggerating. But he was spot on. That guy is an odd duck."

"Odd is putting it lightly. He's creepy. Psycho. Surprised he isn't locked up in an asylum."

"No argument there."

It grew quiet in the cab. Neither of the boys wanted to talk any further about the cobbler. He gave them the heebie-jeebies.

Andy steered their conversation in a different direction. "What do you think of Irina's performance?"

"Not too shabby for a rookie."

"My sentiments exactly. Do you think she's ready for the Russia mission?"

"Yeah. While it's a tough mission for a greenhorn, I think she's got the right stuff."

"Hey," Andy said, pointing to a truck stop on the outskirts of Hebron. "Pull into the TA. It's nearly ten. I'm ready for a real meal and some shuteye. Can't handle another granola bar or bagel."

"I'm tracking with ya," Tony replied. "Even a cheap steak sounds pretty high-speed right now."

Irina didn't even look up from her biography of General Zhukov when the two strode into the camper.

"We're going to get a bite to eat," Andy said. "Can we bring you something?"

"A shrimp basket with extra cocktail sauce," she replied as she flipped the page.

"You got it." He turned and started for the door, then turned back. "I know you're getting antsy, Irina. But resist the urge. Don't go anywhere."

"I know. I know," she muttered. "Never put the mission at risk."

A couple minutes after the boys had left, Irina closed her book and slammed it on the table. "Can't stand being cooped up in here," she grumbled as she stood up. "There's no room for stretching, much less martial arts or dancing." She paced her cramped confines. That only increased her agitation. Four steps were all she could manage before she had to turn around. *This is absurd. I need some fresh air. Some exercise. Get the blood flowing.*

She yanked aside the curtain on the table window and peered out. A sea of tractor-trailers greeted her. She moved to the sink window. Nothing but an empty lot with scattered bushes. The window on the back door revealed only the rear of a dry van. She could scarcely believe her luck. The camper was parked in a favorable location for a stealth operation. She could sneak out, get fifteen minutes of fresh air and exercise, and slip back in. No one would notice. The boys would never know.

Irina cracked the door and peered out an opening in the hinge. The coast appeared to be clear. She slipped out, scampered to her right, and angled around the corner so the camper would shield her. Then she turned toward the field. Within two steps, the crumbling asphalt gave way to compacted dirt and trampled weeds. A few more steps brought her to ankle-high grass. She took in a deep breath and pirouetted under the stars, arching gracefully backward. For a few minutes, she was free. When she stopped spinning, her eyes were fixed on the heavens above. Even in light-polluted regions like Ohio, where you can only see a fraction of the stars that you can see in Montana, the Creator's handiwork left her in awe.

She sped through her ballet stretches, then threw down a

series of ballet steps and leaps. *Wish I could dance the whole time.* A favorite stretch of dance from Swan Lake somehow transitioned into a review of her basic blocks, blows, and kicks. Finally, she attempted the Krav Maga spin kick which Tony had recently introduced. After messing it up twice, she stopped and mentally walked herself through the move several times. Then she crouched, exploded into the kick, landed, and ... found herself facing two girls in hippy-looking outfits that reminded her of Ariele.

Before she could react, the shorter one spoke up. "We're looking for a ride out West. Saw the Montana plates. Can you give us a lift?"

Irina froze, paralyzed with fear. Remorse body-slammed her heart. *What was I thinking? Should have listened to the guys. How do I get out of this mess?* Flight seemed the only sensible option. She darted past the girls, stepped back inside the safety of the camper, and shut the door behind her. She plopped down at the table, cradled her now cold cup of coffee, and tried to pray. The cup was shaking, and coffee slopped onto the table. Her hands were trembling like a California temblor.

The door opened and the shorter gal poked her head inside. Irina's heart raced. She fought back the panic and tried to stay calm. The gal eyed her. "Are you headed West?" she asked.

Irina didn't respond.

"Will you take us out West?"

Again Irina said nothing. The gal's eyes made her nervous. They weren't pleading. They were ... confident.

The gal somehow knew that she had the advantage. Fear and rage welled up in Irina's breast. She jabbed an angry finger in the air. "Get out of here! Scram!"

But the gal didn't budge. Instead, she stepped up onto the stairs, leaned against the doorway, folded her arms, and stared at Irina. Irina bolted to her feet and took a couple menacing steps toward her. The gal stood her ground and calmly reasoned with her. "You can't afford to get in trouble with the law, now, can you? That might throw a monkey wrench in your efforts to fly under the radar. Am I right?"

Irina returned fire with her own piercing glare but had nothing to say. The gal had her pegged. But was it a lucky guess or a solid case? It probably didn't matter. Regardless of what she did or said, she was in deep trouble with the guys. Worse, if she played her cards wrong, she was also going to get the whole team in trouble with the law. But how was she supposed to play her cards right? The deck seemed stacked against her.

Disoriented, she stepped backward, found the table, and balanced herself on it. The gal boldly stepped up into the camper, her companion right behind her, and pressed the attack. "Why didn't you go inside with the guys? Why did you stay on the dark side of the camper? Why did you run from us? What are you hiding?"

Irina looked away.

"I knew it!" the gal exclaimed. "I knew it! I had a feeling there was something suspicious about you. When the truck stopped, two hunky guys with military haircuts hopped out, went inside the camper, exited less than a minute later, and walked to the diner. If you were legit, you would have gone with them. So what's your story?"

Irina thought her heart was going to stop. She slumped onto the bench. Her world was spinning out of control. The gal approached her. "You don't seem like a criminal. So what are you? One of the fugitives wanted for Homeland Security violations?"

Irina jerked as if she had been shot, then laid her head on the table and stifled a sob. The gal stepped closer and touched her on the arm. "Whatever your secret is, hon' it's safe with us. We're not gonna turn you in. We've got our own troubles with the government."

The two sat down across from Irina. The one who had been doing the talking set her hand on Irina's. "I'm Henna."

The gal next to her added, "I'm Anise."

Irina raised her head and stared blankly at them.

Henna ignored the coldness. "A couple years back, we became aware of the growing New World Order nonsense that's spreading like gangrene in our land. Shortly after that, we heard about the Rogue and the government cover-up."

Irina stiffened and broke eye contact.

Henna sensed she had scored a direct hit and continued. "I know you know what I'm talking about. The comet that's headed for Mars and is likely to create havoc here on Earth what with asteroids getting knocked loose, and maybe even planets."

Irina dropped her head again. She wanted to crawl under a rock.

At that moment, the camper door swung open, and

Andy's large frame filled the doorway. His jaw dropped, and shock sprawled across his face. Irina looked at him with tear-filled eyes and shrugged her shoulders. His surprise turned into a glare. He warily eyed the two newcomers who had turned around in their seats.

Tony brushed his way around his brother and stepped up to the girls. "Who are your friends, Nikkie?" he demanded.

At a loss for words, Irina dropped her head and wrung her hands. The shorter gal jumped to her feet and faced him. "I'm Henna and this is Anise. We need a ride as far west as you're going."

"We aren't giving any rides."

"That's a pretty lame way to treat your allies."

Tony winced. "Allies?"

"We know all about the Rogue, and we're just as opposed to the government's cover-up as anyone in the country."

"Rogue?"

"Don't pretend that you have no idea what I'm talking about. A pickup camper pulls into the truck stop. Two hunky guys who look like the military-type head for the diner. A gal stays behind in the camper. When we approach her, she oozes fear, not of us but of the potential consequences of being discovered, which suggests that she is hiding from the law. Since none of you seem like the criminal type, the most likely explanation is that she's a Rogue fugitive. Am I correct?"

Tony felt trapped. His mind raced, trying to process the situation. What was he going to do?

"So, you actually believe the tall tales on the internet?" Andy chided the sprite as he edged his brother aside.

Anise bolted to her feet, bumped in front of Henna, and got in his face. "They're not fairy tales," she insisted. "Look me in the eyes and swear before God that you think the reports are pure nonsense with no truth behind them at all."

Andy met her fiery gaze, determined to maintain his ground. But he hesitated. It pained him to lie to those sparkling blue eyes.

"I knew it," she announced triumphantly. "You do believe in the Rogue."

Tony fumed and clenched his jaw. She had him and Andy over a barrel.

She continued. "We know you can help us. Your plates are from Montana. And you are definitely headed west. When you stepped out of the camper and headed for the diner, one of you said they would drive the next stretch to Indianapolis."

Bewildered, Tony looked at Andy. His brother offered nothing but a frustrated shrug. Tony was seething. They didn't have time for this snafu. He had to do something. The problem wasn't going to go away by itself. His frazzled mind weighed three options. One, they could get rid of them the way the mafia gets rid of its problems. But that would only compound their problems. Besides, that route was unthinkable. Two, they could kick them out of the camper. But that was a risk he didn't want to take. He didn't trust them. Three, they could give them a ride. That bought them time and gave them a chance to get to know them. He turned back to Henna. "Tell you what. We can take you as far as Billings, Montana."

Henna seized his arm. "Thank you! You won't regret this."

He pulled his arm away from her clutch. But as she turned away from him, he grabbed her arm and spun her back around. "There are two conditions. Any infractions, and we'll dump you on the side road in the middle of nowhere in the middle of the night. The first condition is that you two are gonna ride in the cab with Andy and me. The second is that both of you are going to turn your phones off and keep them off."

A playful smirk crept across her face. "Not a problem, big guy."

Andy tossed one of the two boxes under his arm onto the table in front of Irina. "Here's your shrimp basket." She didn't look up. He eyed his brother and jerked his head toward the door. "C'mon. Let's hit the road. I'll take the wheel."

Uncomfortable tension reigned in the cab for the next half hour. The brothers were steamed and didn't feel like talking. Henna determined to break the ice. She leaned on Tony's seat so she was close enough for him to feel her breath on his neck. "Sorry that we got off on the wrong foot."

He merely shrugged.

"Can we start over?"

He shrugged again.

"How did you guys find out about the Rogue?"

"The internet," he replied coolly.

She waited for him to elaborate and give her the details. He didn't. She took the initiative. "We first learned about the comet at the 2018 South Appalachia gathering."

"The South Appalachia gathering?"

"Every year the Rainbow Family has a national gathering. In 2018 the gathering was held in Chattahoochee National Forest in northern Georgia."

"What's the Rainbow Family?"

"A loose-knit movement that believes in things like world peace and ecology and rejects society's infatuation with money and material things."

"So, you're counterculture? Like hippies?"

"Yeah. Kind of. But we're a pretty diverse bunch. Hippies. New Agers. Mother Earthers. Native religionists."

"So how did you hear about the Rogue in that kind of setting?"

"We ran into some cool guys who told us about the Rogue and the end of the world. According to them the ancient legends of many cultures teach that the current age must end with an apocalypse before the new age can start. That was really wild. Like most of the Rainbow Family, we always thought that the world would slip into the New Age more or less painlessly.

"That led us to start reading on the internet about the Rogue, prepping, and the apocalypse. Our research convinced us that the Rogue rumors on the internet were true and that the government was covering up the threat. After that, our relationship with the Rainbow Family started to cool. Our friends in the movement say they're cool with our new path, but it's obvious that they think we're crazy."

Tony was puzzled. "Seems like a big jump from peace-loving hippies to end of the world preppers."

"Yeah. It is. But facts are facts. It's a fact that a massive comet will cause chaos in the solar system. It's a fact that the history of the world is a history of war and exploitation by the powerful. It's a fact that the world is racing for a one-world economic system, one-world government, and one-world religion. That's world totalitarianism, not world peace."

Tony sensed agitation in her voice.

"The Rainbow Family," she continued, "live in their own little world. They have no solutions. Holding hands and singing isn't going to fix anything." She stopped to collect her thoughts. "Maybe the Christians are right after all. Maybe God needs to come down here and clean this mess up himself."

"My dad thinks so," he replied. But he didn't pursue the point. "So how did you girls get involved in the Rainbow Family?"

"We both ran away in 2016 when we were sixteen and went to live with a commune populated mostly with Rainbow folks. That's where we met. We lived there until a year ago."

"So you left the Family?"

"Yeah. We eventually figured out that their approach to peace is pretty much just a sophisticated method of sticking your head in the sand. We still have friends on the inside, but we're on our own journey now. Searching for the truth. Trying not to ignore plain facts."

"Where are you headed?"

"Whidby Island in Puget Sound. Gonna work for some friends who run an organic raspberry farm."

"Doesn't sound like a safe place to be if the end of the world stuff is true. You know. Asteroids and tsunamis."

"Yeah. We don't intend to stay long. Just long enough to make some cash and figure out our next step. Hopefully, we can link up with like-minded folks before the poo hits the fan."

As the conversation continued, Tony felt his heart drawn to the green-eyed vixen with chestnut locks. She had a lot more common sense than he had given her credit for. And she really did appear to be a genuine Rogue believer. Perhaps she was even Rogue Underground material. But he kept his thoughts to himself.

***

On Saturday evening, the boys pulled into the Flying J truck stop in Billings to fill up. Andy turned to their passengers in the back seat with his heart in his throat. He had warmed to the interesting young ladies. "Sorry, girls. This is the end of the road." Then he and his brother climbed out of the pickup. Andy headed to the pump, Tony to the window washing station. Without a word, the two gals grabbed their bags and followed the guys into the chilly evening air. There was an awkward moment of silence when the four met near the driver's door. No one wanted to say goodbye. Andy, ever a man of duty over feelings, broke the uneasy quiet. He handed Anise a fat envelope. "There's five hundred bucks in here. Enough for a few hotel stays and meals."

Her face melted into a tear-filled smile, and she took him by the arm. "If you two ever find yourselves in the Puget Sound area and need some help, give us a call. We want to return the favor if we can."

"We just might do that."

She handed him a bookmark. He flipped it over. Her name, email address, and Signal number were on the back. Out of the corner of his eye, he noticed that Henna had handed a similar bookmark to Tony.

While Andy wondered how to move past the stalled goodbye, the girls launched themselves at their favorites, threw their arms around their necks, and planted tender pecks on their cheeks. Like a handful of grass in a fire, the excitement was over in a flash. The two hippie chicks picked up their bags and walked away at a brisk pace, not even looking over their shoulders.

The brothers looked at each other in bewilderment.

"She's definitely your type," Tony quipped.

Andy blushed but said nothing.

"Wouldn't you like to see her again someday?"

"Maybe, but right now I'm focusing on the mission."

Tony grinned. "I've got a feeling that destiny placed them in our path for a reason."

Andy just shrugged his shoulders and turned toward the gas pump. Tony focused on washing the windows.

About an hour later, as they neared Broadview on Highway 3, Tony turned to Andy. "Something on your mind, bro? You haven't said a word since we left Billings. I got a couple of grunts out of you, that's all."

"Yeah. Been thinking about the situation. We gotta do something about the chicks."

Tony grinned. "You're really stuck on Anise, eh?"

"Stop with the teasing already. I'm serious. We gotta get on top of this situation before it becomes a colossal problem."

"You're right. Been thinking about that myself. Got a plan?"

"I think we should address it at the team level. We don't want to bring it up with Dad and the guys at the Compound."

"Why not?"

"I'm afraid they would pull the plug on Irina. A couple of them were borderline on whether or not she should be allowed on the team. If it hadn't been for Woody, she wouldn't be. He backed her, and they relented. We can't lose her. We really do need her."

"Do you still trust her?"

Andy exhaled. "I do. I think she learned some hard lessons here."

Tony was silent for a few moments. "I'm pretty peeved with her. But yeah, you're right. We need her. Especially her language ability. Still, I'm uncomfortable keeping the guys in the dark on this part of the mission."

Andy turned away from Tony and looked out the window. Tony's guts wrenched. He hated it when there was discord between them.

A few minutes later, Andy turned back. "Remember the mission in Kunar when things went south? When we gave our report, we left out a few details because we didn't want good men to get a five-hundred-pound butt chewing for a fifty-pound mistake."

Tony pondered that for a few seconds, then relented. "Okay, bro. I'll trust your judgment on this one. You've trusted mine a few times."

Andy simply nodded. He didn't want to talk about the subject anymore.

When they rolled into Broadview, Andy pointed to the Fleet and Farm. His brother jumped on the brakes and turned into their parking lot. Irina's heart sank. She knew the boys well enough to know that stopping this soon meant bad news. And the bad news most likely had something to do with her indiscretion. Fears began flying around in her head like a cloud of bats. Would they holler at her? Would they boot her off the team? Would they report her to the folks at the Compound? Her nerves were a frazzled mess when the boys burst into the camper.

"We need to talk," Andy began, as the two sat down at the table.

Before he could say any more, she burst into tears. "I'm sorry for screwing up. I shouldn't have gotten out of the camper. You taught me to never deviate from the plan unless it was critical to improvise for mission success. A small deviation, no matter how insignificant it appears, can put lives at risk and hamper if not scrub a mission. I didn't listen. I figured a little fresh air was insignificant. Now we're paying for it."

"Yeah. You did mess up big time."

Her chest heaving, she stammered out, "I'm sorry."

Andy reached out and touched her hand. "Apology accepted."

She sat in silence for a few moments, chewing on her lip, then she asked, "So what are we gonna do about the girls?"

He shrugged. "There isn't much we can do. They saw your face, a face that's plastered all over the country as one of the most wanted by the FBI. They saw our license plate. They spent two days in the cab with Tony and me. They have money with our fingerprints on it. If they are undercover agents, then the entire Compound is screwed, and there's nothing we can do about it. We probably don't have twenty-four hours before the Compound is swarming with federal agents."

He let the words sink in, then continued. "Fortunately, I suspect that the girls were legit and we don't have anything to worry about. However ..." His words trailed off, and he pounded his hand lightly on the table a couple of times, obviously perturbed. Irina nervously swirled the cold coffee in her cup, sensing that he was about to drop a bomb. "I'm just gonna blurt it out. We can't let anyone know about the girls. Not my dad. Not Woody. Not Red. Not anyone. The guys would go ballistic. We're gonna have to keep this to ourselves. Let's just count this a lesson hard learned and move on."

Irina was both pleased and confused. She looked over to Tony. He nodded his head in agreement. "As dad would say, We're just gonna have to trust God. Trust him to overrule any mistakes that were made and keep us from harm. Trust him to bring good out of this mess and somehow work it back into his plan."

"I appreciate that, guys," Irina said, brushing the tears out of her eyes with her right hand. She continued swirling her cup. "But why are you so sure that the girls were legit?"

Tony smiled, reached inside his leather bomber jacket, and set a tiny unit on the table. "This suggests that they weren't agents."

"What is it?"

"This," he said with a grin spreading across his face, "is a portable RF monitor. It picks up every effort to send or receive radio frequency communications whether phone, text, or wireless transmitter. If the girls were undercover agents, they would most likely have either been wired or attempted to make radio contact with their handlers. And they would have tried to plant tracking devices. This baby was on five seconds after I stepped into the camper and realized we had company. But it never went off once in the past two days. They were clean."

Relief sprawled across Irina's face, and she shook her head in wonder. "That was brilliant!" As Tony returned the unit to his pocket, she deferred to the boys' judgment. "Whatever you two decide to do in this matter, whether tell or not tell, I'm with you."

"Well, that settles it," Andy said slapping the table.

Tony jumped up and grabbed the coffee bean grinder. "How about a fresh pot of Sumatran before we hit the road again?"

As the coffee perked and its aroma filled the camper, the tension that had tied Irina's guts in knots began to ease. As far as the guys were concerned, her stupid mistake was water under the bridge. But she didn't want to be in this hot seat ever again. Their rule was now her rule. *Never compromise the mission!.*

12

the Compound
Sunday, November 10, 2019

Tony pulled up to the lodge in the wee hours of Sunday morning, so wicked tired that his eyelids hurt, like a headache sitting on his nose. *Getting tired of this road-warrior stuff.* Nobody rushed out of the lodge to greet them, and he didn't care. The only thing on his mind was his pillow. He and Andy had agreed earlier that evening that they weren't going to call ahead so they could maximize the rack time they were going to get that night. Visiting and celebrating could wait until later. He heard the camper door slam shut and watched Irina disappear into the lodge. Then he dropped the truck into second gear and goosed it up the road toward the barn.

Irina halted halfway across the great room. While crawling into her own bed sounded inviting, she knew that her inner conflicts would probably chase sleep away. With a sigh, she dropped her bags into a chair, pulled her hat down over her ears, zipped up her jacket, and headed out into the autumn chill.

As she strolled up the road, the beauty of the heavens transfixed her. The nearly full moon hung low on the western horizon, dappling the snowy mountain tops in moonglow. Orion stood like a sentinel in the south, his dagger as bright as she had ever seen it with the naked eye. Canis Major and Sirius guarded his flank. Ursa Major manned the northeast. And the Leonid meteor shower was giving its best show for centuries.

She prayed. *God, you are beyond amazing. The universe stretches out for infinity in every direction ... trillions of galaxies, each with billions of stars, yet you are in complete control. And you are in complete control of our circumstances. Thank you for watching over our dealings with the mafia, protecting us despite my stupidity, and bringing us back to the Compound safe-and-sound. But I'm still uneasy about the hitchhiking girls. Should I let this issue go as the boys suggested? Or should I tell Woody about it? I need your mind.*

Deep in thought and prayer, she was startled when the beehives appeared on her right, a kaleidoscope of soft pastel shades glimmering in the moonlight. She had walked farther than she had planned. With a heavy heart, she turned back. But she had only retraced a few steps when the solution crystallized in her mind. Her cue was the bees, among the most efficient team players on the planet.

In the big picture, the most critical concern for her was working in harmony with the boys. Though it felt less than forthright to not tell Woody about her security breach or the quirky girls they had given a ride to, they couldn't afford discord on the Russia team. A wedge between her and the boys was a threat to the mission. If the mission failed, the entire Compound would feel the loss. Her duty was clear. She desperately wanted the mission to succeed. So did everyone at the Compound. That meant she had to set aside her transparency concerns.

The decision didn't relieve all of her qualms, but it did enable her to go forward with confidence. With the matter settled, peace reigned anew in her heart, and she quickened her pace with the vigor of renewed hope. Now she set her sights on her own bed … after she had indulged a cup of hot chocolate made with half-and-half.

***

The next evening after dinner, everyone gathered in the great room for the Compound meeting. After the stragglers had settled in, Jordy pulled his podium out of the corner and began. "The first item of business is the mirror for the telescope. If you haven't already heard through the grapevine, we can't get the 60-inch mirror we had planned on unless we're willing to wait more than two years. But we can get a 72-inch mirror with almost identical specifications for the same price. Irina, can you fill us in on the details?"

"I called Alluna Optics on Wednesday morning to place an order for the 60-inch Zerodur that Blake had in mind. Alluna gave me two pieces of bad news. The first was that they were backlogged over two years on orders. The second was that they no longer took rush orders.

"I asked if there was any way we could get a mirror sooner. She said the only option was if I was interested in a

72-inch Zerodur with low thermal expansion that was almost identical to what Blake was looking for. I told her I might be, but I would have to sit down with my engineering team and see what they thought."

Blake was grinning like a kid let loose in a candy store with a twenty-dollar bill. "That's actually great news. I wanted to go bigger than 60 inches, but when I contacted Alluna, that was the largest size they made, and no one else offered anything larger than 50 inches. The 72-inch mirror would give me a lot more area." He pulled out his phone. "Hold on while I run the numbers." After fiddling with his buttons, he slammed his phone down in frustration. "Forgot to charge it last night."

"We don't need a calculator," Andrius popped off. "It's just basic math that anyone can work in their head. We'll get close enough for a general idea if we ballpark the math. Round Pi down to 3. The radius of the 60-inch mirror is 30 inches. The radius squared is 900. Pi times 900 is 2700 plus some change.

"The bigger 72-inch mirror has a radius of 36 inches. The radius squared is 1296. Let's round that to 1300. Pi times 1300 is 3900 plus some change. The big mirror with 3900-plus square inches of surface area has somewhere north of 40 percent more real estate than the small mirror with a surface area of 2700 inches. That's a huge gain in light gathering ability and magnification."

"BOOM!" Ariele exclaimed, spreading her hands up and out like a mushroom cloud. The room laughed.

"I wasn't asking whether you liked the idea," Irina said,

scarcely able to contain her laughter over the antics of Andrius and Ariele. I was asking whether you could retrofit your plans and frame to handle the larger mirror."

"No problem," Blake replied. "It would require some minor changes, but—"

"Speak for yourself," Andrius interrupted. "The larger mirror is going to weigh forty-five to fifty-five percent more than the mirror we were planning on using, depending on how much thicker it is. And while you only have to design and weld a slightly larger frame, I have to worry about dozens of engineering considerations that need to be reconfigured including the need for heavier hydraulic pumps, rams, and lines, beefier tires, increased tire pressure, increased wattage on some of the electric motors, and rebalancing the cab. The fact is, it will take me weeks to rework my calculations, locate the replacement parts, and order them. Not to mention, a huge pile of parts will be going to waste." He paused for a moment, shook his head, and griped, "Corporate America has nothing on us."

"But you can make it work, right?" Irina probed, attempting to mask her annoyance with a smile. Sometimes, he was such a whining weiner that she could hardly stand it.

Andrius dropped his head, frustrated that everyone seemed to take his heavy lifting for granted. He tapped his pen anxiously on the table for a few seconds, then glared at her with angry eyes and fumed, "Yes. I can make it work."

"Good. We really don't have any other options. We have to make this 72-inch mirror work." She looked around the table. "Does anyone else have thoughts or questions on the mirror situation?" She waited for a few seconds. If anyone did, they held their peace. She turned to Jordy. "Back to you, boss."

He looked over to Blake. "Any updates on the telescope project?"

"We've pretty much settled on the chassis design. And we've located sources for everything that we need. Now we just need to plan a couple trips to go get the stuff."

"What about the liquid hydrogen project?"

"We procured two Dewar tanks from a big welding supplier in Williston. That's enough to last us for a long time. We picked up the pipe and fittings we need from a company that specializes in industrial gases. And we have a solid lead on an electrolyzer, two compressors, and four heat exchangers in Wyoming. Got that from a friend of a friend."

"How far off the radar are they?"

"About as far as you can get. They were retired fifteen years ago, sold for scrap metal, and taken off inventory. But they didn't make it to the scrap yard. The purchaser sold them for a profit to a friend who has had them in his barn ever since. His hydrogen dreams never got off the ground."

"Sounds good to me. Well, let's move on to the last matter this morning, bringing everyone up to speed on the *Down the Rabbit Hole* program.

"Woody and I interviewed several parties over the past few days who were interested in being the program host. Our favorite is Vitaly Petrov in Magadan, Russia. He's been a regular listener since Krake started. He's fluent in English. And he's enthusiastic about the switch to a human voice.

The computer-modified voice, in his experience, made it hard to focus on the material.

"His only concern is that he speaks English with a pronounced Russian accent. I told him that I didn't think it would be an issue, but I would talk it over with my board before making a final decision. So what do you guys think? Are you okay with the English version of the *Down the Rabbit Hole* program being delivered with a strong Russian accent?"

"Since the message is going out worldwide," Blake replied, "and not merely America, it doesn't really matter what kind of accent the English is spoken with. As long as hearers can understand him, I could care less if he speaks with a Martian accent."

The others voiced hearty agreement.

"Then I'll text Vitaly, Jordy announced, "and let him know that the position is his."

"Will he be using his real name?" Blake asked.

"No. He'll be using a studio name. And he won't be disclosing his location either. The last thing we want is Russian agents or American operators taking him out."

13

the Compound
Sunday, November 10, 2019

Irina stood in the rear barn door, indulging the warmth of the sun on the brilliant fall afternoon. The thermometer had risen to sixty, and there was no wind to speak of, though occasionally she could hear the rustling of stubborn leaves still hanging on the aspen trees. She called to Blake, who was loading bales of hay onto a hay wagon. "Hey!" she called. "We should do a trail ride today. We may not get another gorgeous day like this until next year."

"You're right about that," he replied as he wiped a strand of hay off his cheek. "We could take the ridge trail to the cabin, circle around the backside to Red's place, then return on the old wagon track that parallels the road. I was thinking of riding up to the crest anyhow to look for elk sign. Why don't you check around and see if anyone wants to join us?"

She unhitched his UTV from the hay wagon and scooted off. Ten minutes later, she returned with Ariele, Joby, Kit, and Andrius, the latter badgered into coming by the girls. Though he had ridden a few times since his arrival, he was still nervous around the horses.

Joby and Ariele chose Pepper and Cayenne, black and red bays known for their spirited personalities, and began brushing their backs. Blake handed Irina the reins for Ginger, a yellow dun. She shook her head, walked over to the palomino, and patted it on the shoulder. "I want to ride Sundance." Blake shrugged his shoulders and walked the yellow dun over to Kit. Next to her, Andrius was awkwardly combing Sage, a beautiful rose grey. It was the least temperamental horse in the stable, and the only one that Blake dared to put Andrius on.

When the last saddle was inspected, they led their horses out of the barn, mounted up, and headed for the nearby tree line, Blake leading the way on Blue Moon. Recent drone and chopper flights in the area had made everyone more cover conscious, especially the fugitives, so they no longer rode across the open pasture. The group caught the trail that ran along the west side of the pasture and turned northward. A hundred yards in, the silence of the woods was shattered by the chatter of two squirrels and the raucous commotion of a party of grey jays, called camp robbers by the locals. The trail never failed to deliver on the sights and sounds of the woods.

At the far end of the pasture, the riders followed the switchbacks up the hillside to the crest of the shoulder, then turned uphill toward the main ridge where Blake's cabin stood. Halfway up the shoulder, Blue Moon stopped, snorted, and pawed the trail. Irina pulled up next to Blake. Her horse was shaking its head and trying to spin. It was all she could do to keep it pointed up the trail.

Blake scanned the area, looking for whatever critter was

making the horses nervous, expecting to see a lone cougar. His heart skipped a beat when he saw the culprits, four wolves off to their left, milling around a deer carcass. As he pointed them out to Irina, they began to growl and snap at the intruders who had interrupted their feast. Irina shuddered.

Snarling behind him on the other side of the trail made Blake even more uneasy. He turned in his saddle. Two wolves were trotting alongside the trail, apparently wanting to join the pack but nervous at the presence of the intruders. Suddenly, one of them changed course and attempted a shortcut through the line of horses, which was strung out on the trail. He was headed for the opening between Ginger and Cayenne. Ginger panicked, tossed Kit, and bolted back down the hill. Pepper and Cayenne spun and followed the yellow dun, with Joby and Ariele hanging on for dear life, shouting, and trying to rein them in.

Loud yowls brought Blake's focus back to the thrown rider. He handed his reins to Irina, jumped off his mount, and ran to Kit. She was sitting on the ground next to a large rock, writhing in pain, and clutching her left leg.

"Bad news!" Blake announced when he noticed bone protruding through her jeans. "She's got a compound fracture of the tibia."

A fresh round of growling erupted. All six wolves were huddled together now, thirty yards away, teeth bared, snarling, and inching closer. He stood up, made eye contact with them, waved his arms, and hollered. "Scram! Git!" Undeterred, they continued forward, oddly unafraid.

He sprinted to his horse, which was nervously pawing the ground, yanked his Weatherby .270 Magnum from his scabbard, chambered a round, aimed at the chest of a large black male which he figured was the alpha, and squeezed the trigger. The crack echoed in the hills, and the beast tumbled backward in an explosion of fur.

The other wolves hesitated. Blake didn't. He chambered another round and dropped a large, tawny specimen that he guessed was the beta. The four remaining creatures sniffed and whimpered at their fallen comrades for a few moments, then hightailed it up the ridge yipping and barking.

Blake jammed the rifle back into his scabbard and scrambled back to his injured friend. Andrius was sitting next to her, and she seemed to have calmed down. That worried him. She was probably going into shock. His mind was buzzing. How was he going to get the injured female out of here? They might be able to get a UTV up here with a small trailer behind it. But evacuating her on a utility trailer would be a bumpy ride. That would have to be a last resort. Could they carry her out in a makeshift stretcher? That was probably the best solution, but he would have to go back himself or send Andrius and Irina. He wasn't comfortable with either of those scenarios. They were going to have to get Kit out with what they had—three horses for four riders.

He exhaled slowly. They were in a predicament. Then again, so were Joby and Ariele. Neither had much experience with horses, and they probably wouldn't be able to stop their spooked mounts until they had reached the barn, assuming they were able to stay on their mounts.

He looked at the injured gal, her jaw clenched and face ashen. The ugly truth was, they didn't have any good options. She was going to have to ride back. He took Kit's hands in his. "If I lift you onto Sage, can you stay in the saddle and ride back?"

"I think so," she moaned with tear-filled eyes.

He walked over to the rose grey, grabbed her reins, started to turn her, and noticed that she was limping. A red mat revealed an oozing wound on its shin. *Wonder how that happened? Spun into a rock? Kicked by another horse?* He turned back to Kit. "Change of plans. You're gonna have to ride Sundance."

She nodded sullenly. She didn't care what horse she rode. She just wanted to get out of here.

Irina dismounted and walked Sundance closer to the injured young lady. The cowboy scooped Kit up and carried her a few steps to Irina's horse. "Okay, can you raise your right leg?" he asked.

With a groan, she raised it as far as she could, but only managed a few inches. Andrius gently lifted her leg and pushed it over the horse while Blake guided her onto the saddle. She tried to adjust herself, winced in pain, and shook her head. "It's not gonna work. I won't be able to keep my balance. My leg hurts too bad, and I feel light-headed."

Andrius took her by the wrist. "Would it help if I rode behind you and kept you upright?"

"I think so," she replied, smiling feebly. "I would appreciate that."

Blake helped Andrius mount up, and he slid in behind

Kit, high up the cantle. He reached around her and locked his hands on the horn, bracing them both. The cowboy tipped his hat to them. "We'll be right behind you." Andrius nodded back, nudged the horse lightly with his feet, and they began the slow ride home.

Irina watched the two start down the trail, wrestling with her perceptions. *Nerdboy can be awfully sweet. Just wish he could figure out how to jettison the intellectual superiority stuff.*

Blake touched the arm of the brunette that gave him heart flutters, interrupting her cogitations. "Guess you'll have to ride with me. Hope you don't mind."

"Not at all," she replied. *The same way I don't mind ice cream or chocolate.*

Blake watched as the graceful female mounted. Then, trembling in self-conscious anticipation, he placed his hands on her hips, put his boot in the stirrup, raised himself, tossed his leg over, settled in tight behind her, and wrapped his arms around her waist.

As the horses worked their way down the switchbacks, she picked his brain. "What do you make of the wolves, Blake? I thought wolves, like wild animals in general, were afraid of human beings, especially groups of people."

"Usually they are. I see wolves in this area from time to time, and they have never acted like this, even when I'm alone. This was really bizarre. My mind keeps running to Revelation 6:8, 'Behold, a pale horse. And the name of him who sat on it was Death, and Hades followed with him. And power was given to them over a quarter of the earth to kill with the sword, with hunger, with death pestilence, and with the beasts of the earth.' Many prophecy teachers have taught based on this verse that wild animals will go crazy and be filled with blood lust in the last days, wreaking havoc around the world. Maybe this was a foretaste of that."

"I hadn't thought about that before. That's super spooky. So the world doesn't just face wars, famine, and asteroids from heaven in the last days, they also face wild animals gone bonkers. That gives me the creeps."

"Me too. My skin is still crawling. That's the scaredest I have ever been in the woods, and I have had several run-ins with angry moose and grizzlies."

When they arrived at the lodge, the boys stationed themselves on either side of Kit. "Just lean down," Blake encouraged her, "and I'll catch you."

She was hesitant. But Andrius lifted her right leg and pushed it over the horse. She lost her balance and started falling off. Blake swooped his right arm under her torso and his left arm under her legs, and she toppled into his arms with a cry of mingled fear and pain.

The cowboy, with Irina in tow, carried the forlorn maiden into the lodge and set her on her bed. Moments later, Woody, Jordy, and Red burst into the room. "Joby and Ariele just told us what happened," Woody exclaimed. "They took a UTV down to the construction site and filled us in."

"We can't take her to the hospital," Jordy pointed out. "That would be disastrous for all of us. We're gonna have to set the bone ourselves and put a cast on her leg."

Nobody stepped forward. Kit bit her lip. Broken bones were

not usually home-remedy situations. And the hesitancy in the room to undertake the project added to her uneasiness.

Woody shook his head in frustration, grabbed the medical bag, yanked the zipper back, pawed around, and fished out the scissors. After kissing his daughter on the forehead, he exhaled deeply, cut her jeans up the outside past the knee, and pulled the flap of material away. A jagged fragment of bone jutted up out of the wound, exposing blobs of subcutaneous material. The whole area was surrounded by hideous greens and purples. The sight haunted him. It had been a long time since he had seen anything like it—an evening in the Balkans when a friend had been lacerated by shrapnel from a mortar round.

The stricken man handed his daughter three Tylenol 3 tablets and a bottle of water. "We'll give the medication a half hour to numb you up. Then we'll set the bone." He turned to Red. "We're gonna need padding, plaster of Paris rolls, and a few other things." Red nodded, and the two made their way to the supply room in the basement.

When it was time to set the bone, Ariele sat beside Kit and held the trembling gal in her arms. Woody ran his fingers over the area of the break, trying to conceptualize the lay of the fracture. "I think I need to pull back and rotate slightly to the left," he muttered to no one in particular. He positioned himself for the best leverage and gripped her leg above the ankle tightly. But he didn't move.

Irina wiped away the tears that were streaming down his cheeks and laid her hand on his shoulder. *The old toughie is a softie. The best kind of man.*

Woody calmed himself, double-checked his grip, yanked Kit's leg back hard, and rotated it about thirty degrees counterclockwise. She yelped as if she had been shot, and sobbed on Ariele's shoulder. While she wept, he daubed the wound with antiseptic wipes, cleaning up the dried blood and yellow crusties, then he smeared it liberally with triple antibiotic ointment. Next, he opened the roll of leg sleeve, cut a three-foot length, pulled it over her foot and up her leg to mid-thigh, and worked the wrinkles out. He covered that with two wraps of leg padding.

Red placed a chair next to the bed, and Andrius set a large mixing bowl on it filled with warm water. After he tested the temperature with his finger, Woody pulled on a pair of latex gloves, dipped a roll of plaster bandage, squeezed the excess water out, and began to wrap her leg. His stomach knotted up with apprehension. He knew in theory that the wrap should be firm but not too tight. But what this meant in any measurable way, he had no idea.

When the cast was finished four rolls later, he stripped his gloves off, and tossed them on the bed, relieved that the task was done.

"I guess," Kit exclaimed, with tears in her eyes, "that I won't be part of the Louisiana team after all."

"I'm afraid so," her father answered. "You aren't going to heal before Thursday." He touched her cheek tenderly, then retreated to the kitchen, sat down at the table, and stared off into space with his head propped in his hands. He hated pain. It always took the wind out of his sails when family or friends were feeling pain. And he always felt awkward trying to comfort them, like he was putting a bandaid on something that needed much more than he was capable of giving.

A hand settled on his shoulder and a steaming mug with a familiar scent was placed on the table in front of him. Woody turned his head.

Joby stepped back and smiled. "I knew I wouldn't be of much use in the first aid department, so I made rolls and coffee. Figured folks would need some encouragement once the ordeal was over. And I made you a Cinnamon Griz', just like the old times."

Woody lifted the cup toward his lips, drew in its unique fragrance through his nostrils, savored it, then took a cautious sip. It was too hot to drink, so he set the mug back down and reached for the platter of caramel rolls that the young man had just set on the table. As his teeth sank into the thick caramel slathered with melting butter, he sensed his equilibrium returning. Few things helped him find his sea legs in the storms of life faster than friends and comfort food.

***

The next morning, Ariele brought Kit breakfast in bed. "Sorry that you don't get to go with us on the Louisiana mission."

"Me too. I had my heart set on it. But I did some thinking last night. The more I think about it, the more I suspect that I'll be more valuable off the Louisiana team than on it."

"How's that?" Ariele asked? "You're more of a country girl than I am."

Kit smiled. "True. But it'll take more than a smidgen of country girl to succeed on that mission."

"So what are you going to do?"

"I'm gonna use my recuperation time to catch up on my reading. I've got a long list of titles that I'm going to knock off one by one in such fields as young-earth creationism and anomalous discoveries in archaeology and paleontology. I'll feed my discoveries to Pastor Jordy, and he can use the material in his teaching on the *Down the Rabbit Hole* program."

"Anomalous discoveries?" Ariele enquired. "What's that?"

"Evidence that doesn't fit the theory of evolution."

"Such as?"

"Human footprints found with dinosaur footprints, unfossilized dinosaur bones with intact red blood cells, fossilized trees standing upright through multiple layers of coal, and ancient technology found deep in coal and limestone mines."

"Wow! That sounds fascinating. I definitely want to hear more."

"Then let's plan on it when you get back from Lousiana."

"Absolutely! You've got a date, girl."

14

the Compound
Monday, November 11, 2019

After a light lunch of tuna spread and cheese on whole wheat, Irina walked back to the barn for her afternoon session with the Backstrom boys. But her mind was elsewhere.

She was troubled by the horse ride. Pangs of remorse, even guilt, racked her heart. Kit was going to be laid up for months and wouldn't be able to go on the Louisiana mission. Maybe she should have taken Ginger and let Kit ride Sundance. But this solution went nowhere too. She probably couldn't have handled Ginger either. What if she had been the one with the broken leg? Then she would be off the Russia team, and the boys would be without a Russian-language expert. That could be catastrophic for the Russia mission.

But it was her relationship, or lack of relationship, with Blake that was the biggest issue eating her. *There seems to be chemistry between us. So, why isn't he taking our relationship to the next step? Is he making up his mind? Is he balking at commitment? Is he clueless on how to read girls? Do I need to give him bigger hints that I'm interested in him?* She kicked at a loose rock and watched it tumble into the grass and weeds on the side of the road.

Two hours later, while executing a spin kick, Irina noticed Blake leaning on the top rail of the pen, watching her. Their eyes locked for a half second, and her kick sailed wide, barely nicking the pad that Andy was holding. Her trainer shook his head in disgust and signaled for her to try again. Venting her frustration, she unleashed a barrage of punches and kicks. "That was garbage," Andy complained as he lowered the pad. "Your aim and timing are way off. You need a break. Whatever is bugging you and ruining your concentration, you need to either let it go or resolve it."

Irina flung her gloves to the ground—disappointed with herself, mad at Andy, frustrated with Blake—and strode over to the waiting cowboy.

He watched her approach, his hat in hand, his guts tied in knots, uncertain what to think. The fire in her eyes and fury in her steps didn't help anything. This new version of Irina was still the classy woman that he had fallen for. But her already high intimidation factor had risen dramatically. She was even more assertive than before and crazy good at martial arts. When he attempted to think logically about his relationship with the pretty brunette, everything seemed to argue that she was out of his league. He was just a cowboy and roughneck. She was like a majestic mountain, inspiring men to rise to the challenge, yet humbling all who tried.

Irina stood before him with arms crossed and stared him down, inviting him to either talk or disappear. Even when drenched in sweat and smudged with grime, she was stunningly beautiful.

His courage stuck its tail between its legs. "I ... um ... I just wanted to say that ... I'm ... well, I'm worried about you going on the Russia mission. The new cold war is getting pretty hot, and the US and Russia are involved in several proxy wars. The mafia there is ruthless. Anti-American sentiment is skyrocketing. Maybe you could stay home and let the special operations guys handle this."

Irina glared at him. "Staying isn't an option. I have to go."

"You don't have to go."

"I think I do."

"But you're risking imprisonment or death."

"Dangerous missions do tend to be dangerous."

"What if you don't come back?"

"I try not to think about it. Besides, I think that the odds are pretty good that I'll make it back to Montana."

"I sure hope so," he replied, with voice cracking and eyes misting.

Surprised by this display of emotions from the normally stolid cowboy, her mouth dropped open, and her countenance changed to wonder.

"If you didn't come back," he continued, "I would feel like I was living in a world without sunshine."

The development caught her off guard. "What ... what are you trying to tell me?" she stammered.

"I don't want to lose you."

"Well, you can't lose me if I'm not yours."

The reply shocked and confused him. He stared at her in silence.

"You can only lose me if I'm yours," she clarified. "Are you telling me that you want me to be yours ... as in your girl?"

Blake could feel his whole body trembling with emotion. He swallowed hard and forced the words out of his mouth. "Yes, I want you to be my girl."

"Then do something about it!"

He was puzzled. "Like what?"

"Generally, the guy buys the girl a diamond ring."

He stared at her in shock, this turn of events entirely unexpected. What should he do next? Hug her? Kiss her? Irina relieved him of his dilemma. She cocked her head slyly, gave him a heart-melting smile, and turned to go back to her workout.

He called after her, "Do you want to go for a horseback ride this afternoon?"

"Four will work for me," she replied, without looking back. "And by the way, I want a champagne diamond."

The stunned cowboy put his hat back on and walked away with his head in the clouds. But now he was wrestling with a new dilemma. What in the world was a champagne diamond?

15

FEMA 286, Syracuse, NY
Monday, November 11, 2019

Jack and Sally settled into tattered stuff chairs in the newsroom and placed their dinner trays on the scuffed end table between them. Jack stuffed a few fries in his mouth, then took a bite of his mushroom and swiss burger. "Definitely horsemeat again, and the fries are freezer-burned as usual. Good thing we only see this stuff on Monday nights."

"It's the pudding that's bugging me," Sally grumbled. "I used to love pistachio pudding, and it was a special treat at first. But every lunch and dinner for over a month! That's not meal planning, not in my book anyway."

"Hate to be a bearer of bad news, but I was talking to Frenchie the other day. He said that Camp 286 had procured a hundred cases of pistachio pudding for a song from an overstock supplier and that he had only used twenty cases so far. That's means we're facing another four months of pistachio pudding."

Sally groaned at the bad news. She groaned again when

Jack picked up the remote. "Let me guess," she drolled, "We get to watch more unsettling news in America, Europe, and the Middle East?"

"You got it," Jack replied. "Our daily update on the world going down the toilet."

"Our world news headline story," Geoff Seaworthy intoned, "is Germany's departure from the EU and NATO. This morning she gave these organizations formal notification that she will be leaving them Friday at 9 a.m. Central European Time. She has given the United States and NATO 180 days to wind up operations, remove their staff, and vacate their military bases.

"Even though savvy experts—like the European desk here at CVN—saw the writing on the wall over two years ago and warned about the political winds blowing in Germany, this announcement has taken the West by surprise. Politicians and newscasters on both sides of the pond have responded to this development as if it came out of the blue. But when you see what you want to see, you can't see what you need to see. The widening cracks were there for anyone with open eyes to examine.

"Germany's departure is a heavy blow to the EU and its dream of a unified Europe. They had already lost the second biggest economy in the union with the departure of the UK, and now they're losing the largest. It looks like the writing is on the wall for the EU. It's highly doubtful that the economies of France, Italy, and Spain will be able to carry the rest of the EU on their backs. If the union collapses, the former Soviet-bloc members would likely follow Germany into the arms of Mother Russia while the western members would likely turn their eyes toward the UK and the US.

"The economic pressure that Germany's departure has put on the EU is is already evident in the stunning collapse of the euro since the announcement this morning, dropping from 1.02 to 0.85 US dollars under exceptionally heavy trading. The euro is currently hovering just above the psychologically important bottom of 0.83 it made in 2000. If, or perhaps I should say when, it breaks below that support level, there will be blood in the streets. Some pundits are already predicting that the euro will fall to 0.50 over the next few weeks.

"Two other German developments are in the news tonight. The first is that the longstanding feud between Turkey and Germany is over. A memorandum of cooperation between the nations was signed this morning just hours after Germany gave notice of her departure from the EU and NATO. Highlights from the memorandum include military and economic cooperation and a promise from Germany to return the throne of Zeus and other important cultural artifacts that are housed in German museums.

"The second is that new details have come out regarding the trade agreement which Germany and Russia signed last August. Not only does the agreement grant Germany coal and natural gas at bargain prices, but it also awards her contracts for Meyer Werft to build twenty-four warships for Russia: four carriers, ten nuclear subs, eight destroyers, and two resupply ships."

"I find it amazing," Jack exclaimed, "that Jordy predicted over twenty years ago that England and Germany would leave the EU and that the EU would collapse."

Sally rolled her eyes. "So I suppose I get to hear a rerun of your thoughts on the future of Germany and Russia for what—the tenth or twelfth time?"

"Probably the twentieth to be honest," he replied, chuckling. "I guess I just find the prophetic passages of the Bible to be an endless source of fascination. Those who take their testimony at face value can make accurate predictions about the geopolitical situation in the last days." He launched into a detailed outline of the developments that were likely to be seen in the build-up to the Gog and Magog War in Ezekiel 38 and 39. But he stopped in mid-sentence and focused on the television.

"Big news on the science front tonight," Geoff continued. We received a newswire less than an hour ago informing us that the ExoMars probe failed to land on Mars. Initial reports from the ESA and NASA are blaming the failure on a syntax error in a single line of code, which resulted in the thrusters failing to fire in the manner needed for the probe to enter into Martian orbit.

"Reports have leaked out which claim that both space agencies are brainstorming, hoping to come up with a Plan B that would enable them to salvage the mission. As officials have already reported that it would be impossible to return the probe to Mars, this has left many wondering what the mission officials mean by salvaging the mission."

Jack nudged Sally. "I'll bet a thousand dollars that the

mission didn't fail and that this scenario was planned. They are intentionally using Mars like a slingshot to send the ExoMars probe to the Rogue. My guess is that they'll probably try to intercept it somewhere in the vicinity of Jupiter. Now they're pretending to go back to the drawing board to see if they can come up with an alternative mission that has a ring of plausibility to it."

"When I was still on the team," Sally replied, "the tentative plan was to pretend a Trojan asteroid mission."

"That's what I was thinking."

"What's a Trojan asteroid?" asked brunette Joyce, who often sat next to Sally in the cafeteria and the newsroom.

"They're asteroids that orbit with Jupiter in its orbital path around the sun. They're massed at two main points: Lagrange 4, which is sixty degrees ahead of Jupiter, and Lagrange 5, which is sixty degrees behind it."

"Are there many of them?"

"There are over 7000 known Trojans, but experts estimate that there are more than a million over one kilometer in diameter."

"Wow!" Joyce said as she shook her head in amazement. "I never heard of Trojans before. The more I learn about our solar system, the more amazing God gets."

Jack nodded in agreement. "The more you learn about any field—language, music, culinary arts, mathematics, physics, chemistry, biology, or what have you—the more amazing God gets. 'Fearfully and wonderfully made' doesn't just apply to man. It applies to every work of God's hands in the whole of Creation."

16

the Compound
Thursday, November 14, 2019

The lodge was buzzing with activity. The members of the mission teams stood by their assigned tables in the conference room, gear spread out, waiting for inspection. Jordy and Red moved from table to table, verifying that every item on their mission checklists was in their kits. Woody followed behind, inspecting the equipment to verify that everything was in working order. The other members watched the process from the sidelines, trying to stay out of the way.

After the inspection was completed, Woody squeezed in between Sam and Ariele and took them by the arms. "Are you gals ready?"

"What do you think?" Sam teased. "You and Red both gave me a thumbs up a few minutes ago."

"I was thinking about you, not the gear."

"I'm not scared if that's what you're thinking. This won't be as dangerous as situations I faced in Africa and the Amazon."

"Well, I'm still nervous for you. There may be more danger than you think. The federal government has been stepping up patrols and checkpoints in rural parts of the country, trying to catch fugitives and terrorists."

She shrugged her shoulders. "If we get caught, we get caught, and my life won't be going the way I would like it to go. That wouldn't be the first time."

"Just be careful, girls, to follow mission protocols. Wear your sunglasses and contacts at all times. Stay away from major highways. Follow the route or the alternate routes that Andrius plotted—"

"Dad!" Kit complained, interrupting. "They've heard the safety lecture ten times already."

He grinned sheepishly. "Nothing personal. Not doubting anyone's intelligence. That's just the military vet in me, double-checking and triple-checking everything before the mission."

When the teams had finished repacking their kits and were ready to roll, Jordy asked everyone to join him in prayer. "In a few minutes, Lord, two grand adventures will begin. We look to you for protection. Bless our efforts to procure the telescope components that we need. And help us to warn the world of the awful things that are coming from the heavens above. Amen."

The room seemed frozen in place. Nobody was eager for the unavoidable departures. Ariele, hating the awkward waiting game, grabbed her bags and bolted for the door. The others followed suit.

Sam and Ariele tossed their gear into Blake's truck. They would be driving down to Effie, Louisiana, where they would contact Lobo, trade the truck for a set of wheels with Louisiana plates, and continue to the Atchafalaya area.

The three members of the Russia team loaded their equipment into the Backstrom's camper. They were headed to Palm Beach, Florida where they would board Mikhail Egorushkin's yacht for the long voyage to Sevastapol. Blake was riding along with them so he could drive the truck back to Montana.

Kit watched from the sidelines, tears streaming down her cheeks. Ariele noticed her forlorn friend, walked over, and took her arm.

"What's with the sad face, Bonedigger? I thought you were over the fact that you don't get to go?"

"I'm over that. But I still feel like I'm not pulling my weight. Everyone has something important to do except for me."

"Just take it from God, Kit. He has a purpose for everything. He has a role that he wants you to fill, a role no one else can. Just trust him, wait on him, and do whatever your hands find to do. Focus on your books like you said."

"I know. It'll just take time to adjust. The hardest part for me will be sitting around. I like to be outside doing stuff."

"If you read half the books you said you wanted to read, you won't be just sitting around. Plus, you can switch things up. Read by the fireplace, read in the greenhouse, read in the hay piles in the barn, read in the Hallelujah Tavern."

Kit laughed. "Good thing I love reading."

"I know, right!"

The two embraced, then Ariele scampered back to the campers, where she and Irina shared a long, tear-filled hug.

"Promise me that you'll pray for me every day!" Ariele pleaded.

"I promise."

As the team members started climbing into their trucks, a voice shouted, "Wait!" Ariele retrieved her foot from the running board and faced Joby, who was wrestling to keep his emotions in control. "Close your eyes," he said, "and hold out your hand."

She complied. Something light and delicate dropped into her palm. Or was it two things?

"You can open your eyes now."

"Wow! They're beautiful! I love earrings. And I love the star of David" Where did you get them?"

"I carved them for you out of sandalwood—a reminder to keep your eyes on Yeshua."

She lifted them to her nostrils and inhaled the fragrance. Then, to his pleasant surprise, she flew into his arms and kissed him on the cheek. After a brief but tender embrace, she whirled around, climbed into the cab, and shut the door.

Moments later, the pickups headed down the road and disappeared around the bend, leaving nothing but a lingering dust cloud. Woody wistfully watched the swirls until the last vestiges had dispersed. Saying goodbye was always hard. Saying goodbye when you might never see them again was as bitter as death itself.

17

**Palm Beach, FL
Tuesday, November 19, 2019**

The Bahia Mar Yachting Center was a hive of activity—cars, people, and boats. Nonetheless, Blake found an empty parking spot that was facing the Intracoastal Waterway. "Can't believe I got this lucky," he remarked to Tony. "Usually I end up parking a country mile from where I need to go."

The operator, too anxious for small talk, smiled, grabbed his bag, and headed for the camper. As he had suspected, he didn't need to wake his brother. Andy had already stowed his pad and sleeping bag and was sitting up at the table, rubbing the sleep out of his eyes. He continued to the sleeper over the cab and shook Irina.

"Time to roll, Nikita," he whispered.

She stretched, yawned, rolled out of the bunk, and downed a bolt of cold espresso from her travel mug, trying to clear the fogginess. *Blah! Even premium coffee tastes nasty when it gets old.*

"Time to lose our comfortable footgear," Andy grumbled

as he removed his right boot. "It's not gonna be pleasant dressing like FSB agents. The clothes would be okay," he continued as he slipped on a leather coat over the European-cut trousers and shirt he had donned at their prior stop, "if I only had to wear them once in a while. But the shoes pinch my toes."

"I hate the shoes too," Tony replied. "But once we leave Moscow, we can probably dress more comfortably."

"I hope so. I sure didn't sign up for this."

Irina huffed. "What's up with masculine guys and poor taste? I think guys look hot when they're dressed up."

Tony snorted. "Guess hot just ain't my style."

She rolled her eyes, then slipped off her flats and strapped on a pair of low heels. "Not bad," she remarked as she stood. "A little tight, but they're leather, so they'll stretch a bit."

When they were dressed per FSB regulations, they checked each other's wallets to confirm that everything was in order. It was. They were carrying counterfeit Russian passports, driver's licenses, and Federal Security Service IDs on their person. Their real IDs were hidden in concealed pockets in their leather suitcases.

Irina retrieved her secure phone from her Lola Brown purse and dialed the oligarch's steward.

"Yuri, here."

"Hi Yuri," she said, speaking in Russian. "This is Aleksandra, Konstantin's friend who is looking for passage to Sevastopol. We're at the marina and would like to board."

"Ah, Konstantin's friends in the FSB. Did you bring the cash?"

"Yes."

"Good. Find the dock that faces the Intracoastal Waterway and follow it to your left, all the way to the end. The *Ekaterina* is the last berth on the right, number 505."

"Thank you."

"You're welcome." Irina waited seven or eight seconds in case there were further instructions, but he was gone.

Tony picked up his suitcases. "Let's get the show on the road," he announced with enthusiasm and bounded out the door. The others followed on his heels.

Blake met them on the asphalt outside.

"You still planning on driving a little farther tonight?" Tony asked.

"Yeah. Hoping to get a couple hours north before I stop for the night. But I'll play it by ear. Don't want to drive tired." He stuck out his hand. "Guess this is it. Good luck."

"Thanks," Tony replied, giving his hand a firm squeeze. "Have a safe journey home."

Andy pumped Blake's hand vigorously and slapped him on the shoulder. "Stay safe."

"I will," he assured him.

Blake turned his attention to Irina and her blazing blue eyes. Their eyes locked. He reached out his hand, but she was oblivious. He stretched it farther and touched her arm. She looked down and stared wide-eyed at the engagement ring—rose gold with a stunning three-carat champagne diamond.

"How did you know that I love rose gold?"

"I didn't. But I prayed for wisdom, and the gal at the

jewelry store helped me pick out a ring. I told her that I needed a ring for a woman who loves champagne diamonds and has refined taste. She told me that rose gold makes a stunning setting for fancy diamonds."

Irina snatched the ring from his hand and jumped into his arms. After a few seconds of bliss, she pulled away, dropped the ring in a side pocket in her purse, picked up her suitcases, and headed for the berth at a brisk pace. She didn't want Blake, or anyone else, to notice the tears rolling down her cheeks.

Blake turned for the truck with a bounce in his step. By the time he was behind the wheel, however, his heart was in his throat. What if something happened, and she never came back? He forced himself to concentrate on his part of the mission. Get back home in one piece and stay busy on the telescope. As he turned the key, he prayed. *She's in your hands, God. There's absolutely nothing I can do.*

Yuri met the guests at the bottom of the gangplank and gestured for them to follow him up the ramp. The three hesitated, mesmerized by the gargantuan ship which loomed over them. "It's enormous," Irina whispered. Tony whispered back, "It's longer than a football field." Yuri smiled and gestured again. He had seen this wonder many times before. He would see it again.

At the top of the ramp, an overweight, but distinguished-looking gentleman greeted them with a booming voice. "Welcome to the *Ekaterina*. I'm Mikhail Egorushkin." He embraced each of them warmly then gestured toward the door. "Follow me. I'll show you to your quarters. You can drop your bags there. Then I'll give you a tour. You're free to go anywhere you please except the engine room, my quarters, the crews' quarters, and the guest rooms."

The vessel was as magnificent as it was massive. It wasn't a millionaire's yacht. It was a billionaire's yacht. Over the next half hour, they were shown the ornate lounge, the swimming pool, the hot tubs and saunas, the large gym, the well-stocked galley, the movie theatre, the main passageways, the dozen guest cabins, the spacious decks for strolling and lounging, the engine room, and the heliport. But the team members had mixed feelings about their accommodations. While they would be the nicest they had ever enjoyed, they all sensed that danger lurked in the background.

After the tour Mikhail escorted them to his quarters and seated them in plush velvet chairs. "Let's open a bottle of vodka and share a toast to the success of your venture."

"Thank you," Irina replied, as she handed over the bag with the cash, "but none of us drink."

He nodded with an odd look on his face. She couldn't tell whether it was surprise or disdain. The cheerful man caught himself and changed the subject. "Konstantin tells me that you're with the FSB."

Irina fretted. *Is he just playing along with our cover story, or does he really believe that we're with the FSB? How much did Konstantin tell him?* "Konstantin should learn to keep his lips zipped."

"Vodka loosens the lips," he laughed.

"Indeed it does."

"Ginger ale?" he offered, holding up a bottle of Blenheim.

"Please," she replied.

Mikhail filled three iced copper mugs with the stout beverage and handed them to his companions, then mixed himself a Russian Mule. "Cheers," he said, raising his mug for a toast.

"Cheers," they replied in unison.

"Wow, that's hot," Irina exclaimed, her eyes starting to water.

"Awesome!" Tony added. "I never had a ginger ale with so much kick."

"Unfortunately, nobody in Russia makes world-class ginger ale," Mikhail observed. "This stuff is made in South Carolina. Whenever I'm in America, I pick up several dozen cases."

Their host engaged them in small talk: European politics, Russia's involvement in Syria, the Kontinental Hockey League, and the odds of SCKA Moscow repeating as the winners of the Gagarin Cup. But Irina grew tired of the mindless chatter and steered the conversation back to the matter weighing on her mind. "I understand that our trip will take about four weeks."

"That's correct."

"And you plan on departing tomorrow?"

"Correct. We'll leave in the morning after I have indulged in a leisurely breakfast with a business associate. Our first stop will be Bermuda. Then we have stops in Barbados, Cape Verde, and the Canary Islands. From there we'll pass through the Straits of Gibraltar into the Mediterranean, then through the Straits of the Dardanelles and the Bosporus Strait into the Black Sea, and then arrive in Sevastopol, Crimea."

"Sounds exciting. I can't wait to see the Caribbean and the Cape Verde Islands. But I'm especially looking forward to seeing Crimea again."

"So you've been to Crimea before?"

"Yes. My family spent a few summer vacations there when I was a child."

"Do you have travel arrangements from Sevastopol to Moscow?"

"No. Not yet."

"Don't worry about it. I'll make arrangements for your travel to Moscow once we arrive in Crimea."

"Thank you. I would greatly appreciate that."

"Can I fill your mugs one more time?"

Irina checked her watch. "We're going to pass," she replied as she stood up. "It's nearly two in the morning, and we've had a long day. But thank you very much for the lovely evening."

"My pleasure."

As the three exited the room, Viktor, Mikhail's bodyguard, gave them some serious evil eye. Irina ignored him and walked right past him. But his vicious glare made her apprehensive. Several times on the way to their rooms, she looked over her shoulder. To her relief, he didn't follow them. When they turned the last corner, her concerns proved justified. The goon was standing at her door with his arms crossed. "FSB agents who don't drink vodka!" he sneered. "Never heard of such a thing. That's like a literature professor who's never read Dostoevsky!"

"Nyet! It's more like a professor who doesn't drink vodka."

He ignored her retort and snorted. "I've never heard of FSB agents working in SVR territory. Since when do domestic intelligence agents operate in Foreign Intelligence Service territory?"

Irina met his glare. "We don't do SVR work in SVR territory. We do FSB work in SVR territory."

Viktor looked at her dumbfounded.

"We spy on spies. Our job is to make sure that Russian agents, whether SVR or GRU, don't become double agents."

"I spent a decade with military intelligence in the GRU after I transferred from the Spetsnaz. I never heard of such a thing."

Irina met his gaze with a cold-steel glare. "You must have been pretty low on the food chain when you were in the Main Directorate."

He flushed with anger. "I've got my eye on you three."

"We have our eyes on you too," she replied briskly, brushing off his warning. "Reports are circulating …"

He tensed his jaw, clenched his fist, and took a step closer to her.

Tony attempted to step between them, but Irina closed the gap too quickly and faced the man nearly nose to nose, glowering back.

"Don't try and intimidate me," he roared.

Irina coolly replied, "No intimidation here at all. Just a friendly reminder that you may want to be careful. You wouldn't want to have enemies in the FSB when this ship docks in Sevastopol."

Viktor glowered at her for a few seconds, then turned and stalked away, cursing and muttering.

Andy put his hand on Irina's shoulder. "I have an awful feeling that we haven't seen the last of him."

18

road trip to Casper, WY
Saturday, November 23, 2019

A road-weary Blake arrived back at the Compound late Saturday evening and drove straight into the barn. Dead-on-his-feet exhausted, he had zero interest in human interaction. The only thing on his mind was grabbing some quick grub and hitting the hay. As he stepped out of the camper with his duffel bag, someone shouted, "Hey!" He turned his head toward the voice. Andrius, panting hard, was running toward him

Dread fell upon Blake like a smothering blanket. *Must be an emergency. Can't imagine him running for any other reason.*

The young man stopped next to him, gasping for air, and held up his hand for the cowboy to wait while he caught his breath. After thirty seconds or so, he wheezed out, "Can you take me to Casper in the next few days?"

"Seriously, dude?" Blake replied. "You ran over here just to ask me that? It couldn't wait until tomorrow?"

Uncertain how to respond to the frustration that was practically dripping off his friend's face, Andrius steeled himself and plowed forward. "I'm really worried about my books and tools in the storage unit. The books will be ruined if they get moldy and mildewy. And some of the tools could be damaged by excess moisture."

Blake just stared at him, simmering.

"To make matters worse," he added, hoping to strengthen his case in Blake's eyes, "I saw on the news this evening that there has been a rash of storage-unit break-ins across eastern Montana and Wyoming and western North Dakota, South Dakota, and Nebraska."

The cowboy was unfazed.

"I'm pretty worried about my stuff getting stolen," he continued, clarifying his point. "That would be a tremendous loss, not merely for me but also the Compound. Those tools hold immense value for the telescope project."

Blake, feeling bludgeoned with an issue he didn't want to deal with right now, scorched the young man with a glare. "Andrius," he pleaded, trying not to sound as angry as he was. "Try to look at this from my perspective. I just finished a long trip. I'm exhausted. I don't feel like making another trip any time soon. And I don't feel like talking about another trip right now. I just want to heat up a couple burritos, chase them down with a glass of milk, and crawl into bed."

"You do realize how late in the year it is, right?" Andrius posed, playing the ace up his sleeve. It would be to your advantage to get this trip out of the way before winter hits. Just last week while welding on the telescope, you told me some hair-raising tales about how brutal the Wyoming highways can be in the winter—high winds, monster drifts, and bitter cold. Twice you had car trouble there in the winter, once being forced to ride out a three-day blizzard in a sleeping bag. And I distinctly remember you saying that you would just as soon never face that again."

Reluctantly, Blake caved. "Got me there. Tell you what. If we left Monday afternoon, we could empty the storage unit that evening, drop the key in the office slot, spend the night at a cheap motel, and return on Tuesday. One whirlwind trip. Get it over with. No more worry about mold on your books. No more monkey on my back."

"Wow ... thanks ..." Andrius stammered, blindsided by the agreement to an immediate trip. He had expected something more like a wait-and-see for a possible trip three or four weeks down the road.

"Don't mention it," Blake replied as he turned and walked away. Looking over his shoulder, he added, "We can talk more tomorrow. I'm going to bed."

***

Monday after lunch, the two dropped the Backstrom's camper onto its storage rack, installed Blake's topper, tossed their gear in back, and hit the road. To Andrius's frustration, Blake put on a playlist of Christian country and bluegrass music. To Blake's disgust, Andrius kept his nose glued to a textbook on advanced TIG welding, coming out of his burrow from time to time just long enough to regurgitate a section on welding with rare-earth alloys.

That evening, a half hour south of Sheridan, his belly full

from a sirloin steak dinner, Blake was fighting the nods. After the rumble strip on the shoulder gave him a nervous start for the third time, he vented at his partner. "Can you set that stupid book aside for a while and carry on a conversation like a normal human being? You need to help me stay awake, or we're going to end up in the ditch."

"Just drink some caffeine. That always helps me. Want one of my energy drinks?"

"If I drank an energy drink now, I wouldn't fall asleep until long after midnight. And tomorrow morning, I would feel like I got hit by a train."

Andrius looked genuinely puzzled. "Energy drinks don't keep me awake at night."

Blake wasn't interested in turning caffeine into a discussion. Once his nerdy friend got rolling on a subject he liked, trying to nudge the conversation in a different direction was like trying to throw a sumo wrestler to the ground. If he wasn't careful, he was going to get an earful on the chemistry of caffeine and the other beneficial alkaloids in coffee.

An act of God saved him. A brilliant flash of green arced across the sky in front of them as they were leaving Banner, coming out of the southeast and traveling northwest.

"Whoa! Did you see that?" Andrius exclaimed.

"See what?" the cowboy teased.

"The shooting star!"

"Dude. We have had shooting stars almost every night for months now. It's probably the precursor to the wave of comets that shall bombard the earth in the last days. Like the asteroid or comet impacts in Revelation."

"I've heard the wave lecture a dozen times," Andrius retorted. The planet that once orbited between Mars and Jupiter was smashed into smithereens by another planet. Some of the fragments stayed in the asteroid belt. Some were captured as moons by the planets. Some became the Trojan asteroids in Jupiter's orbital path. Some became the centaur asteroids that orbit between Jupiter and Neptune. Some became Kuiper Belt objects. Some became the short-period comets, which bombarded Earth regularly until she finally swept her orbital path clear. Now we're waiting for the wave of long-period comets, which could begin any time. But, dude, while I think the theory is probably true, it isn't the topic of the conversation."

He stared at Blake, hoping for some kind of intelligent response. When the cowboy didn't respond, he continued his tirade. "Blake. How could you have missed it? It was huge—at least five times bigger than any shooting star that I have ever seen before. And it was green!"

"Yeah. I gotta admit, that was pretty amazing," he deadpanned, then cracked a smile.

"I hate it when you do that," Andrius spat back. "I never know when you're joking or serious."

"My bad. But it's fun to tease you. You get so worked up over little things. True confession—from time to time I intentionally put one of your tools in the wrong spot in your toolbox just watch you throw a conniption fit."

"I don't know what's worse. You being stupid and not knowing where things go, or you being mean and intentionally putting them in the wrong place." He stewed in silence for a minute. "It's hard going through life when nobody around you feels order and numbers like you do."

"You do trust facts over feelings, right?"

"Always."

"Here's a fact on human nature for you to file away. Mean-teasing and friend-teasing are two different animals."

The young man stared at his feet.

"Do you believe me, Andrius?"

"Yeah, intellectually. But I'm having problems reprogramming my value judgments so I can somehow regard your disorderly conduct as decent behavior."

"Good for you, bro. Keep at it. If you can reprogram yourself, it'll be much easier for you to get along with those of us who aren't half as smart as you are."

After a few minutes of silence, Blake restarted the conversation on comets and the end times. "Do you believe the theory that an exploded planet was behind the wave of short-period comets in the ancient past and will result in a future wave of long-period comets?"

"It seems plausible. Something obviously happened up there that resulted in all the fragments. And I suspect that Irina is correct that it happened post-flood. If the flood is true, then all of the impact craters on the planet, even the massive ones that are tens of kilometers across, were made by post-flood impacts."

"What about the idea that Mars and Venus used to orbit the sun in elliptical, comet-like orbits that intersected with Earth from time to time, creating havoc down here?"

"I have more trouble with that theory. It seems far-fetched."

"You do believe in catastrophism, right?"

"Absolutely! The universal flood in Noah's day far better explains the geological features we see on Earth than the slow, incremental processes of the uniformitarian theory."

"Okay. So how do you explain the surface features that can't be explained by the flood?"

"Such as?"

"The post-flood burn layer that smothered hundreds of ancient cities in the Mediterranean, the Middle East, and North Africa in a layer of ash that's laced with extra-terrestrial impact indicators like high-grade sulfur, iridium, hexagonal diamonds, and impactites like tektites and Libyan glass."

Andrius hesitated and shrugged his shoulders. He felt trapped and didn't want to answer.

"Come on, Bud! You're the smart one in the bunch! You already grant recent creation. You already grant catastrophism and the flood. Now you have evidence of huge post-flood catastrophes. What caused them? You can't hide your head in the sand."

"You obviously want to enlighten me, so enlighten me."

"The planetary visitation theory explains the devastation of the cities destroyed in the burn layer including Sodom and Gomorrha. It explains how Antarctica and Siberia went from temperate climates to cold. It explains the ancient accounts around the world which claim that the sunrise and the sunset reversed and reversed back again. It explains the ancient pagan religions, which worshipped these planets as terrifying gods who visited the earth from time to time."

"So, you really believe the theory that errant planets on highly elliptical orbits rained fire, brimstone, and rocks on Earth and caused polar shifts and polar reversals?"

"I do. It's a simple matter of trusting ancient history and rejecting the revisionist history of the evolutionists. Not to mention, there's no competing theory which even begins to explain and harmonize all the data ... well, apart from the brute-force application of evolutionary theory, which tortures the contrary evidence on the rack and forces it to testify on the behalf of evolution."

Andrius sat in silence, mulling this information over. "So, you're suggesting that the burn layer and the polar shifts and reversals, just like the impact craters, are indicative of catastrophism that's distinct from the flood?"

"Exactly. The same kind of God-orchestrated catastrophism that we see in the flood except that it involves a series of smaller-scale, post-flood events."

Andrius screwed up his mouth, an indication that he was weighing the observations.

Blake continued. "The ancient mythologies aren't fiction stories, but representations of events that men witnessed in the heavens, especially those involving the pantheon of gods—the sun, the moon, and the five visible planets. This is why the mythologies of the major cultures around the world often feature the same stories with only the names and minor details changed.

"Further, the ancients weren't worshipping the tiny red star and the benign morning star that we're familiar with, but two planets that terrified them. Men trembled at Mars because he trampled the nations with stones from heaven. This devastation induced the Romans to worship him as the god of war. They even borrowed the idea of using launched stones in warfare from him. Venus was feared as the two-faced woman, sometimes beautiful, sometimes terrible. When she was angry, she would throw fire and brimstone upon the inhabitants of Earth."

"Eventually, these religions introduced idols that represented the planet gods, and after the planets obtained their current benign orbits, the idols remained. To regard these idols as the sum and substance of the ancient religions is to disparage ancient man as whopper-telling liars."

"If this Mars and Venus stuff is true," Andrius challenged, "how do you square it with the worship of Baal and Ashteroth that we see in the Old Testament?"

"Baal was Mars. Astheroth was Venus."

Andrius bobbed his head back and forth, then steered the debate in a different direction. "Apart from the ancient stories, what evidence is there that Mars made close passes to Earth?"

"The length of the year."

Andrius looked at Blake as if he were pulling his leg. "What does that have to do with anything?"

"Because the length of the year has changed. Up until the time of Uzziah and Isaiah, the ancient civilizations used a 360-day calendar which was divided into 12 equal months of exactly 30 days. Around 750 BC, Mars made a near pass of Earth, bumping Earth slightly farther from the sun, which lengthened the year to 365.25 days, and nudging the moon closer to Earth, shortening the lunar month to 29.5 days. At the same time, Earth bumped Mars into its current orbit, or at least into a trajectory that led to its current orbit.

"Many ancient cultures recorded this event in their mythologies, typically representing it by two gods fighting. When the fight was over, and the dust cleared, the year was longer, the month was shorter, many stars had fallen from the heavens, and many new stars were seen in the heavens.

"This created havoc for the priests. The solstices and equinoxes were no longer lining up with their calendars. All their holy days were thrown off. It was at this time that the Stonehenge-type structures were either made or remade trying to rectify the situation. For years the nations added five days to the end of the year as a makeshift way to balance the calendar. Eventually, Solon, one of the wisest men in the ancient world, received the equivalent of a Nobel Prize in science for determining that the year was 365.25 days long."

"But," interjected Andrius, "if the calendar really did change in the Iron Age, how come we don't hear about it in school?"

"Evolution!" Blake exclaimed. "Revisionist history starts with the assumption that the length of the year hasn't changed for billions of years. This requires them to treat the ancients as dimwits who were blissfully unaware that the year was actually 365.25 days and not 360. But this is unjust. The ancients weren't stupid. The ancient Sumerians and Babylonians, for instance, used simple calculus to calculate the orbit of heavenly bodies."

"So, you're saying that we don't hear about the calendar change because the evolutionists approach ancient history with the same unbelief that they approach the biblical record?"

"That's exactly right. The evolutionists treat the catastrophes recorded in ancient history with the same disdain that they treat the catastrophes recorded in the Bible."

"Well, I have to admit," Andrius confessed, "that it is difficult to fathom how ancient man could have believed for thousands of years that there were 360 days in the year when there were actually 365.25 days. It doesn't add up that the entire planet could be wrong for millennia until Solon finally noticed the error. That's like the whole world believing for thousands of years that humans have eight fingers and toes until a scientist made the stunning observation that they had all been counting wrong."

Blake laughed at the analogy.

Andrius stared out the window, stroking his chin for a moment, then he spun back around. "On top of that, a year that's exactly 360 days long composed of 12 months that are exactly 30 days long seems to correspond better with God's wisdom and precision. Makes you wonder if ancient man came up with the idea of dividing a circle into 360 degrees because the year actually was 360 days."

"I have a hard time seeing how man could have figured it out any other way."

"Okay. I'll give you that one. But let's take this one step further. Assuming that you and Irina are correct, what does a calendar change in ancient history have to do with Bible prophecy?"

"Because history tends to repeat or revisit things. And when we come to the book of Revelation, the year is once again 360 days long. This we know because—"

"Because," Andrius interrupted him, "the length of the second half of the tribulation is stated in three ways: three and a half years, 42 months, and 1260 days. And the correlation between the three implies that the year is 360 days in length."

Blake nodded.

"So you think," Andrius asked, "that the 360 days is the actual length of the year, and that something drastic is going to happen between now and then that will change the year back to 360 days?"

"That's exactly what I'm thinking. The same kind of planetary interference that changed the length of the year during the Iron Age. I suspect that Venus, the figurative morning star, will be approaching Earth at the same time that Jesus, the literal morning star, gathers his church in the clouds.

"Sometime after the rapture, Venus will bump Earth—magnetic field against magnetic field, not surface against surface—knocking it into a slightly altered orbit that will change the length of the year back to 360 days. And Venus will be the source of the fire from heaven which destroys the Russian juggernaut in Ezekiel chapters 38 and 39 and wreaks havoc on Magog and many other nations."

Andrius stroked his chin, weighing this information. "That makes sense. Many teachers believe that the rapture and the destruction of the Russian juggernaut happen around the same time—the rapture shortly before the fire falls. And it fits better with the Old Testament accounts of fire falling from heaven."

"I think it's a better fit too. Personally, I'm uncomfortable with the understanding that the fire is caused by nuclear weapons. The fire is a definitive act of God. By one act that God sends from heaven with his own hand and not the hand of man, Israel is baptized by fire and her enemies are destroyed. This is analogous to her baptism in the Red Sea, which delivered her and destroyed the Egyptians."

Blake was encouraged to see Andrius warming to the subject, and the two continued their discussion, almost oblivious to where they were in their journey.

"Hey!" Blake exclaimed. "Did that sign say, 'Casper, next four exits?'"

"Couldn't tell you. I was busy processing the information that you unloaded on me."

"What exit are we supposed to take?"

"Second one when coming in from the north."

Blake took the next exit, and Andrius directed him to the storage business. "My stuff is over there," he said, pointing to the far unit, "in building six, unit eleven."

When Andrius raised the door, Blake whistled at the mountain of boxes, buckets, and crates. "Dude! I'm not sure we can fit all this in the truck."

"We're gonna have to make it fit," Andrius insisted, "because I know you don't want to make a second trip down here."

Blake poked around in one of the crates. "Nice! Angled

solder tips. Mirrors on adjustable arms. Solder and flux up the wazoo. Small brass and steel brushes. Tiny pliers in various designs. You got every kind of cool tool that a guy could want for soldering." He hoisted the heavy crate, lugged it to the truck, and shoved it into the back left corner. Andrius followed with a lighter crate.

After three rounds, Blake ran out of patience for telling Andrius how to stack and cram to the optimum advantage. They switched to Andrius ferrying and Blake squeezing and stuffing. Two hours later, the entire pile was in the truck except for a few empty buckets, which they left in the shed, and two boxes of magazines. Blake made a few last-minute adjustments to the load, then he raised the tailgate and slammed his weight against it a few times until he heard the metallic click. Relieved, he picked up the two remaining boxes and handed them to his sidekick. "These are gonna have to either go at your feet or go in the trash."

Andrius grumpily stacked the boxes on the floor of the cab next to the console. "My feet are going to be cramped."

Blake laughed. "Suck it up, Android. In this life, there's no gain without discomfort."

19

Atchafalaya Swamp, Louisiana
Thursday, November 21, 2019

The girls arrived in Effie, Louisiana a few minutes before noon, and Ariele parked the truck in a convenience store lot. She stared out the window at the torrent pounding their windshield with a staccato blast and watched a cigarette filter get driven across the asphalt. *What a miserable day.* When the clock on her phone showed noon, she called Lobo. An intriguing, slightly husky male voice answered.

"Lobo, here."

"This is Orange Stimulator, Tenkara's friend."

"Good to hear from you Orange. Are you ready to take notes?"

"Yes. I have you on speakerphone and Jungle Queen is ready."

"Speakerphone?"

"No worries. We're in a nearly empty parking lot in a tiny town in a driving rainstorm."

"Gotcha. Step one is to swap your vehicle for one with Louisiana plates. Go south out of town, turn right onto 454, and look for a driveway about three miles out on the right with a blue 60s-era International pickup parked by the intersection. About a quarter mile up the two-track, you'll find a rundown farm close to the river. Leave your car in the barn and borrow the Taurus.

"Step two is the Tupelo Inn in Butte La Rose, east of Lafayette. Take your time. Don't arrive in town until late in the evening—eight o'clock or later. See Maria at the front desk. Tell her that Lobo sent you. She'll assign you a room near the back door and a garage bay to park the car out of sight. Don't take anything to your room except what you'll be taking into the swamp.

"Step three is the building exit. Maria will give you a wake-up call at one o'clock—that's a.m. Make sure you have all your bags. Exit out the back door. Turn right and hug the house. Crouch to stay below the windows. Keep close to the shrubs as you move from the inn to the garage.

"Step four is the trek in the woods. The tree line is fifty feet past the garage. Head straight into the woods. In two hundred yards, you'll cut a rough two-track. Turn right. After that keep to the left at every fork. Walk quietly. You'll pass several private campsites. They may be occupied despite the lateness of the season. After a half mile or so, the track intersects the main road. Turn left. A short ways down you'll see a pickup parked on the left in an opening fifty feet off the road. Throw your stuff in the back and climb in.

"Step five is the canoe trip. We must leave Gator's landing by 1:30 because we need to be deep in the swamp, past the well-known trails, when the early morning fishermen get going. It's three hours of hard canoeing to the platform where you'll meet Rat."

"How will we recognize you?

"Look for a lanky cowboy wearing a tan cowboy hat, blue jeans, a western shirt, cowboy boots, and a woodsy-green Duluth Trading Company vest."

"Like I'm going to see all that in the dark."

"You'll see good enough. Nobody else is gonna be parked at the pick-up sight at that time of the night. Well, gotta go. I have other business to take care of. Drive safe. Stay safe. See you tomorrow morning, bright and early."

More like dark and early, Ariele muttered to herself.

The gals had no problem finding the farm, though it lacked the Southern charm that they had expected. Broken windows, a sagging door, ragged curtains, rusty vehicles, tombstones in unkempt grass, and a weathered windmill squeaking in the stormy weather gave the place a haunted-house atmosphere.

The moment Ariele stepped out of their vehicle, she sensed they were being watched. Ignoring her crawling skin, she tried to roll the barn door open. The weathered colossus didn't budge. Sam lent her shoulder to the effort, and the two of them, grunting and slipping, managed to force it open a few inches at a time. The rusty rollers did more sliding than rolling.

Ariele skewed her mouth in bewilderment. The Taurus had a layer of dust on it. And it was a beater—lift kit, cargo rack on top, door and quarter panels in different colors, cracked windshield. She shook her head, hopped in, and turned the key. The car sputtered and coughed her first three attempts. The fourth time, it kicked over with a billow of exhaust. She dropped the swamp wagon into drive and … *What in the world?* … a shadowy movement in one of the upstairs windows of the house distracted her. Bang! Scraaaaaaatchtch! Infused with adrenalin, she cranked the wheel hard away from the post she had just sideswiped.

Clear of the barn, she jammed on the brakes and sat, trembling. She was so unnerved by the apparition that she didn't dare leave the car or take her eyes off the window. Sam parked the truck in the barn, then went after the stubborn door with an oak 4X4 that she had found in a musty pile of lumber. She slipped one end under the bottom corner and pushed the other upward. The door crept forward five inches. She repeated the process again and again until the rusty roller was snug against the stop. Relief washed over Ariele when Sam slid into the passenger seat. The jittery gal took her foot off the brake pedal and hit the gas. *Not looking forward to coming back here.*

They reached Butte La Rose around 8:30 that evening, rejoicing that they had made their destination. But their mood quickly soured when they turned at Doucet's Grocery. A pair of black SUVs were manning the intersection, scanning the traffic. Ariele watched them warily in her rearview mirror. Headlights flipped on, and one of them pulled out and began following them. She slammed her fist on the steering wheel. "Nuts! Stick a fork in our Tupelo Inn plans."

"There's nothing to worry about," Sam encouraged her.

"It's just a bump in the road. Every mission has them. The agents saw a vehicle that they didn't recognize, so they're going to tail it and call it in.

"Awesome theory, but what do I do right now?"

Hang a right, right here on Parish Road 196. We'll circle around and try again in an hour or so."

Ariele's jaw was clenched, and she was gripping the wheel tight. "Relax," Sam encouraged her. "If Lobo and his pals did their job, we'll be just fine."

"If they did their job right!" she spat back. "Why are we driving a redneck special that sticks out like a sore thumb?"

"It doesn't stick out down here, hon', not like it would in L.A."

Ariele huffed and said nothing.

A few minutes later, they crossed the pontoon bridge and turned south on Catahoula Levee Road. They hoped that the Tahoe would turn around and head back to Butte La Rose. It didn't. It stuck with them for another five miles. It wasn't until they rounded the Catahoula corner that the headlights behind them receded, jockeyed around, and turned into tail lights. "YES!" Ariele shouted, breaking out her air-drumming moves. "That's what I'm talking about!"

"Stay on this road," Sam instructed, interrupting her celebration. "It'll go through Catahoula and take us to St. Martinville. From there we can catch 31 to New Iberia … and maybe a bite to eat."

On the outskirts of New Iberia, Sam pointed to a sign—Catfish Dinner Special! Ariele shrugged her shoulders, drove into the supper club lot, and took the first open parking spot. "You've got to be kidding!" she gasped. The Taurus was nosed up to a black Tahoe, and the driver was eyeing them in his rearview mirror. Her blood ran cold, and she tried to put the keys back in the ignition with a shaking hand. Sam pretended she was retrieving something from the back seat and whispered, "Just act normal. Let's go inside and get a bite to eat, just like we had planned."

Forty minutes later, when they exited the club with their bellies full of catfish and chips, the SUV was still sitting there. Sam ignored them and nonchalantly tossed a bag of muffuletta sandwiches into the backseat—their breakfast for the next morning.

"What's the next step?" Ariele sputtered.

"Get on US 90 and head north to Lafayette," Sam replied. That'll buy us some time. We'll think of something." She turned on the radio, found a Bluegrass-Cajun station, and sat back in her seat, rocking to the music and sipping the Cajun coffee she had ordered to go. "Wow! Who would have thought that mixing molasses with your cream and coffee would taste so good? It's way better than I expected."

Ariele looked at Sam and shook her head in wonder. *The woman is made out of cold steel. Nothing seems to faze her.* Feeling unsettled herself, she started the car, backed out, and pulled onto the street. Their pursuers followed. "Here we go again," she muttered.

The black SUV stayed with them when she turned north on the interstate, though it hung back five or six car lengths. Sam tried to engage her friend, maybe ease her tension.

"Getting tailed once or twice shouldn't come as a surprise. The operations order warned us that this area was crawling with agents."

"Crawling was no exaggeration!" she groused. "Like maggots on roadkill!"

Sam looked away and folded her arms. Talking to the spitfire when she got prickly was like finding grit in your oatmeal.

Ariele's conscience smote her. *Get a grip, girl. Jitters and panic don't help matters. Neither does irritating a friend.* She reached deep and forced herself to sing along with the catchy bluegrass song that was playing on the radio—"I'll fly away, oh, glory, I'll fly away ..." Sam smiled and picked up the tenor part.

"Hey!" Sam shouted, startling Ariele. "Did you see that sign?"

"Which sign?"

"The one for Escape Room Lafayette?"

"No. I missed it. Too busy thinking about things."

"Quick! Take this exit right here, the Louisiana Avenue exit! Then make a left turn on Johnston, a right turn on North College, and a left turn on West Congress."

Ariele cocked her head at Sam. "Seriously? We've got federal agents on our tail, and you're thinking of doing an escape room?"

"Trust me."

Ariele rolled her eyes and turned up the ramp. "So what were those directions again?"

"Simple. The turns are 'left, right, left' like a drill sergeant calling cadence. And the streets are 'Johnston went to College so he could be a member of Congress.'"

The SUV followed them up the ramp and stayed with them when they turned down Johnston. At the North College intersection, Ariele timed the light, hitting the intersection two seconds after it turned red, hoping she might lose their pursuers. But the SUV ran the light too and stayed on her tail all the way to the parking lot for Escape Room Lafayette.

Ariele found an open parking spot near the building. When she glanced into the mirror to check her hair, she noticed the SUV backing into a slot behind her and one car down. She looked over to Sam. "What are we gonna do?"

"Up for some fun?" she replied with a grin, offering up her hand for a high five.

Tapping into her friend's positive energy, she clapped the offered palm. "Let's do this!"

As they walked toward the building, Sam explained her thinking. "I know this is a wild idea. But it just might shake our followers. I noticed that the dude in the passenger seat was on the phone when we were parking, likely talking to his boss. I'll bet this kind of activity doesn't fit the FBI profile for Underground members. In fact, I'd bet a hundred bucks that they won't be here when we come back out."

"So this is like a smokescreen?"

"You got it. In the military world it's called misdirection."

Sam's intuition was correct. When they exited the building at 11:30 p.m., laughing over the fun they had had, the agents were gone.

The girls walked into the Tupelo Inn in Butte La Rose at a quarter past midnight. No one was at the front desk. They rang the buzzer. No one answered. They rang it again, but this time let it buzz for five seconds. Someone stirred in the back room, and two feet hit the floor. An elegant Creole flashing a broad smile appeared through a side door. "Hi. I'm Maria. How can I help you?"

Ariele whispered, "I'm Orange Stimulator. This is Jungle Queen. Lobo sent us."

"Glad to meet you two. Sorry that I fell asleep on the couch." She stepped out from behind the desk and handed Ariele their room key and garage key. "Follow me," she said as she headed down the wide corridor toward the rear of the building. "I'll show you to your room." When they reached the intersection of the rear hallway, she pointed straight ahead. That's the rear exit. If you take that door and turn right, the garage is about forty feet past the end of the building. Your stall is number four, which is the farthest one." Then she turned to the right and pointed to the first room on the left. "That's your room. Number seven." After flashing a brilliant smile, she mouthed "Good luck," and walked away.

The girls parked the swamp wagon in the garage, lugged their duffel bags to their room, and dropped them on the floor. Ariele flopped down on her bed and grumbled. "Guess we can forget about sleep tonight. It's already past 12:30."

"Look at the bright side," Sam offered as she lay down herself. "We'll sleep good tomorrow night."

Ariele shook her head vigorously, trying to break free of

the fog. If she could figure out what the awful noise was, she might able to turn it off so she could go back to sleep. But the sound didn't repeat itself. Instead, a voice that sounded familiar muttered a groggy "Hello." A cheerful but distant voice replied, "This is your wake-up call. It's one o'clock." That struck a familiar chord, and the fog began to lift. They were in Louisiana on a mission, and it was time to roll.

Five minutes later, the two left the warmth of the inn and stepped into the cool, damp air of the autumn night. Sam ducked under the windows, used the shrubs for cover, skirted behind the garage, and plunged into the cover of the woods. Ariele was on her heels, copying her every move. Once they were safely obscured by the forest, Sam pulled out her compass, set a south bearing to catch the two-track, and struck out through the brush-laden upland.

"Sam!" Ariele rasped as loudly as she dared. "Slow down a bit." The older woman relaxed her pace and chided herself for not thinking about her companion. Hiking in a pitch-black forest on a moonless, overcast night was old hat for her. And this jaunt was a stroll in the park compared to many treks she had made in the jungles of Africa and the Amazon. But Ariele was struggling. She had no experience with walking through a gauntlet of obstacles in the dark: branches, underbrush, fallen timber, and roots. Her face and hands were taking a beating, and she had stubbed her toes a few times. The worst part, however, was the psychological undertow of listening to her footsteps crunching leaves and twigs. No matter how hard she tried to walk quietly, she sounded like an elephant barging through the woods.

After skirting the trees and pressing through the undergrowth for two hundred yards, they broke out on the two-track, faring nothing worse than minor scratches. As they started down the road, Ariele whispered a prayer, "Thank you, Yeshua, that we didn't lose any eyes." She smiled at the irony. *First time that name has ever rolled off my lips in prayer.*

Although Sam had intentionally slowed down, Ariele still had a hard time keeping up with her. They had anticipated that this stretch of road would be easy, but that assumption had been a pipe dream. While the high spots were relatively dry, they were few and short, and the low spots were a gumbo nightmare, pocked with mudholes and ruts. Frustration soon surpassed her weariness. *The gal is an Amazon*, she grumbled under her breath. *Twice as much bike riding and dancing wouldn't have prepared me for this.*

By the time she had slogged halfway through the second stretch of muck, Ariele's socks were soaking wet, and her mud-caked shoes felt as heavy as bricks. Misery was going to be her companion for a while. Most likely, there would be no dry shoes or socks until they reached the platform.

Her foul mood wasn't helped by the haunting call of a screech owl that seemed to be singing dark fears into her mind. *Things are gonna go from bad to worse ... you're gonna go the wrong way and miss your rendezvous ... you're gonna get caught.* She shuddered and gave herself a mental tongue lashing. *Stop worrying. Just focus on where your feet are going. Sam will catch the forks.*

Over the next few minutes, the road alternated between

muck and damp earth. Then it abruptly rose out of a boggy stretch and turned sandy. When the easy surface continued for over a hundred yards, and the only difficulty they faced was the mud that was still squishing around in their shoes, Ariele began to wonder if their fortunes had changed. Maybe they would enjoy smooth sailing from here on out.

While her thoughts were wandering, a dog erupted in a barking frenzy in front of them. She almost jumped out of her skin. It wasn't a high-pitched yap, but a husky bark accompanied by a deep, throaty growl. The canine was not a lap dog. The girls froze and looked at each other. Was it chained or loose?

A voice hollered out, "Stop barking at the shadows, Mitzy, or I'll feed you to the wild hogs." Sam crossed to the far side of the road and hastened forward. Ariele followed. The barking stopped for a few seconds but started up again when they reached the animal's turf, a large camper trailer parked about forty feet off the road. The growling cur, which appeared to be a German shepherd, lunged savagely against its chain, barking and snarling furiously.

The door banged open, and a man shouted, "Who's out there!" The girls broke into a jog. "Who the tarnation is out there!" he shouted again. A few seconds later, they heard him holler, "Go, get 'em Mitzy!" The beast went boiling down the road. When they heard him barking too close for comfort, they turned to face him. Sam drew a pistol from a concealed holster and raised it to firing position. Ariele put her hands over her ears when she saw the weapon coming up. But the report never came. When the dog was five feet away, he lunged at Ariele and slammed into her, knocking her to the ground. Panic-stricken, she pushed the animal away from her, rolled to her side, jumped to her feet, and prepared for another attack. It didn't come. Sam was standing over the beast, which was crumpled into a whining heap.

"Grab your stuff! We gotta get out of here fast!" she whispered to Ariele as she reholstered her weapon. Ariele picked up her bags and hastened after her. Forty yards down the road, Sam careened off to the left, taking a fork. The road dipped and changed to slippery clay. Ariele fell muddying her hands, jacket, bags, and face. She wiped the mud off her brow, looked down the road, and couldn't see Sam, though she could hear her distant footfalls. Her heart pumping with exertion and with fear that she might get lost if she didn't keep up, she scrambled to her feet and raced forward in the darkness.

Two minutes later, she caught up to Sam, who was standing at the side of the road, partially bent over, clutching her side. Ariele dropped her bags, fished out a bottle of water, and downed a hefty chug. Then she turned to Sam. "I'm whipped. My whole body feels weak."

"Me too."

"How far do you think we ran?"

"I'm guessing maybe a quarter mile."

"Do you think we're being followed?"

"I suspect not, but I don't know for sure." She put her finger to her lips for silence, and they listened. No threatening sounds pierced the deathly quiet—not vehicles, not dogs, not voices, not footsteps. Nothing but an occasional bird. After thirty seconds, Sam flashed her the okay sign.

Ariele breathed a sigh of relief. "What did you do to that dog?"

"Shot him with a stun gun just as he was leaping at you. He's probably okay by now. But he won't feel like chasing us anymore." She picked her bags back up and nodded her head in the direction they were headed. "Come on. We have to keep moving."

Seven minutes later, they reached the graveled road they were headed for and turned left. About a hundred yards down, they rounded a corner, and the outline of a truck appeared on their left, obscured by the fog that was thickening as they neared the river. As they had been instructed, they tossed their bags in the back and climbed into the cab.

Lobo eyed them, and his eyebrows arched a tad, but he said nothing. He simply started the truck and put it in gear. Once he was on the road that followed the bayou, he broke his silence. "I'm not being unsociable, just focusing on the job at hand. We'll have plenty of time to talk later. By the way. You girls look like you competed in the mud-wrestling contest at the county fair."

Ariele wondered how she might answer such a statement without appearing stupid, but she was distracted when the truck rounded a curve to the right, then cut sharply to the left, tossing her side to side. The smooth ride on the blacktop turned into a rough ride on dirt. A minute later, he stopped in front of a garage, pressed a remote door opener hanging on the sunshade, and drove in. "Grab your stuff and follow me," he ordered as he exited the cab.

He grabbed two duffel bags from the box and headed for the cabin, his long strides quickly eating up the ground. On the backside of the home, he bounded up the stairs onto a porch that faced the river, unlocked a cabinet, and grabbed a life vest and two paddles. When the girls reached the porch, he was already on the dock, where a pontoon boat and two canoes were tied up. They picked up their vests and paddles and hustled toward the river. At the top of the dock, he brushed past them and took off running for the truck.

When he returned with another duffle bag and a propane tank, the girls were sitting in their canoe, arranging their gear—Sam in the stern because she had more experience. He tossed them a handful of cinch straps. "Get your vests on and secure your bags." Then he jogged back to the truck for a third load, which turned out to be fishing equipment. After lashing down his gear, the groceries and supplies for his friends in the swamp, and a propane tank for the platform, he settled into his seat and donned his jacket. Then he whispered to the girls, "It's 1:31. Time to go." Without waiting for them to respond, he shoved off, and his smooth strokes rapidly propelled him away from the dock. The girls—one by no means an expert, the other a raw rookie—followed as best as they could.

Within a few hundred feet, the bayou bent northward, away from the road and civilization. As they paddled into the wilderness, Ariele was overwhelmed with a complex sea of emotions. Discouragement because she was shivering, and her feet were wet and cold. Frustration because her strokes were poorly timed and awkward. Relief because they were putting distance between themselves and the agents who were swarming the edges of the swamp. Reticence because they were leaving civilization behind. And fear. She had a foreboding that this journey into the depths of Atchafalaya Swamp was going to take her to a dark place. Yet danger was unavoidable. Whether inbound or outbound, she was headed for things that posed a threat to her. *Stop with the psychoanalysis and focus on your job—consistent strokes.*

She timed her strokes with Lobo's. The gentle repetitions of canoe paddles dipping and drawing in the silence melted away her tensions. She embraced her fear with stoic resolve and trusted God. Confidence flowed into her strokes. She began to match Lobo almost effortlessly. A smile creased her tired face. She was made for this hour.

Her resolve was soon challenged, however, when Lobo turned east up a smaller bayou. Soon the path was a gauntlet of standing trees, fallen trees, overhanging brush, vines, and mats of lily pads. Their pace slowed. Her mind reeled. *So much for my big talk about my lifestyle preparing me for this trip. Organic food, local trails, and bike riding just don't prepare you for this kind of raw wilderness experience.*

Around two o'clock, while in a wide stretch, the heavens cleared and the stars gleamed overhead. Polaris and the front lip of the Big Dipper were almost directly in front of her, indicating that the voyagers had turned northward at the last juncture. A red shooting star flashed. Fifty feet later, the trail narrowed to six feet on average, and the starry display was covered by a curtain of foliage. Over and over again, they were forced to duck under branches, a few scraping their backs. *This is crazy. If Lobo wasn't leading the way, I would have never believed that this was a passable route.*

A few minutes later, the bayou widened into a moon-dappled lake about an acre in size. Lobo, not far in front of them, hugged the right shoreline. Halfway across, he stopped alongside a thick, tangled wall of cypress roots. Quick as a cat, he tossed his bags up onto the land a few feet over his head, stepped out onto a knee, dragged his canoe out of the water, leaned it against the wall, scrambled up the roots, and dragged his vessel up on top.

"Just do what I did," he advised the girls, who had watched the unexpected development from ten feet away. "All you gotta do is lug your gear and canoe up on top. Then we got an easy-peasy two-hundred-yard portage."

"There has to be an easier route to the platform," Ariele protested.

"There is. But this route knocks four to six hours off the trip to the wildest part of the swamp where the platform and Burt's cabin are hidden. And it goes off-trail in the first half hour, reducing the odds of observation. Fact is, I don't think anyone knows about this route. I've never seen a man or a sign of man back here. Neither has Rat."

The girls paddled over to the gnarly cluster of roots, hesitant. Sam wrapped her arms around one to steady the vessel, while Ariele stood upon the unstable platform. One by one, she heaved their bags up on top, falling awkwardly into the roots with every toss, bruising her arms. When all four were on top, she tossed the paddles behind them.

When their gear was topside, she placed her right foot on a knob just above the gunwale, located two handholds, took a deep breath, and began to climb the jungle gym from purgatory. Her first move went smoothly, and she pulled herself up onto the knob, balancing on her right foot. After testing several potential footholds for her left foot, she settled on a knob that offered less bite but was closer, moved her hands higher, shifted her weight to her left leg, and tried to pull herself up. Her left foot slipped off its perch into thin air. "Stinkin' bug guts!" she shouted as gravity dragged her fingers from their holds. Sam watched, horror-stricken, as she tumbled backward. The small of her back slammed against the outer gunwale, rocking the canoe savagely. The vessel would have capsized if Sam hadn't maintained her armlock around one of the roots. A groan exploded from Ariele on impact. Her feet arced upwards over her bruised back, her head keeled downward, and she disappeared beneath the inky waters.

"Get the canoe out of the way," Lobo barked, fear adding volume and bite to his tone. While Sam pulled the canoe forwards, frenetically grabbing at the roots, he scrambled down to a low knee with a paddle in hand and anxiously scanned the surface. Though it had only been ten seconds since she went under, it felt like a decade of gray hairs.

A hand shut up out of the water, frantically grasping for anything, then Ariele surfaced, sputtering and coughing, standing in neck-deep water. "Over here!" Lobo called. She looked over her shoulder and struggled to turn toward the voice. But she was held fast by the boot-sucking muck which had swallowed her feet. Lobo stretched out the canoe paddle toward her. She reached for her salvation, but it fell a couple feet short. He retracted the offer, yanked on a thin root in front of him, decided it would hold his weight, leaned forward as far as he dared, and extended the paddle once again. This time her outstretched fingers were tantalizingly close. But three inches short might as well have been three yards.

Failure knifed at his guts. In frustration he lobbed the paddle back up on top and shinnied up the wall in a frenzied burst of anger. He rummaged around in his kit bag, dug out a hank of nylon rope, hastily tied a big loop in it, and scrambled back down to the precarious knee. The situation had deteriorated. Ariele, struggling to free herself from the murky jaws of the swamp, had sunk deeper into the silt. The water was now to her chin, and she was starting to panic. "Get me out of here!" she called. Her words fell on his ears like emergency sirens, haunting him. If his plan didn't work … he didn't want to think about it.

"Grab hold of the rope with both hands," he called as he tossed the loop.

It splashed off to her side a couple feet away. She twisted her torso and snagged it.

"Now lean forward and let the water take some of the weight off your feet." The request fell on her ears like a prison sentence. The solution sounded almost as bad as the problem. But she trusted him, resisted the fears that besieged her, and surrendered to the embrace of the very waters she was trying to escape.

Lobo pulled the rope taut, grabbed a firm hold on it as far out as he dared, locked his knees, and leaned back, putting his whole weight into the effort. At first, it was like a stalemate in a tug-of-war. Nothing moved except his quivering arms. Then he shot backward, and the corners of his mouth curled up with satisfaction. The swamp had surrendered its prize. But his celebration turned to concern. He was falling ... backward. A knob on a knee caught him squarely between the shoulder blades, knocking the wind out of him. He slumped to his side and fell into the murky waters.

Ariele dog paddled up to the knee where Lobo had been standing and tried to pull herself up. But her aching arms and stiff limbs refused to cooperate. All she could do was lean her shivering body against the mass of roots and wait. This was a bizarre turn of events. Moments ago he was looking for her. Now she was looking for him.

Lobo tried to take in a breath, but his mouth and nose filled with liquid. Things were fuzzy and dark and cold. It was a familiar feeling. He tried to place it. *Oh yeah. The rodeo in Casper, Wyoming, when the Brahma bull stepped on my chest and my face, and my lungs and mouth and nose filled with blood.* Scenes flickered haphazardly in his mind like an old 8mm movie with jumbled frames running slow. The angry bull's hooves. A clown calling for help. The ambulance. The surgery. The hospital room. The deathly silence in his room except for the haunting sounds of the monitors. The scene changed. Throwing a rope. Pulling on the rope. Falling backward.

His brain realigned with reality. *I'm underwater. Got to stand back up somehow.* He pressed himself up with a sturdy root, brought his feet underneath, and erupted from the belly-deep water gasping for air. His head was pounding and spinning, and his right arm and shoulder blades were on fire. But his attention was elsewhere. *The girl. Gotta find the girl.*

Several minutes later, after a bit of coaching and coaxing, Ariele stood on a boxy knob three feet above the water with her heart in her throat. Once again, she was waiting on Lobo. A massive hand reached down from the top. She extended her arm, and Lobo's fingers locked onto her wrist with a vise-like grip. In other circumstances, it would have been regarded as painful. Now it was welcome—like the belly-crushing seatbelt that held you in the bosom of a helicopter. Two seconds later, she tumbled onto the jumble of cypress roots, dirt, moss, and matted grass—overcome with an emotion-charged appreciation for *terra firma*.

"Hey you," Lobo called out to Sam. "Get this girl into dry clothes while I portage the first load of our gear. Maybe get something hot in her belly, too."

"It's not, 'hey you,'" she replied with a huff. "It's Sam. And her name is Ariele, not girl." The cowboy, at a loss for words, shrugged his shoulders, picked up the heaviest duffel bag and the forty-pound propane tank, and vanished into the darkness.

When he returned, Ariele was sitting on a log, pulling on a pair of dry socks while Sam was setting up her stove to boil water for coffee. Without saying a word, he picked up two more duffel bags and his fishing gear and plunged back into the gloom. When he reappeared again, Sam was handing Ariele a steaming cup of coffee. He nodded at them, picked up Sam's bags, and headed back into the bush.

For the last portage, Lobo lashed the paddles to the thwarts, then he and Sam lifted the canoes onto their shoulders and moved out. Ariele drained a final gulp of coffee, stuck her tongue out in disgust, and poured the last third on the ground. *Don't care what anyone says. Instant ain't coffee.* She stuffed the cup in a side pocket, picked up her duffel bags, and hustled after Sam and the cowboy.

Sam quickly grew frustrated. She found it hard to discern where she should place her feet on the tangled path. The canoe blocked what little moon glow made it through the forest canopy. In the first minute, she stumbled twice, banging her shins on roots. *This isn't a trail. I've been on trails before. This nightmare is worse than the Amazon.*

Five minutes later, a branch that was resisting her progress slipped under the canoe and smacked her in the face, adding to her collection of scratches. Incensed, she barged through the obstacle. *I'm tired of fighting brush. I just want this monkey's butt of a portage to be over as soon as possible.* She heard the branch whip back into place behind her as she pulled her arms and elbows in front of her face, ready for the next assault. But no more thickets confronted her. To her relief an open stretch beckoned. She took a couple steps forward on the easy surface, then hesitated. Moonlight doesn't glisten on grass like that!

"Break!" a voice whispered.

Sam turned to the voice and saw Lobo seated on a root

next to the narrow bayou.

"Get some water and food in your bellies," he continued. "In ten minutes, we'll move on again. From here it's much easier going."

She lowered the canoe to the strip of sand and grass under her feet, dropped her hind end on a damp, moss-covered log, leaned against a tree, and groaned. Her shoulders ached from the awkward load. Her long pants had provided little protection against the blackberry thorns and no protection against the locust thorns. Then there was the matter of her palm. It had been giving her fits since she had reached out to steady herself and poked it on a locust tree. Getting to the bottom of that had priority over food and water.

She fished her tactical-red mini flashlight out of her jeans pocket and examined the wound. No wonder it hurt so bad. The thorn had broken off under the skin and was embedded so deep that it was still seeping blood. She placed her light on a nearby root, bent down to get her hand in the light—a somewhat awkward position—and grabbed the spiny invader with the tweezer from her Swiss Army Knife. A blast of red-hot pain shot from her hand to her eyeballs, and she grit her teeth. Unfortunately, the thorn only retreated a quarter of the way. She steeled herself and tried again.

When she finally held the offender in the tweezers after her sixth attempt, she leaned back against the tree, shaking like a leaf in the breeze. Exhaustion, cold, and pain were taking their toll. She reached in her bag and retrieved a chocolate bar. *Time for some sugar.*

They climbed back into their canoes at 3:15 and pushed

off. Ariele settled into her seat with a groan.

"I'm feeling ya," Sam replied. "My backside got sore too. Change things up. Try kneeling."

For the next half hour, they followed a narrow bayou as it snaked through alternating stretches of marshland and islands of upland. Then the bayou widened out, allowing them to travel at a faster pace. They passed through a one-acre pothole, then a second. At the far end of the third, Lobo stopped, and the girls paddled up beside him.

"These three potholes," he informed them, "are how you know that you're in the right bayou. By the way, all three are spring-fed. Pure water and excellent fishing—full of bream."

Ariele opened her mouth to ask what bream were, but he turned and paddled away.

Sam, her lips pressed together in wonder, mused over their silent guide. *At least we got a glimmer of the talkative cowboy that Woody met on the train.*

Shortly after four, they nosed into a narrow lake that was densely treed along the shoreline with bald cypress and tupelo on the water and thick stands of swamp pine and oak on the upland. They turned left and canoed along the shore. Two hundred yards up, Lobo turned toward shore.

Where is he going? Ariele wondered. *Nothing over there even remotely resembles a canoe trail.*

Lobo ducked low, and his canoe disappeared under a mass of vines that sprawled across the tangled roots. The girls ducked and hoped for the best, but Ariele didn't bow low enough. A protruding branch slapped her head and knocked her hat off. It disappeared over the side. They glided forward through the quasi-tunnel, with vines dragging across their backs and roots banging against the side until the canoe halted. Now what were they going to do? There was no room to sit up, so they couldn't paddle. Ariele reached out, grabbed a root, and pulled them forward. "This is getting catnip bonkers," she grumbled, loud enough for Sam to hear.

When they exited the inky-black tunnel, the maze of cypress trees was still so thick that the canoe barely squeezed between the knees. After several minutes of frustration in the gauntlet, they nosed into a fairly wide bayou. The easier water coupled with the fact that they were nearing Lobo's estimated time of arrival brought an ember of hope that the hard part was over or nearly so. But she couldn't quite bring herself to indulge the expectation. This swamp was a dream dasher. But when the bayou fed into a small pothole, hope stirred her soul like a spring breeze.

Halfway across the small lake, Lobo stopped and pointed to their right. Ariele breathed a sigh of relief. Her hunch had been right. Their nightmare was over. "See that gnarled oak tree between the clumps of cypress?" he asked.

"Yeah," Sam replied.

"See the S-shaped branch about fifteen feet off the ground sticking out sideways?"

"Yeah," Sam replied.

"Set the wendigo on that branch, up against the trunk. Wedge him in between the two nubs so he can't fall out."

"You mean we have to climb the tree?"

"Yep. Wait till daylight so you can see better."

"Wouldn't have it any other way."

"Now look off to our left. About a hundred and fifty feet up that little channel is the platform. You can't see it from here because it's hidden by pine, vine, and moss. But from there, using binoculars, you can see this opening and the wendigo."

Lobo dipped his paddle, spun the canoe about, and headed for the channel. After fighting the low-hanging brush, the bayou widened at a bend, and the girls found themselves under a canopy of trees. Instead of following the curve, their guide continued straight, ducked low, and disappeared under a low-hanging canopy of pine branches and vines. Ariele sighed and muttered, "Here we go again!"

She was beginning to wonder if Lobo had underestimated the distance when the canoe shot out from the tunnel of branches and the platform materialized ten feet in front of them. "Kowabunga!" she exclaimed, her frustration giving way to jubilation as the bow rammed into the deck. Giddy with delight, the girls tied up their canoe, tossed their bags out, and stepped onto the deck. Sam checked her watch. It was 4:32. Lobo had nailed his time estimate.

Their guide turned on an LED nightlight on the wall by the table, which barely illuminated the room. The shack was rustic but efficient: ten feet by feet on the interior, a six-foot-deep deck across the front, a peaked roof that extended over the sides, small storage lofts over the front and rear doors, a narrow bunk bed on one wall, and a counter and a table on the opposite side.

"This is pretty cool," Ariele noted.

Lobo shrugged his shoulders. "Don't know about that. It does what it needs to do."

"How secure is this place?" Sam inquired.

The cowboy cracked a wry smile. "This place is two miles as the crow flies from the nearest canoe trial. It can barely be reached by canoe, and it can't be reached by land. Nor can it be seen from the air. It's surrounded by massive, moss-laden cypress trees and covered by two giant pine trees which lean over it from the upland. Someone long ago bent them over and forced them to grow over the top of the building. The camouflage is completed with sprawling vines, three different species so disease isn't likely to wipe out the cover."

"So what is this place?"

"Don't really know. Rat and I stumbled upon it a few years ago. We suspect it may have been a moonshiner's hooch. But it could have belonged to a poacher. At any rate, we realized that it was an ideal location for secrecy and tore down the rotting remains of a small cabin. After many night trips in canoes loaded with materials, we built the new structure. It's now the main connection point and supply depot for Burt and two other fugitives who live in this part of the swamp. I and a few others make canoe trips into the swamp disguised as camping and fishing trips, but our real purpose is to drop off supplies, mail, and messages, and then pick up anything that Burt or the other two might be sending out. It's also set up to be an emergency hideout for us runners if worst comes to worst."

"Worst probably is going to come to worst," Ariele stated. "My friends believe the apocalypse is on the way. To be honest, I'm starting to think they might be right."

"That's our suspicion, too. But we're prepared. We have several months of supplies stored in the loft and more buried in the upland in three caches. We can add a third level to the bunk with parts that are stored in the rear loft, and there are hooks to hang two hammocks. This place could house five, though not comfortably." He halted, obviously peeved with himself. "Almost forgot. The outhouse is out the back door and fifty feet up the hill between the pines."

"So who is this Rat?" Ariele asked.

"Burt's courier and handyman. He brings Burt his supplies and packages, keeps his hut maintained, and watches out for him."

"How will we recognize him?"

"He's hard to miss. He's a big guy. Stands six foot two, weighs at least two hundred forty pounds, has a crooked nose that was broken in a fight, sports a military-style crew cut, and wears a battered grey-felt swamp hat with a band of cottonmouth skin around it and a few turkey feathers in the band. He's quite the character."

Ariele almost laughed out loud. *Like you're not a character?* "So what's the deal with this wendigo thing?"

Lobo grabbed a chair, used it as a stool to reach the entry loft, reached into a wooden box, and handed the wendigo to Sam. "Here you go. Take care of him. When you're done with him, put him back in his box."

The girls stared in shock at the ugly thing in Sam's hands. It was a doll with a gaunt-looking human body that had long, skinny arms and legs, three bony fingers on each hand, three finger-like toes on each foot, a wolf-like head with oversize teeth, and antlers like a nontypical swamp buck. The ten-inch-tall creature sported a red bandana around its neck, which probably marked it as Lobo's.

Ariele grimaced. "That's beyond ugly. What in the world is it?"

Lobo laughed. "A wendigo. In Algonquin tradition the wendigo is an evil spirit that dwells in the Northwoods from the Great Lakes region eastward. Burt grew up in the Ely, Minnesota area and has an affinity for Algonquin lore. He bought a few of these dolls for the runners like me. Each of them has distinctive markings so Rat knows who is or has been here."

"So we get to borrow your dolly and return it when we're done playing with it?" Ariele teased.

Yep. Something like that."

"And what are we supposed to do with your dolly?"

"As I said, set him on the S-branch in the oak tree, wedged in between the nubs, so he won't fall. Then return to the platform and wait. Within a few days, Rat will paddle by in his canoe, see the wendigo, and show up here at the platform." He's going to be a bit nervous. Not only has Burt never received visitors before, but you two are the first outsiders to ever see the platform or even know of its existence."

"Why can't you take us to Burt yourself?"

"Because I have never been there and don't know the way. That's the protocol established for runners. If a first leg runner gets caught, he can't be tortured into giving up the location of the second leg runner or the fugitive he's working with because he's never been to either location."

"That makes sense. What do we do with the wendigo when we're done?"

"Put him back in the box over the door. Then send me a text that says, 'Wendy is back in his nest.' I'll find him."

"Are you going to stay here until Rat shows up?"

"Nope. I rarely actually meet him. Usually, I just drop the goods and mail, pick up outgoing items if there are some, and go my way."

"Why can't you stay until Rat shows up so you can introduce us?"

"Because I have another mission that I need to attend to."

"Can you just text Rat and let him know that we're here at the platform?"

"He already knows that he's supposed to pick up two visitors and some supplies. He'll come as soon as he is able."

Ariele frowned.

"Sorry. That's just the way it is. We don't normally coordinate dates. I could be delayed or hurried by a day or two, and so could he. We both have other Rogue obligations including packages and mail for the Underground Mailroad. And we both have been forced at times to delay a run because of heavy agent activity."

"Listen, girls, I'm sorry, but I don't have time to answer any more questions. I have to hustle back for a different mission. So I'm gonna show you the ropes and then skedaddle." He didn't wait for an answer but started pointing out things they needed to know about using the platform: where things were located, how to light the propane stove and change the propane tank, how to fill and use the one-gallon water filter, how to store or retrieve water from the two five-gallon jugs, the silence protocol, and what to do if they heard an aircraft overhead. His spiel took five minutes. When he finished, he shook the girls' hands and wished them luck, stepped back into his canoe, and paddled away. In two strokes he disappeared under the tangle of vine and pine. A shiver crept up Ariele's spine. They were all alone ... in a desolate swamp ... with the ugly wendigo.

Ariele turned to Sam. "So what do we do now?"

"Well," she responded. "It's nearly an hour and a half until it's light enough to put Mr. Ugly in the tree, so I vote for making a pot of coffee and rustling up some breakfast while we wait for dawn. Then we can paddle over to the oak tree, and one of us can do the climbing thing."

"Sure hope it ain't me."

"I was hoping the same thing," Sam retorted. They laughed, then laughed some more as they debated whether climbing the tree or holding the wendigo was worse.

At 6:25, when it was light enough to see clearly, the gals paddled over to the wendigo oak. Ariele didn't want to climb the tree but figured that since she was sprier and younger than Sam—though not as tough—she ought to do the climbing. She inspected the uneven ground, eyed the lowest branch on the tree, which was about seven feet off the ground, and jumped. Her hands caught the top of the thick branch, and she thought she had nailed the attempt. But when she did a little kip to help pull her body up to the branch, her feet shot too far in front of her, her hands slipped off the branch, and she crashed to the ground. The roots of the oak tree dug deeply into her back, knocking the wind out of her. She rolled over on her side, gasping for air, and groaned. Sam rushed to her side.

Ariele forced herself to stand up, wiped the tears out of her eyes with a dirty finger, and tried to walk the stiffness off. Her back ached, she had a knob on her head and a bruise on her leg, and she was still struggling to catch her breath.

"Maybe I should climb," Sam said, moving toward the tree.

"No. I got this." Ariele insisted.

"But you're hurt."

"I said I got this!" Ariele retorted, exasperated. She stepped in front of Sam and eyed the tree once again. This time she chose a route up the trunk. She placed her left hand on a knot about five and a half feet off the ground and her right on another about six feet up, tested her holds, put a foot on a knob about two feet off the ground, and started her climb. When she reached the first branch, Sam tossed the Wendigo to her. After eyeballing her route, she scrambled to the S-branch, wedged the ugly creature between the two branch nubs, and flashed a thumbs up.

Back on the ground, Ariele brushed the grit off her pants and sweatshirt, while Sam combed flecks of bark out of her hair.

"OUCH!" Ariele hollered.

"Sorry! Just noticed that you got a nice bump going here. It's bleeding and gonna need some attention."

Back at the platform, Sam dressed Ariele's knob with antibiotic and gauze and pulled a stocking hat over her head to hold the bandage in place. Then they closed the shutters on the windows and crawled into their bunks. Exhausted from a journey that had been far more difficult than they had anticipated, both were sound asleep within a few minutes.

Neither one stirred until two in the afternoon. After downing a pile of mac-and-cheese and taking kettle showers on the back porch, they moved two chairs to the deck and began the waiting game. Luckily, they had brought reading material. Ariele opened a copy of the Jewish New Testament, the Brit HaHadashah, that Joby had given her. Sam started an interesting volume that Kit had loaned her, *Forbidden Archaeology* by Michael Cremo.

As dusk settled upon them, they set aside their books and soaked in the natural beauty that surrounded them. The pungent aromas. The orange glow of a southern sunset that had bathed the swamp in almost magical hues. The raucous chorus of birds and chorus frogs that had exploded upon them when the sun had dipped low on the horizon.

"I had no idea," Ariele marveled, "how enchanting the swamp can be. This sunset is amazing."

"I was thinking similar thoughts," Sam replied. "This is quite the orchestra. I have never heard so many different kinds of birds at one time, not even in Africa."

Ariele jumped up from her seat. "Nuts! Forgot about the water I put on to boil!" A minute later, she returned with two cups of steaming cocoa. As she handed one to Sam, she asked the question that had been festering in her mind all day. "How long do you think we're gonna be waiting here?"

"Got no idea. A day or two. Maybe three. But this isn't a bad place to wait if we have to wait."

"You got that right. Way better than a bus terminal or airport."

20

Atchafalaya Swamp, Louisiana
Sunday, November 24, 2019

Early Sunday morning, the sound of footsteps on the deck woke Sam. Fear coursed through her body. She tried to pour the cold water of reason on the hot fire of emotion—after all, they were expecting Rat—but the fire prevailed. She retrieved the stun gun she had stashed beneath her pillow and stationed herself at the door. *Better safe than sorry.* The shuffling continued, but it sounded like no effort was being made to gain entrance to the cabin, at least not yet. Judging by the heaviness of the footfall and the creaking of the deck boards, the person was bigger than Lobo. She sucked in a deep breath, tried to relax, and peered out the porthole. Nothing was visible except the shadowy outlines of the porch posts, deck roof, and tree branches.

The footfalls approached the door and stopped. Rap! Rap! Rap! A heavy fist was pounding on the door. She stepped back several paces, raised the gun to ready, and asked, "Who is it?"

"It's Rat."

"How tall are you?"

"Six two"

"How much do you weigh?"

"At least two hundred and forty."

"How—"

"Stop with the questions already. You two need to get dressed in a hurry. The bus leaves in eighteen minutes. It's 1:57 now, and I'm leaving at 2:15. We need to be at Burt's before it gets light. We can't risk being seen by aircraft in this part of the swamp. As soon as you're decent, let me know. I have a few items that need to go inside."

Sam heard a racket on the deck and figured that he was dropping off an empty propane cylinder and picking up the full one that Lobo had left by the front door. She flipped her flashlight on. Ariele was sitting up and rubbing her eyes. Without saying a word, her younger companion dropped to the floor from the top bunk and reached for her jeans. Less than a minute later, when both gals were dressed, Sam cracked the door and whispered, "We're ready!"

Rat burst into the room. He really was big and scary—a crooked nose, a military-style crew cut, and a battered, tan swamp hat with a band of snakeskin. He reminded Sam of the creepy bad guys in B-grade movies set in the Deep South. The burly man grabbed the two duffels of groceries that Lobo had deposited by the front door and lugged them to his canoe. Then he rushed back in, removed a package from the mailbox on the side of the counter, shoved two letters inside the battered unit, and exited again. On his return, he stood over the girls like a drill sergeant. "Don't get too picky about packing. Just jam stuff in. You can sort it later. We got to move like greased lightning if we want to stay on schedule."

When the frustrated gals exited the tiny cabin carrying their bags, Rat quickly inspected the room, turned the propane off, and closed the door. Moments later, the two canoes shoved off and squeezed under the overhanging foliage.

On the wendigo pond, Sam listened to Ariele's paddling with an appreciative ear, as a music lover might listen to the efforts of a budding classical musician. Her strokes were smooth and strong. A smile softened the older woman's jawline. Generally critical of the younger generation, she had come to appreciate the young fireplug, despite her hippie streak. *She's got the right stuff. Intelligent. Tough. Resilient. Adapts.*

When the canoes finally stopped for a portage after two and a half hours on the water, Ariele was more than ready for a change of pace. Her body was taking a beating. Her bottom was sore. Her knees were tender. Her shoulders ached. And she had added several scratches and bruises to her collection. This stretch had been the same brand of misery that they had experienced on the route to the platform—a bewildering maze of trees, narrow passages, low branches, thorns, floating logs, and submerged logs.

When she stepped out of the canoe, the spongy ground tried to swallow her shoes. *So much for a change of pace.* The despondent gal picked up her two bags, grimaced at the stab of pain that shot down her right arm from her shoulder, and struck out after Rat. The spongy ground never turned into upland. For three hundred miserable yards, the trail relentlessly sucked at her feet, often coming over the top of her shoes and filling them with cold ooze. Several times she stepped into a muck hole that engulfed her leg up to the calf. Unable to extract herself, she had to set her bags down, and wait for Sam to pull her out.

The third time the swamp held her captive, she had a lightbulb moment. Don't seek happiness in a change of circumstances. Don't let circumstances rob you of happiness. Seek happiness that endures no matter what. That pointed to God. As Joby had expressed to her on several occasions, happiness in God is the only happiness that lasts in times of trial and disappointment. Armed with this thought, she began to hum the few bars she could remember of "Gadol Elohai," Joby's favorite messianic worship song.

The portage proved to be the last hard stretch. From there the canoe trail followed an easy bayou, then angled up a narrow side channel lined with grass and brush. While the trail was disguised in several stretches with low-hanging branches, the passageways offered sixteen inches or so of clearance over the gunwales, enough to pass through relatively unscathed.

Two hundred yards up, the channel widened into a small pothole ringed with cypress trees and surrounded by a horseshoe of upland that was thick with pines and live oaks. On their right they spied the cabin. Similar to the platform, the cozy outpost was nestled between two cypress trees and concealed by the interlocking branches of three massive pines. A sprawl of vines added to the camouflage.

Sam checked her watch. It was 5:42. *Almost exactly three and a half hours since we left the platform. Gotta hand it to them. These swamp boys have their route times down pat.* Rat's haste hadn't been overkill. Darkness was now in full retreat and a reddish-orange hue teased the eastern sky. Another ten or fifteen minutes, and they would have lost the cover of night.

Ariele jumped out before Sam could even grab a porch rail. While the two secured the canoe to handy cleats, the door of the cabin swung open, and a pretty gal on the pudgy side welcomed them. "Hi. Come on in. I'm Peggy Sue, Rutherford's wife."

The girls looked at her, puzzled.

"You likely know him as Rat, which is what everyone has called him since he was a boy. He took to the swamp like a muskrat." She led them to the couch and chairs squeezed into the corner on their left. "This is the living room," she said, laughing. "It's cozy with just the three of us, so it'll be real cozy now."

The girls dropped into the chairs, their shoulders and arms aching. Ariele glanced around at their accommodations for the next few days. It was a castle compared to the platform. Not only was it significantly larger—sixteen feet by sixteen feet, it featured amenities like an oven and a fridge. Her eyes were transfixed by the espresso maker sitting on the counter. *Boy, does that sound good right about now.*

Peggy Sue deposited herself on the couch and began talking about the pros and cons of life in the swamp. After Rat finished hauling the groceries and other supplies in, he rustled about in the kitchen for a few minutes, then returned with coffee cake and fresh coffee. As he handed the first cup to Ariele, he said, "I seen ya eyeing my espresso maker, so I figured you was probably hankerin' for a cup of real coffee."

"Yeah, it's been a few days."

After serving the ladies, he served himself, then joined his wife on the couch. Turning to the newcomers, he informed them, "I know y'all came to see Burt, but he usually spends the mornings up in his study reading and writing. We probably won't see him until lunch."

"That's fine," Ariele replied. "We're not in that big of a hurry." She nodded toward the kitchen. "That's a cute little wood stove that you got there."

"Yeah, we love it. But we only use it on cool nights when there's a stiff breeze blowing. A column of woodsmoke could give our location away."

For the bulk of the morning, Rat kept them entertained with his keen sense of humor and a large stock of lore on the weather, flora, and fauna of the swamp. It was hard to believe that the man in this conversation was the same one that had banged on the platform door a few hours earlier. Despite his tough-as-nails appearance, he was a Southern gentleman with a soft heart and an infectious smile.

But Ariele was not fully engaged in the conversation. Her mind was elsewhere—contacting Joby as soon as possible. In the middle of a discussion on such swamp delicacies as frog legs and crawdad tails, she blurted out her concern. "Do you have cell phone service out here?"

He laughed. "Yeah. Tolerable. We installed an enhancer

in one of the big pines that overshadow the cabin."

"How do you power it?"

"With deep-cell batteries that are charged by solar panels on the roof."

She screwed up her mouth and eyed him as if she questioned the wisdom of solar panels on the roof of their hideout.

"The panels are jet-black and nonglare. On top of that, they're covered up pretty good by branches, vines, and camouflage netting."

"Then how do they work?"

"Inefficiently. They're only working at about a quarter capacity on sunny days and less on cloudy, but we get plenty of juice in the battery bank to charge our phones and laptops and run the enhancer and radio."

Burt came down from his attic hideaway as Peggy Sue was setting corn fritters and andouille jambalaya on the table. After some small talk on current geopolitical events, he brought the conversation around to the purpose of the visit. "I hear from Lobo that you folks in Montana are interested in my last two infrared sensors."

Ariele smiled. "That's correct. We were hoping to pick them up this evening and leave first thing in the morning."

"Well, I'm afraid that's not going to happen."

"Oh," she replied, worried. "Why not?"

"Because our turkey is way too big for three people. So you can't leave until after Thanksgiving."

Her face wrinkled in a faint smile at the unexpected humor. But the wit didn't take the sting out of the truth.

"The truth is. I don't get any visitors, much less astronomers, so I want to take advantage of this situation. I want to pick your brain on the Rogue, the unusual meteor shower we have been experiencing, and the theory of a coming comet wave."

Ariele's heart sank. Staying for Thanksgiving torpedoed her plans to get back as soon as possible. But instead of moping, she found herself revisiting her experience that morning. *Treat this like the mud. Don't let circumstances rob you. Rob them for everything you can.* If her swamp friends were going to detain her, then she would make the best of the situation. She forced a smile and accepted the invitation. "Thanksgiving in the swamp sounds like a wonderful treat."

21

Atchafalaya Swamp, Louisiana
Thursday, November 28, 2019

"Hey, Honey!" Peggy Sue bellowed from the tiny kitchenette, where the ladies were scurrying about, preparing their Thanksgiving feast. "The turkey is stuffed and ready. Is the deep fryer hot yet?"

"It sure is Queenie," Rat whooped as he jumped to his feet. He grabbed the bird, hustled out the front door, and dropped the prize in the fryer with an explosion of sizzling and popping.

Ariele marveled when they sat down an hour later. The spread was unlike any Thanksgiving dinner she had ever experienced—a bacon-wrapped Turkey, spicy bean salad, cornbread, stuffed peppers, sweet potatoes with brown sugar and pecan slivers, side dishes like mirlitons and armadillo eggs, and two pies: pecan and pumpkin.

As he looked around the table at his companions, a happy glow spread across Burt's careworn face. "We have all faced trials over the past few years, and we have all tasted God's goodness amid those trials. How about we all share one or two things that we're thankful for?" He turned to Ariele, who was seated to his left. "Why don't you go first."

"I'm grateful that God allowed me to elude the feds and make it to Montana, and I'm thankful for my all friends in the Underground, both at the Compound and here in the swamp."

The others gave similar answers. When Burt's turn came around, his eyes misted up. "I'm thankful for the love that God has expressed to man in Jesus. It's truly mind-boggling that the eternal Son of God, who spoke the universe into existence, was clothed in human flesh, walked on this planet as a man, died on the cross for the sins of the world, rose from the dead as the first fruits of the resurrection, and now sits in heaven as the ideal bridge between God and man, waiting for the day of his return when he'll clean this mess up and take his throne over the nations."

He bowed his head and prayed. "Father in heaven, we thank you for all the good things you have given us, physical and spiritual. We thank you for another day, for the food you have set before us, and for the hands that prepared it. We especially thank you for your Son and eternal life. Guide us and provide for us in the days ahead. In Messiah's name, Amen."

Ariele was both intrigued and moved. This wasn't the cranky old-timer that Woody had described. This was a gentle, broken man. The simplicity of his prayer reminded her of Joby's prayers. No religious pretensions. Just giving thanks for stuff and asking for stuff. She wished that her prayers were more like that. Talking to God rather than reciting formal prayers. But it was his jarring thoughts on who Yeshua was that jarred her the most. A human being forever. The ideal bridge between God and man.

During the meal, Burt made a concerted effort to engage Ariele. While working on his second helping of candied sweet potatoes, he shared his testimony with her. "When I arrived in the swamp, I was a bitter old man. Filled with anger over the stupidity of our government. Shortly after my arrival, Rat showed me from the Bible what was really going on in the world and that Jesus was the only solution. As a trained scientist who had studied the order evident in the universe, I was attracted to the idea that there was a designer behind the design and that the designer had a plan for fixing the chaos we see in this world. I started reading the Bible for myself, beginning in Genesis. By the time I finished the gospel of John, I had become a follower of Jesus. Now I read the Scriptures daily. And I have become an avid student of prophecy."

She nodded appreciatively.

"How about you?" he probed. "Do you have a testimony?"

"Not really. But I am searching. I started reading the Tanakh and the New Testament with my friend Joby who is working on an online degree to become a Messianic rabbi, and I am considering the claim that Yeshua is the promised Mashiach."

His eyes twinkled with delight. "Good for you! I'm glad to hear that you're searching. Jeremiah 29:13 says, 'You will seek me and find me when you search for me with all your heart.' This is a promise from God, and he keeps his promises. If you seek God with your whole heart, you will find him. And when you find him you will discover that he is way more satisfying than the meaningless life and hopeless death of atheism—we all turn to dirt and cease to exist. Jesus offers eternal delight instead of eternal dirt."

"That does sound way more attractive than evolution. I want to believe that there's more to life than just our short little time on Earth. I want to believe in Mashiach and all the promises made to Israel. But I still struggle with the conflict between science and religion."

"Take it from a man who spent over forty years in the field of science. There is zero conflict between science and religion. The only conflict is between the religion of evolution and the religion revealed by God to man. Science does not support evolution. Science points to intelligent design. The theory that the universe sprang from nothing out of a Big Bang without a cause is a religious fable.

"Science has never observed an explosion which releases creative power rather than destructive power. And the notion that the scattered atoms of this explosion arranged themselves into amino acids, which arranged themselves into simple single-cell life forms, which evolved through quadrillions of positive mutations into all the living things we see today is contrary to the second law of thermodynamics. In nature, we see decay. Things go from order to disorder. We see mutations that are harmful 99.9 percent of the time. We don't see evolution. We see devolution.

"On the other hand, science has observed a vast array of evidence in the universe that shouts intelligent design. And where there's intelligent design, there must also be an intelligent designer. For example, the DNA in the simplest creatures contains vast amounts of complex information which could only have been encoded by a sophisticated coder. Random chance could never do that. Not in ten quadrillion years."

Ariele soaked his wisdom in like a sponge. Creation did make sense when you looked at the raw observational facts without the evolutionary spin.

***

That evening, shortly before nine, Burt, giddy with excitement, gathered everyone around his laptop for the *Down the Rabbit Hole* program. A loyal listener for years, he had appreciated Krake's new program more than the original and had been grieved at its demise in September. Rumors had been circulating on the internet that it was going to return from the dead once again, and this had been confirmed by a recent post on the *Rogue Runners* bulletin board from the new producer which stated that the program would return on November 28—this evening—with a new format and a new host.

"Good evening," the man began, speaking English with a distinct Russian accent. "My radio name is Cheslav Alexeyev, which means *noble defender*. I'm the new host for the *Down the Rabbit Hole* program. I apologize if you have trouble with my accent. Hopefully, you'll get used to it and be able to understand me. I'm broadcasting from Russia, one of the last lands in the world where men still have a little freedom. The American government has been covering up the approaching comet with strong-arm tactics that have robbed its citizens of many of their former freedoms. We feel for them. Sadly, we're beginning to experience a similar crackdown here in Russia. We haven't yet figured out whether our government actually believes in the Rogue or whether they're merely trying to contain the unrest that the Rogue reports have caused. When we have some answers, we'll update you.

"What my real name is will remain a mystery. Whether this program is live or prerecorded, I will not say. What time it is here will go unrevealed. Nor will I say from where this program is being broadcast. This is not so much because I fear the Federal Security Service, but because America has been sending agents from the CIA and operators from Delta and SEAL Team 6 into far-flung lands to eradicate apocalyptic-warning groups like the Rogue Underground and freedom-of-information groups like Anonymous. Authorities caught them on Russian territory on several occasions in the past year. Unfortunately, they have been far more successful than our pathetic government cares to admit, executing a couple dozen men and women who were prominent in leaking or reporting information in forums available to the American public.

"I will say that we have set our English broadcast time at an hour that's convenient for the vast majority of Americans and Canadians so they can listen in the evening after they have finished their dinner. Friends in the West, you can count on *Down the Rabbit Hole* to give you up-to-date information on the Rogue and faithfully unfold the prophecies of the Bible."

Ariele glanced at Sam. "Jordy definitely made the right choice when he decided to go with this guy." The older woman nodded in agreement. "I think so, too."

Burt turned to Ariele with a quizzical look on his face. "Jordy?"

"Jordy Backstrom," Ariele replied. "The pastor at the Compound in Montana. He took over the program when Burrage Krakenhavn was unable to continue."

"So, the *Down the Rabbit Hole* program is now being put together at your home base in Montana?"

"That's right."

"But how? What's the connection?"

"Irina Kirilenko, who first discovered the comet, was in FEMA 286 at the same time as Burrage. She helped him set up the *Rogue Runners* bulletin board, the *Rogue Underground* website, and the *Down the Rabbit Hole* program on her Buster account on the deep web. When she escaped the camp, she took the login information with her to the Compound."

"Wow. This is incredible! So, you folks get to listen to this kind of ministry in person?"

"We do! But some of us are just getting our feet wet."

"So how does Jordy keep track of the Rogue and geopolitical developments from the Compound? And how does he disseminate his discoveries? That's a mighty big task to evade the NSA and the FBI."

"Andrius, one of the young men at the Compound, set him up with a high-tech office in the basement of the lodge. His traffic is masked with TOR, VPNs, and deep-web servers."

Burt was fascinated and wanted to continue the conversation, but the introductory theme music was playing, so he turned his focus back to the laptop.

"Welcome to the third iteration of *Down the Rabbit Hole*. Our ministry focus is unchanged: preaching the gospel, teaching Bible prophecy, and warning the world about the planet-size comet known as the Rogue.

"To those who love this world and its vain pleasures," the young man stated, "Bible prophecy and the gospel promise of eternal life in God's utopia seem like a journey down the rabbit hole in *Alice in Wonderland*. But for those willing to investigate, these things prove to be as real as pain and love.

"Our approach to prophecy is strictly literal. For instance, when the Bible says that fire shall fall from heaven and destroy both the Russian juggernaut and those that dwell carelessly in the isles, we believe that this is actual fire from heaven, not nuclear weapons. We refuse to explain the prophecies of the last days with the same kind of human reasoning that the rationalists use to explain the miracles in the Old Testament.

"Well, that should give you an idea of what our mission is and how we approach Bible prophecy. Let's move on to today's message, which is the phrase 'of that day and hour no man knows' found in Matthew 24:36. As clear as this verse is, most prophecy teachers misunderstand it, and draw ideas from it that God never intended it to suggest. Let me give you four observations that will help you understand this verse better.

"First of all, the phrase 'of that day and hour no man knows' does not mean that no man can know the decade or century. By what principle of interpretation do men suppose that the time limitation *day and hour* means *decade and century*? This phrase means exactly what it says—day and hour. Not more. Not less. It doesn't say that we can't see the time approaching. It merely says that no man can know the day and hour.

"Secondly, Luke 21:28 says, "When these things start coming to pass, look up because your redemption is drawing near." This clearly encourages us to look for signs which indicate that the Lord's coming is approaching. In the face of such clear testimony, how does anyone conclude that we can't discern the approach of this time?

"Thirdly, it's impossible for the prophesied events of the last days to occur without being preceded by signs. The last days are not going to suddenly appear out of the blue. Like all great events that transpire on the world stage, they'll be preceded by a period of preparation. And this stage setting will be seen and recognized by everyone who loves and understands the prophecies of the Bible.

"We have already witnessed the rebirth of Israel as a nation in 1948. This was a stage-setting necessity because many prophecies assume the existence of Israel as a nation in the last days.

"Everywhere we look, the major players on the world stage are getting ready for their parts in the last days—Islam, Israel, China, the fractured Roman empire, Russia and her allies.

"Everywhere we look, the stage is being set for the final act of the late great planet Earth—the mystery of iniquity, political correctness, technological advancements employed for the invasion of privacy and Big Brother control, preparations for rebuilding the temple, the world economy, the apostasy of the church.

"Fourthly, men are mistaken when they think that they can easily calculate the day of the Lord's coming by using the major landmarks of the seventieth week. I refer to counting seven years from the day when the antichrist ratifies the seven-year treaty or counting three and a half years from the day when the antichrist sits in the temple in the middle of the seventieth week and declares himself God—Daniel's abomination of desolation.

"This easy-count theory starts with the assumption that the last days do not involve disruptions in the heavens that will throw off our ability to calculate time. Is this a wise assumption? I don't think so. Things are going to go haywire in our solar system, and these malfunctions will mess with the means we use to measure time.

"I would draw your attention to the fact that the length of the year in Revelation is 360 days. Why is this? Because this is the original length of the year, as evidenced in Genesis and ancient history until the 8th century BC, and it is the length of the year that God is going to use in the millennium and eternity. This implies that something terrifying will happen in our solar system in the last days that will bump Earth back closer to the sun, shortening the year and bringing the planet back to its original Edenic climate.

"Are there any clues as to what this event is? We think so. We have already pointed out before on this program that the Bible teaches in Luke 21:25-26 that the powers of the heavens shall be shaken from their orbits. These run-amok planets will terrify the inhabitants of Earth. We suspect that the first terror to visit Earth will be Venus. At the same time that the literal morning star, Jesus the Messiah, will appear to take his people out of the world, the figurative morning star will make a terrifyingly close pass of the earth, electromagnetically bumping this globe and returning it to its original 360-day orbit around the sun—giving us the year length that we see in the book of Revelation.

"This interaction with a planet is not unprecedented if we trust ancient history as it is written. The major cultures of ancient times are all agreed that Venus and Mars were running amok on eccentric orbits until deep into the Iron Age when the last near pass of Mars bumped Earth and changed the length of the year to 365.25 days. The terrible interactions of these planets with the world—raining fire, brimstone, and stones down from heaven and triggering earthquakes, tsunamis, and volcanic eruptions—explain why the ancient peoples were terrified of the planets and worshipped them.

"The intellectual elite of the world, not surprisingly, reject the catastrophism of ancient history with the same disdain that they reject the catastrophism of the Bible. World-shaping, kingdom-wrecking catastrophes in recorded history corroborate the Bible and the God of the Bible. That's the ultimate taboo. So unbelieving scholars give us a revised version that has been baptized in the waters of evolution and uniformitarianism.

"Now, what would happen if a planet did visit Earth in the last days and bumped it into a 360-day year? That would throw off our calendars! But that's not the only thing it would do. The odds are pretty high that in the wild gyrations of this change, Earth's spin would also be affected. Depending on the angle of the passing planet, Earth's spin could be either sped up or slowed down significantly for a while. This would either shorten or lengthen the days. And when things settled down again, we would face two problems—calendar location and length of day.

"What day is it? Where are we on the calendar? Is it Tuesday or Thursday? Do we go with the day that our watches say it is? Or do we count all the shortened or lengthened days as full days, landing us on a different day on the calendar than our watch would?

"Do we keep the old hour and minute, and assign the day a new length, which may be more or less than 24 hours? Or do we adjust the length of our hours and minutes to the new lengthened or shortened day? Either solution involves colossal headaches for recordkeeping.

"On top of these headaches, Earth will be visited yet again at the midpoint of the seventieth week when the great red dragon (which we think is Mars) makes a near pass of Earth and precipitates a polar shift, causing one-third of the stars in the heaven to fall below the horizon and be replaced by others, giving mankind new heaven in the sky at night. Stars and constellations that used to be seen in the northern hemisphere will now be seen in the southern hemisphere, and vice-versa. This polar shift, potentially accompanied by a change in Earth's tilt, will also change the seasons instantaneously. We suspect that this catastrophic change is what is behind the admonition in Matthew 24, "pray that your flight be not in the winter."

"We could add more material, like the testimony of Isaiah 24:20 that Earth will weave and totter like a drunk as the second coming approaches, but this should be sufficient to demonstrate that there will be tremendous upheaval in our solar system in the last days. Scientists will be scrambling to adjust our clocks and calendars. Our sunrise and sunset tables will be wrong. Our tide tables will be messed up. Our work schedules will be screwed up. Do we count days according to the new reality or the old reality? There will be mass confusion with no easy solution. And when the scientific community has finally settled on a solution, can we be certain that we're calculating with the same clock and calendar that God is calculating with?"

Burt slammed his hand down on the table, startling the others. His wry smile and the twinkle in his eye indicated that the demonstration was not from disagreement but excitement. "That was some seriously good ministry."

"It was paradigm shaking," Ariele replied. "What did you think of the new format and narrator?"

"It's a huge improvement. A real voice is way better than a computer-masked voice. And I like this young man. His personality is exceptional, and he's a natural narrator."

Sam agreed. "I like him, too. Even though he sometimes

accents the wrong syllable and that he Russianizes the pronunciation of the vowels and a few consonants, he's easily understandable."

Burt was staring off into space. Sam nudged him and caught his eye. "What are you daydreaming about old-timer?"

He grinned broadly. "This program brought back some good old memories. Things I haven't thought about for decades. Back when I was in junior high school, when I still had some religion and hadn't yet been defiled by the religion of evolution, I wondered why the year was 365.25 days long. The length seemed awkward to me and hard to work with. Why wasn't the year a straightforward and intuitive 360 days? And why didn't the 12 months each have exactly 30 days in them? I concluded that the current length of the year had to be a result of the curse that we had learned about in Sunday school. I thought my solution was pretty brilliant. But when I brought this idea up with the parish priest, he laughed at me and told me that the length of the year hadn't changed but had been 365.25 days long for billions of years. His reply left me confused. I stewed about the matter for a few years, then forgot about it until this evening's program stirred up the memories. It confirms the instinctive insights I had as a young man about the orderliness of God. Our God is an awesome God!"

22

Atchafalaya Swamp, Louisiana
Friday, November 29, 2019

Sam and Ariele were kneeling on the edge of the deck, securing their gear in their canoe. A thick fog shrouded the cabin like a blanket, limiting their visibility to only ten or twelve feet. Their Mini Maglites cast an eerie red glow on the canoe and the swirling mist. Somewhere in the distance, the haunting cry of a screech owl added to the spooky aura. Ariele shuddered. She hadn't liked coming here in the dark, and she wasn't looking forward to leaving in the dark, especially not in the fog. She glanced at her watch. It was 12:32. Their departure was twenty-eight minutes away. She sighed.

"I'm not looking forward to this either," Sam remarked. "It's bad enough canoeing in the dark, but with the fog, it's gonna be brutal."

"I had an awful dream last night."

"Oh?"

"I was in the garden with Adam and Eve in the middle of the night, and we came upon the serpent. I looked into his awful red eyes. That was a mistake. I couldn't look away. Then I felt fire in my bones and darkness swallowed me."

Sam laughed. "You probably just had too much sugar last night. You were getting a little greedy with the lemon-coconut bars."

Burt came shuffling out of the cabin. "Looks like you girls are gonna be paddling in Stygian darkness. The weather report says the pea-soup fog isn't going to dissipate until after sunrise. And the moon won't be much help either. It doesn't rise until 3:30. And when it does, it'll only be a fat crescent.

"Yeah. Not looking forward to this trip," Ariele snarked. "Think I'd rather lick the warts off a toad."

Burt said nothing. He knew how frustrating it was to fly blind. Twice, while a chopper pilot in Viet Nam, his instrumentation had gone out in low-light situations. Throwing up a silent prayer for the sassy lass, he handed her a small nylon duffel bag. "Here are the sensors: one is 19.5 microns, the other 12.2 microns. I included a few other items that might come in handy including three schematics for infrared telescopes, a controller board, and a handful of electronic components that are common in telescopes."

"Thanks. Blake will appreciate this." She opened the duffel bag she had just lashed down, retrieved a waterproof pouch which she had stashed just for this occasion, worked the nylon bag inside, and sealed the pouch. After several mashings, she managed to squeeze the pouch into her already stuffed duffel bag.

Turning back to Burt, she inquired, "Where did the

controller board come from?"

"It was supposed to be for a fifty-four-inch infrared project at the University of Wyoming that some of my Ph.D. students were working on. But I appropriated it when I went on the lam. I figured it might come in handy."

Rat finished his inspection of the girls' canoe and jumped to his feet, rubbing his belly. "Good to go," he announced. "Now it's time for coffee cake!" Without waiting for a response, he strode back into the cabin. *Men and their stomachs*, Ariele mused to herself. But she had to admit, Peggy Sue's coffee cake was a homerun.

When the moment of departure came, Burt huddled them to pray for journey mercies and mission blessings. Though Ariele felt self-conscious when the believers wrapped their arms around each other's shoulders—a display of affection foreign to her upbringing—she joined in. But she wasn't concentrating on the prayer. Her mind was grappling with the love that the followers of Yeshua showed to each other. It drew her in the same mysterious way that Yeshua's promises to Israel drew her. She thought about surrendering right there on the spot, but fear and doubt held her back.

After a round of hugs, the gals and Rat donned their life vests and climbed into their canoes. Rat pushed away from the deck, spun his bark with a powerful draw stroke, and began to paddle away. The gals followed one length behind.

As the canoes disappeared into the misty bank, pangs of sadness wrenched at Burt, trying to dissolve his stony exterior into tears. He hadn't had any company besides Rat and Peggy Sue for a long time, and his new friends had invigorated his spirits. He wiped his eyes on his sleeves, prayed that God would bring them to faith in the Messiah, and retreated to the cabin with a lump in his throat.

Some hundred yards down the narrow channel which led away from the cabin, Rat anxiously scanned the shadowy trunks passing on his right. He could barely see the front of his canoe, and he needed to find the burl which marked where the channel cut steeply to the right. If he missed it, they would enter a meander which led to nowhere. The protuberance shot by on his right, and he hastily executed a pair of pry strokes, swinging the bow under the tangle of low-hanging branches that covered the next stretch.

As he ducked to protect his head, a flicker of movement caught his eye before it vanished overhead. "Snake!" he hollered as he frantically spun around to see if the serpent was still on its branch or if it had dropped into his canoe. He saw no sign of it. Now he wrestled with shame and fear—shame for breaking his own order for strict silence and fear for the girls.

Sam snapped her headlamp on as soon as she heard Rat yell, and Ariele followed her lead. A few seconds later, the snake appeared at head height just in front of Ariele. Panic-stricken, she raised her paddle to protect herself and ducked low. She heard Sam scream. The shrill cry seemed distant. Something wasn't right. Fire engulfed her left calf. "It bit me," she shrieked as she fell forward onto the bow, her entire body convulsing in pain and fear.

Sam had watched the writhing serpent drop into the

canoe behind Ariele, igniting an unspoken, unadmitted fear. The seemingly fearless woman was terrified of snakes. But when the reptile bit her friend, her fear turned into anger. Animated with a rush of adrenalin, she stepped over the stern thwart, leaned over the yoke, and jabbed the serpent hard with her paddle, pinning it six inches behind its head. Keeping the pressure on, she stepped over the yoke with her heart in her throat and pressed down with all her might until the head was partially severed. Then she bashed away at the flailing head, smashing it a half dozen times. Her heart beating wildly, she dragged the writhing pieces backward until the bloody mess was sprawled under the yoke.

She looked up from the gore. Ariele was lying across the bow, weeping and convulsing in anguish. She looked back down at the snake. What was she going to do? Vipers were still capable of reflexive striking and biting for ten or fifteen minutes after their death. Though it was probably a hundred percent fear and zero percent reality, she didn't dare turn her back to the creature until its head was somehow contained.

"Hey, what's going on?" Rat called out in a subdued voice. "Is the snake dead, or gone, or what?"

"I think it's dead," Sam responded with panic etched in her voice. "I cut it nearly in half with my paddle. But I want to isolate those fangs before I start paddling."

"I got a water jug you can use," he replied. "But you'll need to back up so I can get out of this tangle. Then I can get it to you."

She paddled backward a couple canoe lengths.

"That's far enough," he called out as he emerged from

the foliage tunnel. "Hang on while I empty the jug." Two quarts of lemonade hit the swamp with a swoosh. A few moments later he called out again, "Heads up! Jug on the way."

The container sailed over Ariele, landed on the deck with the dull thud of plastic on plastic, skittered over the reptile's bloody remains, and stopped in front of her. She picked up the blood-spattered jug, unscrewed its lid, and stepped over the thwart. Trembling head to toe, she crouched down, slammed the jug down over the serpent's head, twisted the plastic vessel back and forth until the head was completely severed from the body, used the lid to scoop the head into the jug, then screwed the lid back on.

Her heart racing ninety miles per hour, she tossed the jug toward her seat and called out to Rat. "Got the head secured. I'm gonna kneel backward on my seat and paddle back to the cabin."

"I'll be right beyond you. What kind of snake is it?"

"Do I look like a herpetologist?"

"Was it more coppery colored or more blackish colored?"

"I wasn't concerned about what color it was. I was only worried about killing it. Besides, the red light doesn't reveal much color detail in the dark."

"No worries. I'll look at it when we get back."

Ariele whimpered, "My leg is on fire, and my whole body feels nauseated."

"We need to get her back in a hurry," Rat exclaimed. "She needs an antivenom shot, ASAP."

Sam paddled with a fierce determination that she hadn't

felt since she and Kit were kayaking on Flaming Gorge Reservoir in the storm. She feared for Kit's life. Though she had not known her long, she had grown to love the spunky gal, like the daughter she had never had.

"When you get back," Rat called out, "center Ariele in the landing between the posts and secure both ends of the canoe. Then grab the jug and set it on the kitchen table. After I've secured my canoe, I'll carry Ariele into the cabin."

"Gotcha."

By the time the canoe bumped against the deck, Ariele's breathing had become labored and raspy. That rattled Sam, and she fumbled over the cleat hitches that she could normally tie with her eyes closed. She had seen two people in South America die from snakebite with a death rattle in their throats. She didn't want Ariele to join them.

As Rat lifted the whimpering gal from the canoe, Sam prayed silently to the God she rarely called on, asking him to have mercy on the sprite. When the brawny swamp man stumbled through the door with his limp load, Peggy Sue's face went ashen. He motioned to the couch with his head. "Clear the pillows." Peggy Sue tossed them onto one of the chairs. The Southern gentleman set Ariele down gently and leaned her against the couch arm. "Sit next to her," he directed, "and keep her propped up."

He turned to talk to Ariele, but she was in shock and delirious. He turned back to his wife. "No matter how awful she feels, don't let her lay down. You have to keep her sitting up. We need to keep the affected limb, her left calf, as low as possible relative to the rest of her body. Oh, and get her vest and sweatshirt off. I'm gonna need to check her pulse and blood pressure."

Sam watched the ongoings from a few feet away. "Bring the jug over here," Rat barked. She bristled at his tone but immediately regretted it. He wasn't being mean. He was just a frantic man in a scary situation. She handed him the jug. He removed the lid, picked up the head, and groaned. "That's what I feared. It's a water moccasin. They're often active at night in warmer weather, and the past few days have been unseasonably warm."

"How can you tell? It just looks like an ugly snake to me."

"The white mouth is distinctive, at least among North American snakes. That's why folks also call them cottonmouths."

After dropping the head back in the jug and screwing the lid back on, he handed the vessel back to Sam. "Dump the head and body in the outhouse and wash the jug out really good with hot soapy water followed by hot bleach water. Then hang close in case we need you for something." She nodded and rushed off.

Burt arrived in his elk hide slippers and University of Wyoming sweatpants and sweatshirt, just as Rat was slitting Ariele's jeans up to her knee. He pulled the flaps aside, revealing her left calf.

"Man, that's ugly," the old-timer exclaimed.

Two puncture marks, oozing clear liquid mingled with blood, were centered in a patch of black and purple larger than an orange that was swollen and tender to the touch. The surrounding area that wasn't discolored was getting puffy.

Burt shook his head. "That doesn't look good at all."

"It's not good," the young man replied. "Get the CroFab! And grab the first aid kit!"

Burt rushed to the fridge, grabbed the CroFab, and started reading the instructions.

Rat shouted, "Don't bother reading the instructions. I know them by heart. Mix six vials with six ounces of sterile, slightly saline water."

Burt grabbed a bottle of water and a table glass and started to pour.

Rat nearly melted down when he heard the sound of water being poured into a glass. "Don't guess, Burt!" he bellowed. "Ten or twenty percent off could result in disastrous results. You should know that as a scientist. Use the three-quarter-cup measuring cup from the utensil drawer. That's six liquid ounces when filled to the brim."

"Gotcha," he replied, ashamed of his misstep. He fetched the measuring cup, filled it, poured it into the glass, added a half teaspoon of salt, then added the contents of the six vials. "Added all the ingredients. Now what?"

"Stir it until the salt and antivenom are thoroughly dissolved."

After a few minutes, Burt complained. "It sure ain't stirring in very easy."

"No worries. The literature says that antivenom can be hard to mix. But you're gonna have to stir until the antivenom is dissolved. That could take up to fifteen minutes."

Sam finished washing the pitcher as she had been directed and set it on the counter to dry off. Burt nodded to her. "Can you grab the first aid bag out of the cupboard by your feet and carry it over to Rat. He's going to need it."

"On it," she replied.

"How are we coming, Burt?" the young man called out.

"The stuff is nearly dissolved."

"When it's thoroughly mixed, suck up 250 milliliters into a syringe. Then gently tip the syringe back and forth for a couple minutes, just to make doubly sure that the antivenom is thoroughly dissolved and mixed."

"Gotcha boss."

"Sam," Rat directed. "Find a 250 milliliter syringe in the bag and bring it to Burt. But don't open the package yet."

She pawed through the kit, found the syringe, and set it on the counter next to Burt.

Five minutes later, the antivenom was finally dissolved. Burt filled the syringe, tipped it back and forth a few times, held it needle up to gather any air bubbles, squeezed a drop out of the tip to ensure there were no air bubbles in the antivenom, then carried it over to Rat and stood at the ready.

"Set the syringe on the end table and grab a notebook and pen. I need you to take medical notes as I call out information. We need to keep track of this stuff so we can see whether she's getting worse, stabilizing, or getting better."

While Burt trotted off to get a notebook and pen from his study, Rat pulled the stethoscope out of the medical kit and placed the diaphragm on Ariele's chest. His wife and Sam looked on, hoping for the best. Disappointment showed on Rat's face. "Not good. Her pulse is 143 and weak." He turned to Sam and handed her the stethoscope. "Set this on the coffee table for now and hand me the blood pressure gauge."

He wrapped the cuff around Ariele's arm and squeezed the bulb. His countenance dropped even further. "She's in worse shape than I thought. Her pressure is only 55 over 35."

"That explains why she's so faint and pale."

"No doubt about it." He removed the cuff and handed the blood pressure unit back to Sam. "Keep this handy, and hand Peggy Sue the syringe when she's ready. I'm gonna trade places with her since she has experience with nursing. She'll do a much better job at finding a good vein in the arm and giving the injection."

As Peggy Sue stood over Ariele, she noticed that her friend was starting to bleed from her gums and nose. She kissed the gal on the forehead and stroked her head.

Ariele moaned in a raspy voice, "I feel nauseated and dizzy. And the red-eyed serpent is staring at me. I can't get away from him." Rat and his wife shared a pained look. Their friend was delirious.

Peggy Sue wiped the tears from her cheeks on her sleeve. She was more tense than she had ever been in a medical setting. In the past, she had always had doctors and hospitals backing her up. There was no backup now. If she made a mistake, or the antivenom didn't work, she could easily lose her patient. With a sigh, she grabbed the scissors from the kit, cut Ariele's sleeve to the shoulder, snipped the dangling cloth, cleaned her arm with an alcohol swab, and prepped the syringe.

"Don't administer it all at once," Rat advised his wife. "Give her a microdose over the first ten minutes, about ten milliliters total. I'll keep track of the time. If she doesn't show an allergic reaction to the antivenom, then we can give her the rest of the syringe over the next fifty minutes."

Stepping back, she took a deep breath, pressed the plunger until a drop of liquid seeped out of the needle, stepped back in, and retreated again. "This ain't gonna work. I won't be able to stand at that angle for an hour. Burt, hon', will you fetch me a chair, please?"

The old astronomer dragged the end table out of the way and set a chair next to the couch. Sam set a pillow on it, raising the seat height. Peggy Sue sat down, took a deep breath, isolated the vein, inserted the needle, and pressed the plunger with the faintest pressure. "Count off the minutes, darling," she requested, "by thirty-second intervals."

"I'm on it, Babe."

As the minutes ticked by, the friends watched Ariele for signs of allergic reaction. To their relief, none were evident. When the mini dosage test was completed, Peggy Sue began injecting the rest of the syringe at the rate of 5 milliliters per minute.

Halfway through, Rat turned to Burt. "Hey, bro. Can you make another batch of antivenom using the same recipe?" The older man nodded and hasted to the kitchen.

When the injection was completed, Peggy Sue checked Ariele's vitals again. "Pulse is steady at 138, and blood pressure is unchanged. She seems to have stabilized." But no one smiled at the news. They all knew that the young lady wasn't out of the woods yet.

Burt's forearm was cramping up by the time he finished mixing the second batch of CroFab. Because he couldn't hold the syringe in his hand, he gave the job of filling it to Sam.

After the second course of antivenom, Peggy Sue checked her patient's vitals once again. "Praise the Lord!" she exclaimed. "Her pulse has slowed to 115, and her blood pressure has risen to 70 over 45." Rat placed his hand on his wife's shoulder, and a tear coursed down Sam's cheek.

"Okay, folks. Here's the plan," Rat announced. "We have three more rounds of antivenom to administer. Two vials in six hours, two more in twelve hours, and the final two in eighteen hours. That dosage schedule is sufficient for most pit viper bites. So that means we have six hours until the next administration. Grab a bite to eat and get some shuteye. The next twenty-four hours are gonna be rough."

He grabbed Burt tenderly by the arm. "In five and a half hours, which would be about 9:30 am, make another batch. But use two vials per batch instead of six."

"Whatever you say, chief."

Ariele slumped on the couch the rest of the night and through the day, barely able to sit up, always nauseous, often enduring spasms, occasionally vomiting. The gals took turns encouraging her to sip water. But they didn't try to get her to eat. They knew she wouldn't be able to keep food down.

That evening around eight, Peggy Sue brought Ariele a four-ounce cup of chicken soup. "Just take a little bit," she prodded. "It's mostly broth. You need food in your stomach." Ariele weakly nodded her agreement, and Peggy Sue put a spoonful in her mouth. When she seemed to handle it okay, she gave her another. When that stayed down, she proceeded to give her a spoonful every minute or so until the cup was gone.

Halfway through the cup, Ariele's phone chirped. It was a text from Joby.

Peggy Sue read it to her. "Hi, sis!. Hope everything is okay. I woke up last night with a strong urge to pray for you. Think of you every day. Miss you." It didn't ease her pain, but it did help her to bear it.

Ariele dictated back. "I got bit by a water mocassin and feel like death warmed over. Gonna be out of commission for a while. But don't worry about me. I'm in good hands." She asked Peggy Sue to add a couple heart emojis and hit *send*.

He wrote back again. "There are no hands like Yeshua's. Adorned with carpenter's calluses and nail holes. Always extended to sinners, unbelievers, and backsliders. Always damp with wiped tears. Always bloody from fighting on our behalf." It closed with a half dozen heart emojis and some red roses.

Sleep stole over her while she was reflecting on her plight and her friendship with Joby. Her last conscious thought was the paradox of feeling this happy while feeling this crappy.

***

The next morning, while nibbling away at a slice of cornbread soaked in molasses and honey, Ariele asked Rat, "How long will it be until I'm ready to go?"

Rat replied, "Hate to break the bad news to you, but you aren't going anywhere soon. My guess is that you're probably gonna be laid up for a good month, if not more. The swelling and nausea can stick around for weeks, and your leg could take a couple months to fully heal."

"That means that I'll be here through Hannukah and Christmas," she complained.

"I'm afraid so. You won't be leaving here until sometime after New Year's Day."

Ariele's already sallow face sank in dejection, and she hung her head. After wrestling with the matter for a few moments, she lifted her head and nodded her agreement. "I know," she said with lower lip trembling and tears running down her face, "that I'm in no shape to travel, much less make the difficult trip out of the swamp. I just had my heart set on things happening in a certain order."

"You're just gonna have to take this from the Lord," Peggy Sue chimed in. "Trust him. He knows what he's doing. He has a reason for this. He has a reason for everything."

Ariele nodded her head. "Joby said the same thing when Kit broke her leg and was unable to go with us on this trip."

"We feel a lot less torn up inside if we accept open doors and shut doors as direction from the Lord."

"So what am I going to do for the next month?"

"You don't have to worry about that," she replied as she handed her a thumb drive. "There's a lot of good teaching on here by a number of my favorite prophecy teachers. This will keep you busy for a while. If you finish them, Burt and I both have more."

23

FEMA 286, Syracuse, NY
Tuesday, December 3, 2019

Jack changed into his sewer clothes with happy anticipation. If all went according to plan, today would be his final preparation trip in the foul abyss. Only three bars—the top three—stood between them and freedom. But he wasn't going to cut them all the way through. He was going to leave a thin strand of metal in each to hold the grate in place.

After pulling on his sweater, he stepped around the wall of pallets beaming broadly, settled into a hamstring stretching position, and began to work the tightness out of his legs.

She shook her head at the tunnel rat. "You're grinning like a kid who just found out that he's going to the pizza parlor for his birthday. What's going on? Did a screw come loose?"

He shook his head. "Just enjoying the fact that I can see the light at the end of the tunnel."

"I feel it too. Kind of like watching Christmas getting close."

Jack repositioned himself for a kneeling stretch and began to work the kinks out of his quads.

"Not hearing near as much groaning as I heard a few weeks back."

"I'm feeling better," he replied. "The pain and stiffness in my back, hip, and knees have let up. But my right shoulder and upper arm are still pretty tender. I'm guessing it's repetitive stress from the cutting."

"Awww. Does the big, bad SEAL guy have an owie?"

He rolled his eyes at her.

She smiled back, stifling a laugh. "I gotta hand it to you. You're holding up dang good for an old man."

"To be honest, I'm kind of surprised myself that my body is still functioning when you consider how badly I abused it in this project."

"The human body has amazing powers of adaption, recovery, and healing," she quipped.

He shook his head in mock disgust.

"A frogman once told me that over hot chocolate and popcorn."

Jack groaned with that odd mix of frustration and laughter that fairer-sex teasing sometimes produces. Nothing like a witty female to make an above-average male feel average.

A few minutes later, he donned his outer gear, flashed a smile to Sally, and descended into the darkness. As the shlunk-shlunk sound of his rubber waders faded, she pondered the change in her partner. He had a different spirit about him. For weeks he had seemed to be fueled by a stubborn refusal to give up no matter the odds. Now he seemed to be fueled by confidence.

Jack himself sensed the change. But the significance had escaped him until he realized, about halfway through, that he was crawling at a very brisk pace and hadn't yet stopped or checked his watch. With a shrug of his shoulders, he decided to maintain the momentum. When he arrived at the grate, he was shocked to realize that he had finished the crawl in record time, shaving over ten minutes off. He stuck a piece of hard candy in his mouth and—his heart glowing with the hope that they were on the cusp of escape—attacked the grate with the same vigor that he had attacked the sewer.

As the blade flew back and forth, and grains of iron dust dropped into the cold waters below, Jack pondered the seeming absurdity of the situation. If you had asked him a decade earlier if he could imagine America imprisoning men over apocalyptic warnings—whether true or false—he would have laughed at the idea as lunacy. Freedom of speech defined America.

A season of martial law after a massive comet impact or EMP? Maybe. That might be necessary to keep society from melting down. But jack-booted agents knocking down doors without warrants and Soviet-era-style informants reporting classmates, workmates, and neighbors? That was unthinkable. The government painting patriotic, law-abiding Americans as terrorists because they truly believed in the Constitution or because they had taken it upon themselves to warn the world about the dangers that the Rogue posed to our nation, indeed the entire planet? That was incomprehensible. And yet ... that was America's current plight. It was totally unlike the America he had grown up in and had pictured himself retiring in. *How thou art fallen O Lady of Liberty!* He would have spit in disgust, but his mouth was too dry.

When the cuts were about ninety percent through, he retrieved his shoe polish container, pressed his reddish-black wax mix into them as he had done with the prior cuts, wiped off the excess, and daubed the wax with rust and scale from the grate. He chuckled to himself. *Who knew that toilet-bowl wax was so useful?* His home-scientist mix was working pretty well. If anyone performed a visual inspection from ten feet away, the cuts would be indistinguishable from the rest of the grate. It would be a different story, of course, if someone did an actual physical inspection up close. But the odds of that were pretty low.

He sat back on his haunches with his back against the wall and relaxed for a moment, massaging his sore arms and wincing from the spasms in his back. *Gonna be a miserable trip if the cramps don't settle down.* Motion in his peripheral vision startled him. He tensed and turned his head slowly. False alarm. Two ducks had landed and were swimming along the eastern shore, silhouetted in the moonlight. Despite his resistance to supposed signs, it was tempting to take it as a providential intimation from the Lord that he and Sally would soon be basking in freedom themselves.

Better get moving before I stiffen up. He scarfed an old Clif Bar, downed two outdated vitamin-C tabs for his cramps, and drained the rest of the energy drink in his water bottle, an odd tasting mix from South Korea which had arrived the prior week. Then he got down on all fours and began his last journey back.

Waves of nostalgia flitted back and forth in his mind during the crawl, the same kind he had felt at various stages in his life. His last mission in Iraq. He relived the bullets ricocheting off the Humvee. His last mission in Bosnia. He recalled his trek in freshly fallen snow, the crack of a distant sniper rifle, and several 7.62 rounds whizzing overhead. His last day in the Navy and his final visit to the supply room. Turning in his gear had been a bittersweet moment. He had left a part of his heart with DEVGRU, indeed with the entire SEAL culture, and he would never be going back. But he would still be a SEAL till his dying breath.

Jack lost track of time and distance. He just kept his legs and arms moving, pushing through the numbness and pain, alone in the umbra of the twilight zone. A soft glow in the distance pulled him back into reality, and he unconsciously picked up his pace. When he realized that he had done so, he decided not to slow back down again. The effort felt good, like the sprint at the end of a race. When he finally placed his hands on the ladder and pulled himself erect, joy flooded his inner man. The next crawl, the Lord willing, would be outbound only. He could already taste freedom!

24

Atchafalaya Swamp, Louisiana
Friday, December 6, 2019

"Hey, it's nearly seven!" Rat exclaimed, springing up from the table with the slab of pecan pie that had just been dropped on his plate. He grabbed his laptop from the charging station on the counter, set it on the coffee table, and booted up. Then he opened his TOR browser, navigated to CVN, dropped back into the well-worn couch, and hollered at his friends, "Y'all better hurry up, or yer gonna miss the news." Then he picked up his pie and chawed off a massive bite.

Over the next few minutes, the others joined him, either cozying up on the sofa or taking a cushion on the floor in front. Ariele hobbled over on her crutches and took a seat next to him, grimacing slightly but not groaning or complaining. He was impressed. Though she still felt weak, her leg still burned, and she still had shortness of breath and nausea, she was trying to stay active and productive. No doubt about it. She was one tough chick.

Peggy Sue set a serving tray on the coffee table. Ariele

stared in delight. *So this is the cool gift that Rat had hinted was coming!* On the tray were five stainless-steel travel mugs, each one personalized with a nickname: Rat, Daisy, Renegade, Safari Queen, and Moxie.

Rat handed the redhead her mug. She lifted it to her lips, savored a mouthful of Cajun coffee, then pondered her nickname. Moxie had always warmed her heart. But ever since Woody had uttered it with tears in his eyes when he advised her to flee to Montana, it had held a hallowed place in her psyche. It had become her handle of defiance. She had never been very political or religious. Now she had a cause that transcended policy and religion—truth. The truth of the Rogue, the truth of the prophecies of the Bible, and her growing suspicion that Yeshua might actually be THE truth, as he had claimed in the New Testament.

Her mind turned to her Torah-loving grandfather who had scorned politics and religion. In his estimation both practiced the dubious art of misrepresenting the opposition to make them look worse than they were and misrepresenting one's own party to make it look better than it was. This was throwing mud on the opposition and whitewashing your chosen party. Nobody seemed to have a conscience against this. Everyone seemed to think that you weren't loyal to the truth if you didn't defend the truth with this kind of information manipulation.

The program jumped from the introductory soundtrack to the newscaster's voice, startling Ariele out of her reflections.

"Good evening. It's 8 p.m. here in the Big Apple. This is

THE RUSSIAN RUN

The World Report, and I'm Tom Overbright.

"Our headline story tonight is a massive comet that slammed into the Indian Ocean just over an hour ago. At 5:48 a.m. Bangladesh time, several dozen passengers on board the *Lucky Jasper*, a cruise ship sailing from Sri Lanka to Singapore, observed a gigantic fireball pass overhead. Here's a brief video shot by one of the passengers."

The clip showed a brilliant ball of bluish-green streaking across the sky for several seconds before dropping below the horizon. Then it panned back and focused on its trail, a mingling of glow and smoke which lingered for a couple minutes. Tom continued, "There are also reports of sightings from Sumatra, but it has not yet been confirmed whether these involve the same comet or a different one.

"Initial estimates from experts who have seen the video suggest that the comet was approximately the size of the Xingu bolide that wiped out sixty square kilometers of jungle and three small villages in the Brazilian state of Pará in April."

"Like the other large comets that made impact in the past fourteen months, the Sri Lanka comet approached from behind the sun, making it hard to detect, and traveled in a northwesterly direction. It was not observed until it was a mere fifty-seven minutes from impact.

"Two observatories in Australia, which managed to track the comet for over forty minutes, have calculated that the comet slammed into the deep somewhere in the Ceylon Plain southeast of Sri Lanka and west of Sumatra, close to the equator. A tsunami watch has been issued for Sri Lanka, the southern and southeastern coast of India, and the western coast of Sumatra. But it's not certain that the impact will create a tsunami. While the waves at the impact site were probably well over a hundred meters high, and any ships in the immediate area would have been in danger, it is expected that these waves will have dissipated by the time they reach the shores of Sri Lanka and Sumatra, some six or seven hundred miles away.

"As we speak, government officials from India, Indonesia, and Australia are holding a video consultation to plan a joint response involving both civilian and military representatives. One Australian source indicated that this coalition will involve research ships, support ships, submersibles, and a carrier with helicopters. No specifics have been released as of this time. We will bring you further details and developments as they become available.

"On the European front, the shock of Germany's departure from the European Union continues to rock the remaining nations ... Excuse me ... Hold on ... A high-priority bulletin just flashed on my teleprompter. It appears that two commercial satellites were knocked out by the tail of the comet, one owned by the Chinese government and one by India. No further details are available at this time." He flashed the standard painted smile. "It's time for a word from our sponsor. Stay tuned to CVN and *The World Report*, and we'll keep you up to date on all the biggest stories unfolding in the world."

Burt ran his fingers through his thinning hair and whistled softly. "That's the fourth major impact in just over a year! If that's not a sign of the times, I don't know what is."

"The heavens are definitely going crazy," Ariele agreed. "But I'll bet the authorities just pooh-pooh it like they did the previous three."

"No doubt in my mind. May God help Jordy and Cheslav in their efforts to let the world know that the fireworks are just beginning."

25

**FEMA 286, Syracuse, NY ... near Elmira, NY
Saturday, Dec. 7 to Sunday, Dec. 8, 2019**

Late Saturday afternoon, Jack checked the weather forecast on the computer in his maintenance cage to verify that it was still favorable for their breakout attempt. He breathed a sigh of relief. The National Weather Service, Accuweather, and Weather.com agreed that the snowstorm which had reached Syracuse that morning would continue to pummel the region through Monday afternoon. It was expected to dump more than two feet of snow by Sunday evening. *Thank you, Father. Your mercies are new every morning.*

The timing was ideal. An escape attempt on a Saturday evening was their preferred option. For one thing, the evening director on the weekends, Bradley Nelson, was the least professional of the directors. They had never seen him making rounds. He just sat at his desk playing computer games. For another thing, Jiffy LTL was closed on Sundays, reducing the odds that a missing truck would be discovered before they were out of the area.

Confident that the mission was a go, Jack sent a runner

to summon the entire maintenance department for a 4:15 team meeting. While he hadn't wanted the department-head slot which had opened up after Bryce's transfer to a 300-series camp, he had accepted it. Now it was obvious that the position had been the provision of God. It fit their escape plan hand in glove.

When the last stragglers arrived, he informed the team that he and Sally would be performing maintenance on the boiler and pipes in the north warehouse that evening from lights out to well past midnight. This late-evening arrangement for maintenance had been adopted so it wouldn't interfere with activities like showers and laundry.

At supper Sally gave the same heads up to brunette Joyce, who oversaw the women's dorms, and Jack informed Jeremy Hendricks. The de facto pastor also supervised the men's dorms.

At 6:15, Jack poked his head in Bradley's office and advised the director that he planned on doing boiler maintenance that night so he and Sally wouldn't be in their racks when headcount was taken at 11. The director looked up from his game and nodded. Jack added, "Please don't forget to call the guard shack and give them a heads up so they won't get nervous if they see activity on the warehouse cameras after curfew. It was a fiasco last time we pulled boiler maintenance on the weekend." Bradley dipped his head almost imperceptibly and went back to his game. Jack walked away shaking his head. *Don't understand why anyone wastes their time on those stupid, mind-numbing games.*

At 6:30, Sally stacked four dining-room chairs on her

cabinet cart and pushed the load to her studio. This time, Jack wasn't inside. He was troubleshooting a control module for the boiler, hoping to leave a working spare on his workbench for his friends. Upon arrival she stacked the chairs out of the way, donned a dust mask, put a strip of 120 grit on her sanding pad, and began sanding a coffee table she had stripped earlier that week. She shook her head at the irony of putting so much effort into a project that she wasn't going to finish. But she needed to kill time until 9 p.m.—mission rendezvous time.

As the hour drew near, Jack pushed a tool cart to the western end of the north warehouse where several steam-pipe issues needed to be resolved and left it sitting there. Then he returned to maintenance where he and Sally loaded a cabinet cart with steam-pipe tools, tape, joints, sections, and the bags for their mission. After dropping the bags off in Sally's studio, they pushed the steam-pipe cart to the area where Jack had left his tool cart. Sally spread out some repair supplies while Jack dug out a few tools and left them lying on top of the cart. Then he poured himself a cup of coffee, a classic Melmac mug which he hated to leave behind, took two big swigs, and left it sitting two-thirds full, hoping it would look like they had walked away in the middle of the job.

Back in the studio, Jack double-checked their sewer clothes, dry clothes, supplies, and tools. He was most concerned about the latter, especially the hacksaw, boltcutter, and padlock. If they got left behind or weren't in working order, the mission would likely fail.

Assured that everything was ready to roll, he hustled behind the pallet-stack wall to change into his sewer outfit, while Sally stayed in the studio to do the same. When she was ready, she whistled, their agreed-upon all-clear sign, and they met at the manhole. Jack dropped his bag of street clothes next to their mission bags and gestured for Sally to do the same. Their street duds were going down with them but would be left a few feet from the shaft, where they wouldn't be seen if someone looked down the manhole.

Jack jammed the pallet jack under his manhole-cover lifter that was disguised as a parts crate, pumped the handle furiously until the cover was five inches off the ground, then dragged it backward until it only covered a quarter of the manhole. He checked his watch—it was 9:34. They were running behind already.

He pointed to his watch. "Time to go, Sally."

She gingerly maneuvered her way into the manhole, took three tentative steps down the ladder, and looked over her shoulder at him. Fear was written on her face, and she was visibly shaking. Jack could empathize. He had faced down fear before. A shudder rippled through his body as he recalled his own efforts to quell panic after his air hose had been ripped off at three hundred feet and he was forced to buddy breath back to the surface, stopping at each decompression stage. He flashed her a smile and a wink. "No need to worry. The dungeon is perfectly safe. I already killed all of the dragons with my bare hands." A feeble smile creased her face. That was a good sign. There was still some fight left in her. She bit her lip and descended.

When she reached the bottom, Jack called down, "Back up into the tunnel and give me some room. I'll toss our stuff down, then climb down myself."

The first gear bag splashed into the nasty soup and peppered her goggles. She pulled it in, pinned it to the wall with her left knee, and attempted to wipe the slimy drops off of her goggles. But her rubber glove only smeared them and added to the mess. Worse, bringing her sewage-covered gloves close to her nose was a big mistake. A wave of nausea washed over her. *This is going to be the worst trip of my life.*

When all their bags were in the hole, Jack donned his hardhat, switched his lamp on, and strode over to the pallet jack. He stared at the contraption and hesitated. This was the only part of the mission that scared him. He had practiced this step dozens of times, but the valve was cantankerous. He cracked the release valve a smidgeon to where he figured the pallet would slowly drop over thirty seconds or so, then raced to the opening, scrambled down the first five rungs, and whirled himself around on the ladder.

Nasty bug guts! The crate was descending too fast. In a frantic, adrenalin-juiced effort, he shot his hands out palms up, found finger holds on the backside of two of the bottom ribs of the manhole cover, and pulled the heavy load toward him. His forearms strained, instantly filling with blood and pain. It was going to be close. With a half inch of daylight left, he tugged the cover one last inch, and … it dropped into place with a cold, metallic thwunk.

Though he was thankful that the cover had come down

perfect, he descended with a sinking feeling. Their fate was sealed. There was no going back now if they changed their minds, or forgot something, or ran into problems. No matter how this played out—whether they made it to safety, whether they ended up in a 300-series camp, or whether they died—they had left 286 for good.

Jack hung the bags they were leaving behind on an exposed rebar five feet from the shaft, then placed his hand on his companion's shoulder. "You can do this, Sally. Just grab your bags by the handles, keep them out in front of you, and push them one after the other. That'll keep your hands out of the water, which will help keep you dry and warm. Don't worry about the duffel bags. They're gonna take some serious abuse, but the stuff inside is double wrapped in garbage bags and should stay dry."

She took her first hesitant waddles forward in the noxious slop. Jack resisted the urge to check his watch. He didn't want to aggravate his sense of urgency over the slow pace she was setting. Once she got used to it, she would go as fast as she could.

About two hundred feet in, she huffed, "I can't handle the stench down here! It's beyond putrid. It smells like chemicals, dead stuff, and poop."

"Hate to break it to you, but that's precisely the witch's brew that we're crawling in. But you'll get used to the smell after a while."

She snorted.

A couple minutes later, she stopped and tried to adjust her waders. "I hate these things," she grumbled. "I wish I had never found them in the warehouse. They're the most uncomfortable things I have ever worn. You can't move in them. And they're rubbing my hips, legs, and chest raw."

"Just keep moving Sally. The faster we crawl, and the fewer times we stop, the sooner we get out of here."

"Can we take them off? Wouldn't it be easier to crawl without them?"

"Just get moving!" he barked. There wasn't time to lecture her on the value of the waders as protection from hypothermia, illness, and infection. Besides, there was no talking to anybody when they got irrationally frustrated like that.

At the tee, Jack checked his watch. It was 10:07. *Rats.* A half hour to get this far. They were moving slower than planned.

"How much farther?" she complained.

"We're only a quarter of the way. It's a long way yet."

She stifled a sob as she turned right. "My legs are starting to feel cold. And I don't know how long I can keep this up."

"Just keep moving. Think about the warm truck we'll soon be riding in and the hot coffee when we get to the hideout."

"Warm places and hot drinks won't do me any good if I die before then," she whimpered.

"As long as you still feel cold," he encouraged her, "you aren't dangerously cold. It's when you stop feeling cold that you need to worry."

As she slogged ahead, Sally tried imagining herself sitting in the truck cab with the heater running full blast, but that didn't help. She switched to romanticizing about sitting in front of a roaring fireplace, wrapped in a thick blanket, with the man of her dreams at her side, arm around her waist. She pictured the flickering flames and watched them dance. Soon it was just her and the fire. When the fire grew low, she added another log or two. When the flames didn't seem to warm her as they had been, she dragged herself closer to the fireplace.

She thought she heard someone talking to her. "Are you still with me, Sally?" The fire started to fade and she was back struggling along in the cold water and frigid air. "I ... I ... I'm still ... moving ... can't ... f ... f ... feel my feet ... m ... m ... my hands ... are numb," she stammered out, teeth chattering.

Jack was worried. She was shivering uncontrollably. He helped her kneel upright and placed her hands against the surface of the four-foot pipe so she could steady herself. Then he rummaged in his supply bag, found the box of handwarmer packets, activated twenty of them, and placed five in each leg of her snow pants inside her waders. Next, he dropped a half dozen down the back of her shirt, hoping they would nestle at the small of her back. Then he put two in each breast pocket on her wool shirt. He touched her shoulder. "We gotta get moving, Sally."

She shook her head *no*.

Jack knew that was not an option. They had to get moving again. The handwarmer packets alone weren't enough to stabilize her body temperature. He grabbed the struggling woman, helped her back into a crawling position, and patted her on the back. "You're doing great, Sally. We're halfway down this stretch." She moaned and began to shuffle forward unsteadily.

At two minutes past midnight, Sally stopped five feet short of the grate as she had been directed, and Jack scooted past her. They had been crawling in the sewer for two hours and twenty-five minutes, the last forty-five minutes at a turtle's pace. Sally was so stiff and cold that she could hardly move. And her shivering had become violent. "Hang in there, Sally," he encouraged her. "We're past the hard part. We're on the home stretch now."

Jack started to listen to make sure that the coast was clear, but decided that no sane person would be out in this weather. Besides, Sally's precarious condition required immediate action. He put his shoulder to the grate and pressed until his shoulder went numb. It didn't budge. *Bugger! I should have cut a little deeper.* Furious, he placed his feet on the lower edge of the grate, gripped the strip of metal still clinging to the bottom of the pipe, and pressed his legs outward with all his strength. The grate moved a half inch. Again and again, he exerted himself, until every muscle involved in the effort was trembling in exhaustion.

When the grate had moved six or seven inches, the unit began to yield ground more easily. Jack took heart and continued pressing until his weary limbs, at about seventy percent horizontal, couldn't budge the grate any farther. Like any good soldier would, he adapted. *Guess a two-foot gap is gonna have to do.*

Ignoring the light-headedness that was trying to push his

wussy button, he tossed their bags to the shore on the left and watched them drop noiselessly into the new-fallen snow. Then he turned to Sally. "Time to get out of here. Turn yourself backward, work your legs out over the lip, grab the grate remnants on the bottom, balance on your belly, then push away and drop. The drop will be three or four feet to the water. I'm guessing that the water will be two or three feet deep. If you get the push-out-and-drop maneuver right, you won't get any sewage down your waders. But don't panic if you screw up and get doused. We got dry clothes."

The distraught female nodded glumly, turned around awkwardly, and clumsily worked her way out over the grate bottom. Shins. Knees. Mid-thigh. Hips. Finally, her waist rested on the toothy remnants of the grate. Trembling with cold and exhaustion, she attempted to push herself out and drop, but the arm strength wasn't there and the kick was feeble. She came back down hard on her chest, her feet swung forward, she lost her grip, and she fell backward into the foul water with a weak scream.

Jack spun around, scooted his legs over the jagged bottom until his belly was resting on it, pushed himself outward and swung his legs sideways, released, and dropped. Flash memories of scuba jumps from storm-whipped choppers ricocheted in his cold-fogged brain. His legs plunged into the waist-deep water next to Sally, and he prepared to meet the bottom. The moss and silt found his feet before he was ready, and his legs slid out from underneath him. He was going down, partly sideways and partly backward. His arms shot out to catch himself but found nothing except frigid waters. An explosion of ice-cold water washed over his head and neck. Instinctively he tucked, got his feet underneath himself, and stood upright. He took a three-second inventory of his situation. Legs and arms okay. Face and ears numbing up. Chest, back, and butt soaking wet. Pride bruised. Mission still a go.

But there was no time to worry about himself. Sally was on her back in the frigid water, floundering, trying to stand up. But her waders were too full, and she was too numb, tired, and disoriented. He grabbed her suspenders and tried to raise her to her feet. The grommets ripped out of the rubber, and she flopped back into the chilly bath. He waded around behind her, tucked his arms under her armpits, locked his hands across her chest, and started to drag her to shore.

The heavy load beggared belief. *Definitely waterlogged. She's twice as heavy as I'd expected.* He dug his heels into the bottom to get traction and struggled backward. His calves burned. His upper legs stabbed with pain. Every step was a battle of the will against odds that seemed nearly impossible. By the time he dragged her onto shore, his legs were trembling like jello and barely responded to command. He lowered her into the snow, hobbled around to her front, and nearly panicked when he saw her pale face and glassy eyes.

Gonna have to act fast and creatively, or her hypothermia is gonna pass from life-threatening to fatal. He squeezed as much water as he could out of her dripping hair, placed two handwarmer packets in a wool balaclava, and pulled it down over her head and face. With his folding knife, he sliced her waders down to her calves, unleashing quarts of icy water. Then he pulled the waders off, freeing her limbs from their rubber coffin.

Next, he stripped off her wet jacket and placed an air-activated MRE heater on top of her wool shirt against her belly. "Hold this in place," he advised. "Move it around if it gets too hot." While she clutched the heat source with alternating hands, he bundled her back up with a dry ski jacket and cinched the hood tight.

He turned his attention to her lower body. The soaking wet ski pants needed to come off or her core temperature was likely to drop further. Several long rips with his knife set her free from their chilly grip. He placed his hands on her thermal-underwear-covered thighs. They were cold to the touch. His hands, stiff from the relentless cold and wind, fumbled to open a handwarmer packet and taped it to her left leg. He raised a silent plea to God for help and willed himself to press forward despite the stinging pain. *Task first. Comfort later.* With awkward efforts, he managed to tape six handwarmer packets to each leg. It didn't look pretty, but aesthetics were far from his mind. He finished up by sliding her into dry snowmobile pants, dry wool socks, and insulated boots with three hand-warmer packets in each.

His next concern was the grate. He surveyed the situation and shook his head. *No way I'm gonna be able to pry that down now. No time and no strength. Gonna have to stay that way.*

He struggled out of his own waders and wet top layers and pulled on dry pants, boots, and jacket. Then he transferred their mission gear to two clean duffel bags and left their waders and wet clothes where they lay. Originally, he had planned on stuffing them into the dirty bags and tossing them into the brush, but the breached grate already gave them away, so he didn't worry about their abandoned gear.

His watch revealed that it was 12:29. He exhaled in resignation. They were behind schedule. And there was nothing they could do to catch up. Sally was barely able to hobble. He wasn't in great shape either. The weather was miserable. *Oh well. It is what it is. When the going gets crappy, the tough get scrappy.*

Jack took the exhausted woman by the arm and raised her to her feet. He contemplated holding her up and carrying her duffel bag but vetoed the idea. This was not the time to play the gallant gentleman. The best thing he could do for her under the circumstances, though it felt hard-hearted, was force her to pull her own weight. The more active she was, the sooner she would warm up.

Feeling like a scoundrel, he offered his arm. She took it with a feeble grasp and struggled to maintain her balance. Alarmed by her weakness, he broke off a chunk of a chocolate bar and stuffed it in her mouth to help keep her blood sugar up. Then he began walking up the snow-covered path toward the access road, which he estimated was about a couple hundred feet away. Sally hobbled at his side, tottering, teeth chattering, mumbling. He kept a wary eye on the bag in her right hand. Her stiff fingers couldn't close around its handle, and it dangled precariously from her crooked digits. It would be costly if it slipped from her grasp and neither of them noticed.

On the access road, they no longer had to fight the brush, but the unimpeded wind blasted them, stinging their faces with the whipping snow. And the bigger drifts, which were knee-high on Jack, were too deep for Sally to walk through. She couldn't lift her feet high enough. Instead, she shuffled through them, a slower process. After struggling in this manner for several hundred feet, they reached the fence.

Jack looked down the fence line in both directions, looked at the locked gate, looked at his limping partner, and hesitated. He had planned on cutting an opening in the fence away from the road. Now he was tempted to cut the chain on the gate. That was fast and easy. And he could justify it. Sally was in bad shape and they were behind schedule. But his conscience nagged him to follow the operation order that he had contrived in relative calm.

He sighed, headed off to his left, and nipped a flap with his cutters fifty feet off the road where the fence was obscured by chokecherry bushes. Sally tried to kneel, but her legs didn't cooperate. She lost her balance and began falling toward the fence. Jack's heart skipped a beat as he let go of the flap, sprang halfway off his haunches, and caught her. As she tumbled into his arms, searing pain erupted in his quad and hip.

Wincing at his new problem, Jack helped her crawl through the opening, raised her to her feet again, and led her back to the access road where they continued their plod toward freedom.

Several hundred feet and three massive drifts later, a pronounced rise announced what the white-out conditions had obscured. They had reached the main road. As he had anticipated, they had come out near Sonny's Salvage, where old man Johnson had amassed acres of piles of scrap iron and steel.

Sonny's main building and yard light were barely discernible off to their right, fading in and out of view according to the folly of the wind. *Guess glassing for security cameras is a no-go. But it probably doesn't matter. If we can't see the cameras because of the snow, most likely they can't see us either.* He looked to the left and couldn't make out anything at Jiffy LTL where they were headed.

Jack took Sally by the arm, and they hobbled across the road as fast as she was able. Several steps down the bank on the other side, he moved in front of her and bulldozed a path through the waist-deep snow in the ditch. Four times he had to turn around, walk back to her, and drag her through the gauntlet of white. When they finally reached the fence line, he was out of breath. *Thirty seconds for a blow. That's all you get.* A trickle rolled down his forehead and brow. *Slow down, Jack. Sweat is your enemy.*

What? Crud! Headlights flickered on the edge of visibility. What now? There wasn't enough time to cut an opening. They couldn't risk staying put. Trying to hide on this side was almost as problematic. Getting over the seven-foot fence was their only option. Jack squatted and grabbed Sally by the ankles. "Keep your knees stiff and put your hands on the top," he advised. "I'll lift you up and toss you over." Before she could protest, her feet left the ground, and she was accelerating upward. Her hands shot out and found the top just in time to cushion her chest as she tumbled over. While she was still falling, Jack lunged sideways and upwards, grabbed the top, kicked his legs up high, and vaulted over … almost. He came down hard straddling the fence, catching his jacket and pants in the process. With a furious effort, he tumbled off the top and landed in the snow, sprawled out like roadkill on the highway.

Spitting out a mouthful of snow, he craned his head toward the lights about fifty feet away. They raced past them, leaving a spray of snow in their wake. *A snowplow! Should have figured.* He followed the taillights until they disappeared in the snowstorm. No brake lights appeared. They were safe. The driver likely had his eyes glued to the road and didn't notice them or their tracks in the ditch.

"Thank you, Lord," he uttered, more out of habit than conscious intention. He was too exhausted to operate at full mental capacity. They were being pressed to the limits of human endurance.

Jack heard crying. Sally was kneeling, trying to wipe the snow off her balaclava, hood, and coat. He helped the trembling woman to her feet, brushed her face off, and embraced her. "I'm gonna get you out of here, Sally. All you gotta do is trust me and not quit on me."

"I'm not gonna quit," she whispered, sniffling. "I think I'm doing a little better. My arms and legs don't feel as cold as they did."

He popped another chunk of chocolate into her mouth.

She's gonna need more than a little improvement and a little sugar. We need to get in that truck soon and get the heater on.

They angled their way through the snow-covered piles of metal for several hundred feet before they saw the faint glow of the yard lights at Jiffy LTL. From the cover of a pile near the edge of the lot, Jack scoped the building with his naked eyes and with his binoculars. The storm had let up a little, allowing him a tolerable view of the building. Thankfully, no cameras faced them. There was one on the front corner that covered the driveway approach and another on the back corner that caught activity in the back yard.

After weighing his options, he determined to make a beeline for a door near the center of the wall. Though the direct route left them more exposed, the other options weren't much better. And under the circumstances, speed trumped modest improvements in concealment.

To the right of the door, an electrical conduit ran up the wall, then ran sideways to a light housing over the entrance. He figured that was his ticket to the top. From the top of the light, he should be able to reach the parapet. A convenient dumpster would give him a headstart on the conduit climb. Maybe three or four feet less to climb.

Between them and the door, however, stood a ten-foot-high chain-link fence. They scurried across some fifty feet of open ground to the barrier, and Jack pulled out his wire cutters. He made a dozen snips behind a post, pulled the flap up, and nodded to Sally. This time she was able to kneel and crawl through the small opening on her own—a great relief to Jack. Before he crawled through, he untwisted a wire tie from higher on the post. He used it on the other side to secure the cut near the bottom. *No one's gonna notice unless they look closely.*

Down the slope they charged, the taste of victory in their mouths, only to find themselves in chest-deep snow at the bottom. Jack forced a path through to the asphalt, and they hustled across the narrow strip to the dumpster. He pointed to the downwind side of the garbage bin. "Wait here while I do my thing."

"I'll be fine," she said, as she sat down. But her voice hinted more of dejection than confidence.

Jack said nothing. There was nothing he could say. At this point she needed rest, heat, and warm liquid more than empathy. But he did hand her the rest of the chocolate bar.

An inspection of the conduit revealed that his chosen route wasn't as workable as he had anticipated. Its small diameter and tightness to the wall made it a logistical nightmare. But there was no turning back. And there was no Plan B. It was do or die.

He exhaled in a frustrated huff, dug out his lineman's pliers and multi-tool, traded his warm gloves for a thin leather pair, climbed on top of the dumpster, grabbed the conduit—his fingers barely found a bite underneath—and gave it a hefty tug. It felt like it might hold his weight as long as the screws held. Keeping the handhold, he leaned back, placed his feet on the wall straddling the conduit, and began walking up with short steps and alternating hand slides.

Two minutes later, after several breaks to flex his stiff hands, his left hand found the top of the light housing. He brushed the snow off the top, wedged his fingers behind it, and lodged his right hand next to his left. *Rat raisins.* The position was awkward, and it didn't give him half the leverage he had hoped. Only his left forearm was resting on the housing. His right barely caught the edge. But there was nothing he could do to improve the situation. He counted to three and muscled himself up, straining until everything in his body hurt. The last two inches brought him close to blacking out, but he managed to get his right knee on top, transfer his weight to his leg, and rest. Fighting waves of light-headedness, he questioned his plan. *This is bonehead crazy.* But there were no other options.

The next stage was nearly as daunting. He raised himself on his right knee, got his left foot on top after a struggle, and shifted his weight to his left leg. He counted to three again, leaned into the wall, let go of the housing, spread both hands out against the wall, and stood erect on the tiny platform. His heart was racing—as much from fear as from exertion.

On his toes, his hands barely reached the top of the parapet. He brushed off the snow that he could reach, got as sure a grip as the icy concrete offered, prayed for strength and safety, pulled his way up with shaking arms until his chin was level with the top, shot his right arm over the parapet and found a grip. Then he got his left arm over, dragged himself over the lip, and flopped onto the roof. He lay in the snow for a minute, his arms burning with exhaustion. *Don't think my arms have been this tired since DEVGRU selection.*

Fighting the wind-driven snow that was stinging his eyes,

he cautiously walked to the rear of the building, located the coaxial cable that fed the near-corner camera, and snipped it. Then he continued along the rear parapet, snipping the cables for the camera in the middle of the wall and the one in the far corner. Relieved that the job was done, he shoved his pliers back into his coat pocket and hustled back to the spot where he had climbed up.

When he peered over the edge on his hands and knees, his joy evaporated. Negotiating the route up had been one of the hardest things he had ever done, certainly the hardest thing since his CIA tour in Afghanistan. Going down would be even harder. The fact is, going down by the same route wasn't going to happen. He thought about jumping but vetoed the notion. Trying to land on or in a dumpster only worked in the movies. He racked his mind for ideas. *C'mon Jack, think ... If I had a rope, I could rappel down ... but I don't have a rope ... wait a minute ... the coaxial cable.*

He raced to the cable he had snipped in the near corner, picked up the loose end, and followed it to its source, a housing which fed wires to the cameras, satellite dish, and who knows what else. He snipped the cable a few inches from the housing, looped it around the leg of the satellite dish bracket, lined up the two ends, walked to the parapet, and dropped the loose ends over. They touched the dumpster. *Should be long enough for a field-expedient rappel.*

He straddled the rope with his back facing the wall, reached his right hand behind, grabbed his makeshift rope, and brought it around his right hip, over his left shoulder, across his shoulder blades, and under his right arm. Then he wrapped a single loop around his forearm and gripped the cable tight in his right hand. With his heart in his throat, he stepped up and backward onto the parapet, got positioned, and started slowly letting himself down into a classic rappel position. From there he would let himself down in a controlled manner.

Things didn't go as planned. The cable offered far less friction than a rope, and he couldn't grip it tight enough to stop himself. He was falling in slow motion. The ends sailed through his right hand, and he grit his teeth. Whump! His back slammed into the dumpster lid, and he slid off and tumbled to the ground.

Sally had watched the situation unfold, first in admiration, then in fear. She loped to Jack's crumpled body and checked for a pulse.

He opened his eyes and brushed her hand away. "I'm alive Sally, just give me a minute."

He checked his limbs and appendages one by one: hands, feet, arms, legs, neck, head. Everything seemed to be in working order. He sat up with a weak smile, one of those forlorn grins that peeks through the pain. "All systems go. Banged up but not broken." With a groan he stood up, climbed back on top of the dumpster, grabbed one end of the coaxial cable, pulled the whole length down, and coiled it up. Then he jumped down, tossed the coil into the dumpster, grabbed his duffel bag, and nodded to his partner. "Time to move."

They walked to the row of trucks parked along the back fence and began looking for truck number 21. They found it toward the far side of the lot. It was an older MV series International with a 20-foot box, likely an '08 or '09. Jack tried the door handle. It was locked—as he had expected. He peeked in the window. *Sweet!* Manual windows and locks. *Love it when truck companies go cheap and practical!* He bounded around to the front of the truck, opened the hood, pulled out his tiny flashlight, located the fuse box, pulled the fuse for the alarm system, and dropped the hood again. Then he jogged back to the door, pulled a coil of heavy wire out of his gear bag, molded it into a lock picker, poked it through the seal over the window, fished the wire downward, made a few false passes at the lock, then hooked it and pulled it up. BINGO! he shouted quietly.

Sally climbed in and scrambled over to the passenger seat. Jack tossed their bags in behind her, depositing them on the floor between the seats. Then he reached under the dash, pulled out the ignition connector, poked a hoop of copper wire into the top two pinholes, pressed a small screwdriver to the top pinhole on the bottom, and lowered the screwdriver to the wire. The truck struggled for a few seconds to turn over, then sprang to life. "Praise the Lord!" he shouted as he pumped his fist.

Heat and windshield were next up. He turned the defroster on high, dug out the 12-volt dash heater that Sally had packed, plugged it into the cigarette lighter, and aimed the unit at the windshield above the steering wheel. Behind the seat he discovered a snow brush that he used to clear the snow off the windshield, the side windows, and the mirrors.

The last item on his mental list was exiting the yard. He

fetched the bolt cutter from his gear bag, hustled over to the rear gate, cut the chain, swung the gate open, and jogged back to the truck. Joy flooded his soul when he released the air brake, put the truck in first gear, and they began rolling forward. After he had exited the yard, he ran back, swung the narrow gate shut, and looped the chain around so it looked locked.

Back in the cab, he smiled reassuringly at Sally, put the truck in gear, and drove as fast as he dared in the snow on the utility road. Though it was 1:35 Sunday morning, and they were well behind schedule, things weren't looking too bad. First light wasn't until nearly seven, and it was snowing and blowing pretty hard. If they could get to the hideout by five, the wind and snow would likely cover their tracks before daylight.

He began to pray, thanking God for his help so far, and asking that no policeman or highway patrolman would see the truck and wonder why it was out on delivery at this time of the day, on Sunday no less.

Once he was on Highway 5, he picked up his burner phone and dialed Woody's contact number that had been included in the prison-break package.

"Tenkara," Woody answered.

"Hi. This is Western Style. We're on the road."

The lump in Woody's throat made it hard to talk. "Roger that, Western Style. Glad to hear you're safe. Do you have your directions down?"

"Directions were clear. Directions are memorized."

"Copy that. Have you called your extraction contact?"

"Negative. I'll call Bullseye upon arrival at our destination."

"Copy that. Give us a call as soon as you get there."

"Copy that. Out." Jack hung up and dropped the phone into his coat pocket.

"Can you put the heater on higher?" Sally inquired. "I'm not warming up very fast."

"Sorry. I got the heater on high and the blower set for max. But something is out of whack. We got lukewarm air and slow flow. I need to keep the little heat we have focused on the windshield so it stays clear. We'd probably be screwed if you hadn't thought to bring the 12-volt dash heater just in case."

"So what am I gonna do? I'm not warming up at all."

"Dig out a space blanket and the MRE heaters from my bag, wrap yourself up snug, and activate one of the heaters. When it cools off, activate another one. The blanket will keep the heat close to your body. You should notice a difference."

Fifteen minutes later, Sally, feeling some warmth returning to her body, leaned her head on a spare jacket propped against the window and closed her eyes. She was more tired than she had ever been in her life—utterly exhausted, physically and emotionally.

***

Sally woke in a fog. A hand was shaking her. A distant voice was speaking unintelligible words to her. She sat up and rubbed her eyes.

"We're at the hideout," Jack informed her. I gotta get out and open the gate."

She yawned and stretched, struggling to gain full consciousness. "What time is it?"

"4:58"

"Are we on schedule?"

"No. Way off," he said as he reached for the door. "My target was 3:30. But we got a late start, and the roads were ugly."

Snipping the lock went fairly easy, but he struggled to open the gate, gaining maybe one foot at a time as he slammed it through the deck of white. After he had driven through the gate, closed it, and secured it with the new lock, he didn't return to the truck right away. Instead, he walked up the road for around a hundred and fifty feet, inspecting the conditions. It didn't look promising. They faced sixteen to twenty inches of fresh snow, plus drifts, and it wasn't always clear where the road was. *Hope I can actually make it to the barn.*

His fears were not amiss. Eleven times, the truck bogged down, and he had to rock back and forth until the tires found solid ground. Twice, he had to kneel in the snow and dig the truck out when it got buried in a drift. Thankfully, he had found a shovel strapped to the wall in the back of the truck. Moving that much snow with his arms would have been a nightmare.

Relief flooded his soul when the headlights gleamed off the barn door. The wet, the cold, and the endless frustrations had worn him down. Now the odyssey was over. All he had to do was find the outhouse, and he could rest. When he rounded the corner of the barn, his heart sank once again.

The wind had wrapped the outhouse with a thick blanket of snow nearly six feet high. He traipsed back to the truck for the shovel, returned to the privy, and attacked the pile. In two minutes of fury and sweat, the door was open, and the key was in hand. It had been hanging, as the directions had claimed, over the door on a cup hook.

The key turned easily in the lock on the entrance door of the barn, and the metallic click of the retreating bolt fell upon his ears like the joyous call of the last trump. He pushed the door. It didn't budge. He put a light shoulder to it, and it still refused to move. *Toad warts. The stupid door is swollen tight.* He backed up, lowered his shoulder, and barreled into the stubborn door like a lineman throwing a block. It burst open, and he sprawled across the concrete hands first.

He picked himself up off the floor, ignored the scrapes and bruises he had just added to his collection, and limped to the utility door. The lift chain resisted his tug. He wrapped it tight around his hand, raised his feet off the ground, and bounced. It moved a few inches. *You've got to be kidding! Now I got to deal with a stuck lift mechanism?* He bounced a second time, gained a few more inches, and took a higher bite on the chain. Over and over again he jerked on the chain until his hands were raw and the door was high enough to pass under.

At 5:48, Jack drove into the barn, steered along the left wall, and nosed the truck up to the hay pile. Sally stumbled out and headed for the apartment on the far end of the barn. Jack returned to his current battle—the door chain. He looked at his torn and tender hands. *Need to find a new method.*

A short chunk of pipe leaning against the wall caught his eye. He wrapped the closure chain around it five times, crossing it over itself a few times to keep it from sliding. He hung his weight on his makeshift handle. The door dropped a few inches. He tried again and gained maybe an inch. His third and fourth efforts, he tried to bounce. The effort was in vain. *Need more height and force.*

He carried two hay bales over, stacked them, and climbed on top. After eyeballing the situation, he raised his handle about eighteen inches and jumped off. The handle tilted awkwardly, and he slammed into the wall. Nothing gave. The little patience he had left evaporated. "What else can go wrong in this stupid night!" He climbed back up and made a second attempt. This time a loud PING echoed inside the lift mechanism, and both he and the door came crashing to the ground. Jack picked himself up, massaged his tender knees, shook his head at the door—indeed at the crazy string of things that had gone wrong that night—and limped off to find Sally.

She was sitting at the picnic table in the kitchen with her head propped in her hands, staring blankly out one of the picture windows that overlooked the barn interior. Pity tore at his heart. He had long been inured to hardship. But this night had been her baptism by fire, and she had plumbed the depths of utter exhaustion. Now she needed some heat, some grub, and some shuteye as soon as possible.

He located the utility room just off the kitchen in the

tiny hallway, turned on the breakers for the apartment, and set the furnace at 72 degrees. It had been set at 44, just high enough to keep the plumbing from freezing. The pantry just beyond it was nearly empty, but he did find three sleeping bags and several boxes and cans of foodstuffs. He didn't bother to check the expiration dates. He already knew the verdict, and he didn't care. Within a few minutes, canned ham-and-eggs was sizzling in a frying pan. When they were nearly done, he dropped two pop tarts into the toaster and set the table.

Sally scarfed down her breakfast like a hungry wolf. Jack was impressed. The taste and texture of the ham-and-eggs reminded him of the C-rations his father had given him as a boy. Edible, but not enjoyable. But her countenance soured when she picked up one of her pop tarts.

"Eww! Tastes like 286!"

"It's pretty much the same thing," he replied with a laugh. "They likely passed their expiration date long ago. But they're not half bad if you wash them down with coffee."

"Instant coffee doesn't deserve the name coffee," she complained.

"I'm with you there," he replied, glad to see the sass, which implied she was getting her strength back. "But all good soldiers learn to drink pseudo-coffee. It's part of their discipline."

She rolled her eyes, shoved the pop tarts away, and yawned. Her exhaustion, enhanced by a full stomach, had returned with a fury.

"I set you up in the second bedroom with a sleeping bag,

an extra bag for a quilt if you need it, and a hot water bottle."

Sally nodded, got up from the table, and disappeared down the big hallway.

Jack finished Sally's pop tarts, then he pulled out his burner phone and called the extraction contact he had been given in the prison-break package. There was no answer, so he left a message. "Hi, Bullseye. The birds have flown the coop. Call back on a secure phone."

Five minutes later, his phone vibrated. "Jack, great to hear your voice. Are you at the pick-up site?"

Jack was dumbfounded. He recognized the voice. Bullseye was Spencer Anderson, an acquaintance from Hershey, Pennsylvania that he visited with several times a year at regional shooting competitions. Spence was a retired sniper from the Marine Corp: first with Force Recon, later with MARSOC. Whenever they bumped into each other, they always went out for prime rib and talked shop—guns, special ops, geopolitics, and prophecy. "Wow, Spence! Didn't see this coming. Anyways, here's the scoop. My partner and I broke out of FEMA 286 last night. Right now, we're holed up at the designated hideout near Elmira, NY. I was told to call this number for a pick-up."

"We have a team ready to roll. But we won't be picking you up immediately. We'll wait until the cover of night."

"Understood."

"Look for us at 1 a.m. We'll be driving a Ford Raptor with a snowmobile in the back. But don't interpret the mission as a no-go unless we're not there by 3 a.m. Things could get pretty hairy. We could have twenty-four or more inches of fresh snow by then. That's doable as long as the snow stays in the powder range. If it turns to wet slop, we may have to improvise."

"Like pick us up with a snowmobile?"

"Exactly."

"Where do we meet you?"

"Keep going past the driveway about a hundred yards until you come to a stream. We'll be waiting there just off the road. We were told there's a turnout on both sides for stream access, so you should have room to turn around. Don't worry about the mailbox up the road. The owners, or so we were told, live in New York City and never show up in the winter except for a few days at Christmas."

"Okay. Got it. A stream a hundred yards past the driveway. Easy peasy."

"What's your signal?"

"We'll stop on the road at the creek, turn our lights off, flash our lights three times, wait for five seconds, then flash them three times again. After the second set of flashes, come out of the woods."

"Gotcha."

"Again, our planned pick-up is one o'clock, but don't abort unless we don't show by three o'clock. Copy?"

"Copy that. See you soon, Recon."

"See you soon, Sixer."

Tired as all get out, Jack yawned and checked his watch. It was 6:45. He needed some rack time. But he was uneasy about their tire tracks. He knew he wouldn't be able to sleep until he checked, so he pulled on his insulated pants and coat and slipped out the door to walk the road. He would have to hurry. Dawn would come soon.

In the densely wooded stretch near the barn, the tracks were nearly half full. In a few more hours, they would be completely covered. Farther up the road, where the forest opened up a bit, the tracks were around three-quarters full. At the first open area, where the old deer stand was, the tracks were already hidden all the way across. That was the encouragement he needed. It would be the same for the gate and the open stretch after it. He turned around and headed back.

**

Jack woke with a start. Something was moving. He cocked his ear and listened intently, trying to identify what the sound was and where it was coming from. He relaxed when he realized that it was a tree branch scraping the roof of the barn. The wind had kicked up. It sounded like a full-on blizzard. He checked his watch—11:32. Over four solid hours of sleep. Not too bad considering the circumstances.

He wandered into the kitchen and began preparing lunch. His eyes felt as heavy as lead, and he wished that he could go back to bed, but there was a ton of work to do.

Several minutes later, Sally stumbled into the room. Jack glanced up from the canned ham-and-eggs crackling in a skillet. "Good morning, Sleepyhead. You look like disaster on steroids!"

She giggled. "I don't even dare look in the mirror."

"Here's the plan. We're gonna get some food and coffee

in our bellies, then hide the truck in the hay pile so it can't be seen through the windows, then shower up. After that, we might be able to get another couple hours of rack time."

"A shower? Are you pulling my leg, Jack?"

"Nope. Got the water heater going. And it's a big tank, so you can lollygag all you want while you get the sewer funk and hay dust off."

Jack nodded to the table, and she took a seat. After giving thanks and serving up the eggs, Jack picked up the teapot to pour water for his instant coffee, set it back down, bolted over to his gear bag on the counter, rustled around, and returned triumphantly with his favorite mug from 286. It sported DEVGRU on one side and the Trident on the other side. Sally's eyes misted up at the sentimentalism of the old warrior and the fact that he reminded her of Woody.

After they had filled their bellies and drank a couple cups of not-so-coffee, they went to work on hiding the truck. Over the next three hours, they made a massive opening in the hay pile. Then Jack tucked in the side-view mirrors and drove the vehicle into the maw, snugging the driver side against the bales stacked on the outside wall. After double-checking the cab to make sure nothing was left behind, he rolled the passenger window down and climbed out.

Covering the truck was harder. While it went fast at first, once the pile got higher than Jack could reach, he had to carry each bale up the stair-stepped pile. He also stuffed as many bales as possible inside the van box so the hay pile would be as close as possible to its original size. Four hours later at 7:15, Jack stacked the last bale behind the truck, and the two stepped back to admire their handiwork. If someone happened to look in a window or even walk around inside the barn, they would never suspect that a box truck was hidden inside the pile.

The two of them sat down on the bales, bone-tired, with itchy hay residue sticking to the prior day's grime.

"If you let me take the first shower," Jack pleaded, "I promise I'll be fast. And when I'm done, I'll make dinner and dessert, and I'll wash the dishes."

"You've got yourself a deal," Sally replied with a knowing smile. *And while you're washing up, I'm going to selfishly demolish the bag of Peanut M&Ms that I saw in the pantry.*

At eight o'clock, the escapees sat down for their last meal at the hideout, another round of ham and eggs and a pudding-like dessert which Jack had cobbled together from pumpkin pie filling, dried out brown sugar with lots of hard chunks, and sweetened condensed milk. When Sally was full, she went straight to bed. After he finished the dishes, Jack set the alarm on his phone for 11:45 and crawled into his sleeping bag, completely whipped. *Three hours of sleep if I fall asleep fast.*

26

**near Elmira, NY
Monday, December 9, 2019**

Jack was on the run, trying to escape the invading Russians who had overrun his position in the Golan Heights in Israel. Hi-tech laser weapons were flashing all around him in the darkness. A bolt made his side tingle. His body went limp, his legs turned to jelly, and he collapsed. His consciousness started slipping away. The battlefield became dreamy and hazy, slowly morphing into somewhere else. His eyes opened in a dark bedroom. Confusion and panic knocked on the door of his heart. *Where am I?* Several chaotic seconds elapsed before things pieced together. He was at the hideout. He hadn't been hit by some hi-tech Russian stun gun. The alarm on his phone was going off in vibration mode. It was 11:45 p.m. He unzipped his bag, rolled out of bed, and planted his feet on the floor. It was time to get rolling if they were going to make the pick-up site at the appointed time.

He hustled to Sally's room and shook her awake, a task easier said than done. After a hasty breakfast of instant coffee and the last of the pop tarts, they divided up the tasks. She emptied the tea kettle, washed the breakfast dishes, returned them to their places, wiped the surfaces, and swept the floor. He stowed their sleeping bags, turned off the water heater, and turned the furnace back down to 44 degrees. Then he packed the trash bag. It would be going with them. No trace would be left behind that someone had borrowed this place.

As they donned their winter clothes, Jack felt a tinge of pride. He enjoyed planning and executing missions, and this one had been going fairly well despite a ton of small things that had gone south. But the mission wasn't over yet. It wouldn't be over until the rendezvous crew had picked them up, and they were well on the way to wherever they were going.

He picked up his duffel bags and stepped out of the comfort of the barn into the howling storm. Sally followed. After he locked the door, he turned to his companion. "Wait here out of the wind while I return the key to its hiding place." *Seems funny*, he mused, *to be concerned about the key when the world is coming to an end. Then again, right is right, regardless of the circumstances.*

At 12:20, on schedule for the first time on the mission, the two began trudging up the road, resisted by the howling wind which tried to bowl them over, the driven snow which stung their eyes, and the thigh-deep snow that hindered every step. Several times, Jack had to force his way through drifts over waist-deep. When the deer stand appeared off to their right, they turned toward it and quickly found themselves facing more deep drifts as they crossed the field. At the stand, they entered the woods, and the going became easier. When they reached the brook Jack motioned with his hand, and they turned downstream. A few minutes later at 12:51, he halted behind a small pine that was about thirty feet from the road. "We'll wait here. We can use our duffel bags for chairs."

Their ride didn't show at one o'clock. Nor 1:15. Nor 1:30. When 1:45 came and went, Jack began to worry. He hadn't expected Bullseye to be this late. At 2:27, when hope was starting to fade, and they were doing knee bends to stay warm, a pickup approached their position slowly, slogging through snow that reached the door panels. It stopped where the creek ran under the road. They watched with bated breath. The vehicle's lights turned off, stayed dark for a few seconds, then flashed on and off three times. The vehicle went dark again, then flashed its lights again in the same pattern. Jack whispered "Hallelujah!" tapped Sally on the shoulder, and said, "Go!" She picked up her bags and dashed through the snow. He followed right behind her.

The man in the passenger seat saw them coming, jumped out, and opened the rear door for them. They tossed their bags in and climbed after them. Using the pullout, the driver jockeyed the vehicle back and forth in a five-point turn, then headed back down the treacherous road.

The man in the passenger seat turned around. It was Bullseye—Spencer Anderson. He reached out his hand to Jack, and they shared a warm shake.

"Arrangements have been made," he said, "for you two to stay with some biker friends in a quiet neighborhood on the outskirts of Meyersdale, Pennsylvania. Once there, you can plan the next leg of your escape at your leisure."

"Sounds like a deal to me."

"The apartment isn't much. It's a small studio over a garage, with two tiny bedrooms, a bathroom, a kitchenette, and a sitting room. The ceiling is only six foot four, and the knee walls are only a foot high. So there isn't much headroom."

"Not too worried about that," Jack replied. "Our Lord didn't even have a place to lay his head."

"Got that right."

"Anything on the news about our escape?"

"Only that there were two escapees from a federal detention center in Syracuse. One is a former SEAL, who should be regarded as armed and dangerous. Both are guilty of mishandling national secrets. Local, state, and federal law enforcement in the area were put on high alert Sunday morning. Officials doubt that you went very far in this storm or that you had contacts on the outside who could have aided you. Teams are combing the entire Syracuse area, and the authorities have set up roadblocks thirty miles out of town. Every vehicle going in or out is being stopped and searched. The authorities are predicting that you'll be captured within forty-eight hours."

Jack chuckled. "Looks like our ploy is working."

"Yep. A good plan stacks up pretty well against incompetence. It never dawned on them that you might get a hundred miles away in this kind of weather."

The two chatted for a few more minutes, then Jack's eyelids started to droop, and he joined Sally in fitful sleep.

27

**Atchafalaya Swamp, Louisiana
Wednesday, December 11, 2019**

The three gals relaxed on the deck, their morning coffees in hand, discussing the cultures and cuisines of the Deep South. While Peggy Sue patiently explained the differences between Cajun and Creole cooking, Ariele's mind drifted away, though she did catch that Creole cooking uses tomatoes while true Cajun cooking doesn't.

The majestic wilderness held her spellbound. A glorious sunrise was bathing the swamp in tangerine hues. And a grand symphony was greeting the morning. Hundreds of birds were singing, chirping, and warbling. A woodpecker was hammering away for his breakfast. Two squirrels were chattering up a storm in the woods behind them. A chorus of bullfrogs was croaking in staccato bursts.

While her native California—with its sunshine, deserts, beaches, and redwoods—would always be her first love, the swamp country of Louisiana had grown on her. There was much to love. The scent of pine and oak mingled with pungent earthiness. The sights and sounds. And the glorious isolation. Neither road nor trail led to the cabin. It was accessible only by canoe.

Her mind turned from the beauties of the present Earth to those of the coming kingdom—delightful thoughts she had heard from Joby who had learned them from his favorite Messianic rabbi. He loved to talk about the bodily resurrection and the fact that man will still be man. He doesn't cease to be human. He becomes a glorified man. He will still have a body. But what a body! Not susceptible to pain, injury, sickness, or death. Able to interact with physical creation, but not limited by it. The lack of pain was particularly attractive to her. She was tired of pain: physical and emotional.

A hand touched her shoulder. It was Peggy Sue. "I saw you shivering, so I grabbed this blanket from the porch bureau."

"Thank you," she replied. "I thought I was over the chills and that my coat would be enough. But the clamminess is still lingering." She leaned forward and Peggy Sue draped the comforter across her back and shoulders.

Ariele stood up, wrapped the blanket tight across her front, walked over to the railing, and took a closer look at the sun's rays trying to peak over the treetops. "I love sunrises," she exclaimed, with a burst of her native enthusiasm. "They remind me of Joby's descriptions of the Messiah's return in glory."

Peggy Sue, who had been babying Ariele since her snakebite a week and a half earlier, was pleasantly surprised. The redhead had been moody and subdued, and it was nice to see her warm personality resurface. "They remind me of that day too," she replied. "One of my favorite verses is in Malachi, 'the Sun of Righteousness will rise—'"

"With healing in its wings," Ariele responded heartily, finishing the verse. "Joby quotes that one all the time."

The Southern gal spun around and squinted at her. "You seem different. Has something changed?"

Ariele smiled. "I trusted Yeshua."

"When?"

"Last night."

"I want to hear about it!"

"Well, the *One for Israel* videos that you have had me watching really got me thinking. Last night, I was laying in bed wrestling with the apparent conflict between being Jewish and believing on Yeshua. The light came on suddenly. Believing in Yeshua doesn't make you non-Jewish, it enhances your Jewishness. Yeshua is the promised Maschiach. He is the access to the true Holy of Holies in heaven so we can have fellowship with God. He is the door to all the promises made to Israel. We don't inherit our promises through keeping the law under the old covenant. We inherit them through the new covenant mentioned in Ezekiel and Jeremiah. And this covenant is in the blood of Mashiach. He is the suffering Redeemer in Isaiah 53. He was wounded for our transgressions and bruised for our iniquities. Joby had shared all this with me in the past, but it never sank in. Now I understand."

Sam rose to her feet without saying a word, tossed the last few swallows in her cup over the railing, and walked back into the cabin. Ariele shot a pained look at Peggy Sue. "She's still uncomfortable talking about God."

"I get it," she replied, touching Ariele's arm. "I responded that way too, at first. It took a while for my heart to thaw out." She looked intently at Ariele. "So, you're a Christian now?"

"I guess that's what I would be called. I didn't have an emotional experience like you and Rutherford talk about. The light just came on and I couldn't walk away. I wanted to bask in its warmth."

"We don't all have emotional experiences. But we all turn to the light of the world."

"I just feel bad that it took so long for the truth to open my eyes."

"Seeds don't spring up immediately when they're placed in the dirt, and neither do spiritual seeds when they're sown in the heart. Sometimes they germinate fast, and sometimes they take a while."

Ariele sighed. "I'm not sure what to do from here, though."

"What do you mean?"

"Well, I feel drawn to Messianic Judaism. I don't think I could do the Baptist-type Christianity and feel comfortable, though I appreciate it immensely."

"So …?"

"But am I right to feel this way? Should I fellowship in Christian circles? All of the believers I know except for Joby gather with home churches of some sort."

"You have an obligation to follow Jesus according to his

teachings in the New Testament. You don't have an obligation to change your culture any further than your culture is departed from the revealed will and ways of God."

The door opened, and Rat appeared in the opening. But he said nothing. He just stood there, unwilling to interrupt their conversation. Peggy Sue laughed. "I think we're being politely summoned to the breakfast table." As they stood, they were waylaid by the wafted scent of biscuits and bacon gravy. Ariele rubbed her stomach. Her appetite had returned, and she had come to love Southern food.

When all five were seated, Peggy Sue suggested that Ariele pray. Burt nodded his agreement. She bowed her head. "Father in heaven, we thank you for family, friends, and fellowship, for the food on the table, the air we breathe, the water we drink, for this amazing planet. Most of all, we thank you for Yeshua, your eternal Son, the promised Memra, in whom alone your people find redemption and receive their national promises. May your name be glorified forever. Amen."

28

Sevastapol, Crimea
Sunday, December 15, 2019

The three team members stood at the railing of the *Ekaterina*, enjoying Sevastapol's skyline. Though dawn was creeping over the horizon behind them, it was still dark enough for the city lights to twinkle like thousands of gems spilled out of a chest. No one said a word. Irina wrestled with a tumble of emotions—relief that this leg of their journey was complete, apprehension at what lay before them, and nostalgia at reconnecting with her past. She looked over at the guys standing a few feet to her right. *Wonder how they're doing?* Their expressionless faces didn't offer much for clues, but she could see that they were chilled. The winter air had reddened their Scandinavian cheeks. She brought her mittens to her face and covered her own cheeks.

Her thoughts were interrupted by Mikhail's imposing voice. "I stopped by your rooms to say goodbye, and you had already vacated them. Now I find you at the rail with bags packed. Have I been such a poor host that you can't get off my yacht fast enough? You ignored me on our voyage except for an occasional dinner together, and now I catch you trying to sneak away without saying goodbye."

The accusation wasn't strictly true, for they had joined him for dinner on every occasion that he had invited them—a whopping three times. But it did contain an element of truth. They had spent most of their time holed up in their rooms, focusing on their Russian studies. They had only left for meals in the cafeteria, gym time in the morning, occasional strolls to the deck, and watching Russian movies in the theatre in the evening. They had treated him more like a transportation service than a friend. But in reality, that was all that he was.

Irina flashed him one of those frowny smiles that many members of the fairer sex have mastered. "You were a wonderful host, and we greatly appreciate your hospitality. Unfortunately, we were unable to capitalize fully on your kindness because we were busy preparing for our business in Moscow."

He smiled back, a weak effort that spoke more of politeness than affection. "I understand. Business before pleasure. Every successful person approaches life that way." He turned around to head inside, then turned back again. "I apologize for Viktor. I know you didn't get along with him very well, and I don't blame you. He can be a pain in the backside. Sometimes he looks out for my interests with too much machismo and aggression. But he's good at his job. He's one of my most trusted men."

"Yeah. We didn't appreciate his nosiness and attitude. But I do appreciate his service to you as a bodyguard."

"Don't underestimate Viktor. He's far more than a bodyguard. He also helps with business expansion, accounts receivable, and heavy housekeeping."

Irina sensed that this comment was intended as a veiled threat. But she ignored it and changed the topic. "Did you finish arrangements for our transportation to Moscow?"

"I did. Sergei will meet us at the dock and drive you to Moscow. He's already there and waiting."

"Thank you," she replied. "Your kindness is greatly appreciated and won't be forgotten."

Their concerns addressed, the two entered into polite small talk. They were discussing Russian cuisine and the best places to eat in Moscow when the yacht halted alongside its berth. Two deckhands tossed heavy ropes down, and two pier employees secured the vessel.

When the gangplank settled on the concrete below, and the First Officer opened the gate, Mikhail picked up one of Irina's suitcases, took the brunette by the arm, and escorted her off the ship. The guys followed close on their heels. Halfway down the ramp, Tony glanced over his shoulder and shot Andy a knowing look. His brother nodded back with his jaw clenched. Neither trusted the Russian businessman.

On the pier, Sergei greeted his boss with a backslapping hug and a broad smile. "Good to see you, Mikhail."

Mikhail embraced him warmly. "Good to see you too, Seryozh."

The scene strengthened the negative vibes that Irina was feeling. Something didn't add up. Drivers don't greet their billionaire bosses with such familiarity. And billionaires don't greet their drivers with diminutives. Whoever he was, Sergei wasn't Mikhail's driver.

Before she had time to process her fears, Sergei opened the trunk of the BMW, a black M760i, tossed her luggage in, and nodded for the guys to do likewise. Mikhail embraced her, an uncomfortably tight squeeze, and kissed her on each cheek. As she pulled away, he held her arm tight, peered into her eyes, and gave her instructions as if she worked for him. "I made arrangements for your stay in Moscow and contacted several longtime associates about lucrative opportunities. I will be in touch."

The offer unnerved Irina. She peeled his hand off her arm, backed away, and latched onto Tony's arm. The magnate's painted-on smile broadened into a smirk as if he enjoyed making her feel uneasy. He fixed her with an icy look, then turned away, refusing to acknowledge the boys' presence or significance, and headed back up the gangplank.

Sergei motioned for the boys to climb into the back seat. Then he took Irina by the arm, escorted her to the other side of the vehicle, and opened the front passenger door for her. She slammed it shut again and reached for the back door. Sergei eyed her with cold disdain. She didn't see it, but Tony did. As she scooted in next to him, he touched her arm, reassuring her. She appreciated the gesture. *Glad to know that the Delta Boys have my back.*

The BMW backed into a ninety-degree turn, and Andy, facing the ship, noticed Viktor leaning over the rail, giving them a menacing glare. He stared back defiantly until the departing sedan pulled away.

They drove through Sevastapol in dead silence. Irina was frazzled and didn't feel like talking. The boys were occupied with analyzing the situation. Things were not what they superficially seemed. Sergei was no chauffeur. He lacked the social graces and refinement. His cold stare and erstwhile broken nose suggested that he was mafia. And if he was mafia. So was Mikhail.

As verbal communication was out of the question, Tony moved his hands out to his knees and flashed the sign language symbols for "hot," "jump," and "hot." Andy knew he meant "out of the frying pan and into the fire." He signed back "yes/agree" twice for emphatic agreement. Unbeknownst to them, their agreement for a convenient lift from the States to Moscow had come with fine print written in invisible ink. Now they had to figure out a way to nullify the contract.

Shortly after they crossed the Chorno River, Sergei finally spoke. "Mikhail has arranged two dacha stops on the way to Moscow to break up the long drive. Upon arrival in Moscow, you'll be dropped off at the Hotel Presnensky, where he has reserved a luxury suite for you. All of your expenses, including room service and meals, will be on his tab. He'll join you in in a few days."

"Mikhail's generosity knows no bounds," Irina replied. "I look forward to seeing him again." But that was disinformation. She had no interest in seeing him again, and they wouldn't if she could help it. Her instincts warned her that the hints of trouble would soon burst into flame. *As daddy used to say, where there's smoke, there's fire.*

29

Moscow, Russia
Tuesday, December 17, 2019

Irina's heart waltzed with contrary emotions as the luxury sedan negotiated the busy streets of Moscow—now a warm-fuzzy sense that she was returning to her roots, now a pragmatic realization that this was not her home. Red Square was grand, even magnificent. But she was an American and felt the draw of the American vision, at least what it was in its halcyon days.

Sergei drove into the Tverskoy District north of Red Square and double-parked the BMW in front of Hotel Presnensky, drawing the ire of a taxi driver behind him who honked, then sped around him. Irina stepped out of the car and stared down the sidewalk, mesmerized by the large snowflakes that were swirling in the breeze. The falling flakes had glazed the fur hats and coats of the pedestrians with white frosting. The scene was postcard perfect.

But the weather brought chill as well as charm. Shivering, she hurried into the building, Sergei and the Backstrom boys right behind her. They almost ran into her when she froze in her tracks in the lobby. She swiveled her head and drank in the grandeur of the older hotel. The crystal chandeliers, green-and-gold motif, and white grand piano with gold trim seemed too ornate to harmonize with her father's descriptions of Moscow's bleakness before the old regime fell.

"Most of the Cold-War-era hotels are drab," Sergei observed, noticing her wonder. "But several, including this one, were frequented by party officials. They used them when they wanted to meet in more secrecy than they could get in Red Square and the adjoining districts."

"Officials trying to avoid other officials?"

"Yes. And the eyes of the KGB."

Sergei continued to the front desk and informed the receptionist that Miss Aksakova and her assistants were guests of Mr. Egorushkin.

"Ah, yes," the young man replied. "His secretary called yesterday. Their suite is ready. Room 40 on the fourth floor. It's the first room on the right when you exit the elevator." He handed two room keys to Irina.

Sergei placed his hand on Irina's arm and advised her in a fatherly tone that bordered on stern. "Don't disappoint Mikhail. He despises ingratitude. He expects those who receive his favors to respond with gratitude. And he doesn't give second chances." He waited for a reply.

She met his eyes and coolly replied, "We honor our friends."

He nodded as if that were the kind of answer he was looking for and walked away. There was no goodbye or good luck. Irina and Tony looked at each other and shrugged.

As they waited for the elevator, a slow and ancient unit, Irina pondered the oddness that had unfolded during the two-day trip to Moscow. Sergei had spoken to them only when necessary. When asked a question, he had replied in the briefest manner possible. At Belgorod he had detoured thirty minutes out of the way and stopped for the night at a country dacha with sentries at the gate and armed guards roaming the grounds. He had made a similar detour to another guarded estate Monday night in Kutepovo when he could have easily made it to Moscow.

Tony must have been reading her thoughts. After they stepped onto the elevator and the door closed, he whispered into her ear, "I got a gut feeling that the silent treatment and the visits to the dachas were efforts to intimidate us."

She nodded back. "I think so too."

When Irina pushed the door for their room open, she discovered that it was much heavier than she had anticipated. She stopped to caress the thick slab, its oak grain showing through the fading stain. The boys pushed past her. The sitting room was appointed in classic Soviet-style with ornate molding. Straight ahead, a hallway ended at a window that overlooked the alley. On the left side of the hallway, a narrow kitchen could be seen through an archway. On the right a narrow hallway led, presumably, to the bedrooms.

The crew dropped their suitcases next to the sofa and huddled. Andy started to say something, but Irina put her finger to her lips to shush him. Ignoring his puzzled look, she pulled out her cellphone, tapped a brief message, and showed it to them. "Something not right. Don't trust Mikhail. Hotel likely bugged." She then backspaced over the unsent message.

The boys nodded their agreement. "Got a plan?" Andy mouthed, barely audible as a whisper.

She nodded *yes*, walked around the corner, and headed down the bedroom hallway. The boys glanced at each other, shrugged their shoulders, and followed. She walked into the far room, opened the window, stuck her head out, scanned both directions, pulled her head back in, and closed the window most of the way, leaving a small gap. The guys stared at her, puzzled. "Let's go shopping," she announced brightly and loudly, flashing a mischievous smile.

"Any place in particular?" Tony asked.

"No. Just want to get a feel for the neighborhood and pick up a few things we'll need for our stay."

"Sounds good to me," Andy responded.

Irina hustled into the kitchen, rustled around in the cupboards, and found a coffee pot and three cups, which she set on the counter. "I'm figuring we'll be gone three or four hours. While we're out, we can pick up some groceries so we can make sandwiches and coffee when we get back."

When they exited the building, Irina turned right and walked briskly down the sidewalk to the far corner on the next block. While they waited for the streetlight, she divulged her mind. "Here's my plan. We'll continue down the street a few blocks, mingle in a crowd, and hail a cab. Andy and I will get in and go look for a flat in the Cheryomushki District. I doubt anyone would look for us there, and if they did, they would have a hard time finding us. Tony, you're gonna take the cross street down one block, then make your way back to the alley behind the hotel and climb the fire escape to the fourth floor."

He raised his eyebrows. "I don't like where this is going."

She continued unfazed. "Then you're gonna edge your way down the ledge to the window I left open, climb inside, and wait."

"Wait for what?" he demanded.

"I suspect that our apartment is going to be visited while we're gone. My hunch is that Mikhail has close ties to both the Bratva and corrupt government officials. He wants to use us for his own business. If we don't comply, he'll turn us in. It's a win-win for him. No matter how it turns out, he comes out ahead."

"I'm tracking," Andy replied. "He's curious as to who we are and why we're here. If he figures it out, he can use the information to blackmail us or get us arrested."

"Exactly."

"I had suspicions myself that we might be visited, but I like your plan better than mine."

"What's your plan?"

"Setting up a camera."

"I thought of that too, but recording their visit wouldn't stop them from discovering things we don't want them to know. It would only tell us that we were visited."

"The hard job again!" Tony complained. "Seriously! Why do I always get the hard jobs?"

"Because you're the toughest, and I'm the smartest," his brother replied.

Tony shook his head and continued his tirade. "Edge my way down a ledge four stories above a blacktop alley? What happens if I die while playing Ethan Hunt?"

"You won't die!" Irina assured him. "The ledge is fairly wide, and on all three stretches—the fire escape to the rain gutter, the rain gutter to the bundle of wires, and the wires to the open window—you'll have decent handholds."

He didn't buy it. "Can you tell that I'm skeptical? I wish you had given me a heads up while we were in the room. I would have poked my head out the window and taken a gander for myself. But no, you had to put me in a place where I'm supposed to trust your judgment on a high-risk, special-ops-grade assignment. I suppose I should ask your opinion on whether the M4, the HK 416, or the FN SCAR is better in urban warfare? Or maybe you can give me the low down on the differences between America's RA-1 ram-air parachute and the UK's RT-80?" His glare was as cutting as his frustrated sarcasm.

Irina, teetering between tears and indignation, got defensive. "It didn't seem like a technical matter to me. It looked like it was simply a matter of strength and agility, which you have in spades. You can do almost anything. I just looked at the ledge and thought, yea, he can handle that."

Tony softened his tone. "What if I get up there and discover that the distances between the handholds are wider than my arms reach? What happens if the rain gutter or the wires give way when I put my weight on them?" He shook his head and objected vigorously. "I don't like this plan one bit."

"Do you have a better one?"

"No."

"All right then," she huffed. "Time to roll." She whirled around and hastened across the street.

The boys caught up to her at the curb on the other side, but nobody said a word. Andy sensed the tension between his companions. Irina's jaw was clenched. She was going to need a few minutes to cool off. Tony's fists were balled. That wasn't a good sign. His brother was fuming. Irina blazed on ahead for three blocks, elbowed her way into a small crowd milling around at a bus stop, and flagged a passing cab. She hopped in. Andy looked over to his brother, but Tony just kept on going without acknowledging him. He sighed and climbed in after the angry female. As the cab pulled back into traffic, he watched his brother turn right at the corner and start jogging.

Four and a half blocks later, Tony turned down the narrow alley that passed behind the hotel and … it wasn't a straight shot. *You've got to be kidding me!* he grumbled under his breath. *What's with the hodge-podge streets and alleys in this stupid city?* The alley made a sharp right turn and passed a backstreet tea and coffee shop. When it turned left again, the fire escape was in view. He bounded up the stairs two at a time to the fourth-floor landing, then leaned on the railing to rest his burning legs and lungs and study the route. The first move was a doozy—a seven-foot-plus stretch on an eight-inch ledge to the downspout. *Kangaroo poo!* he fumed. *Why did I let that crazy brunette talk me into this?*

He dropped his coat, climbed over the railing, stationed

himself on the ledge with his belly to the wall, and began edging his way toward the downspout—maintaining an iron grip on the fire escape. Halfway there, he stopped and banged his head on the wall. *I'm facing the wrong stinkin' direction!* With his belly facing in, he would have to reach over the top of the downspout to get a good grip. This would put his center of gravity far enough away from the wall that it greatly increased the risk of a fall. Stewing over his stupidity, he returned to the landing.

After eyeballing the situation again, and traversing the entire route in his head, he gingerly climbed back out on the ledge, this time facing outward. More nervous than the first time, he edged his way toward the downspout. Against his better judgment, he glanced at the ground four stories below. A wave of dizziness hit him, and his rattled nerves began to fray. *This is worse than Aussie rappelling without a belay man.* He steeled himself. *Don't look down, Stupid … just keep your eyes fixed on the goal.* Inch by inch, he slid his feet down the ledge while straining his left hand toward the downspout. He hoped to slide his hand underneath it and grip the far side.

When he reached full extension, he was a good twelve inches short. He sputtered to himself, *I wonder how many brave men have died trying to please good-looking females?* He drew a couple deep breaths, let go with his right hand, and continued creeping down the ledge, as scared as he had ever been. Nine inches to go. Six inches to go. Three inches to go. Contact—his outstretched fingers touched the downspout. *Cold metal never felt so good.* But he wasn't out of the danger zone yet. He executed another slide. His fingers were behind the spout. Another slide. His fingers reached the far side of the spout. A final slide. His fingers got a firm bite on the far side, and a wave of relief washed over him.

But he still wasn't out of the woods. He continued sidling toward the downspout with baby steps until his left arm was pressed against it. *Here goes. It's either triumph or tragedy.* In one seemingly reckless move, he squatted as far as he dared, exploded upward on his left leg, and threw his right leg and body over the downspout. As he made the crossing, he jammed his right hand under the downspout. A fraction of a second later, his right foot caught the ledge. His heart palpitating wildly, he steadied himself and started standing upright. The spout creaked and moved. A fresh shot of adrenalin hit his system.

In one awkward, panic-stricken effort—as two lag screws popped out of the wall near his right hand and a seam buckled—he stood up, retracted his right hand from behind the downspout, extended it, and pressed his trembling body against the wall. He sighed in relief. Somehow, the downspout had held, and he had managed to keep his balance.

But his ordeal wasn't over. He still faced two more obstacles. With his pulse racing, he rotated his left hand from its firm grip underneath the downspout to a less secure grip on its top and began shuffling toward the communication cables.

When he reached full extension, he was again about a foot short of a solid handhold. He sighed, a mixture of dejection and frustration, let go of his grip on the downspout, and slid his way forward, his cheek pressed against the cold bricks, his fingers searching the narrow joints between the bricks for the faintest grip. His view of the situation grew darker. *Just wanna get this over—live or die.*

He made two large, hasty steps, and his fingers touched the cables. But his sense of relief collapsed into the horrifying realization that he had lost his balance. He frantically threw himself sideways and stabbed his left hand underneath the cables. The awkward effort dislodged his feet from the ledge. He was falling. As his body hurtled sideways and downwards, his left forearm passed underneath the bundle, and he crooked it to give himself a little more friction.

A half second later, his body slammed against the ledge and his feet continued swinging downward in an arc. At maximum extension, a jolt of pain rocked his left arm which was holding his weight. Ignoring the throb, he twisted his body and reached for the cables with his right hand. He closed his fingers around several strands and clenched them in a death grip. His feet continued swinging to maybe a forty-degree angle, then pivoted back. On the backswing, he locked his feet on the cables and stopped himself.

Holy buckets. He was dangling four stories above the alley, and his left arm felt like it was going to tear off. Relying mostly on his right arm, he placed his feet against the wall, leaned back to increase his friction, and walked up the wall a foot or so. Then he moved his left hand upward, wincing at the stab of pain. After repeating the maneuver several times, he was able to place his feet on the ledge and stand up. With his throbbing arm locked behind the cables, his muscles trembling with exhaustion, and his heart pounding, he leaned his head against the wall to rest for a moment. But duty pounded on the door. *No time to dawdle. Got to keep moving. Got to get there first.* Even five seconds late could be fatal.

He surveyed the next move. *Only four feet from the window. Would be a piece of cake if my body wasn't so battered.* He withdrew his arm from behind the cluster, grabbed a handful of cables on the front, extended his right arm, and scooted down the ledge. His fingers found the inside of the frame, giving him a bit more stability. Two further slides enabled him to squat, slip his fingers in the gap, and grasp the bottom of the window. He pushed the window upward. It didn't budge. He tried again with all the vigor he could muster. It moved two inches. "Wonderful!" he grumbled under his breath. *The angle is bad. Gotta get better leverage.*

His anger flared, and he shuffled sideways until his left arm was fully extended and his right arm was jammed in the window as far as the narrow gap would allow—nearly to his elbow. Gritting his teeth, he stood up and slammed his right arm upward at the same time. The window flew open. He squatted back down, ducked his head, threw his right arm forward, let go of the cables, and dove in the opening. He didn't make it. His ribs smashed upon the sill, knocking the wind out of him, and his left arm, already tender, got slammed against the frame. Wiggling and worming the rest of the way, he crumpled on the floor, frazzled.

While he lay there, a metallic click startled him and raised the hair on the back of his neck. *The deadbolt!* Someone was opening the suite door. He sprang to his feet, crept to the bedroom door, and listened. The sound of the door shutting echoed hollowly. Footfalls crossed the sitting room and stopped near the couch. A suitcase latch snapped open, and the faint sounds of rifling followed.

Tony padded down the hallway, halted at the end, and listened. A second suitcase popped open. He bolted around the corner. The man looked up, startled. It was Victor. With a sneer on his face, the goon rushed him. Tony stopped just in time to respond to the massive right hand hurtling toward his face. He turned deftly—felt knuckles graze his right cheek—grabbed the brute's arm, and used his momentum to propel him headfirst into the oak archway that graced the kitchen entrance. The crown of his head slammed into the post with a dull thud, and he crumpled to the floor. Blood began to ooze from his scalp. The thug pulled himself up to his hands and knees and tried to stand up. A crushing blow to the back of the head crumpled him again. This time he lay still as a stone.

Nervous, Tony put two fingers to his neck. His pulse was present and steady. *Thank you, Jesus.* He didn't want their mission scuttled because he had killed a psychopathic Spetsnaz veteran who had connections in both the Bratva and corrupt government.

What next? He needed to secure Victor. That was obvious. But to do that, he needed his kit bag. The problem was, it was ten feet away on the couch. If Victor woke while he had his back turned, that could be dangerous, especially if the goon was packing heat. A pat-down revealed a concealed-carry holster under his coat. With a low whistle, he retrieved a 9mm GSh-18, the pistol that had replaced the Makarov in the Russian Armed Forces. *Now that's one hot dame.* He pocketed it, the holster, and two extra magazines and continued the search. On the other hip in a tactical pouch, he found brass knuckles, a blade, a garotte, and a taser. *There's no way Viktor was a mere bodyguard. This stash suggests enforcer.* He found the thug's cellphone in an upper pocket and powered it down.

Tony examined Viktor's face and eyes and figured that the lug was unlikely to return to consciousness in the next minute or so. He scurried to his duffel bag on the couch, retrieved his kit bag, and dug out two heavy-duty zip ties and a roll of duct tape.

Two minutes later, the former operator stood over his handiwork. Victor was lying in the bathtub, his hands and feet secured with zip ties, and his mouth duct-taped. *This ought to buy us some time. He won't be going anywhere for a while.* But he didn't gawk long. It was time to beat a hasty retreat.

He closed the bedroom window, returned Irina's belongings to her suitcase, propped the suite door open, staged their suitcases in the hall, pulled the suite door shut, and moved the suitcases to the fire escape door. While the knob turned, the door didn't budge. He checked to see if the latch and the deadbolt were retracting. They were. *Must be stuck from expansion.* He turned the knob and rammed his shoulder into the door. It burst open, and he stumbled into the railing on the landing.

He pulled out his secure phone and called Irina.

"Ballerina here."

"Hey, fancy dancer. You were right. Mikhail did send someone to visit us. It was Victor."

"So what happened?"

"He's taking a nap right now ... in the bathtub."

"Is he secure?"

"What do you think?"

"Sorry. Dumb question."

"No worries. Do you have any leads on an apartment yet?"

"No. We just arrived in the neighborhood."

"Where can I meet you with the luggage?"

"Pamyatnyy Kamen."

"Like I know exactly what you're talking about and where it is," he replied. "Can I find it on the tourist maps?"

"You won't have to find it. It's a well-known landmark. The taxi driver will know how to get there."

"Okay. Call me a taxi, have him meet me at the bottom of the fire escape at our hotel, and tell him where to take me."

"Copy that."

Tony moved the suitcases to the landing and forced the door shut with a brutal kick. After his third brisk trip down the fire escape to the alley below lugging suitcases and bags, he dropped the last two on the asphalt, wiped the sweat off his brow, and slipped his coat back on. The cab showed up before he had time to catch a chill.

As the yellow Camry sped off, Tony mulled the events of

the past hour. *That was way too much excitement. Hopefully, Konstantin kept Mikhail in the dark about the real purpose of our trip and the name of our contact. I'd prefer not to run into Mr. Goon again. Next time, he won't be quite so overconfident. Probably won't be alone either. And I'm gonna have to talk with the brunette about mission planning.*

30

Moscow, Russia
Wednesday, December 18, 2019

Irina's eyes opened. It seemed too early to get up, yet she felt wide awake. She fumbled for her phone on her bedstand. It was only 5:10. With a sigh, she rolled over and pulled her covers over her head. But two minutes later, she flung them aside. *Not gonna work. No way I'm gonna fall back asleep.* That was one drawback to being hardwired for diligence and excellence. Sometimes your sleep took a hit.

She slipped on her robe, padded out to the kitchen, started a pot of coffee in the Moka pot she had picked up the prior evening, then dropped two slices of rye bread into the toaster. At the small table by the window, she soaked in the character of their flat. It was a partially furnished, two-bedroom apartment on the fourth floor of a 1960s-era Krushchyovka in the Cheryomushki District about twenty minutes south of Red Square. The building complex was one of the few older complexes that hadn't been torn down in the urban renewal of the 90s. And the price had been reasonable, 100,000 rubles per month, plus a two-month security deposit. Though the walls and floors were chipped here and there, and the bright-colored paint was fading, it was the kind of apartment she had often pictured in her fantasy of dancing with the Bolshoi Ballet.

When the pot finished bubbling, she poured a cup, took her first sip, savored the body and boldness, sat back in her chair, cradled her mug in her hands, and indulged the sweet movements of Beethoven playing quietly in the background—on Orpheus Radio at 99.2 FM. The music tapped deep into her psyche, and her thoughts turned melancholy. While she appreciated their neighborhood, it had one shortcoming. It was inconveniently distant from the theatres in the Tverskoy District, a half hour by car and forty-five minutes by bus. She had been nursing the hope that she might be able to take in an opera or a ballet performance while they were in Moscow, a love she had been unable to indulge since her detainment at 286. But it seemed unrealistic now. *Okay, Beethoven-girl. Mind off the mundane. Mind on the battle at hand. You have a long, sweet eternity to indulge your penchant for classical music, opera, and ballet.*

She opened her notebook and began jotting down a to-do list for the next few days. The first item was shopping: kitchen stuff, dishes, groceries, and toiletries. The second was calling her secretary at Nebesa Smotret. The third was connecting with her contact for the sensors, Igor Fedorovsky. Hopefully, this contact from Konstantin wouldn't be as dangerous as Mikhail.

Shortly after ten, she called Nebesa Smotret.

"Nebesa Smotret. Svetlana speaking. How may I help you?"

"Hi, Svetlana. This is Aleksandra Aksakova. What's the latest update on the mirror I ordered from Alluna Optics?"

"Glad to hear from you, Miss Aksakova. I just received a call from them this morning. Your mirror is finished, crated, and sitting on the dock. It'll be shipped tomorrow morning. You can expect to receive it within four weeks."

"Fantastic. Say, I'd like to visit the office this afternoon around two and take a look around. I want to get a feel for the location, the layout, the storage cage, the dock, and the nearby restaurants and coffee shops."

"That would be great."

"What's the best way to get from the Cheryomushki District to the office?"

"The Moscow Metro. Take the Kaluzhsko-Rizhskaya line from the Novye Cheryomushki station to the Koltsevaya line. Then take the Koltsevaya to the Krasnopresnenskaya station in Presnensky District. From there you'll only be six blocks from the office which is in the old industrial complex. When you get to Krasno, give me a call. I'll walk over and meet you. It'll be easier to show you the shortcut to the office than describe it to you over the phone."

"Thanks, Svetlana. I'll see you around two."

"Looking forward to it."

After hanging up, she dialed Igor's number—nervous to the point of nausea. After three tones, a gravelly voice answered, "This is Maxim. What do you want?"

"I'm Aleksandra Aksakova. I'm looking for Igor Federovsky."

"What's your business?"

"Several weeks back Konstantin made arrangements for

me to meet with him here in Moscow."

"Konstantin? That tells me nothing. I know a dozen men with that name. Some of them I want dead."

"The pakhan in Atlanta who runs the American operation."

There was a pause on the other end. "Give me a few minutes to verify your story. If you're telling the truth, I'll call you back. But if you're lying to me, I'll find you and teach you not to lie to Maxim and the Solntsevskaya Bratva."

The line went quiet. Rattled, she picked up her mug and tried to relax. But the Rachmaninoff playing in the background wasn't very conducive to relaxing.

Five minutes later, the boyevik called back. "Igor says to meet him at Stolovaya 57, Thursday evening at 6. It's on Red Square near St. Basil's Cathedral, a little way up Ulitsa ll'inka. He'll be wearing a grey suit with a lavender tie. Be early, and dress for the occasion."

"Got it. I'll be there."

Again the line went dead. Irina shrugged her shoulders. *Don't know if this Maxim dude is super busy or super rude or both.* She put him out of mind and shifted gears. *Time for the fun stuff. Time to go shopping.*

***

Thursday evening, the team arrived by taxi at Stolovaya 57 at 5:45 sharp. Tony held the heavy door, Irina gracefully entered, and the host greeted her. "Are you here alone or meeting guests?"

"Meeting a guest."

"Who, may I ask?"

"Mr. Federovsky."

"Yes. I'll show you to his table."

As they followed the host, Irina noticed heads turning. While the attractive brunette was used to attention, she had never experienced this much. Then again, she was being escorted by two handsome, buff blondes, and all three were dressed to the nines. She was wearing a red dress by Versace, ruby earrings by Cartier, and matching Christian Louboutin pumps. The guys were decked out in medium-gray Armani suits with baby-blue shirts, silk ties in a herringbone pattern, and gold Rolex watches. She smiled to herself. *The Delta boys clean up pretty good. They just need a little help.*

The host showed them to their seats at a table near the rear of the restaurant, the waiter handed them menus and asked for their drink orders.

"Three alcohol-free Russian mules, please," Irina replied.

While they were raving over the pungency of their drinks, a man in a grey suit and lavender tie approached their table and addressed Irina. "Cheap vodka tastes like rotten fish."

"What do you suggest?"

"Moskovskaya Osobaya is my favorite."

Irina smiled, and the man took the open chair next to her. "Glad to do business with you, Miss Aksakova."

"Likewise."

"How is my friend Konstantin doing?"

"He was happy and healthy the last time we saw him about six weeks ago."

"Glad to hear that." He gestured to the waiter that they

were ready to order. Then he turned back to Irina. "I recommend the lobster in sherry sauce."

"Sounds delicious. I'll give it a try."

She shot the boys a look suggesting their compliance. They shook their heads. "Steak and potatoes for me," Tony rejoined. "Me too," Andy added.

Igor bore a look of disdain. The boys ignored him. While they did enjoy Tex-Mex, they rarely strayed from straightforward American cooking of the variety that reigns in the Midwest and the West.

After dinner, while they were enjoying baklava and vanilla ice cream, Igor finally broached the subject. "Konstantin tells me that you would like to procure three sensors for an infrared telescope."

"That's correct."

"And the specifications were 10, 4.75, and 2 microns?"

"Correct."

"What kind of time frame?"

"As soon as possible. The board is pushing me to prioritize this project above the others on my plate."

"I have two contacts who might be able to obtain these items. I'll give them a call tonight, and we should hear back in a week or two after they have checked their sources. But I should warn you, that if any either of my contacts can procure sensors for you, you'll be making a trip to a region of the former Soviet Union that is Asia's Wild West."

"Adventure suits me just fine," Irina responded.

A sadistic grin broke across his stoic face. "You may well get far more than you bargained for." He stood up, snatched the tab from the waiter's hand, and dropped it on the table in front of Irina. "I'll call you when I have something definite." Without a goodbye, he turned and walked away.

31

**the Compound; Atchafalaya Swamp; Moscow;
Meyersdale, PA
Wednesday, December 25, 2019**

The Compound members who weren't on mission gathered at the lodge in the early afternoon for a Christmas dinner. The gals bustled about the kitchen, preparing the honeyed ham, candied yams, the various side dishes, and a Mexican apple pie for Woody. Most of the guys were gathered in the great room by the fireplace, cracking nuts and discussing geopolitics and the spiritual decline in America.

"Hey, Andrius!" Betsy hollered out from the counter where she was slicing apples. "Are you picking a salad or estimating how many bacteria are in a cubic inch of greenhouse soil?"

"Sorry, Betsy," he shouted back from the greenhouse. "The wide variety of hot peppers in here got me to thinking about genetics and variety development. Kind of lost myself."

She roared with laughter. "I can't even imagine what it must be like going through life with a head overflowing with information and running a hundred miles an hour."

The embarrassed young man slunk out of the greenhouse and set his basket of tomatoes, peppers, onions, and greens on the counter.

Kit, who was sitting on a stool peeling yams, ribbed him. "Is that dirt under your fingernails? Looks like you might be losing your tech-wonk ways. Or at least moderating them."

Andrius blushed as he picked up an onion and began peeling it. It was true. He had grown to love puttering in the greenhouse and found himself fascinated with horticulture—what kind of lighting is best, what natural fertilizers are best, how to grow hotter peppers, and how to stimulate the beneficial flora and fauna in the soil. But he didn't like feeling embarrassed, so he changed the topic. "So how are you holding up?"

"If you're referring to the fact that going on the Louisiana mission was not in God's plan for me, I'm doing fine."

"How did you learn to handle disappointment so well?"

"Watching my dad. He's endured a lot of pain over the decades. So he's had to learn some hard lessons about letting go of the past and embracing the present. You can't live in the past: not the glorious past, not the painful past. When you do, it disrupts the present. We can't allow the past to keep draining our emotional bank account. We need to seize the day. Make the best of the opportunities it presents."

"I wish I was strong like that." He finished slicing the onion, then turned to her again. "How about the paleontology career that was taken from you?"

"That one's a bit harder. It's taking me a while to get my

bearings. I was a naive young Christian when I embarked on my career path. I didn't realize how opposed the scientific world is to the Bible and anything that substantiates its author or its history. The mean-spirited opposition I received to some of my discoveries and research was unexpected. But it's a moot point now. I won't be going back to paleontology any time soon."

Kit stood up abruptly, grabbed her crutches, and faced him. "I really don't want to focus on my losses right now. I want to focus on my gains. And the biggest gain we have is God's gift of his own Son, born of a virgin in Bethlehem—the gift we're celebrating today. He came into this world to live a life that the world would consider unfulfilling and die a death that the world would regard as a tragic waste. But his death provided man with eternal life. If we truly enter into the spirit of his incarnation—the true spirit of Chrismas—then we understand that our life can still be profitable even if it looks and feels unfulfilling."

Having gotten that off her chest—for her own sake and his—she whirled around, hobbled to the warming plate, refilled her stainless-steel travel mug from the simmering pot of egg nog, and headed for the great room to join the discussion on comet devastation. She had overheard Blake mention a comet called Phaethon, the Libyan glass which it had formed, and the evidence of a formerly lush Sahara that it had destroyed. That sounded too fascinating to pass up.

***

Ariele was too excited to fall back asleep. Today was her first Christmas—her first time observing it. Yeshua made sense now. The Son of God, the promised seed in Genesis who would bruise the serpent's head, had been born into the world to die for the sins of the world. Who wouldn't want to celebrate the day of his birth? So what if we don't know the actual date with any degree of certainty.

She climbed down from the top bunk, pulled on her warm fuzzy socks, grabbed the clothes she had set out, and limped out the back door to the dressing room that Rat had cobbled together on the back porch. "Yikes!" she muttered as she splashed her face. "This water is freezin' cold!" Shivering, she gave her body a fast once over with the washcloth, then wrung it out and hung it on a peg to dry. Dropping into the chair, she pulled up her leg and examined it. The bite site was still discolored, but the tenderness and swelling had gone down a little more in the past twenty-four hours. With a sense of relief, she quickly dressed and pulled on her well-worn Counter Culture sweatshirt. It seemed fitting. She was now counter-culture in more ways than one.

Back in the cozy cabin, she curled up in a chair in the sitting corner and gazed at the bonsai spruce on the coffee table, its tiny LED lights bathing the room in cheer. The idea behind the Christmas tree was intriguing. She knew it wasn't in the Bible, but according to Burt, Martin Luther had started the tradition, using the evergreen tree as a symbol of the eternal life which Mashiach offered to man.

Next to the diminutive tree, a gold-plated menorah lifted its arms toward the heavens. Peggy Sue had surprised her with it several days earlier. This evening at sunset, she would light the fourth candle. Hannukah, too, held deeper meaning for her now. The Maccabees hadn't merely been fighting for their rights as Jews. They had been fighting for the honor of God. *God, help me to have a noble spirit willing to stand for your truth and your honor regardless of the cost.*

"Good morning, Moxie," Peggy Sue called out. "Do you feel up to helping me in the kitchen? I was planning on latke and sufganiyot for breakfast, but I have never made either one before. So I could use some help."

"I would love to help, but I'll probably have to sit down most of the time."

"Not a problem. I'll set you up."

As Ariele mixed the batter for sufganiyot, tears of thanksgiving pooled in the corners of her eyes. God had opened her heart to the true meaning of Christmas and Hannukah. And her friends were going out of their way to bring her Jewish traditions into their celebrations.

Rat's booming voice startled her. "How's the leg feeling?" he asked as he sat down at the table across from her.

"Better every day. The swelling and pain have gone down quite a bit in the past few days. But it still gets tender if I stay on my feet too long."

"Have you started to think about when you might be leaving?"

"Why?" she teased. "Are you getting tired of my company?"

He laughed. "Nope. But missions are missions. And you came here on a mission."

"I'm thinking that we'll probably leave after the New Year. But I'll see how I feel in a week and make a decision at that time."

"That's exactly what I was going to suggest. Say, as long as we're talking on important subjects, can one of you girls slice up the halva?"

***

Irina pulled a tray of tea cakes out of the oven and sighed. It was Christmas Eve, and she was fighting the blues. She had spent a joyous Christmas with her family every year for over twenty-five years. Even in FEMA 286, she had enjoyed the day with her friends: drinking hot spiced cider and cocoa, baking Christmas cookies, and singing carols. Now there wasn't much festivity going on. While the Backstrom boys were more than happy to eat her cookies, they definitely weren't in the Christmas spirit.

She looked across the open living area to the sofa. Par for the course, they were glued to the laptop screen. Earlier, they had checked the news on the Middle East and Russia. Now they were focused on intelligence reports which alleged the transfer of nuclear weapons from a military depot in the former Soviet state of Kazakhstan to the Bratva. The fear was that these weapons of mass destruction could wind up in the hands of terrorists if they hadn't already.

Andy groaned, "This is America's worst nightmare come true."

"Agreed," Tony replied. "Don't see how this can end well."

Irina set a tray with tea cookies and mugs of hot chocolate on the coffee table next to the laptop. They grunted "Thanks" without so much as looking up or glancing at the tray. The apparent ingratitude crushed her. Back in the kitchen, she punched down the dough for the piroshki with more vigor than necessary, venting her frustration.

But as she kneaded the lump, she pulled herself together. *Come on girl! The guys nixed a tree and singing carols for security reasons. We're posing as Russians. It would raise suspicion if we observed Christmas on December 25. Be thankful that they're so focused. They may miss a few social cues, but they won't drop the ball when it comes to the mission.*

Her reflections on men and duty morphed into thoughts of the cowboy in Montana that was waiting for her. The ring! She dashed into her bedroom, retrieved the stunning piece from her purse, slipped it on her finger, and sat on the edge of her bed, daydreaming about her wedding ... a white dress, tons of flowers, and a stunning cake.

***

Jack squelched a sigh. Giving in to Sally's request for a Kurdish Christmas was shaping up to be a royal disappointment. Roast duck just wasn't on the same level as a Christmas ham or smoked turkey. The pomegranate stuffing was so different from the stuffing he knew that he couldn't picture it as stuffing. And it was too sweet to pretend that it was a substitute for cranberry sauce. The garlic hummus was better, but it was no substitute for candied sweet potatoes. The kleicha or date cookies, a foretaste of their dessert, were over the top with the fragrant bite of nigella seeds, cardamom, and saffron. The dolma, biryani, and black tea thick with sugar played out in similar fashion.

Sally pointed to yet another dish, and Jack eyed it with suspicion. Ground lamb with rice, spice, and diced tomato rolled up in a grape leaf didn't sound that appetizing. Who in their right mind would eat leaves anyway? In a survival situation, for sure. But for dining pleasure? It made no sense.

"Come on, Jack," Sally plead. "Just try it. It's a Middle Eastern delicacy. My Kurdish grandmother always made them for holidays and birthdays."

He rolled his eyes, snatched one up, and took a bite. After chewing for a moment, he shrugged his shoulders and forced a smile. "Tastes like a pita sandwich without the pita."

The pained look on Sally's face went home like an arrow, and he looked away, ashamed. Why did he have to be so insensitive? There was no need to telegraph how much he disliked Middle Eastern spices and how much he missed his favorite Christmas dishes.

As he picked at his plate, his duty became clear. In his SEAL days he had been willing to lay his life down for his brothers-in-arms. In the same way, he should be willing to lay down his Christmas for a fellow Undergrounder. He had allowed her to have the Christmas she had wanted, and it wasn't right to merely go through the motions. He had an obligation to help her enjoy it.

He looked up from his plate with a sparkle in his eye. "Can you pour me a glass of that yogurt drink? What did you call it? Mastow? I decided to try it after all. You only live once. Might as well live it on the edge."

The smile on her face said it all. His faux pas was water under the bridge. As he sipped the beverage, actually appreciating the hint of mint and salt in the watery yogurt, he realized that they were going to have a merry Christmas after all. As for his preferences, they could wait till the Compound. Then he and Woody could do a Scandinavian Christmas with all the trappings like rommegrot, lefse, and traditional cookies. He figured nobody there would object to a second round of holiday treats.

32

Atchafalaya Swamp, Louisiana
Saturday, December 28, 2019

Burt came boiling down the stairs from his attic hideout. "Hey, Rutherford, grab your laptop and head to the CVN website! They just posted an update on the Sri Lanka comet!"

Rat, kicking back in his favorite chair, held up his military-grade laptop, a Getac X500 loaded with security hardware and software. "Got it right here, Gramps. Give me a few minutes to reply to Lobo and Mojo on the *Rogue Runners* bulletin board, then we can take a look at the comet news. In the meantime, make yourself useful—put on a pot of coffee and see what Peg has in the oven. Smells like it might be molasses snaps."

The old-timer laughed. "Coffee and cookies coming up." As he pulled out the canister of coffee, he quipped, "What would we do without the nectar of heaven and sugar?"

"Life would definitely be rougher," Rat replied. "The simple pleasures make things a lot easier to bear on the battlefield."

Five minutes later, Burt set a tray on the coffee table with mugs of Cajun coffee and cookies hot out of the oven. A wry smile scrawled across his face. "You were wrong. They're Peg's world-famous Cajun Christmas cookies."

Rat laughed. "That's even better."

As the crew crowded around the laptop, Rat navigated to CVN and located the video that had Burt so worked up. "Whoa!' This has only been posted for twenty minutes, and it already has over one hundred thousand views!"

Ariele scolded him. "Don't just sit there gawking! Play the video already."

Rat hit the play button and dished it back. "Glad to see that you're getting back to your cantankerous old self."

"Good morning. This is Arnot Baudette live in New York City with the weekend edition of *The World Report*. It's two minutes past eleven on a chilly Saturday morning, and we have a breaking story on the Sri Lanka comet that came across the wireless than an hour ago.

"Eight hours ago at 2:05 p.m. Bangladesh time, the research submersible DVS Alvin, after several weather delays in the past week, finally began its anxiously anticipated dive to investigate the comet." He pointed to a pin icon on a map of the Indian Ocean. "It lies on the seafloor, in the vast Ceylon Plain, about four hundred and fifty miles west of the Batu Islands, an archipelago off the coast of Sumatra.

"The crew—a pilot and two scientists— caught their first glimpse of their quarry after a fifty-minute descent, spent four hours making observations and gathering samples, and then returned to the surface. The surprising results of their initial survey have already taken the scientific world by storm.

"One staggering discovery its size—far larger than anticipated. Its base rests on the seafloor at a depth of 14,217 feet or 4306 meters. And its top lies 6101 feet or 1860 meters below the surface. This means that the comet has a height of 8116 feet—approximately one and a half miles. To put things in perspective, that's approximately the distance that Mt. Rainier towers over the mountains around it. Bear in mind, too, that some of the comet's base lies buried in the mud, perhaps another 200 to 400 feet. Maybe even more.

"Another bombshell is its composition. The samples suggest an iron-nickel matrix with inclusions of platinum group metals—similar to the iron-nickel meteorites which originate in the asteroid belt. The scientific community had expected the comet to be a rapidly melting dirty snowball, laden with enough dust and grit from heavier materials to sink it to the bottom. But this finding is only preliminary. Much more work will need to be done.

"The comet is also far more intact than expected. Scientists had expected that it would explode at impact into thousands of pieces and that the search would be for small fragments of ice and scattered grit. But sonar had suggested that a large body remained intact, and visual inspection has confirmed this. An estimated seventy-five to eighty percent of the original mass is resting on the bottom in one chunk like a mountain with a rough pear shape. Dozens of massive fragments, some hundreds of feet high, are scattered around it.

"We now cut to several amazing videos provided by Woods Hole Oceanographic Institution, which allow you to watch this discovery unfold from a front-row seat." The camera switched from a headshot of the announcer to the first video. It opened with a shot of the crew climbing into the Alvin and the hatch being sealed, moved to a clip of the Alvin being lowered into the water from the Atlantis, then a clip of the Alvin submerging, and closed with a shot of the crew watching the light above them fade as they descended into darkness.

The second video opened with a shot of the scientists staring out the portholes and watching their monitors. An inset showed the mission timer ticking: 49 mins 39 secs ... 40 secs ... 41 secs. At 49 mins 53 secs the scientist sitting to the left of the cockpit erupted, "Dude! Do you see that?" He pointed down. "Isn't that the top of the honkin' comet?"

"Holy cow!" the other scientist replied. "The sonar guys were right! If I didn't see it with my own eyes, I wouldn't believe it. We're still a mile and a half from the seafloor. I thought for sure we'd be descending for at least another hour before we saw anything."

"Me too. But this is a hundred-dollar bet I don't mind losing." He paused, then excitedly addressed mission control. "Are you guys getting this topside?"

"Visuals are coming through clear, Zeke," a voice replied. "That thing is a beast. Time to break out the champagne."

"That sure looks like rock, doesn't it?" Zeke continued.

"It sure does," his partner replied. "We gotta get a sample. Bring us in close, Bart, so I can get a core. I'm interested in that lighter-colored spot overhead."

"You got it, Charlie," the pilot replied. He deftly maneuvered the vehicle until the front was only a few feet from the monolith. Then he directed the arm with the core sampler toward the requested spot. "Three, two, one, drill." The three watched the drill work away for a minute, raising a little murk in the water.

Bart shook his head. "Not gonna happen boys. We haven't made a quarter inch. There's no way under the sun that this is dirty ice or any kind of ice. It's definitely rock. Some seriously hard rock."

"No sweat, Bart," Charlie answered. "Take us down. We'll likely find a piece or two on the bottom that are small enough to pick up with the manipulator."

As they descended, Zeke rambled on the ramifications of stone comets. "Dude. Talk about paradigm-changing. The Xingu comet and the Mongolian comet were stone. Now this comet is stone. Do we need to go back to the drawing board and rework our theory of comet composition and formation? Can you imagine the magnitude of the destruction if a stony comet this big hit Manhattan?" He paused. "New York City gone. No more Wall Street. We'd be going back to the stone age."

The third clip opened with the Alvin stopping five feet above the littered surface, jumped to a camera focusing on the base of the main body, and then panned as the Alvin turned around. Two very large fragments came into view. The vehicle headed toward the nearest one. Along the way, the bottom was strewn with fragments that ranged from softball size to automobile size.

"Grab one of those, Bart!" Charlie exclaimed. The video focused on an area of the floor with a heavy concentration of smaller pieces, moved to a scene of Bart working the controls for the manipulator arm, the showed the arm extending, adjusting, picking up a softball-size chunk, and dropping it into a collection basket. The video closed with a shot of Bart and Charlie doing a high five.

The broadcast returned to the studio, and Arnot summarized the events of the past few weeks. "The discovery today is indeed a hallmark moment, but it has a two-part back story—the comet itself and the harmonious response of the nations to investigate this extra-terrestrial invader.

"The story began on December 6 with the massive fireball which enthralled all who witnessed it. The impact was fierce, raising waves over three hundred meters high and splashing water over a mile into the air. Two ships whose last known positions were within twenty miles of the impact are missing: one fishing boat and one pleasure craft. Three other craft that were within fifty miles of the impact were capsized by waves that were reportedly thirty to fifty feet high.

"Thankfully, the waves quickly dispersed, and by the time they had traveled eighty miles, they no longer posed a threat to shipping. Later that day, a small surge that averaged twelve inches high reached the shores of India, Sumatra, and the Maldives. The negligible wave was a tremendous relief as many scientists, influenced by the tsunami model of oceanic impact, had predicted a tsunami over one hundred feet in height. As it turned out, the much-maligned surge model had correctly forecast the size and duration of the waves caused by the impact.

"Within hours after the comet had blazed upon the scene, regional governments—led by Australia, India, and Indonesia—were engaged in a video conference planning their response. Over the next few days, the United States, England, France, New Zealand, Japan, and China offered substantial support, both civilian and military. The nations coming together in this project with united resolve is truly an amazing story. It evokes the hope that mankind will stand together in the future no matter what the universe throws at us.

"Within a week, the first ships had arrived on site, and by the end of the second week, a small armada was on hand including Australian and American replenishment ships and the Australian carrier HMAS Canberra, which supplied helicopters for searches and for transferring goods and personnel between ships.

"During this week the Atlantis, the support ship for the DVS Alvin, also arrived on the scene. Thankfully, at the time of the comet's dramatic appearance, the Alvin happened to be exploring the Sunda Deep in the Java Trench off the south coast of Java, so it was already in the neighborhood. In an amazing show of cooperation, the U.S. Navy and the Woods Hole Oceanographic Institution agreed to loan the Alvin and its support team to Australia for the Sri Lanka comet mission, though they did so with one stipulation, that only Woods Hole pilots would operate it, and a Woods Hole scientist would be on board for every dive.

"During the third week, a large contingent arrived from the U.S. Navy including supply ships and two ships equipped with the most advanced sonar in the world. Their first full day on site was Christmas day. The crews were given four hours off and a ham dinner. Then it was back to the mission. Late in the afternoon on the third day of the American involvement, one of the sonar ships located the comet. The following day, which is today, the Alvin undertook its history-making descent and discovery.

"Sadly, this comet, like the others in the past fifteen months, has spawned a torrent of apocalyptic fearmongering from the religious right and the conspiracy advocates. To help combat this anti-science nonsense, we have asked Dr. Franconi of the Smithsonian Institute to once again dispel fears that the recent spate of comets is a sign that the end of the world is at hand." He nodded to his guest. "Thank you for appearing on the show, Doctor."

"As always, my pleasure."

"To revisit a question that has had Americans riled up for months now, does the fact that Earth has now witnessed a fourth major impact in the last fifteen months have any end of the world implications?"

The learned man smiled and shook his head disparagingly. "None whatsoever."

"What if we factor in the two dozen Chelyabinsk-class impacts, the nearly two hundred minor impacts, and the dozen or so pebble showers that occurred in the past year? There are dozen of reports of damaged homes, buildings, and cars."

"The minor incidents are just as irrelevant as the major ones. And few things are more painful for scientists to watch than unscrupulous apocalypse preachers using the recent impact events as grist for their wild end-of-the-world theories."

"Can you elaborate on why these events are insignificant?"

"Because the earth is billions of years old and will be here for billions more. This planet probably experienced a thousand showers like this one in the past fifty million years. Maybe ten thousand. None of the past showers brought the world to an end, and the present shower won't either."

Rat stopped the video with a snort of disgust. "Sorry folks. I can't listen to his garbage anymore."

"Me neither," Ariele agreed. "He reminds me of the false prophets in the Tanakh who cried 'Peace, Peace' when judgment was on the horizon."

"Ain't that the truth," Peggy Sue chimed in. "The false prophets are busy convincing the public that there's nothing to worry about while the warning signs of the approaching apocalypse are raining down on their heads."

33

Moscow, Russia
Monday, December 30, 2019

Irina pulled her ushanka down lower over her head until it covered her eyebrows and obscured her vision, then jammed her hands back into her muff. Her face was numb from the wind whistling down the plaza out of the northwest. There was no escaping it. When she turned her back to it, trying to give her face a reprieve, it stung her neck. She pivoted once again, this time offering her side to the wind. Her eyes fell upon the Monument to Minin and Pozharsky, the bronze heroes standing undaunted in the wind and snow. Her mind drifted back to a wintry day in her middle school years in Ostroh, Ukraine. She was sitting in her father's chair, reading the account of the merchant and the prince defending Moscow. Their courage had brought tears to her eyes. She had prayed that God would make her brave.

A man walking toward her stared rudely. Indignant, she turned to face St. Basil's Cathedral. *Why was he staring?* She felt conspicuous in the fur coat and ushanka with matching muff and boots. While she loved dressing up, the outfit seemed over the top. But it was what Igor Federovsky had told her to wear when he had called back with the details for meeting their guide for the sensor deal. "Wait near Minin and Pozharsky," he had informed her. "Wear white fur head to toe. Fyodor wants there to be zero chance of mistaken identity. He will approach you and give you the necessary details."

The minutes passed. Irina began stomping her feet, trying to drive the chill out of her toes. She pulled a hand out of her muff and covered her nose, which felt like it was going to fall off her face.

"That's what you get for choosing style over utility," Andy teased.

She ignored him and checked her watch. "Hopefully, he shows. Igor said the window was from 3:45 to 4:15. It's now 4:08."

Several minutes later, a man in a grey wool coat angled in closer to them. Irina recognized him. It was the man who had stared at her when he had walked by earlier. He stopped in front of Irina. "Are you here for business or pleasure?"

"Definitely pleasure."

"What kind of pleasure?"

"My business is my pleasure."

He stuck out his hand. "I'm Fyodor."

"Glad to meet you," she replied as she shook his hand.

"I'm assuming that you all have Russian passports?"

"Yes."

"Good. You can't travel where we're going without them."

"Do we need visas?"

"No. Just your passport." He reached into his pocket and retrieved an envelope. "Here are your train tickets to Dushanbe, Tajikistan. Our train leaves on Saturday, January 4 at 12:15 p.m. Meet me at Central Station at 10:30 for breakfast so we can go over our travel plans and security considerations."

"We'll be there."

"Be forewarned that our source is asking one hundred thousand dollars apiece for the sensors, but he has been known to inflate the price during the process."

"Understood."

Fyodor smiled. "And be ready for anything. The criminals in that neck of the woods know that they're a long way from the law, and they push their way around with impudence."

"Not worried."

Fyodor gazed into her eyes trying to get a read on her. He decided that she probably was as tough as she talked and changed the subject. "Have you tried the food at the Metropol?"

"I have not."

"Don't leave Moscow without visiting. The food is good and the architecture is stunning. I recommend the fried duck with wild-cherry sauce."

"Thank you. I appreciate the advice. Will you join us there for dinner this evening?"

"I'm sorry, Miss Aksakova," he replied. "But I can't indulge the pleasure of your company at this time. I have business to take care of before our departure." He smiled politely, turned on his heels, and strolled away, whistling *Polno vam, snezhochki*, a traditional Cossack folk song.

Irina pondered the tune choice, one often sung before battle. Was that intentional, a Freudian slip, or pure coincidence? Was he subtly conveying a message? She laughed at herself. *Getting way too jumpy. He probably just likes the tune.*

34

Atchafalaya Swamp, Louisiana
Thursday morning, January 2, 2020

"Just try it with one duffel bag," Rat suggested. "See how it goes. You don't want to overdo it."

Ariele shot him a look of defiance, picked up both her bags, and stepped into the girls' canoe, wincing when she lifted her left leg and again when she put weight on it. She wedged one into the bow, pushed the other under the thwart behind her, and secured both with straps.

Rat looked on, apprehensive. Her boundless determination made him nervous. It could put them all in a bad spot. One of his friends, a driven, goal-setting type, had needed four months to return to normal after he had been bitten by a cottonmouth. Over and over again he had pushed himself too hard, the oxygen level in his blood had dropped, and he had gotten lightheaded, passing out on several occasions. If the sassy redhead passed out in the swamp ... that wouldn't be good.

Ariele lowered herself into her seat and practiced the full range of stroke motions she would use as a bowman. Her arms, shoulders, and core felt strong. That was good. That's what she needed the most. The rest of her was iffy. Her left leg still ached, and she occasionally faced headaches, waves of nausea, and lightheadedness. She didn't care that these symptoms would likely increase with activity. God helping her, she was going to make it through the practice run after breakfast, and she was going to paddle out of the swamp at the earliest possible date, no matter how bad she hurt or how sick she got.

Two thwumps behind her startled her out of her cogitations. She whirled around. Sam's duffel bags were sitting on the floor of the canoe, and Sam was smiling mischievously, obviously pleased with the reaction. Before she could say something snarky to her older friend, Peggy Sue's honey voice called from the doorway, "Breakfast is ready! Come and get it!"

Ariele jumped to her feet. A flash of pain erupted in her calf. She tottered, grabbed the railing, and steadied herself. Sam placed a steadying hand on her arm, and the frustrated young lady brushed it off. "I got this! Just gotta slow things down a bit." She ducked under the rail, tumbled to her hands and knees, got up unsteadily, shook off a wave of dizziness, and continued inside. Sam and Rat looked at each other and shook their heads, a mixture of admiration and uncertainty.

As usual, the radio was on for breakfast and tuned to the Morning Show on K279AL, the local Christian station. Ariele took her seat next to Burt and poured herself a cup of coffee. Sam and Rat followed right behind, and Peggy Sue set a mound of corn fritters on the table.

Halfway through the plate of fritters, the broadcast suddenly cut off. For two brief seconds, a serene silence filled the room, then the obnoxious squawk of the Emergency Alert System pierced the quiet. Rat and Burt paid no attention, figuring it was a run-of-the-mill local alert about fugitives, something that happened two or three times per week.

"We interrupt this program to bring you the following special bulletin." A single brief squawk. "This is a Presidential Alert."

A hush fell over the table. Rat and Burt looked at each other with eyebrows raised. Forks were set down, and all eyes turned toward the multiband radio on the counter. None of them had ever heard a national-level alert before.

"A terrorist attack has occurred on American soil. Less than ten minutes ago, at 7:08 am Central Standard Time, an apparent nuclear device was detonated in Port Arthur, Texas. We will bring you more details as they come in."

The radio returned to the local program. "Wow!" remarked Bob Cornuke, the morning show host. "That caught me by surprise as much as it did you. But it shouldn't have taken any of us by surprise. The increasing sophistication of terrorist cells, the rapid expansion of terrorist activity in America, the dramatic growth of ethnos-against-ethnos birth pangs, and the warnings of discerning prophecy teachers all pointed to this day as inevitable."

Burt's chair scooted back with a clatter. Now all eyes were on him. He rushed to his attic hideout, grabbed his secure laptop, hurried back down, set it on the counter, and fired it up. Breathing heavily, he wheezed out, "Gotta check the weather for eastern Texas and western Louisiana. Find out if we're gonna get hit by the fallout."

He tapped a few keys, tapped a few more, tapped a third time, then scrolled. "Praise the Lord!" he announced. "Doesn't look like we have to worry. The wind is blowing nearly due south in our region and is expected to shift to the SSE over the next few hours. So it'll miss us entirely. But the Yucatan could get doused."

Two minutes later, another Emergency Alert squawk interrupted their breakfast table and Bob's impromptu prophetic chatter on the Morning Show.

"This is a Presidential Alert. The White House has confirmed that a nuclear device has been detonated in Port Arthur, Texas and has declared a national emergency. This state of emergency will remain in effect until federal authorities have certified that there is no further threat anywhere in the United States or her territories from weapons of mass destruction.

"Immediate shelter notice. If you are within the blast zone area or the fallout zone, take immediate steps to protect yourself from radioactive fallout by putting dense objects between yourself and the outside. The blast zone is defined as the entire area within five miles of West Port Arthur Bridge. The fallout zone is defined as that area extending southward from the blast zone, reaching as far west as Clam Lake in McFadden National Wildlife Refuge and as far east as Holly Beach.

Fifteen minutes later, while Burt and Rat were polishing off the biscuits and gravy, an Emergency Alert squawked for the third time.

"This is a Presidential Alert. The White House has issued a travel restriction notice. A restriction zone has been declared within twenty miles of the blast. Until further notice, no travel to or from the restricted area is permitted except for authorized emergency and law enforcement personnel. If you live within the restricted area, do not attempt to leave. If you have loved ones in the restricted area, do not attempt to enter.

"Travel restriction notice. All private and commercial flights in the US are banned until further notice. All bus, subway, and train service is canceled until further notice.

"Travel restriction notice. Unnecessary travel on public roadways is banned until further notice. Do not travel on public roads unless necessary. Use is limited to authorized, emergency, and commercial vehicles, and individuals with genuine need. Heavy fines will be levied for all unnecessary traffic.

"Travel restriction notice. All public roadways—federal, state, and local—will be manned with military-assisted checkpoints. All vehicles will be stopped. All passengers will be required to produce a photo ID. Passengers may be required to submit to further protective measures as electronic fingerprinting and facial recognition.

"Active duty mobilization notice. The White House has declared a full mobilization of all active-duty members of all branches of the United States Armed Forces. All pending leave is canceled. All current leave is revoked. Members on leave have 48 hours to report to their unit.

"Reserve and National Guard call-up notice. The White House has initiated a one-hundred-percent call-up as authorized by the Homeland Security Act. This call-up is effective immediately for all National Guardsmen regardless of branch, all Reservists regardless of branch, and the Civil Air Patrol. All members are to report to their unit headquarters immediately.

"This has been a Presidential Alert issued via the Emergency Alert System. It will be repeated twice every half hour. Stay tuned for important updates."

"Wow!" Burt exclaimed, gesticulating with his hands. "Shutting down the country, implementing what amounts to martial law, and setting up roadblocks on every highway. That's unprecedented! They must have their sights on a vast network of terrorist sleeper cells."

"Could be," Rat replied. "Or maybe they're exploiting a golden opportunity to net as many Homeland Security violators as they can, not just the Rogue-aware, but also the patriots, deucers, preppers, and apocalypse preachers as well."

Ariele sat in silence, her eyes moist with tears. Her heart had been set on returning to Montana. Now her plans were dashed to the ground for the second time. Sam placed a gentle hand on her shoulder. "Don't worry, Moxie. We're just gonna have to trust the verse that Jack loves to quote: 'All things work together for good.'"

She nodded and wiped her cheek with her sleeve. "I was thinking of that passage myself."

That afternoon Ariele tried several times to call Woody and Joby on her secure phone. There was no service. She tried again in the evening after supper. Rat watched the frustrated young lady slap the phone shut and slam it into her purse after yet another dead call.

"What in the world is going on?" she asked no one in particular. "No cell service. No internet."

"Well," Rat replied. "I doubt it's a terrorist attack. Most likely the federal government has instituted SOP 303 nationwide."

She looked at him with arched eyebrows.

"SOP 303 is a federal directive that allows federal, state, and local governments and law enforcement agencies to shut down cellular service during emergencies. Folks can still use landlines. And they can still use the internet with a physical connection. But all cell phone towers and non-government satellite communication options have been turned off."

"But why?"

"So terrorists can't use cell phones to communicate with each other or activate explosives."

"So we could be without phone service for days?"

"That's right. Or even for weeks."

"So how am I going to contact Woody?"

"You're not going to. But don't worry. He has the same problem, so he isn't going to fear the worst when he can't reach you or you can't reach him."

"But I would like his advice on what we're supposed to do."

"I can tell you exactly what he would say."

"So what would he say?"

"He would tell you to stay put for now since every road will be manned with roadblocks, every vehicle will be stopped, and every passenger will be positively identified—by identification cards, facial recognition, and fingerprints. They're going to catch a lot of real terrorists, a lot of soft terrorists aware of the Rogue, and a lot of other persons who are regarded as threats to America."

She frowned at him.

"I'm serious, Moxie. There's no other counsel he could possibly give. You have to stay put until this mess goes away."

"I could walk home!"

"Not a ghost of a chance. With the security net they're setting up, the odds are pretty much zero that you could make it back to Montana without running into officers, soldiers, or officials. And with the tools they'll have at their disposal, it won't take them long to figure out who you are. Worse, if they interrogate you, using some of the illegal methods which they claim they don't use, they'll draw out of you the names of every one of your connections in the Underground."

Ariele crossed her arms, puffed her bangs, and looked away. But she knew he was right. It was just going to take her a while to get reconciled to the new reality.

35

Meyersdale, PA
Thursday, January 2, 2020

Jack stuffed the *Motorcycle Digest* into the magazine rack next to the couch, leaned his elbow on the armrest, and stewed. He had read every motorcycle magazine in the place several times. He was tired of playing pinochle and Scrabble. He was just plain sick and tired of being cooped up in the cramped apartment over Romeo's garage. The ceiling was only six foot four inches. The curtains had to be closed at all times. Their only lights were three LED nightlights and two micro-LED flashlights on the low setting. They were obsessed with noise avoidance. They weren't allowed to use the blender or the mixer. Even the dingers on the microwave and the toaster oven had been disabled. They talked just above a whisper. They only took showers, ran the water, and flushed the toilet when Romeo was making noise in the shop below.

It wasn't that the rules were unreasonable. They were necessary. If Romeo's neighbors figured out that someone was living over his garage and contacted the city, and the city sent someone over to see if the apartment met the city's code for rental units—which it didn't—all three of them would be in deep doo-doo. But living under them was getting old. He needed a change of pace—desperately.

But that was not happening any time soon. The plan called for him and Sally to lay low here at Romeo's place for five or six weeks until interest in their escape had subsided. He stared at the calendar on the wall and counted the remaining days for the umpteenth time. Two more weeks of this, and they were out of here.

The plan was for them to ride in the camper trailer being towed by two members of the Calvary Crusaders who were traveling to Eagle River, Wisconsin for the World Championship Snowmobile Derby on January 17-19. On the evening before the Derby, the race fans would find a lonely parking spot at one of the overflow lots, call Jordy, and wait. Red and Jordy would show up late in the evening, and he and Sally would transfer to Red's camper.

In the meantime, Jack needed to let out some steam. He wished he could go for a long hike in the hills or take a swift jog in the streets. But neither was feasible. *Gonna have to settle for fifty pushups and some more time in the Bible. Maybe I'll read Daniel again and then a couple of the minor prophets.*

To change things up, he opted for five-second negative pushups. After struggling through the last set, his arms trembling like jello, he collapsed on the floor. "Are you gonna be done with the laptop any time soon?" he asked Sally, his face buried in the carpet.

"I can be done now," she replied from her stuff chair a

few feet away. "I'm just puttering around."

The laptop was their prize possession. During the first week of their stay, Romeo had procured it with some of the escape-package cash and added it to his network. Since then, Jack had set up a Buster account, and Woody had procured membership for him in the Rogue Underground. Now he and Sally used it for Bible reading and news, along with email and messages on the *Rogue Underground* website.

"Does another round of bacon, eggs, and hashbrowns sound okay, Jack?" she asked as she stood up. "I know I've made the same breakfast every day since we got here."

"No need to apologize. Country breakfast never goes out of style. I could eat it three meals a day."

She marveled as she walked to the kitchenette. *Mom was right. Guys and breakfast are a match made in heaven.*

Jack dropped into Sally's chair and checked the CVN newsfeed. As usual, he began clicking on the links for the latest stories on Israel and the Middle East. Halfway through a story on Syria threatening war if Israel didn't return the strategically important Golan Heights, a newsflash appeared at the top of the page. NUKE DETONATED IN PORT ARTHUR. The white heat of a nightmare scenario coming true overloaded his senses. His body felt numb. His mind fogged.

He tried to click on the newsflash bar. But the cursor responded erratically as if possessed, overshooting the bar several times. *What is going on?* He checked the touchpad. It wasn't the pad. It was his finger. His whole hand was shaking. *Relax. Breathe deep and slow. Moderate the heart rate. This is no different than a sniper mission.* In between breaths and heartbeats, he stopped the cursor on the bar and clicked.

A text box appeared. "At 7:08 Eastern Standard Time this morning, a nuclear device was detonated in the Ship Canal in the refinery district of Port Arthur, Texas. Authorities are rushing to investigate. We have no further details at this time. Further bulletins will be issued as information becomes available."

"Sally!" Jack called out as loud as he dared. "The poo may have just hit the fan. Come check this out!"

The whip she had been using to scramble the eggs hit the sink with a clatter, and she scurried over, taking a seat on the armrest. Curiosity gave way to horror, then frustration and tears.

"This world is coming apart at the seams," she fumed. "I just don't understand all the hatred, fighting, wars, and political maneuvering in the world. To what end? It never fixes anything. It merely changes a few externals and sets up the next conflict."

"Got that right. Only Jesus can fix this mess—"

She finished his thought. "When he comes down, takes out the trash, and establishes his kingdom here on Earth."

"Yep."

"I've been thinking about that a lot lately, to be honest."

Jack wondered if she was finally going to surrender. But she wasn't ready, yet. She sighed, wiped the tears from her eyes, and returned to the kitchenette. Jack took her case before the Lord in silent prayer, confident that it was only a matter of time. She appeared to be beaten ... as beaten as the eggs he could hear sizzling in the hot frypan.

***

Thousands of miles away, Irina was setting the table for an early dinner when Tony exclaimed with unusual animation, "Holy lizard gizzards!" He spun the laptop around so the others could see. A red news-flash bar blared "Nuke Detonation in the USA."

The anchor for Channel One returned. "I was just handed a special news bulletin. Fifty-four minutes ago the terrorist organization Sayf Allah detonated a nuclear device in the United States in Port Arthur, Texas, in the oil refinery district. This is a tragic day for America—9-1-1 all over again. Our hearts go out to them. The American authorities have not yet released any details on the destruction or the death toll, but there's little doubt that the report will be grim."

He elaborated for a couple minutes on the scant details that had trickled out from American sources, then segued into a diatribe against terrorism and religious fundamentalism. Unsurprisingly, he closed his handling of the special bulletin with a sharp rebuke of Washington's double standards. "It's a crying shame that America wants our help in their war against terror, yet they regard our efforts against terrorism in Chechnya as if they were the bungling steps of heavy-handed government."

The boys nodded their heads in agreement, and Andy grumbled, "America definitely fumbled the ball on that regard. We should have supported the Russians in Chechnya. That's my two cents worth."

***

All morning long and through lunch, Jack and Sally monitored the CVN website, hoping to get an update on the tragic news. Other than a regurgitation of the contents of the emergency broadcast message, nothing substantial was available until the two o'clock broadcast.

"Good afternoon from New York City. This is *The World Report* on CVN, and I'm Helen Hewitt. We're going straight to our main story, the nuclear attack on the United States at Port Arthur, Texas.

"This morning at 7:08 a.m. Central Standard Time, a nuclear device was detonated in the Port Arthur Ship Canal in the refinery district. The explosion occurred on a Singaporian-flagged oil freighter registered as the Anubis. The flash was seen over 200 miles away in Shreveport, Louisiana, and the mushroom cloud could be seen as far away as the western suburbs of Houston, Texas.

"The damage is mind-boggling. Facilities operated by Chevron Phillips, KMTEX, Martin Energy Services, and Motiva suffered billions of dollars worth of damage, with two terminals destroyed and three severely damaged. Dozens of fires are burning out of control. Most structures within three-quarters of a mile were destroyed or severely damaged. Windows were shattered up to two and a half miles away. Shipping took a massive hit. The Anubis and another tanker are piles of twisted steel, three tankers are burning, two barges and six tugboats are destroyed, and five tugboats are missing.

"The latest report claims there are hundreds of confirmed deaths, hundreds unaccounted for, hundreds hospitalized with third-degree burns, and thousands being treated at aid stations for minor injuries such as flash burns to the eyes, first and second-degree burns, and cuts and slivers from glass and other flying debris.

"Health officials are requiring everyone who was within five miles of the blast, whether they were outside or inside, to seek medical assistance immediately. FEMA—working with regional hospitals and clinics, first responder units, and the Texas National Guard—has set up dozens of treatment centers outside the five-mile radiation zone.

"Do not assume that you are okay merely because you didn't suffer burns or cuts. There is a threat of radiation poisoning. Don't wait until you develop symptoms like nausea or hair falling out. If you were within two miles of the blast, assume that you have been exposed to radiation until a medical professional has determined otherwise. Officials inform us that all exposed individuals within a half mile received a potentially lethal dose. Anyone up to a mile away that was not shielded faces the danger of acute radiation poisoning. Anyone who was outside and exposed up to two miles distant is still at risk for radiation poisoning. Please seek treatment immediately.

"We can't bring you live footage of the tragedy as no reporters are allowed in the blast zone, and aircraft and drones are banned except for flights by authorized personnel. But we have obtained photos and footage from folks inside the restricted zone who have shared the horrors on social media outlets."

The show cut to a series of shots and video clips

portraying the damage, the injuries, the fires, the billows of smoke, and the massive, burning oil slick blocking the waterway. The segment closed with a video obtained from a security camera on the tower at Golden Pass LNG Terminal two and a half miles southeast of the blast. It caught the explosion, the mushroom cloud rising to a height of four and a half miles, and the blast wind, which was still over 150 miles per hour when it reached the terminal.

"The gentleman who forwarded the blast video," he continued, "is holed up in the facility in a makeshift fallout shelter which he and his associates hastily threw together when they realized that they were in the path of the fallout. Officials are currently trying to figure out how to rescue these folks and many others who are trapped in the danger zone."

"Sayf Allah, or Sword of Allah, has claimed responsibility for this tragedy in a string of anti-American rants on Twitter and Facebook. One chilling example says, "Port Arthur is just the beginning. Death to America. Death to all the infidels. Death to all the Christian pigs." This newcomer to the ranks of Muslim terrorist organizations was upgraded last month by the CIA and is now regarded by them as the most dangerous in the world. Their continual attacks on buildings, stadiums, trains, bridges, and dams in Europe and North America over the past few months demonstrate that their boast of extreme terrorism is no empty threat.

"At this point no information has been released by the authorities on the blast itself, but we contacted several former CIA officials for their perspective. Their consensus is that the size of the fireball, the height of the mushroom cloud, and the extent of the blast area suggest a ten-kiloton device.

"At this point, we can only speculate where and how they obtained nuclear weapons. But rumors have been floating around on black sites and the intel grapevine for the past few months which claim that Sayf Allah had obtained both one-kiloton and ten-kiloton nuclear devices in the past year. This suggests that they have in their possession both Soviet-era RA-115 backpack nukes, which were used by the GRU—the Main Intelligence Directorate—and ten-kiloton RDS-9 warheads from a 53-58 torpedo. The former was the only one-kiloton device and the latter the only ten-kiloton device in the Soviet arsenal. So it now appears that these rumors have morphed into a living nightmare.

"While Russia 'officially' claims that all 250 of the Soviet-era backpack nukes are accounted for and held in retired inventory in secure facilities, inside sources have leaked internal reports which indicate that more than 100 are unaccounted for. The same reports suggest that there was a relatively easy path for backpack nukes to disappear because many were stored on Spetsnaz facilities with security protocols that were not much beyond those used for RPGs, grenades, and mortar rounds.

"How they obtained ten-kiloton torpedo warheads, on the other hand, is the million-dollar question. There are only two theories that our CIA sources regard as plausible. The first is that they obtained them through a powerful black marketeer who bribed a high-ranking officer in charge of a nuclear weapons depot, most likely with a sum north of four hundred million rubles. The officer would have needed sufficient funds to bribe at least two junior officers and four security personnel as well as providing himself with a tidy nest egg.

"The second is that they salvaged them from a sunken Russian sub, like the K-8 which sank in 1970 in the Bay of Biscay off Spain with four nuclear torpedo warheads on board. This theory presents its own difficulties. How did they procure a submarine that can descend to depths of 15,000 feet? Did they buy one, build one, or rent one? And what about the necessary support ship? Our experts suspect that if this theory is correct, Sayf Allah built and manned their own deep-water salvage sub, which would vastly lower the risk of non-radicals blowing the whistle.

"Yet another question is how they armed the ten-kiloton device. Our experts think that the most likely scenario is that the radicals piggyback wired it with the backpack nuke, using the smaller device as the timer and the electronic ignition for both nuclear charges. The backpack nuke was designed to be manually armed, so it would be much easier to arm it and set a timer. And it wouldn't be extremely complicated to connect the electrical ignition device to the initiating charge in the ten-kiloton device."

Helen stopped for a moment, listened to someone communicating with her on her headset, nodded, and then announced, "We're going to cut to Douglas Kirby with KBMT out of Beaumont, Texas for a closer look at the situation. Douglas, what can you see?"

"Helen, I'm standing as close as we can get to the blast zone—twenty miles from ground zero—at a roadblock on the north end of Beaumont on US 96. From here you can't see any of the blast damage, but you can see thick billows of black smoke rising from the area. Recent tweets indicate that five oil tankers are burning and nearly a dozen facilities are on fire.

"There is chaos here at the roadblock as hundreds of folks have gathered on the outside, seeking information on loved ones in the blast zone, and a line of cars nearly two miles long is waiting to exit. Officials have now begun letting vehicles out, but only after extensive identification and security protocols have been satisfied. On several occasions in the past hour, we have observed individuals being hauled away in federal law enforcement vehicles, presumably folks known or suspected to have association with domestic terrorism.

"Another complication here, as a FEMA official kindly explained to me, is that officials are not letting anyone leave the twenty-mile limited access area if they lived or worked within the five-mile blast zone unless they have proof that they visited one of the designated aid stations. Those that don't have proof are being required to pull off to the side of the road and walk to one of the exit-point aid stations, where they could stand in line for hours. Those that are discovered to have injuries or radiation poisoning are being directed to the proper facilities. Several of the worst cases have left here in ambulances."

"Thank you for the update, Douglas."

"You're welcome, Helen."

"Before concluding our report on the Port Arthur tragedy," she continued, "I want to point out two remarkable circumstances which tempered this tragedy—keeping the death toll from being many times higher and vastly reducing the damage to the American oil industry.

"The first is that the device appears to have been detonated before it reached its target. On the assumption that the attackers wished to inflict maximum damage and casualties, we can assume that their intended target was the Chevron pier in the West Basin where their ship, the Anubis, was scheduled to unload. Had the ship tied up at the pier before the explosion occurred, the number of fatalities and the amount of property damage could have been five to ten times higher.

"We asked one of our CIA contacts—a retired Delta operator and CIA agent with extensive training in American, Russian, and Soviet-era backpack nukes—how the Sayf Allah suicide bombers could have accidentally detonated the device. He informed us that the backpack nuke was probably being handled by men who had minimal training with the devices and who were unable to understand the manual—if they even had one—because it was written in technical Russian. Most likely, the militants accidentally detonated the device while arming it. According to our contact, there are two mistakes you can make while arming an RA-115 which will result in express detonation.

"The other remarkable circumstance is that a high-pressure zone began pushing its way south into Oklahoma and Arkansas Tuesday evening, which brought a stiff North wind to the coastal regions of Louisiana and eastern Texas Wednesday evening that has been steadily blowing since then at fifteen to twenty miles per hour. This breeze has pushed the blast cloud and the fallout away from populated areas.

"America ... We dodged a bullet this time around. The odds are, we won't be so lucky next time. Maybe it's time to do something more substantial in our efforts against Muslim terrorism."

Jack turned to Sally. "This is going to turn the election scenario on its head. My money is on Charles Weston now. He won't be polling ten percent behind next week. Swing voters, independents, and moderates won't think his hawkish stance on Islamic extremism is an overreaction after this."

She sighed. "You might be right. But I don't like to think about the future. When I look into the crystal ball, all I see is war, terrorism, violence, and political turmoil increasing."

"The outlook is definitely bleak," Jack agreed. "No matter who gets elected, they won't fix any of the world's problems. They can't. They don't understand the problem. Everyone regards others as the root of the problem. But, as Pogo said long ago, 'We have met the enemy, and he is us.' Until the Messiah descends from heaven and gets the whole world on the same page—his page—the world will be filled with hatred, violence, turmoil, and wars."

***

After an early dinner, Jack and Sally turned to CVN again for an update on the Port Arthur incident.

"Good evening from New York City. It's 5:01 eastern time. I'm Geoff Seaworthy, and this is *The World Report* on CVN. The big story this hour is that U.S. bomb squads—from the FBI, police SWAT teams, the Coast Guard, the Army, the Navy, and the Air Force—found three armed nuclear devices earlier today and have successfully de-armed them. One was in New York City harbor, one at Newport News harbor near the shipyard, and one in San Diego harbor. All three had timers set for 3 p.m. eastern time when the first shift is getting off and the second shift is coming on in most eastern seaboard cities. This would have increased the casualty rate by at least fifty percent in what would have been a catastrophic series of blasts.

"All three devices were positively identified as Russian 10-kiloton RDS-9 warheads from a 53-58 torpedo, which were armed by piggyback wiring them to a one-kiloton RA-115 Soviet-era backpack nuke. This validates the theory offered earlier today that the Port Arthur device was an RDS-9 warhead from a Soviet-era torpedo.

"All three devices were found in unsealed shipping containers on ships registered in either Singapore or Liberia, countries with a large Islamic population that's known to have been deeply infiltrated by fundamentalist groups. One Air Force official who spoke to us earlier, on condition of anonymity, confessed that the search efforts had focused on ships registered in several nations where Islamic radicals had relatively easy access to shipping."

"I won't delve any further into this as Tom Overbright will bring the full story next hour covering the nationwide hunt for weapons of mass destruction in America's harbors and ports, the discovery and disarming of the nukes, and the ongoing hunt for terrorists, especially members of Sayf Allah. Don't miss his presentation. It will include interviews with several of the brave men and women involved.

"We'll close this brief with an update on the transportation bans. Federal officials assure us that crews are working around the clock to return our mass transportation systems to service as soon as possible and that the crews are making tremendous progress. They expect New York City subway service and NorthEast Corridor Amtrak service to resume as early as Saturday afternoon. Within the next three weeks, all public transportation systems are expected to return to full service.

"The Federal Transportation Commission does want to remind commuters that they will encounter heightened security measures—including manned checkpoints, Geiger counters, explosives detection, surveillance cameras, and facial recognition—as permanent features on all public transportation systems as part of a national rollout of Phase Two of FATE, the Federal Anti-Terrorism Effort.

"As for our roadways, please bear in mind the travel restriction that's being enforced nationally during the dragnet. Traffic is limited to authorized vehicles, emergency vehicles, commercial vehicles, and individuals with genuine need. Heavy fines will be levied for non-essential traffic. Officials estimate that the nationwide dragnet effort will last two to three weeks, but caution that the minor inconvenience of random checkpoints will continue for months if not years."

Jack shook his head in frustration. "I guess we won't be going to Wisconsin in a couple weeks as planned."

"So now what are we going to do? Do you have any ideas?"

"None at the moment. But between the guys at the Compound and the Calvary Crusader boys, somebody is bound to come up with a good idea." But the frustration in his voice betrayed the fact that he wasn't as confident as his words suggested.

Sally wasn't worried. His funks never lasted long. They were more like the morning fog that quickly burns off than multiday storm fronts.

"When this initial stage of tight security passes," he continued, "the entire country will be under a state of heightened security for a long time. It's going to significantly change the dynamics of how we get back. Our trip from here was going to be a picnic. Now it's going to be an obstacle course."

"To quote a man I know, whose initials are Jack Lundstrom, we just have to trust that God will provide in his own time."

The irony struck him. The stalwart Spartan needed a word of encouragement from Miss Worrywart.

That evening, the two relaxed with a bowl of buttered popcorn—made earlier in the day while Romeo was running a grinder. But they weren't conversing. Sally was unusually quiet.

"Something bugging you, Sally?" Jack asked.

"I've been thinking about what you said about the world—every last man—being infected with a moral disease that they can't cure. I'm starting to understand. Everywhere I look I see this disease … on television … on the internet … in the people around me … in the entire world … in my own heart."

"It's definitely universal. This spiritual virus was concocted by a spiritual being far more powerful than mankind, and he propagates it with powerful lies that appeal to our lusts and pride. We can't keep ourselves from catching it, and we can't fix ourselves once we get it. We need God's help. Only God can free us from its death sentence."

A tear rolled down her cheek, and her lip began quivering. She pulled her knees up, wrapped her arms around her legs, buried her face, and muttered, "The world is a mess. I'm a mess." She was too distraught to talk about the subject any further. Jack let her have her space. She would come out of her cocoon when she was ready.

That night, lying awake in her tiny bedroom, Sally wrestled with herself and the truth. She was weary of the self-help theories that polished the outside but fixed nothing on the inside. She knew that the evil in the world could not be explained by the theory that man is essentially good and that he just needs an emotional, educational, or financial helping hand. And she was tired of trying to navigate her own way through life. She needed God's help. She asked for it. And she got it.

36

Dushanbe, Tajikistan
January 7-10, 2020

Irina stared out the window at the dreary, monotonous landscape rolling by, bare hill after bare hill, trying to maintain a good attitude. She had looked forward to the train ride, but it had been a miserable three days. The heat wasn't working properly. The bathrooms reeked. And the food was pitiful. They had endured watery borscht over the weekend and bland cabbage soup yesterday and today. *Glad we arrive in Dushanbe tomorrow. I'm so ready for a hot shower and real food.*

She glanced at her traveling companions. Tony was leaned against the window with his eyes closed. Andy was across from her, earbuds in, watching something on his phone. Fyodor was across from Tony, his nose in the latest issue of *Ekspert*, a weekly business magazine published in Moscow. While the three men sitting with her could pass for mere tourists or typical businessmen, and that's what their papers and passports claimed, all three were experts in arcane fields. And she needed all three.

Fyodor was a bit of an enigma, though. Judging by the scraps of information she had pieced together in the past few days, he had begun his career in the Bratva as an enforcer. When his pakhan had figured out that his brains were more valuable than his brawn, he had been promoted to a brodyaga who specialized in the weapons and technology trade in the former Soviet states east of the Caspian. In the three years since then, he had made twenty-seven trips to Dushanbe. This wealth of experience boosted her confidence about their upcoming meeting with Li Qiang, a dangerous black marketeer in a dangerous part of the world that was overrun with bandits, opium, and jihadists.

***

The Russia team relaxed after their arrival on Wednesday and did some shopping on Thursday while Fyodor took care of the necessary footwork. On Thursday evening, he pulled up to the Hotel Taj Palace in a rented Mercedes, and the three climbed in, trying to ignore their butterflies. On several levels, this was the most dangerous part of their trip. After introducing them to Farzann his Tajik driver, Fyodor motioned for the blocky man to start driving. As the sedan pulled out onto the street, their guide remarked over his shoulder, "We're headed for the Limping Camel."

Irina recognized the name. She had read about the place while studying up on Dushanbe's history and culture. The club was located in an older neighborhood and had been a hangout for criminals and ruffians since the 30s. It had been renovated in the 70s with funds from Soviet officers who supplemented their income by smuggling, but the intervening decades had taken their toll.

Less than a kilometer from the club, the taciturn man reviewed the intel for the evening. "Li Qiang is the largest arms dealer in the region, a major player in the opium trade, and the only dependable connection for Chinese and North Korean technology. He's closely associated with the Chinese mafia, has political connections in Beijing, and cooperates with two Russian families who are not friendly with Solntsevskaya Bratva. I have dealt with him on more than twenty occasions. He always shows up with two bodyguards, who reputedly were members of the Chinese Special Forces."

"You gave us this information in the train station over breakfast," she replied.

"I'm just reminding you. The man is dangerous. Watch yourselves and be careful."

"Not too worried," Irina replied. But her guts were churning.

"You ought to be worried. He makes me nervous. I hate coming here."

Irina shrugged, pulled her makeup kit out of her purse, swiveled his rearview mirror toward herself, smiled at him when he frowned, and touched up her lipstick and mascara as nonchalantly as if she were going to the opera.

The club was dimly lit, smoke-filled, and chaotic. Speakers blared the regional equivalent of country music. As the four waded among the tightly packed tables and milling crowd, Irina observed that half of the guests were regional—Russians, Chinese, Afghanis, Turkmens, Kazakhs, and

Uzbekis—while the rest were locals. None appeared to be tourists. The clientele appeared to be every bit as rough and tumble as the intel had claimed—arms traders, black marketeers, drug dealers, and jihadists. She looked over her shoulder at Tony. Vigilance was etched on his face. *He's as nervous as I am.*

They reached a section where the crowd was so thick that the way seemed blocked. Off to the right two tables had been pushed together and several dozen men were haggling in Russian over a business deal. Off to their left another mob was gathered around a table of gamblers, likely playing Trynka. Fyodor barged his way forward. Irina tried to follow, but within several steps, only his head was visible. Then it too disappeared in a blur of commotion. Someone had grabbed him and pulled him aside. Had it been a friend? Business partner? Her heart began to race, and she strove to turn in his direction and find him, but someone behind her pushed her forward. She assumed it was Tony, so she continued straight.

When she finally broke free of the maddening throng, she turned to look for the boys. They weren't there. A large Chinese man in business attire noticed the attractive brunette, stood up, and put his arm around her waist. "Hands off me, you pig!" she warned as she pulled away. When he didn't retract his arm, she spun out of his grip and landed an angry slap on his cheek.

When Tony and Andy heard her cry, they bulled their way through the crowd with a vengeance and burst through the wall of bodies just in time to see the man lunge for Irina.

Tony started for her side, but Andy restrained him. The irate female blocked her attacker's arms upward and landed a punch on his throat. He stopped in his tracks, sucked in a rasping breath, and reached for his throat with hands. Before he could think about his next move, Irina launched a kick into his groin. He yelped, doubled over in pain, and clutched himself.

The Russians and Tajiks at the table burst into laughter. But two muscular Chinese jumped to their feet and rushed Irina. The boys stepped in front of her with arms folded. One of the bodyguards pulled his Glock and pointed it at Tony. Irina tensed. But his boss waved them off and sputtered, "Let them be." They glared at the boys, then returned to their seats, humiliated and itching for a fight. A cloud of tension still hung in the air, and the surprise de-escalation didn't make sense to Irina. But the mystery cleared up when Fyodor brushed past her and the boys, placed his hand on the groaning businessman's shoulders, and said, "Are you okay Li Qiang?"

Irina went numb. *Great. Just what we need. The obnoxious letch is the arms dealer we're supposed to meet.*

She looked at the boys. Tony was clenching his fists. Andy's jaw was tight as a drum. Their edginess had ratcheted up a couple notches.

"Is the feisty tigress with you?" the heavy-set man asked Fyodor rather indignantly.

"For better or for worse."

Li Qiang scowled at Irina, lowered himself carefully into his seat, picked up his glass of baijiu which was two-thirds full, and slammed the rest of the clear liquid, attempting to numb the pain in his throat. He let it burn for a moment, then waved to Fyodor. "Sit down, Mr. Zhirinovksy, my friend, and let us eat. Then we'll talk business."

Turning to the three Russians who were sitting to his left, Li Qiang spoke briskly in broken Russian. "Dmitriy, we'll visit on Saturday or Sunday. I believe we can swing a sweet deal for your AK-200s and your GM-94 grenade launchers. My buyers in this region have deep pockets and are desperate for modern weapons." The man nodded and departed, followed by his Russian associates and two Tajiks.

Irina moved away from Li Qiang, hoping to take a chair as far away from him as possible, but Fyodor grabbed her arm and seated her to the right of the despised wheeler-dealer. Then he took the seat on his other side. Tony watched this drama play out, then took the seat next to Irina. Andy sat next to him.

After a superb Kazakhian prime-rib dinner, which Irina enjoyed despite the awkward circumstances, Fyodor got down to business. "So how do you want to make the swap?"

"Who says there will be a swap." Li Qiang replied. "I said I had the sensors. I didn't say they were yours for the taking."

"Has the price gone up?"

"Let's just say that there's a bidding war, and I'll sell them to the highest bidder unless someone agrees to my buy-it-now price."

"And what is that price?"

"Two hundred and fifty thousand dollars apiece. In greenbacks."

Irina nearly gagged on her sweetened green tea. "Seven hundred and fifty thousand dollars," she stormed, flabbergasted. "That's two and a half times the agreed-upon price!"

"I don't dictate the price. The market does. Take it or leave it."

Their eyes locked in determined combat. Irina started to scoot her chair back as if she were going to get up and walk away.

Fyodor placed his hand on her shoulder and addressed her calmly in English, attempting to defuse the volatile situation. "I understand that you don't like the man, Aleksandra, but trust me."

Irina stiffened, gripped with a sense of vulnerability. *How does he know that we're Americans? Who told him?*

He continued, "Don't let your emotions get in the way of doing business. You won't change his mind. If you need the sensors, take his offer. Don't walk away from your only opportunity to obtain them. He won't give you a second chance."

"There are other sources," she shot back.

"I'm afraid not. He has the Chinese supply locked up, and the Russian supply dried up quickly once the fairy tales about the rogue comet or the rogue planet or whatever it is started making the rounds on the internet. The Russian government has clamped down severely on the black market sale of infrared equipment."

She looked over to Tony, hoping for some sign of support. He gave her a blank stare and shrugged his shoulders as if to say, you're the boss.

"Fine. I'll take it," she fumed.

Li Qiang smirked. "Then meet me tomorrow morning at ten at the abandoned cement plant north and east of town. Drive inside the old warehouse and maintenance building. And bring the cash … all of it. I already don't like you, and you don't want me to like you even less."

***

Friday morning at 9:40, Fyodor's Mercedes raced north out of Dushanbe on M34. Eight minutes later, the black sedan turned east onto a rough dirt road and barreled through a pothole, banging the undercarriage in the dirt and slamming the boys' heads into the roof.

"Hey, watch it!" Tony shouted.

Farzann apologized. "Sorry. This road really bad. Twenty much years past since repaired."

"You can slow down a bit," Fyodor advised his driver. "It's only four kilometers to the old plant. We have plenty of time."

Despite the slower pace, the drive was still jarring. They bounced over rocks and ruts and swerved around the deepest potholes. While rough roads in the twenty to thirty kilometers-per-hour range were nothing new to the guys, it was a painful initiation for Irina.

Ten minutes later, the vehicle rounded the rocky shoulder of a hill, and the abandoned cement plant, a crumbling relic of the glory days of the Soviet Union, loomed in front of them.

"Kingdoms rise and kingdoms fall," Irina remarked to no one in particular. "If the Rogue really is the harbinger of the end times, the rising Russian empire will soon come to an end even more stunning than the collapse of the Soviet Union. The rest of the world won't be far behind."

"I hope you're wrong," Tony replied. "I haven't crossed a single thing off my bucket list yet."

The Mercedes rolled into the plant yard. Irina was captivated by the desolate scene. The rusting equipment and the stark buildings, stripped of most of their windows and doors, seemed like a set from an apocalyptic movie.

Andy swung his head to the left and stared at the building they were passing. He could have sworn that he had seen a figure in the shadow of the door opening, and he was certain that he had seen a glimmer of light as if someone had been watching them through binoculars and accidentally tipped them toward the sun. He tapped his brother on the leg and signed "enemy." Tony nodded. He too sensed danger.

Farzann rolled the sedan into the open bay door of the warehouse, wheeled around, backed up beside a workbench in the middle of the spacious floor, and turned the engine off.

That's odd, Irina thought to herself. *He's tense. Gripping the wheel as if he's afraid or nervous.*

Andy opened his door and climbed out to stretch. He wanted to be limber if something happened.

There was no time to stretch. While Tony and Irina were exiting on the other side, another Mercedes raced into the building, zipped past them, wheeled around, and stopped about thirty feet away on the other side of the bench. Two men sprang out of the back seat and took positions near the vehicle with Kalashnikovs in the ready position—the bodyguards they had met and offended the previous night. Irina tensed. *Not looking pretty.*

The driver, wearing a neat gray suit, bounded out of the vehicle, strode around the front, and smartly opened the passenger door. Li Qiang stepped out. He was wearing a white suit, sporting gold-plated designer sunglasses, carrying an ivory and gold swagger stick, and smoking a cigar. The rotund wheeler-dealer strutted around the car and leaned against it, puffing his stogie and eyeing those who had arrived in the first vehicle.

The driver hefted the briefcase from the backseat, where it had sat between the two bodyguards, walked briskly over to the workbench, snapped it open, and turned it toward their trading partners, exposing three pouches with Chinese writing. He then motioned for someone to come forward. Andy started forward, and the Chinese guards raised their weapons at him. He froze. Irina whispered, "Walk slower, bro. You're making them nervous." He grinned sheepishly and started forward again at a more deliberate pace.

The tension was so thick you could have sliced it. Li Qiang's henchmen were nervously fingering the triggers on their assault rifles. Fyodor and his driver had their hands underneath their coats, likely on their pistols.

Under the watchful eye of the driver, Andy set the briefcase on the table, opened it, and exposed its contents—seven hundred and fifty thousand American greenbacks, mostly in fifties and hundreds. The driver sneered, "It had better all be here," and began the tedious job of thumbing through the packets in each pile.

While the driver was focused on his counting, Andy picked up the first packet. "Hey, Irina," he shouted. "The writing is in Chinese. How do I tell if I got the right stuff?"

"Look for numbers with the micrometer symbol, μm. We need 10, 4.75, and 2.2. Also look for periodic table symbols like Hg which is mercury, or Cd which is cadmium, or Te which is Tellurium."

"This one here says HgCdTe and 4.75 μm."

"Fantastic. Just what the doctor ordered. But go ahead and open the packet just to be certain."

Andy cut the end off the packet with the scissors on his Swiss Army knife, pulled out the sensor, and examined it. "Yep. Same symbols and number."

"Good. Check the others."

He slipped the sensor back into the anti-static sleeve and returned it to the briefcase. Then he picked up the second foil packet, snipped the end off, and dumped the contents into his palm.

"Okay!" The driver declared as he slammed the briefcase of cash shut and closed the clasps with two vigorous snaps. "We're done here. The swap is made." He snatched the attaché off the bench, leaned in toward Andy, and whispered, "Watch your back," then strode back to his Mercedes.

Andy returned the second package to its foam housing, closed the briefcase, and hustled back to their vehicle with their treasure in hand.

While he waited for Irina to climb into the car, he watched Li Qiang's Mercedes speed out of the building and turn east, away from the main road to Dushanbe.

"That's odd," Andy observed. "Why east?"

"Dunno," Tony replied. "What did the driver say to you?"

"Watch your back."

"Any idea what he meant?"

"Got no idea. But it sounded ominous."

"Something doesn't feel right."

"He doesn't trust his boss, and you shouldn't either," Fyodor interjected.

Tony looked over to him, hoping for further commentary, but the Russian turned his back and pulled out his phone. When the other party answered, he began speaking in Tajik.

Irina furrowed her brows. *Tajik?* She had assumed that the call was to confirm the completion of the deal. That, undoubtedly, would have been made in Russian.

He dropped the phone into his pocket, leaned against the vehicle, and folded his arms. Irina approached him when she realized that he had no intention of going anywhere. "Will we be leaving, soon?"

"We need to make sure that the coast is clear," he explained.

Irina shrugged her shoulders and climbed into the backseat. *Until the coast is clear? What does that mean?* The seconds turned into minutes. She began drumming her fingers impatiently on the armrest on the door. Seven long minutes later, Fyodor's phone rang. A voice chattered in Tajik for ten seconds. Their guide answered one word in Russian, "Good," climbed into the sedan, and nodded to Farzann.

As they headed back toward town, Andy noticed fresh tire tracks turning west onto the road at the building where he thought he had seen someone watching them. A sinking feeling wrapped its clammy arms around him. Not long after, he noticed a tan sedan behind them, churning up a cloud of dust. "We're being followed, Fyodor," he informed him.

The brodyaga replied indifferently, "That's just my Tajik bodyguards. Brought them along in case Li Qiang tried something."

But the answer didn't quell Andy's uneasiness. Another quarter mile up the road, the car careened around the shoulder of the hill that hid the plant from view, and ... Farzann jammed on the brakes to avoid hitting a sedan straddling the road. Several men jumped out from behind it with guns drawn. Farzann slapped the Mercedes into reverse and gunned it, but slammed on the brakes again two seconds later and dropped his head on the steering wheel. The tan sedan that had been following them had also angled across the road, blocking their escape. They were trapped.

Andy warily eyed the three men, who were slowly approaching them from the front with pistols in combat-firing position. "Definitely not amateurs. They're approaching Russian style."

His brother, who was watching the thugs that were

approaching from the rear, replied, "Yep. Same here. Gonna guess they served in the Russian-trained Tajik Special Forces."

"Time to chill."

"No doubt about it. We couldn't gun our way out of this with FNs or H&Ks in both hands."

"I would still feel better with cold steel in my hands."

"Amen to that."

One of the men approaching from the front motioned for the folks in the car to step out. The five obliged.

When the three gunmen approaching from their rear joined the others, Fyodor confronted one of them and demanded in Russian, "What's going on, Hamasa?"

"Changing sides, boss man. We were offered better pay from a better man."

Fyodor cursed and spat on the ground. Hamasa's lips curled up in an evil grin, and he slammed a fist into the Russian's gut. He doubled over with a grunt. Hamasa barked orders in Tajik. Two of the gunmen pointed their weapons at Irina and the Backstrom boys, a third secured the briefcase with the sensors, and two others separated Fyodor and Farzann. After slapping them around and searching them, they forced them into the trunk of their own Mercedes and slammed the lid down, entombing them in darkness.

Hamasa motioned to the boys and Irina and gave them instructions in broken Russian. "Hands overhead. Move to hill side of road. Walk twenty paces past the tan sedan. Face the bank. Don't try anything stupid. If you do, I shoot the girl."

They complied. There was nothing else they could do. With their hands in the air, they crossed the road and walked past the vehicle behind them. Two of the armed men stayed ten steps behind them with pistols trained on them. When they turned and faced the dirt and rocks, Irina's heart palpitated wildly. What was going to happen? Were they going to die? If that was the case, her family would never know where she was or what had happened to her. And she would never look in Blake's eyes again.

His head slightly turned, Tony watched out of the corner of his eye as three of the men pushed the tan sedan over the edge of the road. With a series of awful crunching sounds, it careened and tumbled its way down the hill before coming to rest with a mighty crash.

"Don't move until we're gone," one of the gunmen barked. Then the thugs walked backward, keeping their weapons pointed at them. When they reached the nearest Mercedes, they jumped in, and the black sedans sped away. The whine of the engines being revved at high rpm in low gears slowly faded in the distance, then disappeared.

Irina's first reaction was relief. They were safe. But dejection quickly gained the upper hand. They were exposed to the elements in harsh weather. It was 34 degrees Fahrenheit, and the wind was blowing about 25 mph. They were wearing light jackets, not parkas. She was shivering. They had no transportation. And worst of all, they had no sensors.

Her negative reflections were interrupted. "We need to get moving right now!" Andy insisted. "We don't want to be here when those guys decide to come back." He turned and started running down the road toward the old plant at a hefty clip. Tony galloped after him. Irina kicked a stone and hustled after them.

A hundred yards up the road, breathing hard and legs tiring, she caught up to the boys. "Why would they … come back?" she wheezed out.

"I'll explain later," Andy replied.

"Why this … direction?"

"One, it's unexpected. Two, cover and concealment. Three, high ground. Four, the first three buy us time to come up with a better plan."

"Unexpected?"

"They probably expect us to head back to town for security and warmth."

At the first big draw, Andy headed uphill, geared down to a trot, raised his arms to protect his face, and vanished in the thick brush near the wash. Several hundred feet up the draw, sufficiently hidden from the road, he stopped for a quick breather. "Where's Irina?" he asked his brother.

Tony turned around. She was nowhere to be seen. He started to head back down the ravine. Andy grabbed his arm. Tony looked at his brother dumbfounded. Andy cupped his ear. He nodded and cocked his head downhill. But all he could hear was his own heavy breathing and pounding heart.

Below them, Irina was struggling. She was sucking wind hard, her heart was pounding, she felt light-headed, and her legs were quivering like jelly. She stumbled, went down hard on her hands and knees, struggled back up to her feet, and leaned against a juniper. *Never been half this tired in all my life.* On the verge of panic, she scanned ahead for Tony. She had lost sight of him shortly after they had left the road. But there was no sign of him.

She closed her eyes in distress. Thoughts of sitting down and quitting circled in her mind like vultures. But from the inner depths, advice she had received as a young girl from her grandfather percolated up to her conscious mind. She had wanted to quit classical piano because she had hit a wall and felt like she wasn't improving. He had sat down next to her on the sofa, put his arm around her, and encouraged her. One line stood out. *No life skill is more important than the habit of never quitting just because the going gets tough.*

She steeled herself, let go of the tree, and started walking again. *Just gotta keep moving ... up the draw ... till I find the guys ... or they find me.*

Snap! Tony looked to Andy. He nodded back. He had heard it too. Someone had stepped on or grabbed a dry branch in the brush below. Tony wanted to whistle but didn't dare. If the thugs were back and looking for them, any sound that carried could be a fatal mistake.

A minute later Irina stumbled into view, tottered a few more steps, and crashed to her knees. When she looked up to investigate the sound of sliding footsteps approaching from above, she saw Tony reaching out his hand. He raised her to her feet. "Got to keep moving, Nikki. Why don't you take the lead? Just head for the top. Don't worry about finding the best route. Just keep us in cover as much as possible and keep moving. Set a pace that you can maintain."

A half hour later, they crested the ridge, dropped down the other side far enough that they weren't visible from any point on the road, and took a break on a large, flat rock. None of them had water to quench their thirst. But Irina pulled a granola bar out of her purse and broke it into three pieces.

While Andy slowly nibbled his piece, trying to make it last, she brought up her question again. "You still haven't explained to me why they might be coming after us. I'm having a hard time squaring that with the fact that they let us go."

"I think we were just swindled in an elaborate scheme."

"A scheme?"

"Yea. It looked to me like Hamasa pulled his punch when he hit Fyodor. And when Fyodor groaned and bent over, it was a hair too soon. I think the fight was choreographed."

"So you think Fyodor is involved in this?"

"More than involved. Try arranged. I'm guessing he thinks that he's getting short shrift from the pakhan and that he deserves more. So he decided to take advantage of some Americans, figuring they would have no recourse. He can report the sale to the pakhan, send him his share, and resell the sensors on the side for a tidy profit."

"But why go to the trouble of arranging something like this? Why not simply take the sensors from us on the way home?"

"Plausible deniability."

"Gotta admit. That's pretty brilliant. If we complain to his boss, he has a cover story and a bruise or two to back it up."

"Yep."

"Looking back with twenty-twenty hindsight, his sense of self-importance did raise red flags for me. But I didn't see things going in this direction. This reminds me of a remark my grandfather once made when talking about his experiences with officers in the Soviet Army. 'Intelligent men who overvalue themselves are always a liability and oftentimes treacherous.'"

"I've had similar thoughts, though not expressed half so well."

"Hey!" Tony sniped. "Hate to break up this deep philosophical discussion on the ins and outs of Fyodor's criminal mind, but we need to come up with a plan and get out of here."

"Got any ideas?" his brother replied.

"I think we should hug the backside of this ridge until it intersects the ridge behind the mill, follow that ridge to just above the mill, and scope things out. If the place looks safe, we can find cover and shelter there. Then we can figure out the next step."

"Sounds like a plan to me," Andy replied.

"We need to slow our pace, though" Tony added. "so we can dry out. Can't do that if we're humping so fast that we're adding more sweat to the problem. We stopped for less than five minutes, and I'm already shivering. I'm soaked to the bone."

Andy nodded his agreement and headed down the ridge.

Twenty minutes later, laying prone on the cold ground, concealed by brush that reminded them of sagebrush in the

American west, they surveyed the situation around the mill. It was six hundred yards as the crow flies to the nearest building, a gaunt hulk with most of its windows broken out. A quarter mile up the road from the mill, close to the ravine they had ascended, one of the black sedans was parked on the shoulder. Two men stood with arms raised to their head: one scanning the ridgeline, the other scanning the plains south of the road.

"Binoculars won't help if they're looking in the wrong places," Tony deadpanned.

Andy chuckled. "Bet they never figured that we might get this far in less than forty-five minutes."

"What's the third guy doing?" Irina whispered. "It looks like he's looking for something on the shoulder of the road."

"He's looking for something … our footprints. He lost the track. That's why he's gone back and forth a couple times. He'll soon figure out that we left the road."

The three men gathered in the middle of the road. The tracker gestured toward the ridge and then toward the draw. Then he headed up the draw at a quick pace. As soon as the three men were hidden from sight by the intervening hills and ridges, the boys stood up and bolted down the hill toward the mill. "Gonna have to put 'er in high gear," Tony advised.

His brother replied. "Yep. We got twenty minutes max before those guys reach the top of the ridge. Less if they seek a vantage point on the shoulder."

Irina trailed behind, struggling to keep up. Her knees and calves complained as her long bounding steps carried her down the slope, first angling to her right, then back to her left. Halfway down, her left foot landed on a loose rock. It tipped downhill, and fire burst forth in her ankle as ligaments and tendons were strained beyond limits. She was falling. Her right foot came down hard into the dirt, but too close to her center of gravity to keep her balance. She flew into a forked juniper. Her right shoulder exploded with pain as it glanced off one of the trunks. Snapping sounds echoed in her ears. Her head slammed into the dirt. She blacked out.

Tony was shaking her. Her head was ringing. Why were there two Tonys? He lifted her out of the crotch of the tree and helped her to her feet. Holding his arm, she made it down the final hundred yards of the steep slope without serious mishap.

Once they reached the gentler slope, the babysitting was over. "We'll go faster if we walk separately, Nikki, so you're on your own from here. Take the lead. Walk as fast as you can." Too tired to talk, she nodded and pushed her wobbly legs as hard as she could.

Well out in front of them, Andy disappeared down the steep drop that was behind the factory. When he reappeared, he was scampering across the rutted yard, weaving around the scrap iron, the trash, and the remnants of sand and gravel piles. Just as they reached the steep drop themselves, he scurried through a doorway close to the center of the building. Sensing the nearness of their goal, they plunged down the slope and trotted across the yard. A minute later, clutching their sides and breathing hard, they joined him inside the gaunt structure.

Andy gave them thirty seconds to catch their breath, then hastened off to their left. They followed him around machinery and piles of trash, then passed through a doorway into the next building, which was connected to the warehouse where their ordeal had started. He froze and held up a clenched fist, signaling his companions to stop moving and be silent.

A vehicle was approaching the other side of the building. Irina's heart raced in alarm. Tony pointed to the massive cement mixer in front of them, and they darted behind it. But it gave them no vantage point. They couldn't see what was going on. They crept to the side of the machine and stationed themselves behind the two large electrical panels that had once powered the unit. Peering through the narrow slot between them, they watched the partially open bay door.

The nose of a tan Land Rover appeared and stopped. A car door opened and closed. Footsteps crunched in the sand and gravel. The rear hatch opened and closed. More footsteps. Then a tall Englishman stepped through the opening. A camera was draped around his neck, and he held a tripod in one hand and an equipment bag in the other.

Irina stood up and started walking away from the safety of their hiding place, intending to accost the stranger. Andy and Tony looked at each other, but it was too late to stop her. They shrugged their shoulders and waited to see what would happen.

The man, who was busy setting up his tripod and camera, didn't see Irina walking across the open floor. Nor did he hear her. The wind whistling through the building masked the sound of her footfalls. When she slipped into his peripheral vision, he almost jumped out of his skin. She took a couple more steps to close the gap, and he took a couple steps backward to maintain it.

"Can you give us a ride back to Dushanbe?" she implored in a honeyed voice in English with a Russian accent.

As the photographer pondered the mysterious brunette and her odd request, her partners appeared from behind the machinery. His eyes darted from Irina to the other two and back again. "Perhaps. What happened to your car?"

"Our ride left us here," Irina replied, "after they robbed us."

He looked at her with raised eyebrows, obviously skeptical.

She offered her hand. "I'm Aleksandra Aksakova with Nebesa Smotret, a Russian astronomical organization. We were on a buying trip to buy Chinese-made sensors for our infrared telescope project in Siberia. The German- and American-made ones were beyond our budget. We didn't realize how shady our connection was until it was too late to back out. When the dust settled, we were out our money and the sensors."

She watched him, hoping to see a positive response. But he didn't respond. He just continued to eye them like a timid dog keeping his distance from an aggressive one. Irina, hoping to assuage his fears, reached into her purse, retrieved her Russian passport and driver's license, and handed them to him.

He examined her identification and handed it back. A

slight smile warmed his face, and he identified himself. "I'm Harry Wetherington from New Brighton, England, currently on assignment with National Geographic. I'm doing a story on the abandoned Soviet installations in Tajikistan, both military and industrial." As he spoke, he cast several uneasy glances at her companions.

Irina gestured toward the Backstrom boys. "This is Dmitriy Stepanychev and his brother Sergey. They are the security team that my company hired to protect me on my Tajikistan trip and while in the far-flung regions of Siberia."

"I see," he replied, relieved by her answer. Terrorism was on the upswing in the nation, and criminal violence against foreigners, especially those perceived as wealthy, was rising in Dushanbe. He moved forward again and continued setting up his camera, though his trembling hands were hindering the effort. "Can you wait for a couple of hours while I take photographs of the plant? I'll give you a ride back to Dushanbe when I'm done."

Irina grabbed him by the arm. "We can't stay here. The bad guys are looking for us. As we speak, they're scouring the ridge northwest of here, and if they happen to glass down here with their binocs and see your 4WD, you are in as much danger as we are."

The direness of the situation came into crystal-clear focus, and Harry waved them toward his SUV. While they jogged past him, he snapped two quick pictures of the rusting mixers, hastily broke down his equipment, and raced for his vehicle. As he turned the key, he asked, "Where to?"

Irina, who had taken the front passenger seat, replied,

"The Hotel Taj Palace, please."

Andy poked her and shook his head *no*.

"I changed my mind. Take us to the Hostel Doshan."

"Not familiar with that place."

"Take the Gazprom Neft exit off of Abuali Ibn Sino Avenue."

"Can do," he replied as he turned onto the access road.

Andy nudged Irina again, motioned the direction that they were headed on the road, and made a slicing motion across his neck.

She addressed Harry again. "Excuse me. Can you take a different route back to town?"

"An alternate route? You think the mafia guys are watching this road?"

"No doubt about it."

Harry shook his head and exhaled, realizing that this escapade was taking him deeper than he had anticipated. "Yeah, there's a road we can take." A couple hundred yards past the west end of the plant, he turned south. "This track passes an abandoned mining operation and continues to the northeast part of Dushanbe. It's rugged enough that a sedan can't follow us."

"That works for me," Irina replied.

Harry gave Irina a little side-eye. "You speak excellent English for a Russian."

"I did my graduate work in America. Mastered English pretty well. Never did get the American accent right, though." That actually was true.

He laughed. "There is no American accent. Just thirty

different ways to butcher the Queen's English."

The road curved sharply right as it began to climb a small ridge, allowing a view of the road behind them, which had been obscured by their dust cloud. Tony, speaking Russian, broke the bad news. "One of the Mercedes is following us!"

Irina and Andy whirled around. A black sedan was flying up the rutted track and gaining on them.

"If we don't step on it," Tony insisted, "they're gonna catch us."

"Not worried," Harry replied, shrugging his shoulders. "We'll lose them up ahead."

Despite his ambivalent answer, he pushed the pedal down hard. The vehicle lurched forward and bounced wildly across a stretch of boulders. Irina reached frantically for the grab handle, unnerved by the violent motions and the rocks battering the skid plate. She missed, tried again, and missed again. The road cut back sharply to the left, slamming her head against the door. Harry jumped on the brakes, yanked the wheel to the left, and accelerated up the steep, rocky incline. Irina rubbed her jaw. A crimson splotch on her hand arrested her attention. *Must have bit my lip.*

The Land Rover crested the ridge. A narrow valley sprawled out below them with a dry stream bed winding back and forth across the bottom. Harry gunned it downhill, spraying sand and gravel on the corners, taking advantage of the fact that the road was in better shape on this side.

Near the bottom of the descent, the track banked around a small shoulder, and the wash came into view. Irina gasped. The bridge had washed away, and its twisted remnants lie scattered downstream. To make matters worse, the rocky stream bed looked impossible to cross with a car. Her heart sank. They were trapped!

She looked over to Harry. He read the worry written on her face and flashed a wry smile. His reaction puzzled her. Why wasn't he nervous?

Harry locked up the brakes, stopping the vehicle in a cloud of dust, and dropped it into low range. "This Land Rover has seen worse," he said as he shifted into first gear. Then he juiced it, nosed down the embankment, and began the bone-jarring crawl across the boulder-strewn bed.

Near the halfway point, a ferocious bounce slammed their heads into the ceiling. "Mercedes no make here," Andy said, rubbing the swelling knob on his dome. Irina looked back and winked. He wasn't sure if she was laughing at his miserable effort to speak broken English with a Russian accent or whether she was appreciating it.

With a few lurches and bounces, the Land Rover climbed out of the streambed on the other side. Harry stopped and shifted back into high range.

"The Mercedes!" Tony yelled. Irina swiveled around. The black sedan was rounding the shoulder just above the bridge. Harry gunned it up the road. The Mercedes stopped at the dead end, and three men hopped out. They fired a half dozen shots after them, and then the Land Rover disappeared in the forested bottomland.

Irina winced as the weight of the moral dilemma descended on her conscience. *Hope they didn't get Harry's license plate. If they did, his days are numbered.*

Feeling less pressured after he put a ridge between them and their pursuers, Harry relaxed and slowed down. "I don't like it when my adrenalin goes up," he said, turning towards Irina. "It reminds me of being bullied in my school years in inner-city London." He paused and exhaled with his lips pursed. "At least these guys don't have a helicopter as the Chinese did when I was covering the comet story in Mongolia."

Irina turned to him and cocked her head. "Sounds like there's more to the story than made it to prime time news."

"Yeah. National Geographic and Downing Street were trying to avoid an international spectacle, so they silenced me and made me sign a confidentiality agreement. The truth is, two of the choppers at the impact site not only chased us away but followed us. When we were in the middle of a relatively flat area several kilometers later, they stopped us, interrogated us, and confiscated my camera and phone. Luckily, suspecting the worst, I had uploaded several audio files and several dozen pictures while we were on the run. And I had a spare phone and camera back at the ger."

For the next thirty-five minutes, Harry regaled Irina with tales of adventures in far-flung places like Siberia and Tibet. She wondered if this cultured Englishman—who loved assignments in the ruggedest, wildest regions in the world—might someday find himself covering end-of-the-world stories in the Middle East.

As the Land Rover sped across an intersection with a maintained road running east and west, Andy prodded Irina once again. "No go Dushanbe," he demanded. "Go Denau, Uzbekistan."

Harry jumped on the brakes, pulled over to the shoulder, and faced Irina. "I'm tired of this game!"

She pled her case. "Sergey thinks we should go to Denau instead. He says we won't be safe in Dushanbe. Even if the mafia can't track us down in town, they'll be waiting for us at the train station and the airport. They know that the train and the airport are our only options to get back to Moscow."

"You do realize, don't you, that Denau is two hours away?"

"I'm very sorry," she replied. He looked away from her pleading eyes. She leaned in, touched him on the shoulder, and whispered, "Please."

He glowered at her. She continued to plead with her eyes. The driver flinched first. "Buzzard breath! I might as well. This day is shot already." He slammed the vehicle into reverse, pushed the accelerator to the floor, spun dirt back to the main road, jammed on the brakes, spun the wheel around, slapped the shifter back into drive, and hammered the gas.

Irina leaned back in her seat and closed her eyes. *Thank you, Lord. You used the ravens to feed Elijah. You opened the windows of heaven for the inhabitants of Jerusalem. And you put a photographer in our path at just the right time. You are beyond amazing.*

At the border the young Uzbeki guard collected their passports and scrutinized them. Bewildered, he waved for his partner. The other guard, who looked like he was in his mid-thirties, trotted over, and the two conversed animatedly, ignoring the vehicles waiting to enter and exit the country.

After several minutes, the young man turned back around to Harry and pointed to a holding area off to the side. "Wait there," he said. Then he stuffed their passports into his coat pocket.

Harry's heart sank. This didn't look good. He wondered if he had made a serious mistake in agreeing to help his Russian passengers.

Irina turned away from his searching gaze and stared out her window, crushed with remorse. This was her fault. He was in trouble because of her. Yet when she replayed the past few hours, she could find no other viable option. They had been forced to turn to him for help. She swallowed hard. Then she prayed.

Ten minutes later, a smartly dressed officer drove up in a white Mercedes G-Class. After talking with his subordinates and examining their passports, he strolled over to the vehicle and questioned Harry.

"What is the purpose of your visit, sir?"

"We're going to Denau to enjoy some plov with lamb for dinner, then I'm going to drop them off at a hotel and return to my hotel in Dushanbe."

"We don't often see British citizens and Russian citizens traveling together."

"I suppose you don't."

"How did you meet your friends?"

"I met them while shooting pictures for a National Geographic article on the abandoned factories and military posts of the Soviet Union in the Dushanbe region."

"Why are they staying Denau?"

"They were in Dushanbe for business and found out they have a couple of days to kill. I told them they needed to see the bazaar in Denau."

"What is their business in Dushanbe?"

"Their company, Nebesa Smotret, is trying to obtain Chinese telescope parts for an observatory project in Siberia."

The gentleman smiled. "Dushanbe has become quite the hub for Europeans to access Chinese technology."

"Yes. I suppose it has."

"Would you like to make a small donation today to help our border guards promote safety in Central Asia? We keep businessmen safe so they can conduct their business without worry."

"How much is small?"

"Thirty thousand rubles."

Harry didn't have that much money on his person, much less in Russian rubles. He looked to Irina expectantly. She rolled her eyes, dug her emergency fund out of her purse, and counted out six of the orange five-thousand-ruble notes into Harry's hand, who handed them to the officer.

The gentleman smiled graciously, placed his right hand on his chest and made a slight, almost imperceptible bow. Then he waved the car on through.

"Baksheesh!" Irina grumbled as they pulled away. "Fleecing men for basic services that they are guaranteed by law."

"Welcome to Asia," Harry replied.

Forty-five minutes later, Harry parked in front of the Turon Hotel, and the Russia team climbed out of his Land

Rover. Irina started to walk toward the front door, then whirled around and knocked on his window. He rolled it down.

"As big as the Mongolian comet story was, a much bigger story is brewing. It dwarfs the four major impact events we have experienced in the past fifteen months."

He cocked his head and eyed her, wondering if she was going to push the half-baked Rogue story on him.

She was. "There really is trouble coming, and the US government along with the governments of many other nations are covering the story up. If you want real facts and not mere hype, search for 'hairy star + seven sisters' with a search engine like DuckDuckGo. Don't use any of the common search engines. They're completely on board with the government cover-up and the sorry explanation that Russian hackers are promoting upheaval in America and Europe. And they're blocking websites that attempt to share the facts with the public, labeling the story as an empty conspiracy theory."

Harry stared at her blankly, making her feel awkward. She ignored her feelings and continued. "Harry. Real scientists believe. If you do the search I mentioned, you will find material posted by legitimate scientists proving that there really is a massive comet headed for Mars and that it really does pose a serious threat to Earth. It is going to knock asteroids out of the main belt into elliptical orbits, and the collision between the comet and Mars could well knock one or both into elliptical orbits that will intersect with Earth's orbit."

Harry nodded politely, not sure what to make of the warning. He was of the opinion that the Rogue was bad fairy dust. "It would be a fascinating story to investigate. I see fascinating similarities between Rogue believers, Planet-X advocates, and Area-51 fanatics. But right now, I'm too busy to look into the matter. Maybe I'll find the time when I have finished this story on the decaying remnants of the Soviet Empire in Central Asia."

"Promise me that you will do the search I suggested and read the material it brings up—the material written by genuine scientists?"

He nodded. "Okay. Okay. I promise." He put the SUV into gear. "Nice chatting. But I have to go. I need to catch a bite to eat and get back to the border crossing before it closes."

Irina turned and walked inside, joined the boys in the lobby, and paid for two rooms with her Rosselkhozbank debit card.

Ten minutes later, the three sat around the table in Irina's room, drinking bottled green tea and revisiting the day's events.

"This day has been a total disaster," Irina complained, seething with frustration. "We blew through a ton of money and ended up with no sensors. And we probably won't get another opportunity to procure more."

The boys said nothing.

"Why did Fyodor doublecross us?" she stormed. "What did we do to him?"

"I don't think it had anything to do with us," Andy replied. "I think he got greedy, viewed us as easy targets, and figured he could double his money and get away with it."

"But wasn't that risky for him to mess with Russian citizens who are active Federal Security Service agents on special duty?"

"I think he suspected that we were Americans. I thought that the first night in the restaurant."

"I wondered about that too when he spoke to me in English. So you think we got played?"

"Exactly."

"But why did we come here instead of going back to our hotel in Dushanbe? They didn't know where our hotel was."

"I'm pretty sure they did. And if we had shown up, we would have discovered that our room had been ransacked for valuables and that the hotel was being staked out. They probably had a half dozen guys watching for us."

"But why would they be waiting for us? I never quite understood why they were chasing us. They got what they wanted. They got the money and the sensors."

"No, they didn't," he laughed. "They only got the money and one of the sensors."

Tony and Irina stared at him.

Chuckling, he reached up the right sleeve of his oversize wool sweater and pulled out the 4.75-micrometer sensor. Then he reached up his left sleeve and retrieved the 10-micrometer unit.

"What! So that's why they were after us?" Irina shrieked, breaking into laughter and tears at the same time.

"Yep. We outfoxed them."

"Well," Tony interjected, "you did at any rate."

Andy laughed. "I do get a good idea once in a while."

"But they came back so quickly," Tony responded. "They must have only been a few miles down the road when they figured out that two of the packages were empty."

"Yep. It would have been the killing fields if they had caught us."

"But how did you pull this off?" Irina asked.

"Fyodor made me nervous when we first met him, and the night at the restaurant only deepened my suspicions. I didn't know if he was plotting something against us or Li Qiang. At any rate, I decided to wear this baggy wool sweater just in case I needed to slip a sensor or two up my sleeve. When they showed up this morning, the way the driver was acting confirmed to me that something was up."

"But how … when … did you pilfer the sensors?"

"I slipped them up my sleeves while leaning over the briefcase, pretending to return them to their packages. I think Li Qiang's driver noticed what was going on. Just before he returned to his vehicle, he whispered to me, 'You are on your own.' I took that as a warning that he wasn't responsible for the consequences of my actions."

"But why wouldn't they say something to a regular business partner?"

"Perhaps Li Qiang hates Fyodor. Maybe Fyodor slighted him or one of his friends. Maybe he cheated them. I don't know. But their world is a dog eat dog world."

Irina leaned over and gave Andy a sisterly hug. "Well, no matter what the explanation is, God blessed, and it all worked out."

Tony slapped him on the back. "Sly dog. I wondered what was up with the ugly sweater. Not your normal style."

"No doubt."

"So what's your plan from here?" Tony inquired, changing the subject.

"I'm figuring we'll catch the train here in town super early in the morning. The station is just up the street."

"How early?"

"It arrives shortly before two o'clock and leaves at twenty minutes after."

"Another poor night of sleep."

"Yep. Looking that way."

"That gives us a few hours to kill," Irina observed. "So what are we going to do in the meantime?"

Andy replied, "I think we should run with Harry's cover story about a visit to the bazaar. We do need to pick up suitcases and clothes to replace what we left in the hotel. And we should pick up some food for the journey. Not sure I want to gamble on train food again."

"What have you got in mind?" she asked.

"I'm thinking crackers, cured meat and cheese, and some bottled water."

"I'll go along with that. And while we're out, we should snag a bite to eat at one of the restaurants."

"Food sounds like a plan," Tony replied. "I'm famished." Then a Cheshire grin stretched itself across his face.

Irina looked at him quizically. "That doesn't look like a food face."

"I was just thinking about the gangsters back in

Dushanbe. I wish I could see the look on their faces when we don't show up at the train station tonight."

She smirked. "Yeah. That would be a bomb to watch. Wonder what they'll do when we don't show."

"They'll likely suspect that we decided to lay low for the next train or two," Andy surmised. "So I wouldn't be surprised if they watch the train station several more times before they give up."

"Do you think they'll track us to Moscow?"

"Probably. But by the time they figure out that we skipped town and trace us back to Moscow, we will have already left town."

37

Moscow, Russia
Thursday, Jan. 16 to Friday, Jan.17, 2020

Irina faced the raging bull. Its head was down. Its nostrils were flared. Hot snot was dripping from its nose. The stadium reverberated with the blasts of the air horns that the blood-lusting crowd wielded, infuriating the bull even more. He pawed the dust, tossed his head with an angry snort, and charged. She screamed and reached for the top of the wall, trying to climb out of the arena. But her hand, despite her frantic efforts, couldn't find a handhold. She fell backward and tumbled to the ground. Before she could stand up, the bull was on her, pawing at her with his hoofs and hooking her with his horns.

But she wasn't feeling any pain. Her side, though, was vibrating or shaking or something. What was going on? And what was her pillow doing in the arena? The mists of dreamland began to clear, and she realized that she was in a bed. *Where am I?* A look around the room and out the window revealed that she was in their apartment in Moscow. What day was it? Her mind raced through the days of the week. *It's Thursday. We arrived back in town last night on the train from Denau.*

Heart still palpitating, she retrieved her phone, which was lodged against her side, sat up in bed, turned off the alarm, and checked the time. It was 7:03. Her alarm had been playing for three minutes. Too much sugar before bed didn't mix well with bull-fighting music for an alarm. Either the sugar or the alarm had to go. She laughed at herself. *Probably won't be the sugar.*

She stepped into her slippers, donned her robe, and headed for the shower, still feeling groggy. After breakfast—rye toast slathered with butter and Altay honey and a cup of coffee—Irina called Svetlana at Nebesa Smotret. It was a few minutes past eight.

"Nebesa Smotret. How may I help you?"

"Good morning, Svetlana. This is Aleksandra."

"Nice to hear from you. Are you back from your trip?"

"Yes. We arrived last night shortly after midnight. Did my mirror arrive?"

"Yes. It was delivered Tuesday morning and is sitting on the dock."

"Fantastic. I'll get my crew ready to load it on our truck."

An hour and a half later, the team disembarked from the Moscow Metro at the Krasnopresnenskaya station and made the short but chilly walk to their office building. Once they arrived, the boys hopped into their Ural 43206-41, a Russian military truck similar to an American deuce and a half, and Tony fired it up. They had been fortunate to find it. The beast had the 230 horsepower turbo-charged package instead of the standard 180 horsepower. Its oversized fuel tanks would allow them to travel 550 kilometers between fills. And its pedigree was almost too good to be true—assigned to a headquarters unit that rarely used it during a decade of service. The odometer was barely over 26,000 kilometers. The lack of dings on the body and the underside suggested that the salesman was telling the truth.

When the temperature gauge started moving, Tony drove the brawny rig out of the vehicle area and backed it up to the loading dock. Then the brothers surveyed the situation.

"The crate looks sturdy enough," Tony noted. "It should be able to handle anything it faces in its journey across Siberia, the North Pacific, and the Rockies."

"No doubt about that," Andy replied. "But how are we gonna move it? The thing is massive. Seven feet per side. Eighteen inches thick. Weighs over two thousand pounds."

"The forklift can handle it."

"Not too worried about lifting it. I'm worried about the fact that we need to stand it on edge for transport so we have room for our supplies and sleeping space in the back of the truck."

Tony grinned. "Just sit tight and let the pro handle it." He hopped on the ancient propane forklift, fired it up, and pushed the crate to the wall. Then he nosed the forks under the front edge of the crate and slowly raised them while inching his way forward.

Irina watched nervously. "Be gentle with my baby!"

He pretended to tip a cowboy hat. "Yes, ma'am."

The crate stood upright with a clatter a quarter inch from

the wall. Tony spun the forks around, drove over to a pile of pallets, stood seven of them on end on the forks, and secured them with a ratchet strap. Then he drove back to the mirror, snugged his makeshift spacer up against the crate, raised the forks a smidgeon, and crept backward. The mirror rocked. Irina gasped. Tony set the load back down gently and strapped the crate to the pallets. Then he picked his load up again.

Several feet shy of the truck bed, he set the mirror down and scratched his head. "Looks like the canopy is a good six inches short," he called out to Andy. "We're gonna have to raise the arches."

When they had raised the arch legs as high as they could in the stake pockets, which was about eight inches, Tony hopped back on the forklift, raised the crate, and crept forward to test the clearance. They were relieved when the top of the crate cleared the first arch by an inch. He continued creeping forward until his front tires ran up against the back of the truck bed.

Irina watched, puzzled. "How are you guys gonna get the crate all the way to the back? You still have at least seven feet to go, and you can't drive the forklift into the back of the truck. The bed is eight or ten inches too high.

Tony winked at her. "You can unplug your worry unit, Nikki. The experts have everything under control."

The guys stacked a pile of pallets behind the crate for balance and another in front of it for pushing. Tony hopped on the forklift, touched his forks to the bottom of the front pile, and nudged forward until his tires stopped at the truck bed. Then the boys unstacked the rear pile and stacked a second pile in front of the crate. Another round of gentle nudging with the forks pushed the crate against the headboard with a comforting thwump.

Irina got the goosebumps. *Sometimes their ingenuity amazes me.* While the guys were admiring their work, Irina sidled up, glowing with satisfaction. But her expression soured when she noticed blood dripping from Tony's hand. She grabbed his arm and yanked it up for a closer look. "You kept working with an inch and a half sliver in your palm? What's wrong with you! You and your brother ... unbelievable ... too much macho, not enough brains."

He grinned. "A man's gotta do what a man's gotta do."

She tugged him by his arm toward the building entrance. "Come on, big guy. Let's take a coffee break and get this attended to."

"You're just using my hand as an excuse to get out of the cold."

She rolled her eyes. It was hard not to love them. But their boyish banter did get under her skin sometimes.

The boys reluctantly followed her. They were antsy to finish the project.

Forty-five minutes later, the crew was back on the dock. The guys ferried load upon load from their storage cage and stowed them in the back of the truck: folding cots, sleeping bags, foam sleeping pads, blankets, winter clothes; crates of spare truck parts like belts, filters, lightbulbs, and wipers; four spare tires, two spare batteries, boxes of oil and radiator fluid, twenty jerry cans of diesel, three cases of anti-gel; snow shovels, ice spud, axe, chains, winch, blowtorch with a case of one-litre bottles of propane; propane stove, propane heater, propane fridge, ten twenty-kilogram tanks of propane. Their food and clothing were stored in wooden crates that doubled as tables and chairs.

Irina watched the guys find places for the last load of boxes and blankets, impressed with the thoroughness of their preparation and giddy with excitement over their departure in the morning. Everything had come together. Finding the right truck. Getting the truck inspected and outfitted by a local mechanic. Obtaining and loading the mirror. Obtaining and loading equipment and supplies.

"Hey, guys. Let's go back to the apartment and celebrate our last night in Moscow."

"I'm ready to celebrate," Tony replied as he poked at his hand. "I'm ready to be done with Moscow. I've had enough city and enough shopping to last a lifetime."

Andy nodded in agreement. "I'm tracking with you. Shopping is no picnic."

"What are you cooking for dinner?" Tony asked.

"How about that potato soup with sausage that you like so much? I can whip up something yummy for dessert, too … like medovik."

"Medovik?"

"It's a layered honey cake."

"Any dessert with honey in it sounds good to me."

"Does your owie still hurt?" Andy asked.

Tony looked over to his brother and feigned serious pain. "Do you feel like driving the first few days, bro? I think I'm crippled."

Andy laughed. "Man up, wuss!"

Irina walked away. *Boys and their banter.*

Several hours later, after the boys had stuffed themselves with potato soup, Irina set three slices of medovik on the table, poured three cups of coffee, and the team sat down to catch the world news on Andy's laptop.

"Good evening. Greetings from chilly Moscow. I'm Dmitry Stepanovich, and this is Channel One evening news."

Tony leaned over, placed his finger on the touchpad, and added English captions to the broadcast. Irina frowned. "The guy speaks way too fast for me," he apologized sheepishly. She rolled her eyes and turned her attention back to the screen.

The broadcaster began with coverage of the latest Russian and European news. The team only half-listened, focusing instead on the delicious dessert. They were waiting for news that more directly affected them, especially news on America and the Middle East.

"Stay tuned. After this advertising break, we'll continue with our investigation into America's provocative bunker program."

Several commercials later, he was back. "We received reports this week from our undercover investigators in the U.S. that the American government has recently begun construction on two more Cheyenne-Mountain-class underground bunkers: one in the Cascade Mountains near Seattle, Washington and the other in the Santa Cruz Mountains near Palo Alto, California. This brings the total to twelve Cheyenne-Mountain-class underground bunkers that are being built on top of the two that already exist: Cheyenne Mountain itself and the Raven Rock Mountain Complex.

"Another report, based on information gained from an inside source involved in the project, indicates that when the Cheyenne Mountain expansion is completed, the complex will be able to house over 100,000 people. It will be a fully functional city spread over a hundred floors capable of operating for three years cut off from any contact with the outside world. The aim isn't mere survival. There will be movie theatres, gymnasiums, swimming pools, tennis courts, and salons." He sneered. "Another outrageous example of American waste and softness.

"The same source provided a list of thousands of tech and industry leaders, scientists, educators, billionaires, movie stars, musicians, and artists who have been invited to ride out any existential catastrophe within the safety of this ark. The American government, of course, denies this report as fake news dreamed up by delusional conspiracy theorists.

"The massive complexes, however, are just the tip of the iceberg. Homeland Security has been tasked by the Homeland Security Act to ensure that every city and county in the country provides shelter, food, and water for their citizens for two months in the face of disaster. On top of that, sports arenas and event venues are required to supply shelter, either on-site or underneath nearby buildings, for their stated capacity. Homeland Security is currently overseeing the construction of thousands of emergency shelters across America with capacities ranging from one hundred to thousands. In urban areas the larger shelters are often connected by underground passageways.

"Now the American government claims that these shelters have no purpose beyond protecting their citizens from natural disasters and radical terrorists armed with weapons of mass destruction. They appeal to the recent Port Arthur tragedy as a vindication of this claim. But the Kremlin is skeptical. For one thing, there's a substantial body of evidence that Port Arthur was a false flag operation. For another thing, if it's true that they're merely worried about terrorism with smaller nuclear weapons, why are they building a dozen Cheyenne-Mountain-class facilities? Isn't this a bit of an overkill? And why require thousands of small communities that face practically zero chance of terrorism to prepare for terrorism?

"The blunt truth is, their large-scale efforts look like preparation for nuclear war. And if they're preparing for such a war, who are they preparing for war with? Moscow fears it can only be Russia. We are, by a significant margin, their primary geopolitical nemesis. But what are the Americans thinking? Do they fear that we're going to attack them? That's laughable. Why would we start a war which we can't win—indeed which no one can win? The only logical conclusion is that they're preparing for a war with us in which they intend to strike first. This is the view that's circulating in the Kremlin. The Russian government fears that America is planning to launch an attack as soon as her shelter program is completed and her Next Generation Interceptor defense shield is up and running.

"The liberals claim that this fear is far-fetched. But is it? For years now, American politicians and media pundits have criticized Russia with Red-phobic rhetoric over her supposed expansionist ambitions and her unreasonably harsh stance against terrorism. And they have warned Russia that there would be serious repercussions if she did not toe the line on Western demands. The fact is, America is already waging asymmetric warfare against us with harsh measures in the financial and energy markets and with sophisticated hacker squads which are jointly sponsored by the NSA and the CIA. They are crippling our economy so we cannot keep pace with them in the arms race. And when they think that we're weak enough, they will strike.

"Thankfully, our government is making tremendous strides in response to the American threat. Such next-generation weaponry as the Avangard hypersonic glide vehicle, the Kinzhal hypersonic missile, and the Peresvet laser combat system will give us a distinct technological advantage if America goes through with the madness of precipitating a nuclear war. We will stop the vast majority of their missiles, and they will not be able to stop ours."

Andy scoffed. "There's a lot of hype and hot air in their claims of tactical advantage. The truth is, their new systems are still largely unproven and years away from implementation, and when American missiles sneak through their over-hyped missile-defense system, the Kremlin and the Moscow elite will have ready access to the Metro-2, but the population at large will have nowhere to hide except unstocked Cold-War-era fallout shelters, which can probably only hold ten percent of the population."

"What's the Metro-2?" Irina asked, looking at him.

"A secret, deep-underground subway system that leads from the Kremlin and several elite neighborhoods to a series of secret bunkers deep under the suburbs of Moscow."

Irina shook her head. "They probably will have to use their fancy bunker system, but it won't be because America has launched dozens of nukes at them."

"You got that right," Tony responded. "It'll be the aftermath of the Rogue—asteroids and planets running amok."

"And the swarm of long-period comets that's coming."

They returned their attention to the broadcast when they heard Dmitry say something about another American development that had broad geopolitical ramifications.

"America's schoolyard bullying of the world, including her allies, makes my blood boil. Her actions are nothing short of shameless hypocrisy. I am deeply disturbed that the U.S. government complains constantly about Russia's supposedly heavy-handed foreign policy, yet they're guilty of far worse in their dealings with anyone who poses a threat to their self-centered vision of geopolitical order and stability.

"Take, for instance, their recent response to the act of terrorism at Port Arthur. Though that attack only involved a small handful of extremist individuals from Saudi Arabia, Egypt, and the UAE, the United States has chosen to vent its wrath against these nations with an ultimatum. They must quickly and summarily deal with extremism within their borders or suffer serious consequences—no access to America's capital markets, no military or economic aid from the U.S., no trade with the U.S., no American tourists, no airline flights to or from the U.S., and no visas to the U.S.

"With their backs to the wall, and no realistic alternatives, these countries have undertaken a bloody purge of suspected extremists. Had they failed to meet America's demands, they would face the twin devils of financial devastation and political isolation, leaving them to face off alone against their adversaries Iran and Turkey.

"In Saudi Arabia alone, over one hundred were beheaded this week and hundreds more were arrested. In Egypt similar numbers were executed by firing squad. The entire Middle East is in an uproar. Riots have broken out in many major cities, including the normally placid Riyadh. God help the situation.

"My fellow Russians … citizens of the world … take stock of this situation. Don't be deceived by America and her empty promises of goodwill. This is how the self-professed leader of the free world treats her allies."

Tony slammed his hand on the table. "America certainly has her shortcomings, but Russia's expansionism and hypocrisy bother me far more than any of America's problems."

Andy stroked his chin, deep in thought. "Yeah. Me too. But I'm thinking this goes deeper than a comparison of the virtues of America and Russia."

Tony looked at him. "How's that?"

"What if this drove a wedge between the U.S. and Saudi Arabia? That could open the door for Riyadh to become involved in the Psalm 83 War. Dad has always insisted that they would be part of it."

"Yeah, I could see that. If push came to shove, and the house of Saud had to choose between America and her regional allies, it's not too much of a stretch to see her side with her neighbors for an attack on Israel. After all, she values her reputation in the Muslim world as the champion of the faith more than she does her relationship with the United States. Besides, she has the oil ace up her sleeve. No matter what America's short-term bluster is, Riyadh would expect her to ultimately turn a blind eye to Saudi involvement in such an invasion."

"But honestly, I don't think the White House should worry about how the Saudis respond to this crackdown. We ought to crack down not only on terrorism but on the nations that harbor terrorists. It has to be done. Nobody else is going to do it."

Irina turned from the window—and the snowflakes drifting lazily toward the ground—and shook her head. "Wake up, guys. America isn't the good guys in this movie."

They looked at her, puzzled.

"Regardless of how the current situation shakes out, the United States, ultimately, is going to be on the wrong side of God and Israel. All the kingdoms of the earth are going to be gathered against God and Israel at Armageddon."

The boys shifted in their seats. They got uncomfortable whenever Irina spoke too directly about the Bible. Tony changed the subject. "Speaking of being on the wrong side of things, we're on the wrong side of Russia, and we're leaving early tomorrow morning for the right side. Let's wrap his evening up and hit the hay."

***

Irina tossed her two duffel bags of clothes and personal items into the back of the truck. Andy stacked them out of the way with the rest of their gear. "Are there any more bags or boxes coming?" he asked.

"Nope. That's it. The last two."

"Faaantaaaastik. We're running out of space back here."

"Is everything stowed away and secure?" she hollered over the din of the rumbling diesel engine.

"Yep," he replied.

"Then let's roll!"

"Amen to that!" he replied as he hopped out. "Nothing left to do except cinch the tarp ropes down so they don't flap in the wind."

She jumped down off the loading dock, walked to the front of the truck, tossed her purse and their lunch bag onto the floor of the 6X6 near the console, then climbed in and took her place in the middle. Tony was reviewing the gauges and switches on the dash one more time. Russian still seemed awkward to him when he got nervous.

Andy finished his last slip knot on the three ropes holding down the tarp on the back, jogged around to the passenger door, climbed in, grinned at his brother, and gave him a thumbs up. Tony dropped the truck into low, and the heavy unit lurched forward. He found second gear and turned down the wide alley.

Irina checked her watch. It was 5:58, Friday, January 17. "Praise the Lord!" she announced. "Two minutes ahead of schedule. If the weather permits and the roads are in decent shape, we should make it to Madagan in twenty days. That would put us there on Saturday, February 8."

"I'm not gonna hold my breath for good weather in Siberia," Tony countered. "As I said last night, I'm inclined to add fourteen days to our estimation of the trip length."

Irina said nothing. She knew he was probably right, but still, his negativity was hard to bear.

After they had driven a couple minutes in silence, Andy attempted to thaw things out. "Can you pour me a cup of coffee, Nikita?"

"We should wait until we get out of the city," she replied. "This old beast is a rough ride, and it doesn't have coffee cup holders."

"You're probably right. We definitely don't want to spill any of the coffee. It's gonna be hard enough making the two thermoses last. Wish I had thought about installing coffee cup holders. The Russians are even less concerned than the Americans when it comes to comfort and convenience in their military vehicles."

Tony chuckled. "That's one area where the Russians really have passed us up in the arms race."

The boys shared a hearty belly laugh, and Irina laughed with them until her sides ached, though it was more from the contagion of their laughter than from appreciating their humor.

38

Atchafalaya Swamp, Louisiana
Saturday, January 18, 2020

After dinner, Burt hustled up to his attic hideout to fetch his multiband radio so they could listen to the evening news. He set the unit on the counter and tuned in K279AL, the local Christian station. A few minutes into Matt McCoy's coverage of the local news, in the middle of a notice on the local FFA chapter's annual banquet, the program was interrupted by the grating squawk of an Emergency Alert. "At 4:30 p.m. Eastern Standard Time today, the White House lifted the national emergency notice and issued a national heightened-threat notice. Please listen to the following updates.

"Travel restriction update. The ban on travel to, from, and within the twenty-mile restriction zone around the blast area has been lifted, and a restricted-travel notice issued. Commercial traffic, commuters, and family members will be allowed access into and out of the zone. Sightseers will be turned away. Be advised, heightened security measures are still in place and will be enforced. All vehicles will be screened.

"Travel restriction update. The ban on travel within the five-mile restriction zone around the blast area has not been lifted. Entry will be denied for all unauthorized individuals and vehicles. Many areas have dangerously high levels of radiation. Select neighborhoods in the northern portion that are more than three miles from ground zero may be opened in the coming weeks as government officials certify that they're free of dangerous levels of radiation.

"Travel restriction update. All bus, train, light-rail, and subway services have been reopened. Most commercial airlines have resumed service, though flights to and from some nations are either banned or restricted. Most private flights are still banned as the government labors to establish protocols that will safeguard our nation from the threat of private aircraft used for terrorist purposes. Contact your local airport for further information. Be aware that heightened security measures are still in place for all public transportation. You will face delays. Plan your travel accordingly.

"Travel restriction update. As of 9 a.m. Eastern Standard Time this morning, the travel restriction on Federal, state, and local roadways is lifted. Be advised, however, that a national heightened-threat notice is in effect and that random checkpoints will be operated across the entire spectrum of federal, state, and local roads. Be prepared to stop. Make sure that you have all the necessary ID on your person.

"Cellular service update. As of 4:30 p.m. Eastern Standard Time this afternoon, cellular service has been reactivated in ninety-eight percent of the country.

"Military demobilization notice. All active-duty military units not already demobilized will begin demobilization. All units deployed in Homeland Security operations are relieved of duty and will return to their normal duty stations.

"Reserve and National Guard activation update. The White House has revoked the one-hundred-percent activation order and invoked a twenty-five-percent activation order. Units retained will continue with Homeland Security missions including checkpoint duty, FEMA duty, border duty, and assignments with federal and state agencies. Units will serve on three-month rotations until further notice. Check with your unit for information about duty status.

"This is the end of this Emergency Alert System bulletin. It will be repeated once per hour."

The local announcer, Matt McCoy, returned to the air. "Our station manager has decided to delay our normal programming for a few more minutes to bring you a special message from Brett Murphy, an affiliation correspondent who has been traveling across the country for the past two weeks, attempting to gauge America's response to this tragedy. Currently, he's in Tulsa, Oklahoma. Brett, what are you seeing? What are you hearing?"

"Matt, Port Arthur has changed this country. We no longer live in a post-9-11 America, but a post-Port-Arthur America. All across the nation patriots are flying the Red-White-and-Blue and the Gadsen flag. Americans from both sides of the political aisle are once again united against the radicals and terrorists that threaten this freedom-loving nation. Everywhere I go, I see broad support for our military, our law enforcement agencies, and our emergency services. There's a groundswell of gratitude for all who serve."

"That's wonderful news. Thanks for the report, Brett."

"My pleasure. God bless America!"

Matt continued with the theme of thankfulness. "We here in Baton Rouge, indeed all of southern Louisiana, join the rest of America in extending a hearty thank you to all the military and law enforcement personnel who secured our nation's roads, hunted down terrorists, and foiled terrorist threats. Their hard work for the past two weeks in the greatest dragnet in history resulted in the arrest of more than five thousand terrorists and secured our land so we can return to blessings we take for granted, such as using our cell phones and driving on our road system without sitting at checkpoints. Wow! Two weeks was a long time to go without a cell phone.

"We also want to thank all the emergency service personnel who responded to the Port Arthur tragedy or otherwise assisted in the events of the past two weeks." He rattled on in the same vein for a few more minutes, then closed with a hearty, "God bless America!"

Ariele's secure phone vibrated on the table. When she picked it up and put it to her ear, Burt turned the radio off. "Hi. Orange Stimulator here."

"Hey Moxie, good to hear your voice."

"Woodie! Nice to hear yours too. It's been a long time!"

"Yes, it has. But I'm gonna skip the small talk and cut straight to the chase. What are your plans for returning to the Compound?"

"As of right now, nothing firm. We'll probably give the roads a few days to clear the backlogged traffic, then head home."

"We need to come up with an alternative plan to get you two back. There are random checkpoints all over the country, even on county roads. The odds of you getting back without being stopped are almost zero. Jordy also picked up some chatter on the *Rogue Runners* bulletin board and several alternate news sites that thousands of cameras were installed on federal and state highways in the past two weeks."

"That doesn't sound good. So what are you thinking?"

"I'm thinking that we should have Blake and Andrius drive down with the Backstrom boys' F-250. They would pick up Blake's truck, then pick you girls up. Andrius would drive Blake's vehicle back, and Blake would bring you girls back to Montana in the Backstrom's camper. It's a larger unit with a secret hiding space under the sleeper over the cab that you can use at checkpoints and during traffic stops. It's only twelve inches deep and cramped. But it's hard to notice."

"Sounds like a workable plan to me."

"Talk things over with Rat about a departure date that works for him, and get back to me."

"Before you go, what do you make of America's response to the Port Arthur event?"

"While I feel a twinge of patriotic pride, for I am an American, I don't like it. I think Jordy is right that this is going to morph into an aggressive response to everything that can be labeled radicalism. The government is going to pressure radical Islam, but it's also going to put serious pressure on evangelicals, conservatives, patriots, preppers, and conspiracy folks. We're about to go from the frying pan into the fire."

"So you think this is part of the stage setting for the last days?"

"I'm afraid so. Hey, I gotta run, Mox. Have other calls to make. Take care. Hi to Sam and Burt. Hi to Rat and Peg."

Ariele turned to Rat. "Woody wants to have Blake and Andrius meet us at the Tupelo Inn. Andrius would take Blake's truck back, and Sam and I would ride in the Backstrom's camper which Blake would be driving. This would give us fast access to a concealed compartment if we needed it. But he wants you to give him a date when we can meet them at the inn."

"Hate to break the bad news to you, Moxie. But if we aren't going to meet your ride in the next two days, then we're going to have to look at a departure maybe three weeks in the future."

Ariele's lower lip started to quiver, and her eyes misted with tears.

"I'm sorry," he responded. "But I have two Underground missions that are going to tie me up for at least two weeks. I won't even be canoeing in the right direction. I'll be headed to another part of the swamp and exiting on the east side."

Sam's curiosity was piqued. "So what kind of mission? Another astronomer or some media personality hiding out in a secret location? Running medicine? Groceries?"

"Sorry girls. Both of the missions are top secret. I'm not allowed to mention names or places or what I'm doing. The government is starting to play very rough with those they accuse of soft terrorism. If you were ever tortured, you might spit out a name or two that would lead to harm for someone. I have to protect those I serve and those I serve with."

"No worries, bro," Sam replied. "I understand. Been there, done that myself."

The crestfallen girls got up, donned their coats and hats, filled their mugs with Cajun coffee, grabbed a bowl of pecan sandies, and retreated to the porch. There they listened to the songs of the evening birds, gazed at the stars in the moonless sky, and tried to ease their discouragement at yet another unfavorable turn of events. A lump rose in Ariele's throat. There was nothing she could do but wait. *Lot of waiting in the Bible*, she mused. *Men waiting on God for his time. Easier to read about it, though, than submit to it.*

39

**Lake Baikal, Russia
Sunday, February 2, 2020**

"Another beautiful day in paradise," Tony complained. "Forty-five degrees below zero, and the wind is whipping twenty to thirty miles per hour."

Andy tried to be positive. "Look at the bright side. It sure makes you thankful for hot coffee and shelter from the wind."

His brother didn't reply. He just grabbed a couple more Hazelnut Sormovskoe cookies from the package on Irina's lap and stuffed one in his mouth. While he was chewing it up, a cloud of steam exploded out the front of the truck, slammed against the windshield, and frosted it up. "Rotten frog farts!" he hollered as he jumped on the brakes. "Perfect time for a busted water pump!"

Andy cranked his window down, stuck his head out, and called out directions, trying to help his brother stay on the road. "Steer left! ... Doing good ... Little more left! ... Hold 'er."

Irina plugged the portable windshield heater into the

cigarette lighter and aimed it in front of the steering wheel. The small unit struggled to clear an eight-inch patch, and Tony could barely discern the road in front of them. But with Andy's directions, he managed to drive a half kilometer up the road and steer onto a wide shoulder, where he could safely shut the truck down. He sat rigid for a moment, then huffed in frustration and pounded the steering wheel a few times.

"You okay, bro?" Irina inquired.

Andy nudged her in the ribs, shook his head almost imperceptibly, and grabbed a handful of cookies. She got the message. Tony needed a minute to gather himself.

Tony said nothing for a half minute, then asked, "How far are we from anywhere?"

"We've been driving for nearly an hour," Irina replied. "So we're about halfway between Nizheudinsk and Tulun."

He shook his head in frustration, pulled on his coat and gloves, and jumped out of the truck. While he popped the hood and took a look at the situation, Andy fetched the spare water pump from the back of the truck along with the tool kit and propane heater. "Where do you want the heater, boss?"

"To the side of the air filter. Angling down toward the pump will work just fine."

Andy propped it in among the hoses.

"Angle it a little bit more downward."

Andy tipped it a hair more. "How's that?"

"That'll work. Got it blowing right on my hands. Next, I'll need a windbreak. I doubt I can last one minute in this weather with my gloves off."

Andy trudged back to the rear, grabbed a canvas tarp, and lugged it to the front. The two of them draped it over the raised hood, tied two corners to the frame behind the front tires, and pulled the rest forward until it draped nearly to the ground. While it blocked most of the wind, it also made a terrible racket as the wind whipped it back and forth. And it blocked the feeble sunlight. The boys were standing in near dark.

"Thanks, bro. Now I'm gonna need a light."

Andy ducked under the tarp, then reappeared thirty seconds later with a battery-powered lantern, which he set on the air filter. "Voila! Let there be light!"

Tony smiled, opened the cock valve on the bottom of the radiator, and let the coolant drain. "Don't let the EPA know."

Andy cracked a grin. It was good to see his brother indulge a little humor. The moodiness he had been indulging lately bothered him.

While the yellowish-green stream splashed into the snow, Tony loosened the alternator, removed the belt and fan, and disconnected the hoses from the pump. When the flow slowed to a trickle, he put his socket wrench on the first bolt and hesitated. "Hopefully it's not corroded!" he grumped. "It would be a nightmare if it snapped off inside the block." Andy didn't reply. He didn't want to add to his brother's discouragement, and there was nothing he could say at this point that would encourage him. Tony reefed on the bolt. It resisted for a moment, then popped loose and turned out easily. The tension in his jaw relaxed slightly.

He set the bolt on top of the air filter cover and wrenched on the second. To his relief, it also came out easily. But he fumbled when he tried to twist the last bit out with his stiff fingers and remove it. Andy nudged him aside, extracted the bolt, and placed it next to the first. Tony struggled a little harder to break the last two bolts loose, but once they started, they also turned out freely.

Andy stowed the final bolt, and Tony placed his numb fingers in front of the heater and bowed his head slightly, trying to hide the pain on his face from the sting of cold fingers warming up. After a minute, he picked up the scraper and went after the gasket. Three-quarters of it peeled off with a few awkward swipes. But several stretches resisted his efforts. Tony attacked the remnants with a vengeance, skinning his knuckles twice in the process. When the last piece flaked off, he once again warmed his hands, wincing in discomfort.

After less than a minute, he pulled his hands away and turned to his brother. "Gimme the gasket." Andy retrieved the package from his beltline, where he had stored it to keep it supple, tore the plastic with his teeth, and handed the fragile ring to his brother. Tony smeared a little coolant on the backside to help it stick to the metal and set it in place. Then he held the new water pump in place while Andy started the bolts by hand. When the last was ready, he stepped out of the way, and Tony turned the bolts in and cranked them as tight as he dared.

When he set his wrench down after the final one, he didn't stop to warm his hands again. Instead, he unscrewed the lid on one of the antifreeze jugs and proceeded to fill the radiator. By the time he was topping off the reservoir with the third jug, he could barely maintain a grip on the container. The liquid, which was the same temperature as the air, had chilled his hands to the point of near frostbite. When the last of the liquid chugged out, he let the jug slip to the ground and snapped the cap on the reservoir.

With tears in his eyes, he held his hands as close to the heater as he dared, grimacing at the fire in his frost-nipped hands. Andy let him warm his frozen members for a minute, then grabbed his shoulders and steered him toward the truck. "You've been out here with bare hands for twenty minutes. We need to get you in the cab and get you warmed up."

He helped him climb into the driver seat, fired up the truck, and turned to Irina. "Aim the portable windshield heater at his hands until the regular heater kicks in full blast. I've got to stow the tools and tarp and close the hood."

A few minutes later, he climbed into the passenger seat, turned to Tony, and gave him a thumbs up. "Ready to roll boss!"

Tony, his hands practically glued to the portable windshield heater, managed a feeble grin, pointed to the windshield, and gave him a thumbs down. "Not quite. It's your turn to play the hero. You need to wash the antifreeze off the glass, or I won't be able to see the road."

***

"But wouldn't it be awesome," Irina pleaded, "to eat breakfast while we watched the sunrise over Lake Baikal?"

Andy shrugged his shoulders. "Not particularly. A lake is a lake, right? I've seen plenty of lakes in my life."

Irina pressed her point. "Come on, guys. This is a once-in-a-lifetime chance to see Lake Baikal. Will you ever be in Siberia again?"

"No matter how cool it is," he complained, "I don't see how it's worth the extra hours of driving after an already long and ugly day. I think we should stick with the plan we made last night and stop in Irkutsk."

She turned to Tony. "What do you think?"

He said nothing. He hated arguing with Irina. It was always a fight to the death.

"Please," she pleaded sweetly.

He puffed his cheeks out and exhaled slowly, an expression of resignation which Irina did not miss. "Oh, I dunno. Whatever. I guess we can go a little farther."

But the strong-willed brunette felt no joy when she got her way. The poor guy had braved the biting cold for twenty-five minutes this morning while changing the water pump and hadn't warmed up since then. Now she was asking him to delay his hot shower and hot meal?

Irina bit her lip. *How can I stop myself from being this way?* A quote from Pastor Vargas came to mind—"Selfishness is a dragon with ninety-nine lives. You'll slay the beast dozens of times before it rears its ugly head for the last time." That was certainly her experience. She cradled her travel mug, tried to focus on the rugged beauty of the taiga, and hoped the tears wouldn't flow.

Three hours after the boys had glumly watched the last

Irkutsk exit disappear in their side-view mirrors at sunset, the words "Guest House Baikalskiy Rai" flashed in the glare of the headlights. Tony jumped on the brakes and jerked the truck onto the access road. They hit the embankment on the uphill side, bounced off, skidded toward the drop off on the downhill side, then fishtailed several times. After regaining control of the vehicle, Tony muttered, "The way this day has been going, I'm not gonna be a bit surprised if the lodge is closed or the road is impassable." The aggravation in his voice stung Irina. She wished a thousand times over that she had not plied him with her touristy request, adding to the length and difficulty of his day.

Late that evening, their showers out of the way, Irina set a platter of Russian tea cakes and a pot of extra-rich mocha at the kitchenette table where the guys were powering their way through their favorite conservative websites.

"I hope you don't think," Tony snarked, "that sugar is gonna make up for today's management decisions." His gruffness startled Irina, but the impish grin that followed betrayed the fact that he was over the Lake Baikal matter.

"We should catch the late evening news," she replied, changing the subject. "It might be a few days before we can pick it up again."

He stuffed one of the tea cakes in his mouth and navigated to the Channel One affiliate in Irkutsk. "Don't you ever get tired of hearing Russian?" he ribbed.

She didn't bite. She didn't feel like bantering.

"Good evening. This is Channel One evening news broadcasting live from Moscow, and I'm Dmitry Stepanovich, bringing you the latest national and international news.

"President Lebedev continues to make impressive strides in raising Russia's political, economic, and military stature in the geopolitical arena. Earlier today he signed a mutual defense agreement with Germany and Turkey. If any of the three partners are attacked, the others are obligated to—and will—declare war on the aggressor, whoever that may be. In connection with the defense agreement, Ankara granted Russia a fifty-year lease on all six of the former American installations, effective tomorrow at 8 a.m. Ankara time. Advance teams are already on the ground at Incirlik and Izmir to survey the operational potential for Russia's Air Force and Army. This—need I say—is a paradigm-changing development that tips the balance of power in the region.

"In retaliation against the US and her NATO allies for their unjust restriction of ships flagged from nations that they unfairly regard as havens for terrorists, Russia and Turkey demanded five days ago that all NATO ships in the Black Sea depart immediately. Rather than add to the tension in the region which has reached a boiling point, the U.S. and her NATO allies complied and vacated the Black Sea. Since then, the Turkish and Russian navies, along with ships from Syria and Iran, have blockaded the Dardanelles, forbidding NATO access to the Black Sea.

"Furthermore, Moscow and Ankara both released announcements this morning that the Black Sea is no longer regarded as International Waters. It is Inland Waters belonging to Russia and Turkey and their regional allies. The U.S. has moved the USS George H.W. Bush, the USS

Harry S. Truman, and the USS Abraham Lincoln into the eastern half of the Mediterranean, professedly to monitor the situation and protect U.S. interests in the region. Moscow remains skeptical—that's a lot of firepower for a monitoring operation—and they have warned the United States against escalating the situation.

"Two other stories highlight the power shift that's taking place in the Middle East. The first is that Qatar, outraged over the West's blind infatuation with Saudi Arabia, has given the United States and her NATO allies ninety days to leave Al Udeid Air Base. Reports have trickled in that the base will be opened to forces from Russia, Turkey, and Germany.

"The second is that Chancellor Wagner of Germany announced last night that she was sending an armored combat brigade and two Kommando companies to Syria by summer to be permanently based at Khmeimim Air Base, Russia's main military base in the region. They will coordinate and cooperate with Russia, Turkey, Syria, and Iran in their peacekeeping efforts in the region."

Tony groaned. "Talk about a geopolitical coup in Eurasian and Middle Eastern affairs! Where's President Weston? Nobody is outmaneuvering President Lebedev on the world stage right now. These developments seriously erode America's strategic advantage in the region and significantly impact her ability to contain Russia in the New Cold War."

Andy concurred. "Lebedev and his allies keep on piling up the powder kegs in the Middle East. When the pile finally explodes, it'll be one massive fireball."

Tony didn't reply. He was staring off into space. Andy shrugged his shoulders at his brother, then waved his hand in his face. "Still with us, bro?"

Tony smiled. "Sorry. Your comment on powder kegs in the Middle East reminded me of dad. I find it amazing that he foresaw these developments twenty years ago based on the Gog and Magog passage in Ezekiel. Now it's coming to pass. And the economic clout and the firepower of the Russian juggernaut is substantially increased with the addition of Turkey and Germany."

"Yeah. I was thinking about dad and Bible prophecy too. His stand on the future collapse of the EU is pretty impressive when you consider the fact that his preacher friends all regarded him as nuts. Almost to the man, prophecy teachers at the time predicted the death of the dollar, the demise of America, and the rise of the euro and the EU."

"Yep. As dad used to say—"

Andy filled in the blank. "'Big eye on current events, little eye on Bible prophecy.'"

"Yep. And 'too much speculation, not enough Bible.'"

"Too bad that most of those who should be eating crow right now have conveniently forgotten that they should be choking down black feathers."

"Nobody eats crow anymore. It's passe."

"You got that right. You don't have to admit that you were wrong. Just claim that you were advocating a possible scenario."

***

Irina peered out the massive picture window, watching the north wind blast the trees and the cottages with swirls of snow. From time to time, the frozen lake appeared for a moment through the curtain. Or was it her imagination?

"Lovely sunrise this morning, eh, Nikkie?" Tony teased as he walked into the dining room.

"Beautiful view of the lake, too," Andy added.

Their teasing, though good-natured banter, stung. She turned to face them. "I'm sorry, guys, that I insisted that we push on to the lake. I had no idea that a storm front was going to blow in that would spoil my plans."

Tony replied, "No worries. We didn't know either. Sorry that the weather spoiled your plans. If it's any consolation, the weather is going to be a bummer for me, too. We'll likely be fighting finger drifts all morning again."

She nodded, lips quivering. "I really wanted to see the lake. It's been on my bucket list since I was a child."

Tony set his hand on her shoulder, always overwhelmed when her eyes turned red. "It actually would have been a treat to see the lake, Nikita. I had no idea what the fuss was about until I googled it last night. It's the world's largest freshwater lake in terms of volume—more water than all five Great Lakes combined. And it's the only place in the world with freshwater seals."

"Let's talk about breakfast," Andy interrupted, rubbing his empty stomach. "What do you suggest, Miss Aksakova?"

"Blini," she replied, taking a seat with her back to the window, and glad to change the subject. "But I want whipped cream instead of sour cream."

"I'm game if we throw in some meat, like Russian sausage."

Twenty minutes later, Andy stopped a forkful of blini inches from his mouth, held it there aloft for a moment, then set the fork down on his plate. "Holy chicken gizzards!" he exclaimed, staring wide-eyed out the window.

Irina spun around in her chair and gasped. The storm had cleared enough for the sun to appear, low on the horizon over the hills to the East, but it was unlike any sun she had ever seen. It was veiled in an ice fog, surrounded by a large halo, graced with a huge cross, and accompanied with glowing orbs on either side that were nearly as large as the sun itself. It almost looked like there were three suns. Drawn in by the glory of the sight, she rose to her feet and stared in amazement.

"Take it you've never seen sun dogs before," Andy asked.

"Nope."

"Just think. If you had gotten the sunrise that you wanted, you wouldn't have gotten to see this."

She laughed. "So true. Sometimes disappointment is the door you have to pass through to see God's glory."

40

Zabaykalsky Krai, Russia
Wednesday, February 5, 2020

The truck coughed and sputtered as it struggled to push its way through the waist-deep mound of white, and after a few promising lurches forward, the lumbering vehicle ground to a halt. "Nuts!" Tony muttered as he slammed his fist on the steering wheel. "I'm getting tired of fighting these stupid snowdrifts." He slammed the shifter into reverse, and with an angry foot on the gas and tires whining, the truck skittered backward twenty feet or so. Then he slammed the shifter back into first gear and powered the truck forwards, making it about three feet farther. He repeated the process again and again, gaining a few feet each time, and with each gain his temper subsided a little. On his sixteenth attempt, the truck nosed through the far side of the drift, found a little traction, and inched its way out of its clutches.

"I hate to say it," the frustrated driver vented, "but I'm thinking that we should take the next exit or pullout and wait out this storm. The visibility is getting worse, the drifts are getting deeper, and it's only a matter of time before we get stuck so bad that we won't be able to get out. That would be seriously ugly."

Andy didn't reply. He had been having similar thoughts, but he figured his brother wasn't ready to make the transition from venting to planning. He turned his attention to Irina. Her head was hanging, no doubt disappointed that another day had to get cut short. He lifted her chin. "Nikki. I know it's discouraging to have another day go down the tubes, but our progress has slowed to a crawl, the weather and road conditions are getting worse, and the barometer is still falling. Tony is right. We need to find a place to hole up until this storm blows over. It's too risky. Getting stuck on the highway in this kind of weather could be fatal. Not only would we be forced to face the blizzard in the open, but we would be sitting ducks for the big plow trucks when they clear the road."

She nodded and dropped her head again.

"I know you think Tony and I can work near miracles, but it's simply too dangerous to continue. Sometimes the only way to salvage a mission is to postpone it or adjust it. Right now, we need to respond to the situation with common sense and make some adjustments to our expectations and timetable."

"I know," she replied glumly."

"Look on the bright side," he continued. "We actually made one hundred and fifty kilometers despite the heavy crosswinds, massive drifts, and poor visibility. And we can be thankful that we didn't have to shovel our way out of any of the drifts that we got stuck in. Tony rocked us out of all of them."

Irina shuddered at the price the boys would have paid if they had been forced to get out and shovel—frostbitten faces, hands, and feet. But it didn't console her disappointment. It was going to take her some time to adjust her expectations.

They drove in silence for ten minutes, bulldozing through drift after drift. The uneasy quiet was interrupted when Andy pointed and shouted, "Road! On the left!"

Tony had seen the sign at nearly the same time and was already on the brakes. He cranked the wheel hard and aimed for where he figured the center of the road would be. It was almost impossible to tell in the near whiteout conditions. The truck tipped to the right as the steer tire on the passenger side went off the roadbed, throwing the three around like rag dolls and slamming Andy against the door. Tony cranked the wheel back to the left and the tire jumped back up on the road, tossing them all to the left.

The road climbed out of the low spot where the drifting snow had accumulated and a patch of grey appeared. Tony relaxed. The wind, blowing straight down the road, had scoured the surface of all but a few small finger drifts, and here and there patches were bare dirt. But the reprieve was short-lived. The wind picked up with a fury, and the road vanished in a frenzy of white.

"Hey, is that a building?" Andy hollered as they passed a structure on their right.

"Couldn't tell you, bro. I got my eyes glued to the road, straining to catch the occasional glimpse of dirt. We go off the road here, and we'll be stuck until spring."

A lull in the wind exposed a gray strip in front of the truck, which faded into blowing snow some twenty feet in front of them. Tony pressed the accelerator down hoping to take advantage of the moment. A large patch of bare ground passed on his left, confusing him. Had he left the road? Distracted, he didn't notice the massive drift in front of them until Irina screamed. He jumped on the brakes, but it was too late. The truck slammed into the bank of white. When the explosion of snow subsided, Tony flipped on the wipers and cleared the windshield.

They were surprised to see a building about fifteen feet in front of them. They hadn't been on a road after all, but the access road to a gas station and diner, which were closed for the winter. The building blocked the wind that was howling out of the north, but massive drifts had curled around its sides, almost like the horns of a bull. They were stuck in the right horn, buried up to the running boards.

"Where are we?" Irina inquired.

"I'm not sure," Andy replied. "But I'm guessing that we're close to Zabaykalsky Krai. That was our halfway point for the day."

After jockeying around, Tony broke free from the drift, turned the vehicle around, and backed into the narrow space between the horns, getting the rear of the truck close enough to the building that the wind was largely blocked.

The crew donned their parkas over their wool submarine-service sweaters and pulled on their hats and mittens. Irina hated this part of the day—climbing out of the almost warm cab and getting in the back of the unheated, breezy truck.

"What's the matter, Nikita?" Tony teased. "The cold only lasts for a few minutes."

"That's only half of the problem. I don't just hate shivering while we wait for the heater to warm the back of the truck up. I also hate the damp air, the propane smell, and the musty canvas smell once it does warm up. And the breeze that whistles through drives me bonkers."

Tony just smiled and climbed out the driver's door.

Irina sighed, followed Andy out the passenger door, and stepped into the frigid air. At the back of the truck, Tony was attempting to untie one of the ropes that held the flap on the driver's side closed. But it was uncooperative. After warming the stubborn knot with his bare hands and grabbing one of the loops with his teeth, he finally persuaded the frozen knot to relinquish its hold. He decided against attempting to untie any further knots. Instead, he lifted the free portion and made a small opening.

Irina marveled at the manly man working with his bare hands in the biting wind. *How do they do stuff like that?*

He motioned for her to climb in. She scrambled through the opening, and Andy squeezed in after her. Tony clambered in last and tumbled to the floor. His cold hands had failed to get a secure grip on the tailgate or hold his weight off the floor. He stood up and tried to secure the flap. "Nuts," he grumbled as he struggled with the inside rope. "My fingers are way too numb." After three failed attempts, he called his brother Andy. "Hey, boss. Hate to bother you. But my fingers are too stiff to tie the flap down."

Andy hustled to the back and placed his hand on his

brother's shoulder. "No problem, bro. I got the heater going. You go warm your fingers, and I'll cinch this bad boy down."

A minute later, Andy joined Tony at the space heater. He held his hands aloft over the unit, indulging the pleasant sensation of hot air warming cold fingers. "This thirty and forty below stuff is getting old," he complained.

"No doubt," Tony muttered, flexing and unflexing his fingers, wincing occasionally from the stabbing pain you suffer when you warm up fingers that got too cold. "Starting to wonder if we're ever going to make it to Magadan before spring. This is the third storm that we've had to stop for, and we're barely halfway there. We have already lost six days. How many days are we going to lose this time?" He winced, then massaged his left hand with the stiff fingers of his right hand. "I'm seriously thinking about moving to a warmer climate if we ever make it back to Montana alive. Someplace where the winter lows don't drop below the 40s. Like maybe Arizona or New Mexico."

Andy worried about his brother. Since Moscow, Tony hadn't been his usual self. From his childhood, he had never been the melancholy type. He had rarely been discouraged and rarely complained. Now he was nursing the blues. Andy figured that it was more than getting tired of the incessant bitter cold. Something deeper seemed to be eating at him. His "if we ever make it back alive" comment was particularly unsettling. It wasn't merely the fact that he had made it, for soldiers often had a morbid sense of humor in difficult situations. It was the spirit in which he had said it. Fearless Tony was afraid.

"Something on your mind, bro?"

"Nah. Not really."

Andy looked into his brother's eyes and raised his eyebrows. Tony felt like he was naked in the garden in the presence of God. You just can't hide anything from those that know you well.

"Really, it's nothing." he pleaded. "Just been having dreams about drifting in chilly waters all alone—cold, exhausted, no more will to fight, about to go under. But they're just dreams. Not used to dealing with stuff like that. But I'm good. I'll figure it out and get my stuff squared away."

"Okay, bro," Andy replied. "Do what you gotta do. We need your A-game, or we can't pull this off." He started to turn away, then turned back. "I got your back. You know that."

Andy left Tony to his misery and fired up the propane stove that was sitting on the next crate over. After adjusting the flame, he filled the percolator with water and set it on the left burner. Then he opened two cans of diced potatoes and two cans of meatballs, dumped them in a kettle, and set their dinner on the right side. A few minutes later, the coffee began to perk, filling their tiny shelter with its tantalizing scent.

Irina scooted closer to the stove, indulging the homey sound of the percolator and watching the flames on the stove flicker and dance, casting odd shadows on the canvas walls. A smile brightened her face as she recalled her grandfather casting hand shadows on the wall with the light of a flickering kerosene lantern at his dacha in the Carpathian

Mountains in southern Ukraine when she was a little girl.

Andy poured her a cup of coffee, and she cradled the mug in both hands, thankful for the guys and reconciled to the situation. It wasn't as catastrophic as her emotions had made it out to be. It didn't matter whether they were here one day or ten. God was watching over them, and he would bring his purposes to pass in his timing. And if those purposes proved to involve pain or disappointment, that was okay too, for Sweet Everlasting was coming.

41

Meyersdale, PA
Wednesday, January 22, 2020

A quiet rapping on the apartment door stirred Jack from a cat nap on the couch. He tensed and waited in silence. After a pause of six or seven seconds, the knocking returned—the familiar riff "shave and a haircut, six bits." Jack relaxed. That was Romeo's knock.

He jumped up and opened the door. "Hey, Romes. Come on in!" he said warmly, but with a subdued voice.

Their Underground handler handed him two grocery bags. "Got more bacon, eggs, mac-and-cheese, chili, hamburger, cheese, and taco shells for the man tastebuds. And as the lady requested, some fresh veggies and fruit too."

Jack placed the bags on the counter and pointed to a seat at the kitchen table. "Care to stick around for a cup of coffee?"

"Actually, I planned on it. Got a couple things I'd like to pick your brain on."

Romeo and Sally pulled up chairs while Jack poured three cups of coffee, then took a seat himself.

"So what's on your mind?" Jack inquired.

Romeo's face screwed up with his sly, eye-twinkling smile. "I've put some serious thought into your travel dilemma for the past few weeks, and I think I have a workable solution."

Jack eyed him nervously. Romeo had a reputation for being on the reckless side. He raced in the AMA National Enduro Series circuit as well as non-series rallies. Over the years he had been hospitalized six times. He had broken both legs, both arms, many of his ribs, and had cracked vertebrae in his back on two occasions. It was a wonder that he could still walk. Hesitantly, Jack asked, "So what do you have in mind?"

"What do you think about taking the John Deere Express?"

"Somehow, I just can't picture John Deere and express together. But my curiosity is piqued. What are you thinking?"

"An Underground acquaintance in Iowa is looking for a used John Deere T670 combine. I located one for a decent price not too far from here in Shippensburg. I would use my old F-350 and my old lowboy trailer to move it from Pennsylvania to Iowa. When the delivery is done, I would leave the whole shebang there and take the Greyhound back. I've been thinking about parting with the old combo for a while, and this is an opportunity to do so in support of a good cause." He eyed Jack. "So what do you think?"

"Honestly, I don't like it one bit. I can't imagine how it's even remotely possible for us to travel in the cab of a combine and escape notice. We'd be sitting ducks."

"You wouldn't be traveling in the cab."

Jack's eyebrows furrowed. "Where then?"

"Inside the combine."

Jack stared at his friend, mouth agape. "Inside the combine?" he asked. But the grin that slowly crawled across his face suggested that the idea had struck a chord.

"You got it," Romeo replied. "If I took off the side panel, and removed the separator system and straw walker, that would open up a small room inside with about four feet of headroom. Then I could put in a makeshift floor on top of the sieve and the straw chopper with a few 2-by-4s and some plywood. It would be cramped in there, but manageable. You would have room for two sleeping pads and bags, a couple camping potties, and several duffel bags for food, supplies, and clothes. Once you two and your stuff is stowed inside, I would re-attach the side panel."

Jack nodded. "That might work. What about cooking? It would be nice to have a low table for cooking. And a curtain for the portapotties would be a necessity."

"Yeah. I already thought about both. The potty should be on the downwind side and the table on the upwind side. The curtain could be fabricated with a cheap shower curtain and PVC."

"Sounds good to me. And what about the separator system and the straw walker? How are you going to get them to their destination? A combine isn't much good without them."

"I would strap them to pallets and ship them by truck."

"How long do you think this trip would take? Two days, maybe?"

"I'm thinking something more along the lines of six to ten days."

"What? You're joking, right? That's a lot of time to be cooped up in a tiny space."

"We need to get from Pennsylvania to Iowa without hitting any of the random checkpoints. That means I'll have to spend hours every day picking out a route for the next two-hour stretch that will avoid checkpoints and will, at the same time, take us down rarely patrolled roads and avoid restricted bridges and underpasses. Some of these stretches are going to be slow going—unplowed and unmaintained."

"That will lower the odds of hitting a random checkpoint, but how are you going to reduce the odds to zero?"

"The internet. I have uncovered several websites that provide real-time updates on all active checkpoints. You just enter your location by city or county and it gives you a map with every checkpoint in the neighborhood and region, as well as the last known location and direction of checkpoint convoys. On top of that, I'll stop at elevators and diners throughout the day and ask the farmers and truck drivers for the best route to haul a combine to such and such a county while avoiding those pain-in-the-butt checkpoints."

"Sounds like you got those bases covered. What are we going to eat, and how are we going to heat our food up?"

"I was thinking cold food like meat, cheese, and crackers."

"Not gonna work. That would be fine for two or three days. But if we're looking at six to ten days, we're gonna need hot meals and hot coffee to keep the morale up."

"Okay," Romeo replied. "So I go to the Army Surplus store and buy a few cases of MREs and a few cases of heating packets."

"Got no problem with the MREs. But the heater packets are a no-go. When you add water to the packets—which contain magnesium, iron, and salt—the chemical reaction releases enough hydrogen that it poses a risk in confined spaces."

"So what would you suggest as an alternative?"

"The safest option is the new air-activated MRE heaters. I haven't found the military version for sale anywhere yet. So we'll likely have to go with a civilian version like the Firedragon system which comes with a folding stove. The tabs are nontoxic and odorless when burned, and they boil water fifty percent faster than similar products like dry alcohol or hexamine. The stove and tabs, or equivalents, are readily available in sporting goods stores. One distinct advantage that the tab stove has over the units incorporated in the MREs is that it'll allow us to boil water for coffee."

"I'll put them on my shopping list."

But Jack wasn't sold yet on the project. "What are you going to do about the fact that combines are overwidth and require oversize permits? If you go through the permitting process, then you have the Highway Patrol involved right from the get-go, which sounds like a nonstarter to me. And if you skip the permit process, it won't matter one hoot that you have a plan to dodge all the random checkpoints because a patrolman or a sheriff is going to pull you over."

"I'm way ahead of you. My plan is to dismount the combine tires and replace them with sprayer tires in the rear and small tractor tires in the front. I'll probably have to weld up a special hub for each of the replacement tires. This will get me several inches under ten feet so I won't need any overwidth permits. And using my lowboy will keep me nearly a foot under the overheight limits. This frees me up to work myself across the farm belt on county highways and rural roads."

"Are you going to ship the tires too?"

"Nope. I'll chain them down behind the combine."

"Brilliant. And what about the wind running through the machine? How do we stop the breeze and the wind chill?"

"I'll configure some windbreaks. Not really an issue."

So what's your tentative time plan?"

"I can pick up the combine tomorrow, prep it on Friday and Saturday, and leave on Sunday. That would put us in Waterloo, Iowa, assuming my estimates are correct, somewhere between the last day of January and the first few days of February."

"That'll be a cold ride, and we'll definitely get sore from so much lying and sitting."

"Yeah. Thought about that. Not much you'll be able to do for the discomfort except force yourself to stretch a few times a day. The cold will be easier to deal with. I'll make sure you have plenty of cold-weather gear, space blankets, hand and foot heater packets, dry socks, and warm food and drinks." Romeo looked Jack intently in the eye. "So what do you think? Do we got a plan?"

"Not quite. There's one minor detail we haven't talked about yet."

"What's that?"

"How are we going to get from Iowa to Montana?"

"An ice-fishing expedition. The plan is coming together, but the details haven't been nailed down yet, so I can't give you much more information than that."

"No worries."

"Do we got a plan?"

"As far as I'm concerned, we do. But I'm gonna call Woody and run it past him. Then I'll send you a text and give you either a go or a no-go."

"Okay then," Romeo said, standing up. "I'm gonna assume it's a *yes* and get started." He drained the last couple swallows of his now lukewarm coffee, gave Jack and Sally a thumb's up, and hustled out the door.

Sally looked at Jack, worry written on her face. He smiled back. "Look at the bright side, Sally. You get another great adventure story to tell someday."

***

"So what do you make of the idea?" Jack asked his cousin Woody during a secure call that evening. "Do you like it? Does it seem workable to you?"

"I actually like the idea. It's a unique strategy that probably won't attract a lot of attention. Is it workable? That comes down to the Romeo variable. If he really does come up with a half-decent solution to stop the wind from blowing through, then yeah, it's workable. Otherwise, it'll be a death trap.

"As for heating your meals, I've done some experimentation with the Firedragon tabs and a few other brands with similar composition, and I've discovered that they usually take closer to seven minutes to boil water than five, but that shouldn't be a big deal. It's not like you'll be in a hurry in the belly of the green beast."

Jack chuckled. "In the belly of the beast. Funny that you should put it that way. My mind has been going down the Pinnochio path ever since Romeo broached the idea. I keep thinking of Geppetto who got swallowed by the whale and was forced to live in its belly."

Now Woody laughed. "At least you're gonna have a luxury raft compared to his."

42

Meyersdale, PA to Jordan, MT
January 26 to February 5, 2020

Early Sunday morning, a few minutes after two, Romeo rapped on the apartment door. "It's time to load," he whispered when Jack answered. The two fugitives picked up their duffel bags and followed him down the stairs, into the garage bay, and out the side door. But they weren't outside. They were in a tent of blue tarp and 2X4s that extended from the sidewall of the garage to the combine, protecting the Geppetto project from both the snowy weather and the prying eyes of neighbors.

Sally ascended the step ladder first, and Romeo illuminated their temporary home with his flashlight. "Wow! That definitely is a small space," she exclaimed as she peered into the belly of the beast. She looked back to Jack and tried to put on a brave face. But she couldn't hide her concern. He was having his own second thoughts. There was only four feet of headroom, so there would be no standing up. And there was less than eight feet of floor between the utility counter and the potties. They wouldn't be moving around much. She fought the rising panic. *My claustrophobia is going to go full pandemonium.*

Though cramped, the layout was sensible. Their pads and sleeping bags were laid side by side on the floor. The utility counter that ran across the front was twelve inches deep and twenty inches high. It would serve as a table and workstation. Four five-gallon dispensers, held in place by restrainers, provided their water supply. Duffel bags of food, gear, and clothing were stowed on and under the shelf.

On the other end of the floor, two twenty-gallon porta-potties sat side by side, each with its own curtain. Old sleeping bags hung along the walls of their little room to break the breeze and provide a little insulation. Wherever the wind could blow in through openings on the front or the side, Romeo had stuffed foam padding or cheap sleeping bags. It wasn't pretty, but it was effective.

"The front side is elevated a couple inches," Romeo whispered. "That ensures that your head is uphill slightly. The porta potties are at your feet—downhill and downwind."

Sally turned up her nose as she tossed her two bags down by the table and sat on one. "Smelling the blue-goo stink for a week or more is going to be a king-size bummer!" Tears started to well in her eyes.

"It definitely doesn't smell like mom's kitchen," Jack replied, "but I would rather deal with this smell than be back in 286, or worse, a 300 series camp."

"I can't disagree with you there. I'm just whining."

"If it's any consolation, I'm whining too. I just keep it bottled up inside."

Sally rolled her eyes at him. "Yeah, right. Jack and whine mixes like oil and water."

"Just treat this like a camping trip. We get a chance to rough it and catch up on some reading."

"Like I didn't get my fill of reading the past month," she snipped. But immediately she regretted the moody outburst. "Sorry for adding unhelpful negativity to an already difficult situation." She forced a smile. "On the bright side, maybe I'll finally read *Moby Dick* and *The Count of Monte Christo*."

Romeo and Jack shared a firm handshake, then Romeo moved the ladder out of the way and hoisted the sidewall into place with two pullies, bathing their quarters in darkness. Jack turned on his tactical-red mini flashlight, but it did little to quell the feeling of isolation. Moments later, the screech of bolts getting tightened turned the confined space into a torture chamber. After several nerve-rattling minutes, silence engulfed them. Now they were trapped inside, and their fate was sealed—for better or worse. The seconds ticked by. The seconds turned to minutes. Time seemed to slow to a crawl. Sally began to wonder if they were ever going to move. After the longest eight minutes of her life, the combine lurched forward, almost knocking her down, and they were underway.

The two crawled into their sleeping bags and shut their eyes. Jack, long inured to the sounds of noisy transportation like choppers and C-141s, soon fell asleep. But the cacophony of squeaks, vibrations, and whistling breezes kept Sally wide awake. When Jack's snoring added to the din, she unzipped her bag in a frustrated huff, reached for her purse, dug out the earplugs he had made her pack, and inserted them into her ears. While she hated using them with a passion, she had no choice. Sleep was not a luxury. It was a necessity.

***

Four days later, in western Ohio, while Romeo was skirting around the north side of Hicksville on a poorly maintained road, Jack was trying to perk a pot of coffee. But the two efforts proved a miserable combination. Between hitting potholes and swerving around them, the combine was getting bounced around pretty good. That forced Jack to keep his hand on the handle of the coffee pot so it wouldn't collapse the folding stove or tumble off of it. "Nuts!" he grumbled, switching hands. "That's the third time that hot water has slopped out and burned my hand!"

Sally tried to encourage him. "At least the sacrifice is for a good cause. This hotel would be unbearable without coffee."

"Yeah," he replied. "We do need the java."

A minute later, water began bubbling up in the glass dome, the bubblings quickly taking on a brownish tint.

"Too bad we can barely hear the percolator," Sally observed. "I love the sound. It always takes me back to grandma's house."

"I like it too," he replied. "Drippers are convenient, and cold presses make better-tasting coffee. But you can't beat the sound of a percolator."

He filled her travel mug, snugged the lid on, and handed

it to her. "Here you go, Sal. And here's a box of Ginger Lemon Shortbread cookies that I found in one of the food bags. Don't eat them all in one shot."

"Don't hold your breath. At the moment, the only thing going right is the coffee and cookies. My eyes are buggy from trying to read in this bouncy ride. I haven't felt warm since we left. And I have run out of comfortable positions to sit or lay down. So me and my comfort food are getting pretty tight."

"I hear ya. I'm one hurting unit, too." He snagged a handful of cookies from the box he had just handed her, sat down with his back against a mound of duffle bags, slid his right hand through the handle of his travel mug, and returned to the Bible app on his secure phone. "Think I'm gonna tackle Jeremiah again."

***

Romeo eyed the elevator yard warily as he rolled toward the main building. A sheriff was standing next to his squad car, chatting with someone. The officer stared at the F-350 as it pulled up, noting the Pennsylvania plates and the odd load. He said something to the other man, who turned, bounded up the steps, and disappeared inside the elevator. Then he walked over to the driver's side, and Romeo rolled his window down.

"Interesting load you got there," the officer noted.

"Yeah. It was a lot cheaper to haul it myself than pay someone to haul it with a semi. But I didn't want to deal with the oversize permitting process for every state I had to pass through, so I took the field tires off and put narrow tires on. That keeps it under ten feet wide."

"You're coming from Pennsylvania?"

"Yeah. Left four days ago."

"From where?"

"I picked it up in Shippensburg. Here are my papers."

The officer glanced over the sales receipt and shipping forms on the clipboard. "Four days to get here? Why so long? Sounds more like a two-day trip to me."

"I've been mixing business with pleasure. The buyer doesn't need the combine until fall, so there's no hurry. I planned a route that takes me through a lot of rural country and offers stops at state and county parks. If I see wildlife during the day, like foxes or deer, and there is a safe place to pull over, I try to get a few photos. When I pass a park, I make a brief stop for a hike and some photos." He picked up his camera sitting on the passenger seat and handed it to the sheriff. Got some nice deer pics this morning in a cornfield that still had standing corn." The sheriff waved the camera off, so Romeo set it back down.

"It says here that you're headed for Waterloo, Iowa?"

"Yes, sir. I expect to be there in another four or five days unless we get a bad storm."

"Can I see your driver's license?"

Romeo fished it out of his wallet and handed it over.

"Do you have any other identification, like a birth certificate or a passport?"

He retrieved his passport from his truck bag and handed it out the window.

The sheriff walked over to his vehicle and radioed the information in so dispatch could run a background check. Five minutes later, the sheriff returned with his identification and handed it back. "Do you mind if I take a look around?"

"Nope. Be my guest. Is there fresh coffee inside?"

"Yep. Bob just put another pot on."

"If you don't mind, I'm gonna run inside, use the restroom and get a cup."

"That'll work for me."

While Romeo played it cool and casual, the sheriff began to walk slowly around the green giant, tapping on the sides, tugging at chains, and checking the chain binders and ratchet straps. Jack and Sally sat motionless, wondering whether this was the end of the road. They had heard the sheriff's conversation with Romeo, and now they could hear him poking around.

When Romeo returned with a donut and a full travel mug, the sheriff requested a full light test. They ran through the brake lights, running lights, turn signals, headlights, and fog lights. Then he had Romeo test the wipers, the defroster for the dash, and the defroster for the rear window. Then he asked to see his registration and proof of insurance. Then he checked the tread depth on both the truck and trailer tires.

Romeo was starting to get agitated. The guy seemed like he was determined to find something—anything—to write him a ticket, or worse, compound the trailer. But the sheriff wasn't finished. He asked to see the emergency reflectors, first aid kit, and fire extinguisher. Romeo said nothing and produced them, though he wasn't required to carry them since he wasn't a DOT-registered vehicle.

The sheriff looked at him and half-smiled, perhaps as much out of embarrassed frustration as friendliness. "Looks like everything is in order, Mr. Jankowicz. You're free to go."

Romeo thought the ordeal was over and placed his key in the ignition to start his truck, but before he could turn the key, the sheriff leaned on his window. "The roads west of here, in this county and the next, are in pretty rough shape. They should have been repaired long ago."

"Thanks for the heads up." He reached to turn the key, but the nosy officer continued to lean on his window and chat him up, asking about farming in Pennsylvania, the road conditions along the way, the new terrorism threat, the hassles that the new security measures posed for the public, and how those measures had affected him. Romeo sensed that he was being probed. The sheriff was fishing for responses that might suggest that something was off-kilter. He bore with the conversation, forcing himself to make eye contact and not act like he was in a haste.

After six painfully long minutes, the sheriff relented. "Well, I guess I should let you go." He stood up, slapped the side of Romeo's pickup, stepped back, and waved. Romeo waved back, fired up his rig, and pulled out of the yard.

As he accelerated out of town, he started to relax. But a glance in his rearview mirror brought a new wave of worry. The sheriff, like a bloodhound, was tight on his tail. His concern intensified when the patrol car drove past the last few city streets and the county road on the edge of town. For the next six miles, Romeo was on pins and needles, expecting the sheriff to flash his lights at any moment. But his fear didn't materialize. When he finally passed the county line, he checked his side-view mirror and watched his antagonist stop on the shoulder, give him a long stare, and turn around.

***

On Tuesday evening, Romeo drove into Joe Balzar's place, a large grain farm six miles north of Waterloo, Iowa. He stopped in front of the pole barn according to the plan and picked up his phone to send a text announcing his arrival. But Joe had noticed him from the window and was already hustling over. The farmer scooted in the side door and opened the main bay door. Once Romeo had backed in, Joe closed the door, grabbed two socket wrenches off his workbench, tossed one to Romeo, and the two of them began removing the bolts that held the side panel on.

Jack tensed at the awful racket. Why was the side panel being removed? Had they arrived at the Balzar farm? Or were they getting inspected somewhere?

Halfway through the first bolt, Romeo stopped and shouted, "It's us, Jack. We're in Waterloo."

The uneasy passenger breathed a sigh of relief.

The two lowered the side panel, slid it out of the way, and leaned a step ladder against the makeshift floor. Jack and Sally, stiff and sore, could barely climb down. Romeo steadied them and helped their feet find the rungs. Once on terra firma, they gave Romeo a warm squeeze, pumped Joe's hand, then gleefully stretched their limbs. Freedom had never felt so free before.

"Are you two interested in hot showers and pizza?" Joe asked.

"Sounds wonderful!" Sally shouted. Jack nodded in agreement.

"Great. While you two get washed up, I'll order two extra-large pizzas. What do you want on them?"

"Anything but fish and pineapple," Jack replied.

"Amen to that," Sally added. "And no jalapenos for me."

"Then I'll order two extra-large pizzas with the works, double meat, double cheese, no garbage on either, and no heat on one."

"That's a lot of pizza for five."

"It'll go. Trust me."

"Halfway through their feast, Joe's phone chimed. He read the text and smiled. "Bert and Ernie are five minutes away."

"Bert and Ernie?" Jack inquired.

He smiled. "Your ride to Montana."

"Figured that. But Bert and Ernie? Is that dumb luck or humor?"

"Not their real names," Romeo explained. "Ron and Don got their nicknames years ago when they started riding with the Calvary Crusaders. Ron, who we call Bert, is tall, skinny, serious, and a first-class bookworm. Don, who we call Ernie, is short, stocky, and hilarious. He's always telling jokes and pulling pranks."

Jack grinned. "Gotcha! So what's the plan from here?"

"Tomorrow morning after breakfast," Joe replied, "I'll take Romeo to town so he can catch the Greyhound bus back to Pittsburgh, and you two will climb into the camper that Bert and Ernie are towing. They'll transport you to Jordan, Montana, a two-day journey barring problems, where you'll rendezvous with Red and Woody. After the transfer, Bert and Ernie will continue to Hell Creek Marina on Fort Peck Reservoir where they'll participate in the fishing tournament that runs this coming weekend. That's their cover for the trip. From Jordan, you and Sally will have a four-hour ride to the Compound.

"Sounds good to me," Jack answered, as he reached for another slice of pizza.

"Any questions?"

"Nope. There's not much to think about. This leg of the journey will be a picnic compared to the first two legs."

***

A few minutes before midnight on Thursday evening, Bert pulled into an abandoned farmstead that was six miles west of Jordan and several miles off the highway. The camper slowed, and Jack peered between the curtains watching for Red's pickup. A seemingly endless row of long-retired farm equipment rolled past his window—tractors, combines, plows, rakes, balers, trailers, farm trucks, and pickups. When the trailer slowed, and the faded-green F-150 appeared between a Massey Ferguson and an Allis-Chalmers, his eyes moistened. An almost violent desire to rush out the door seized him. But precautions were precautions. He steeled himself to wait for the all-clear message.

After an agonizingly long minute, his phone vibrated.

"Coast is clear. Safe to exit." He bolted out the door and met his cousin Woody at the bottom of the stairs. A few tears flowed down his cheeks as the two shared a back-patting hug, making the moment as awkward as it was welcome. This was new territory for him. He wasn't a weeper. The last time he had cried was at his wife Emily's funeral. Before that, he had no recollection, not even back to junior high school.

While struggling to gather himself, he realized that Sally was at his side, waiting for her turn. Glad for the reprieve, he stepped aside. She and her former colleague shared a fleeting embrace, separated, and stared awkwardly at each other. Woody, not wanting the moment to degenerate into full-blown embarrassment, directed her attention to the sky above.

She looked upward, and her eyes widened. "Wow! That is a lot of stars. You told me many times about eastern Montana's dark skies, but I always thought you were exaggerating. You know … guys and their fishing stories."

He laughed. "The Montana skies are no fishing story. Gorgeous blue skies during the day and jewel-bedecked heavens at night."

Jack stepped between them, grabbed their arms, and pulled them toward Red's truck. "Hate to break up the stargazing party, but we need to roll. You two can indulge your dark-sky passion all you want once we get back to the Compound."

43

the Compound
Friday, February 7, 2020

Shortly after four in the morning, Red parked his F-150 next to the lodge, and four happy souls darted inside. The great room exploded with a flurry of handshakes and hugs as Jack was welcomed by his old friends and Woody introduced Sally. For the next half hour, the two newcomers held everyone spellbound with an abbreviated account of their escape, Jack doing most of the talking, Sally filling in a few gaps and adding her own observations.

Once the excitement had settled down, Woody and Jack migrated to the fireplace hearth for a few moments alone. Sally respectfully gave them fifteen minutes to themselves, but when she couldn't hold out any longer, she strolled over and deposited herself next to Woody.

Slightly perturbed at her intrusion, yet welcoming her presence, he smiled. "Glad you made it here safe and sound."

"Glad to be here. I just wish the girls were here too ... back from their missions."

"We all do."

"What's the latest news from them?"

"The last report we heard from the Russia team was five days ago when they were at Lake Baikal, which is about two-thirds of the way to Magadan. It could be months yet before they make it back. We sent a team of guys to extract the Louisiana team. We expect them to return sometime in the next week or so."

"I wish the girls didn't have to go on such dangerous operations. I've been worried sick ever since I heard that they were on the teams. The Russia mission especially makes me nervous."

"Believe me. If we had had better options, we would have taken them. But they volunteered, and we were convinced that they were more than capable of handling whatever came their way."

"This new America scares me. It puts good people in a bad spot. Do you think she'll ever go back to the way she was?"

"I doubt it. The exponential curve for the stage setting for the last days has turned sharply upward. Things are likely to get even worse from here."

She sighed.

"It's gonna be okay, Sally. We just need to trust God. On the other side of the ugly is the coming of the Lord and his glorious kingdom."

Sally nodded. "That's what Jack's been trying to tell me. I know it's true. But truth is harder to implement than understand."

A smile creased his face. "Trust me. I know that only too

well." He hesitated, made a false start, then spit out the issue that had been festering in his mind. "Speaking of putting folks in a bad spot, I owe you an apology. I put you in a bad spot when I asked for vacation. I have regretted that day ever since."

Sally would have none of it. "My sacrifice at that juncture was small, and it was the right thing to do in the circumstances. I don't regret the choice, and I would do it all over again without batting an eyelash."

"But—"

"Woody, there are no buts. I'm not going to forgive you because there is nothing to forgive. You made a difficult decision, and it was the right one. Granted, it put me in a tough position and forced me to make my own hard choices. But you're not the one at fault here. It was policies enacted by a corrupt government that forced your hand. And if you hadn't forced mine, something else would have come up that would have done so. So stop second-guessing yourself and quit living in the past. There was nothing reasonable you could have done to change things."

He relinquished the point and took up a different question that had long perplexed him. "How come I never got polygraphed?"

A bright smile lit up her face. "I went to bat for you. I told the FBI agents that although you held a few quirky ideas on cosmology, your character was beyond reproach. I used a little reverse psychology too. Twice I asked them to polygraph you. Both times they declined." She laughed heartily.

Woody relaxed. It almost felt like the old times ... like the annual Christmas parties when they had sat next to each other and laughed. But could he relax enough? He hadn't been able to relax enough back then. And that had been a simpler life in a simple world. How was he going to relax enough now? He fled to comfort food. "Should we go make a batch of popcorn?"

She bounced up beaming. "Sounds like a home run to me."

He followed her to the kitchen, perplexed, wondering how a simple man like himself could struggle with such complex emotions.

***

That evening the folks gathered at the lodge for a celebration feast of smoked brisket and grilled asparagus prepared by Woody and Red. Afterward, they gathered around the fireplace for a meeting. Jordy dragged the pine podium out of the corner, placed it to the side of the crackling fire, and began. "The first order of business is the news clip of Jack's capture. We've all seen it and have our own theories on what transpired. I thought it would be illuminating to get Jack's take on it." He dimmed the lights and started the video.

It opened with a clip of an FBI chopper skimming over a highway, though it was not clear whether it was actual footage from the day of Jack's arrest or stock footage. Then a shaky camera zoomed in on the license plate on Jack's Jeep. This was followed by a slightly blurry shot of SUVs moving in behind the vehicle. Then followed a series of movie-grade shots of the SUVs chasing him up the highway, down the road for Manassas National Battlefield Park, and surrounding him in the parking lot at Henry Hill Visitor Center. Some thirty armed men approached the Jeep. An officer raised a bullhorn and shouted, "Step out of your vehicle with your hands up!" But Jack didn't comply. Instead, he leaned over, and an explosion rocked the scene, shaking the camera. The video closed with shots of the chaos—charred bodies and burning wreckage. But some of the shots didn't seem to match the layout of the vehicles in the original parking lot view.

Jordy flipped the lights back on. "What's your take on this, Jack? How much of this is real, and how much is bogus?"

"Several of the scenes are genuine including the shot of me in the parking lot, but most of it is fiction. There was no chase, much less a high-speed chase. Only one-third as many vehicles were involved. Only six men approached the Jeep. And there was no explosion. I stepped out of my vehicle as requested, and they handcuffed me and led me away."

"But why would the government stage a bombing like that?" Jordy asked. "Why would they claim that you died in a suicide bombing."

"A false flag operation. They need to justify the hard-line position they have taken against soft terrorism," Jack replied. "To win this battle in the minds of the public, they need soft terrorism to be riddled with loose cannons who engage in real terrorism. They need the public to regard soft terrorists as lunatics, often armed and dangerous, whose end-of-the-world fantasies must be stopped before they morph into self-fulfilling prophecies."

"What about the fatalities and the wounded?" Woody interjected.

"I wish I had an explanation. The research I have done over the past five weeks since escaping 286 has been inconclusive. I suspect that the bodies and injuries were all staged, however, there appears to be some evidence that the government has sacrificed innocent rookies and recruits on the altar of political expediency. There's no doubt in my mind that the government is corrupt enough to do either."

The group plied Jack with a few more questions on his flight and arrest, then barraged him and Sally with questions on their time in 286, their escape through the sewer, stealing the truck, staying at the cabin, connecting with their ride, holing up in Pennsylvania, and their ride in the belly of the combine.

At 8:30 Jordy rapped his empty coffee cup on the podium. "We need to move on to another vital subject." He turned to Sally. "It's our understanding, which we learned from Irina, that you were a major player in the Minoa project. Tell us about your involvement."

"In December 2017 I was summoned to an emergency meeting in the Cabinet Room at the White House. The president spoke for about two minutes, informing us about the existence of the comet formally designated as RN13 and popularly known as the Rogue, informing us that it posed a serious threat to the world, and informing us that he had declared a national emergency. At that point, I wasn't worried. I figured that we were dealing with something in the one-kilometer range. Then he turned the meeting over to Dr. Goldblum.

"He started by giving us the details on the comet. Needless to say, I was numb when I learned that a rocky comet larger than Mercury was on a collision course with Mars, that it was still too far out to pick up with Earth-based infrared, that its albedo—below 0.015—was too low for it to be picked up with Earth-based optical, and that we currently had no space telescopes capable of observing the comet.

"The initial threat analysis by NASA suggested that there was a slight possibility that either Mars or the comet could be bumped out of its orbit. But they weren't concerned about that. They feared that the comet would knock a few asteroids out of the main belt when it passed into the inner solar system and a few more when it passed out again and that these asteroids would eventually pose a threat to Earth.

"It was a complete surprise to me when he explained— given all the hullaballoo for the past two decades over the danger that the earth faced from NEOs—that the government's greatest fear wasn't the asteroids themselves, but public panic over them. They were pulling out all stops to avoid apocalyptic anarchy.

"Next, he informed us that the government was in the process of organizing a response that had been codenamed Minoa, that he had been appointed director over the entire Minoa response, and that he answered directly to the president. This was shocking to me as I had always regarded him as an overrated, self-promoting opportunist.

"I was even more shocked when he appointed me to be the head of the Minoa Research Team, composed of twenty-four astronomers, astrophysicists, and aerospace engineers. I honestly didn't think I was qualified and figured he was trying to win brownie points with me. But there was no way to turn down the appointment without serious repercussions, so I reluctantly accepted. My team was given six main duties.

"One, monitor and investigate the Rogue through every available means.

"Two, oversee the retrofitting of NEOCam, the refurbishing of Spitzer and WISE, and the Rogue research conducted through these telescopes.

"Three, oversee the renovation of Space Shuttle Atlantis and its subsequent Rogue missions.

"Four, plan and oversee the new mission for the ExoMars probe, which we hoped to land on the Rogue while pretending to land it on a Trojan.

"Five, oversee the six Earth-based infrared telescopes which had been assigned to the Rogue and were currently tracking the Rogue with stellar occultation.

"Six, defend the 'official' explanation of the stellar occultation, which, as you already know, is the shock horizon from the growing jet of a recently formed black hole."

Andrius raised his hand with a question. "Is there any significance behind the RN13 nomenclature?"

"Yes. RN13 is an acronym that stands for Rogue, NEO, and thirteen, the thirteen being a symbol for bad luck."

Woody raised his hand, and she nodded at him. "We were told by several web sources that Space Shuttle Atlantis was refurbished so NASA could refurbish the Spitzer and the WISE space telescopes for cold-body missions. But something seemed amiss in these reports. The Spitzer was about 160 million miles from Earth at the time, which is more than six hundred times the distance to the moon. So it would have been impossible to reach it with the Space Shuttle. The fact is, with current capabilities, any manned mission to the Spitzer is out of the question. So how did they refurbish it?"

Sally smiled. "They used Space Shuttle Atlantis to launch a large robotic satellite that had been designed and built by Dirk West, the maverick scientist and owner of Space Treks. I was in the meeting at the White House in January 2018 when President Weston cornered Dirk and demanded his help."

"I'll bet there were some fireworks there."

"There certainly was. Two of the most arrogant men on the planet going at it. When Dirk balked at the president's request for a special satellite to refuel and refurbish the Spitzer Space Telescope, claiming that he was too busy, President Weston got in his face. 'Listen here, hotshot. You will assemble a team in the next forty-eight hours who can be fast-tracked for Secret clearance and report to Richard Fairchild. You are going to build this satellite for me, and you are going to have it done in six months—launch-ready by the end of July. If you fail to show in two days or fail to perform at any stage, I will make it worse for you than habanero in your jockstrap. No more NASA contracts and no more permits ... ever. End of story.'

"Dirk got red in the face and started to holler at the president. But two Secret Service agents grabbed him. As they were dragging him away, he shouted at the president, 'You can't do that!' The president bellowed back, 'Watch me!'

"And how long did it take Dirk to get the satellite ready?"

"Five and half months."

"How long did it take the satellite to get there?"

"From its launch out of Space Shuttle Atlantis, it took MacGyver, as the satellite came to be called, two hundred and twenty days to reach the Spitzer."

"How long did the refueling and refurbishing take?"

"Six days. The signals took about thirteen minutes to travel to the Spitzer, so all of the operations were prolonged. The software update was relatively straightforward once it started, though it took a while because the motherboard and CPU were slow. The hardest part was replenishing the helium. We had to loosen a cover and swing it out of the way, insert a filling fixture into the fill valve, and turn a lever to allow the exchange of fuel. The process once started only took about thirty minutes."

Andrius had another question. "How come the government didn't use SOFIA or some other high-altitude flight option with infrared capacity to get an early jump on visuals on the comet? They probably would have only gained maybe six months, but for NEO warning, six months is huge."

"President Weston considered this option, but he was jittery about the contrail nutcases. They track all flights that aren't commercial, military, or civilian, and they have become quite sophisticated in their efforts. While most of their theories on these ghost flights are far from the truth, their tracking and sleuthing are causing serious headaches for two top-secret government programs. He decided against giving them more fuel for their conspiracy theories, for that would further endanger the top-secret programs and possibly complicate our efforts to keep the comet under wraps."

Jordy raised another tantalizing question. "How did the White House convince Europe to let us take over their ExoMars mission and turn it into a Rogue mission?"

"That was a tough sell. Ultimately, it cost us several concessions. The first was turning over the proof that a massive comet was going to pass through the asteroid belt, potentially knocking asteroids out of orbit that could threaten Earth for centuries, and then pass close enough to Mars to bump one or both bodies into new orbits, possibly leading to unthinkable scenarios.

The second was promising a massive investment in several NATO allies who were terrified that they might be looking at a post-Germany NATO within a couple years—a fear which has since come to pass.

"The third was underwriting a joint NASA and ESA mission to Mars that would launch supply capsules in 2028 and 2029 and launch a manned module in 2030. Europe was promised that she would supply two of the six crew members.

"The fourth was significant political concessions regarding Israel, human rights, hate-speech laws, gun rights, and global warming. Concessions that would have infuriated his right-wing support base had they known. But President Weston had made it clear to his special envoy that he would agree to almost any conditions, provided that they made were under the table and would not be announced until after the election. So the Europeans made their demands, President Weston accepted, and Europe turned over the project and kept their mouths shut on the concessions. President Weston's followers have no idea how badly he has betrayed them."

"That would be a crushing blow to his loyalists," Jordy observed, "if he re-engineered himself into a populist after the next election. But such a move could broaden and strengthen his base while isolating and weakening both the far right and the far left."

"After seeing President Weston at work in the White House," Sally noted, "I think he has a few surprises up his sleeve for America."

"How about the other nations?" Jordy continued. "How much do they know about the comet?"

"We shared the comet's existence with the heads of our closest allies and the G20 so they could prepare for the coming disaster. We also coordinated with several other nations that have large infrared telescopes to ensure that no astronomers engage in research in Taurus except for those that are authorized. Several large observatories were either leased or purchased outright for exorbitant sums."

"How about timing?" Woody inquired. "When will the comet be visible to Earth-based infrared telescopes? When will the biggest optical telescopes pick it up? And how long until amateurs will be able to see it with legal backyard telescopes?"

"According to the information that was available at the time of my arrest, the comet will first be visible to Earth-based infrared sometime this spring when it's nearing Uranus. It won't be visible to our largest optical telescopes, like the Keck 1 and 2, until sometime in 2023 when it's between Saturn and Jupiter.

"As for the amateur astronomers, NASA says they won't see the comet, though a few might get lucky and notice that something odd is going on in the asteroid belt in March 2024. But NASA will be ready with pre-packaged explanations so they can explain away any occultations and deflections of asteroids that may occur."

Woody was dumbfounded. "Are you implying that NASA doesn't believe that the Rogue will develop a coma?"

"Correct. They're following mainstream science to the letter. According to the common understanding, comets are dirty snowballs, and comet comas and tails are the sublimation of ice. Stony comets don't have ice to sublimate, so they can't develop comas and tails."

Woody shook his head flabbergasted. "Nobody said a word about the occasional asteroid that has displayed a coma? Doesn't that make them worry?"

"Yeah, they brought it up. But no, they're not worried at all. They think the odds are on their side. Fewer than one in a thousand asteroids manifest a coma. And ninety-nine percent of the time, asteroid comas are so faint that backyard telescopes are unlikely to notice them. Since they're treating the rocky comet just like it was a rocky asteroid, they figure there's a one in a thousand chance that the Rogue will manifest a coma and a one in a hundred thousand chance that the coma will be bright enough to be visible with a backyard telescope."

"Wow. They're clinging to the explanation that comas in rocky asteroids are best explained by the sublimation of trapped ice? And they're extrapolating that theory to rocky comets?"

"That's right. They have convinced themselves that there's nothing to worry about."

Woody chuckled. "They're in for a painful surprise that's going to reveal their lies to the world. The Rogue is going to glow in the heavens like no comet has done for nearly three thousand years. A light show for the ages."

She cocked her head slightly. "Jack talked about electrical comets when we were in 286. He said he got the idea from you."

He nodded. "Yeah. We talked about the electric universe many times over the past decade."

"So you think that when the comet gets deep enough in the solar system, the charge imbalance between the comet and the charge flowing from the sun will lead to electrically-induced ionization, and that's what causes comets to glow?"

"Correct. But I would add that the tiny charge imbalance of an asteroid with a slightly elliptical orbit is nothing compared to the massive charge imbalance of a comet that's coming from the depths of the Kuiper Belt. That's why comets glow brighter than asteroids. And when you factor in the size of the Rogue, there will be an insane coma and a tail that stretches across the entire horizon."

44

Atchafalaya Swamp, Louisiana
Saturday, February 8, 2020

Ariele and Sam sat on the deck of the cabin wrapped in blankets, savoring mugs of coffee and indulging the glow of what would likely be their last sunrise at the remote hideout. As the nascent hues spread and brightened, Sam jabbed Ariele with her elbow. "What's eating, you, girl? You've been pretty sullen the past few days."

The young lady turned to her older friend. "I got an email from Joby a few days ago that kind of rocked my world."

"A Dear John letter?"

"No. Nothing like that."

"Then what?"

"He told me that he was in love with me and wanted me to be his wife."

Sam squinted down her nose. "Isn't that what you wanted? An organic, farm loving, Messianic rabbi for your husband?"

"Yea, but … he wants to make aliyah to Israel. And he

wants to join the Israeli Defense Force and make that his job until he finishes his master's degree. I'm torn up. I don't want to move away from my family to a different culture. Especially not if I'm going to be on my own a lot while he's training."

Sam touched her arm. "But you already have moved away from your family. Because of the government's response to the Rogue, you can't communicate with your family without endangering them."

"I know. But living a thousand miles away is hard enough. Living seventy-five hundred miles away would be unbearable. I might as well live on the moon." She swirled her coffee cup on the arm of the rocker, then looked back to Sam. "I know I'm just feeling sorry for myself. Still, the culture change would be rough. All I know is California."

"I think you'd be pleasantly surprised by how well you'd fit in. You grew up in a Jewish community in Los Angeles, exposed to a rich blending of cultures. So you're well prepared for Israel's melting pot of Mediterranean, Middle Eastern, and European cultures and her diverse expressions of Judaism from secular to ultra-Orthodox."

Ariele nodded.

It dawned on Sam that the real issue was Ariele's independence, not Joby or Israel. She was—why didn't she see it sooner?—her mini-me. That called for a different approach. "Sometimes you find more freedom in commitment than you do running solo."

The thought startled Ariele. She turned to her older friend, looking for further light.

"The freedoms you gain in commitment," Sam continued, "often outweigh the freedoms you lose."

Sam found herself staring into bewildered eyes. "I know it seems strange to hear that from me, but it's a lesson that I'm finally learning after all these years, though I still struggle with fear."

"So why do you struggle with commitment?"

"It's a long story. I grew up in a dysfunctional family. My parents' marriage was filled with tension. My grandparents' marriages on both sides were rocky. And the marriages of my aunts and uncles on both sides were unstable. So I grew up fearing commitment. I equated it with pain. By the time I was in high school, I lived in a shell. I had guy friends, but no boyfriends. Not that I wasn't interested—"

The conversation was interrupted by the secure phone vibrating in Sam's coat pocket.

"Jungle Queen."

"Tenkara, here. Good morning, Sam."

"Hey, Woody. Great to hear your voice."

"You too. Say, got a big heads up. You girls need to get out of there ASAP. The Middle East is heating up. Israel has incensed its neighbors with its recent attacks on Hezbollah positions in Jordan, Hamas targets in Gaza, Syrian troops in the exclusion zone in the Golan, and Iranian outposts in Syria. There is troop movement in Jordan, Lebanon, and Syria near the Israeli border. Russia just delivered two massive shipments of equipment to Syria. And Syria is preparing a convoy of equipment that U.S and Israeli intelligence presume is headed for Lebanon."

"Yeah. We caught the story on the news. Do you really think this situation could affect us?"

"Not sure. But the government is still on edge over the terrorist attack in Port Arthur. We don't want to take any chances that things might lock down again over another instance of terrorism. Can't have you getting stuck down there again."

"Yeah. That would be a bummer."

"Are you girls still on target for a departure tonight?"

"We are, unless something significant changes. Rat got back from his mission early this morning and is sleeping now. He plans on taking us to the platform tonight and out of the swamp tomorrow night."

"Sounds good. We've been pretty anxious about you girls."

Sam laughed. "What! You don't think we can take of ourselves?"

"It's not the gender, Sam. It's the danger for all involved."

"I know. Just yanking your chain. By the way, is there any news on Jack and Sally?"

"There is. They arrived yesterday afternoon."

"Thank God! I'll let Ariele know."

"Well, gotta run, Sam. Take care. Say hi to Moxie."

"I will," she whispered. "Bye." She clasped her phone to her chest in trembling hands, her jaded nerves standing a little aloof from the spark of joy as she mouthed the words to herself. *Jack is safe.*

***

"Man, am I bushed!" Ariele complained as she cinched down her bags in the canoe. I didn't sleep at all. I was way too anxious."

"I didn't sleep either, but I'm not feeling tired," Sam replied. "I'm way too wired. But once the adrenalin wears off, I'll be dead on my feet." She tightened the strap securing her duffel bags to the thwart in front of the stern seat. "I hope this attempt goes better than the last."

"Me too! No snakes!" Ariele replied.

The two shared a laugh.

Rat placed his gear bag into his canoe. "Glad we got an overcast sky," he announced. "It'll cover up the full moon."

"I'd rather have the full moon," Ariele snorted, "so I can see where I'm going."

"Clarity is nice, but secrecy is better." The tension in his voice suggested that something was bothering him.

"What's up, Swampie?" Sam inquired.

"The towns along the edge of the swamp and the settlements in the bayous are crawling with agents. "I'm guessing there are twice as many as when you two arrived. And they have started patrolling the outer reaches of the swamp by canoe. We're going to have to exercise extreme caution. No talking. No noisy paddling."

"Understood," she replied. "We'll give it our best." She felt sorry for Rat. They were a liability to him. They slowed him down. They were too noisy. And they were on the Homeland Security registry—Ariele as a known threat, she as a suspected associate. If they were stopped, his cover would be blown. Perhaps they should have just met him at the platform and picked up the sensors there. That would have saved him and them a lot of hassles.

A few minutes later, just before midnight, tearful goodbyes were exchanged, and the trio pushed off. Though they had used tactical-red LED flashlights while getting ready, Ariele's eyes hadn't yet adjusted to the inky darkness, and she struggled to see the narrow channel that led away from the cabin. Tossing her head in a huff of frustration, she discovered that her peripheral vision was better able to catch the outlines of the waterway and the trees and branches overhanging it. She relaxed and focused on listening. Soon the sound of their paddles dipping, pulling, and lifting drew her in like a country song indulging pain and hope. She was leaving friends she had come to cherish—friends who had saved her life. But she was also headed for Montana and a pair of dazzling blue eyes.

They glided out of the channel into the nearby bayou and found themselves wrapped in a thick blanket of fog. Ariele nearly panicked. She held up her hand and made the freeze signal, which Rat had taught them on their inbound journey. Sam stopped paddling. Rat's soft dips and strokes could be heard off to their right. Ariele rolled her eyes at herself. *Should have remembered that we make a right turn here.*

The next hour passed in a blur of bayous, channels, potholes, fog banks, tangles, and swats from branches. She recognized nothing after the first bayou. Fear stretched its tentacles into her mind. *Are we lost? Is Rat taking us on a different route?* Her trepidation eased when he beached his canoe on the shore of a small pothole. She recognized the spot. It was the only portage on this leg of their swamp journey. Now she fought frustration. Normally, a chance to get out of the canoe would have been welcomed. But not today. Not with her sore leg.

Ariele gingerly stepped out of the canoe, hobbled over to a nearby cypress tree, and sat down with her back against its trunk. While she rubbed her tender calf, she watched Rat and Sam ferry loads of gear to a relatively dry snarl of roots, lash the paddles to the thwarts, lift the canoes onto their shoulders, and trudge off into the darkness. As the silence and gloom enveloped her, she turned her attention to her right elbow, which she had cracked hard on a tree. It throbbed with that odd combination of pain and numbness that only the elbow can offer. As she rubbed the aching joint, her fingers found a hard and crusty substance clinging to her jacket. Her first thought was bark. But underneath the flake that had peeled off, her jacket was sticky. Blood! She had split her elbow open.

On the second trip on the portage trail, Ariele limped along behind Sam, carrying her own duffel bags. As she slogged through the boot-sucking muck, her shoes filled with foul-smelling ooze, her left calf throbbed, and waves of dizziness washed over her. Rat had warned her that this sometimes happened even months after a water-moccasin bite. She resisted the dark channels that her mind drifted towards and turned to prayer. *Right now, LORD, the only thing I have going for me is that I don't have it as bad as Job. Get me through this trial and allow me to see your goodness in the land of the living.*

Back on the water, the woeful odyssey continued. The discomfort in her leg became a searing fire, and her right elbow stabbed with pain with every stroke. The intrepid young lady tried to tough it out with silent tears and prayers. But that didn't distract her enough. She began counting her strokes. Soon she was no longer counting the rhythmic sounds but merely indulging them. They pulled at her hypnotically. She relented and slipped into a foggy delirium.

They were paddling across a small lake. Where were they? How long had she been drifting mentally? How much of the trip was left? Where was Rat? She peered into the thick darkness in every direction, but there was nothing to see but the smothering fog. They continued going forward or what she hoped was forward, every stroke adding to her fear and uncertainty.

The mist thinned, revealing the indistinct shoreline on both sides. She was overcome with the sensation that she was in a familiar place. Or was it her mind playing a trick on her? Off to their right, she could see Rat paddling away from them. He disappeared into the shadows of the shoreline. That confused her. But everything made sense when the wendigo oak greeted them on their left, its unique double forks stretching into the sky from the massive trunk.

Sam swung the canoe around, and the girls paddled toward the wall of trees where Rat had vanished. After two false starts—nosing up what looked like an overgrown passage and getting stopped by a wall of vines and roots—they found the opening. Two minutes later, they tied up at the platform. Ariele grabbed the porch rail and pulled herself up on her wobbly legs. She tried to lift her sore leg over the side of the canoe, but throbbing pain kept her from raising it more than seven or eight inches. She tried to stand on her sore leg and lift her good leg over the canoe side, but her bad leg threatened to buckle.

Rat hoisted Ariele onto the deck and steadied her against the rail. "My hat's off to you, girl," he said softly, "for pushing through the weakness, nausea, and pain. That was an outstanding effort. Most of the guys I know couldn't have gutted that out." She managed a feeble smile, leaned over the rail, and retched into the turbid waters.

Sam took her suffering friend by the arm, led her to the tiny table, and forced her to drink some water, take an electrolyte tablet, and eat some chocolate.

When Rat had finished lugging their gear inside, he joined them at the table. The bloody sleeve on Ariele's jacket concerned him. "We need to take a look at that elbow."

When Sam peeled the blood-soaked shirt sleeve off her arm, she gasped. A two-inch gash, still seeping blood and fluid, ran vertically up her elbow. Ariele slumped in her chair and shivered, weak and chilled. The Jews for Jesus t-shirt that Peggy Sue had given her did little to protect her from the chilly breeze wafting through the platform. Sam draped her jacket over her shoulders. Though it was little more than a token effort, Ariele reached up and clasped her hand.

"Yikes!" Ariele exclaimed as Rat lifted her arm to take a look for himself.

He whistled. "That definitely needs stitches." He retrieved a well-stocked first aid kit from the shelf, dug out the topical anesthetic, and liberally swabbed the wound area. Ariele winced.

"Gonna need to let that sit for thirty minutes," he advised. "In the meantime, Sam, get some hot chocolate and crackers in her belly. And more electrolytes."

When the dreaded moment arrived, Rat held Ariele's arm steady while Sam plunged the suture needle into the tissue next to the wound. Ariele grit her teeth. Her elbow was numb, but not numb enough. Tears welled up in her eyes. Sam pushed the needle up on the other side, fished one end through, tied a triple overhand knot, and cut the loose ends. Then she repeated the process until the gash was closed with ten uneven stitches.

"It ain't pretty," she announced, "but it'll get the job done."

The two of them pulled a clean thermal shirt over Ariele's stiff arms, then zipped her up inside her sleeping bag on the bottom bunk with a hot water bottle. Sam touched her cheek and whispered, "Good night, Moxie." Then she climbed into the top bunk, bone-tired herself.

Rat scurried about the cabin for a few minutes, his tiny red light flickering back and forth, running through his checklist of security and safety concerns. When he was satisfied that everything was okay, he unlaced his boots, climbed into his hammock, and listened to the night sounds. Though it was cool, there were still a few chorus frogs and spring peepers exercising their lungs.

"Hey, girls," he announced, interrupting the symphony. "I'll fry up some potatoes and eggs when we wake up in the morning." But nobody answered. They were already in dreamland.

***

The next evening, they retired early, crawling into bed at 8:30, hoping to get a few hours rest before the next leg of their journey. But Ariele struggled to fall asleep. She tossed and turned for an hour. Her leg and elbow throbbed. Her mind ran helter-skelter among a gauntlet of law-enforcement fears: agents patrolling the edges of the swamp, getting stopped at roadblocks, the Compound getting raided. And she was nervous about what her friends at the Compound would think about her exercise to follow Jesus as a Messianic Jew. She hoped they could appreciate this direction. It seemed like destiny was calling her.

She woke in a daze. Someone was shaking her. "Rise and shine," she heard Rat say. "It's 11:45. We're heading out in twenty minutes." She unzipped her sleeping bag, slung her feet out of the bunk, and struggled to put her shoes on, fumbling with the laces like she was all thumbs. Though her weakness and nausea had largely retreated—Sam had kept after her all day to eat, force liquids, and take Vitamin C and ginger—she still felt sore and out of sync. She opened up the sleeping bag to air it out, wolfed down a granola bar, and lugged her bags to the canoe. *Not looking forward to another night of paddling, but it sure will be nice to put this swamp adventure behind us.*

Rat slammed his bags into his canoe, startling Ariele. She looked skyward, noted the cloudless sky, and guessed that his tantrum was over the lack of cloud cover. The girls loaded their gear and took their seats in silence. They knew Rat was in no mood for conversation. He reminded Ariele of her father. When he was grumpy, he wanted to be left alone, and he wanted silence. Without a word, he climbed into his canoe, pushed off from the deck, and started paddling. They followed.

As Ariele passed under the canopy that shrouded the platform, she took a wistful look back. She was going to miss this little outpost in the wilderness. The cabin too. Not miss them like home. Miss them like stops on the wayfarer's journey home. She no longer had a home in this world. Not California. Not the Compound. Her home was in the world to come. She was now a pilgrim and stranger.

The trip went much more smoothly for Ariele than the previous night. Though she banged her head twice while passing under snarls of roots and took a sliver in her palm during the portage while climbing down the wall of cypress roots, overall it was her best night in the swamp. The time passed more quickly too. She was pleasantly surprised when they passed out of a narrow bayou and turned east on the big water.

Twelve minutes later, they tied up at the dock at the cottage where their swamp adventure had begun. She checked her watch. As usual, Rat was on schedule. It was 3:57.

"Canoes go in the garage," he whispered. "Paddles and vests in the cabinet on the porch." Then he grabbed a load of gear and hustled up the dock. The girls followed. After carrying their duffel bags and gear to the porch and storing their canoe in the garage, the girls sat on their bags and waited for their ride. Rat waited with them rather than going straight to bed.

At 4:29 the faint whine of an engine intruded on the quiet. Soon a vehicle appeared on the driveway. Their nerves were on edge. Was this their ride? Was it law enforcement? Or was it rednecks looking for trouble? The vehicle stopped, but no door opened. With trembling hands, Ariele typed the verification text, STETSON? Blake texted back, YES! GIT IN CAMPER!

The girls hugged Rat goodbye, grabbed their bags, darted around the corner, and raced for the truck. Blake didn't get out. There was no time for hugs. They tossed their bags into the camper and climbed in after them. Then Sam tapped on the pass-through window, signaling to Blake that they were ready.

While the truck bounced up the road, the girls took their shoes and watches off and placed them in their clothes bags. Hard objects would make noise if they banged or scratched against the plywood in the secret place if they had to hide. Then they lifted the plywood cover and stowed their bags at the foot end of the hiding place.

Ariele shook her head. "What in the world? They lined the whole thing with heavy-duty space blankets! It'll be unbearably hot in there if we have to spend more than a few minutes inside."

Sam nodded in agreement. "No doubt. But we're just gonna have to grin and bear it. The guys are more concerned about our safety than our comfort."

They curled up in semi-miserable positions at the table and tried to get some shuteye. As Ariele's eyelids began to droop, she noticed that headlights were no longer shining through the back door. She tried to process that information. Why didn't Blake stop to make sure that Android was okay? Or maybe he didn't notice that the brainiac was no longer behind him. Or maybe splitting up was part of the plan? But the fog of sleep overcame her, and she never finished processing the matter.

45

**west of Dallas-Fort Worth, TX
Saturday, February 8, 2020**

Blake trembled with anxiety. It was his turn at the checkpoint. Two soldiers moved in front of his truck and stood with M16s at ready. A Homeland Security agent walked toward him. Blake prayed the same prayer he had prayed at every checkpoint. *Lord, watch over us. Bless our journey home. If you open doors, no man can shut them. If you shut doors, no man can open them.*

The agent motioned for him to roll his window down, the poked his head partially into the truck. "Have you got any passengers with you?"

Blake smiled and patted the empty seat next to him. "I'm pretty much a loner until I get hitched."

"Mind if I check the camper?"

"Be my guest."

The man turned his infrared scanner on and waved it back and forth across the driver's side of the pickup camper, starting low and working his way higher, looking for anomalous heat signatures that could be illegal aliens or

Security Act violators. When he finished that face, he disappeared behind the truck. A couple minutes later, he reappeared in front of the vehicle, holstered his scanner, and gave the guards a thumbs up. The soldiers stepped aside and waved the pickup through.

Blake exhaled. This was getting old. It was their third checkpoint since leaving Butte La Rose, Louisiana. They had been stopped at Lafeyette, again outside Shreveport, and now on the west side of Dallas-Forth Worth. He accelerated to highway speed, set the cruise control, and banged on the ceiling of the cab, his signal that the coast was clear.

The girls were ecstatic to hear the pounding. It was hot and stuffy in the hiding place, and while they probably weren't in danger of suffocating, they did feel overheated and short of breath. With a rush of joyous relief, Sam pushed the plywood up, flung one leg over the lip, and began sliding out. Her exit was interrupted by Blake banging once again on the ceiling. This time rapidly and violently. She froze. The extra banging confused her. Were they supposed to hurry up and get out or hurry up and get back in?

The question was answered by the whoop of a siren and flashing lights shining through the door curtain. "Rats!" Sam muttered, as she retracted her leg, squeezed back into the tight confines, and lowered the plywood. In the darkness, they sensed the brakes being applied fairly hard, then heard and felt the distinct staccato of a rumble strip. Blake was pulling over onto the shoulder.

Mere seconds after the truck stopped, the camper door clattered open, and footsteps barged into the camper. Blake informed them later that the surprise visitor had been a Homeland Security agent. That's why he entered the camper so fast. He didn't have to run the license plate first like highway patrolman usually did. They heard him poking around in the camper, opening and closing doors—the closet, under the sink, the tiny bathroom. Then he checked the storage spaces in the benches at the table. Sam shuddered. *Sure glad we didn't try to hide in any of those spaces.*

He approached the loft bed, pulled out several of the drawers that spanned the front, and slammed them shut. Then he raised the mattress, looked around for a few seconds, and let it fall back down with a thwump. There was silence for a moment. Apparently, he hadn't seen anything that made him suspicious. She was glad for the meticulous effort that the guys had put into the hideaway space, like the inclusion of screws so it looked like the plywood was screwed down.

The agent turned around and addressed Blake, who was standing at the camper door. "Sorry to be so nosy. The agent at the checkpoint recorded an anomalous infrared signature in the loft and another under the sink. We're required by DHS to check every anomaly. We can't make assumptions or exceptions. Every day we catch vehicles trying to sneak people past this checkpoint. I didn't find anything suspicious, but I did notice that your water heater and your electric mattress pad are on. They'll go down in my report as the probable causes. You may want to turn the mattress pad off when you're not using it. They're a known fire hazard."

Sam expected him to leave. But he didn't. Blake started to speak, but he stopped mid-sentence as if the man had silenced him. The two stood motionless. He was listening! Did he suspect something? Sam's heart began to pound, and her anxiety skyrocketed. It was so loud in her ears, she feared it might give her away. She began to struggle. The plywood was inches above their faces. The darkness enveloped them. She felt like she was trapped in a coffin. Worse, her nose and sinuses were plugged from a cold she had been fighting. She felt like she couldn't breathe and was going to pass out. Phlegm was building up in her throat. She desperately needed to cough.

The discomfort and panic grew. The urge to give up and push the plywood away was overwhelming her will. She was losing the battle. Then she did something unusual. She prayed. *God. I know it seems self-serving to pray in a desperate situation when I don't normally pray. But help me. Amen.* The prayer was as terse and to the point as the woman who uttered it. Immediately her pulse slowed, her body relaxed, and her breathing eased. That surprised her. But she knew it shouldn't have. There was a God up there. And he really was God.

But she didn't stop with her temporal need. Once she opened the door, there was no shutting it again. Not for a woman like herself who lived life with near reckless passion. At that moment, in the darkness of her prison, Sam surrendered to the amazing God-Man that Jack, Woody, Kit, and now Ariele had surrendered to. *Jesus. I believe that you are THE way of salvation. Help me to pursue you with the same passion that I have pursued this world's treasures. Help me to fight your battles with the same intensity that I have fought earthly battles. I promise this won't be a foxhole conversion.* A calm descended over her. She could hardly believe that she had prayed the prayer. But she was relieved and glad that she finally had.

Footsteps shuffled across the floor and down the steps. The door slammed shut. Hope began to rise in Sam's breast. The driver's door opened and shut. The truck fired up, started rolling down the shoulder, crossed the rumble strips, and pulled back onto the highway. A few seconds later, Blake pounded on the ceiling for the third time. Sam pushed the plywood up, and the girls crawled out of their tomb, hot and sweaty, and emotionally exhausted. They flopped into their seats and stared at each other.

"I think we need some moral support," Sam suggested.

"Amen to that!" Ariele replied. "You make the coffee, and I'll dig out the dark chocolate."

46

the Compound
Tuesday, February 11, 2020

Blake nudged his tan F-150 up to the log parking rail at the lodge shortly after four o'clock in the afternoon, turned the truck off, and laid his head on the steering wheel exhausted. His hands were jittery from too much caffeine. Empty coffee cups and energy drink cans littered the floor. His tongue was raw from chewing sunflower seeds to help him stay awake.

He pondered the odyssey he had just endured. It frustrated him to no end that a trip that should have been a leisurely camping trip had been a nerve-wracking, high-risk mission. How had this once great nation collapsed into early-stage dystopianism almost overnight?

He knew the mechanisms. The interlaced conspiracies which had taken America down the path of Big-Brother government had been masterfully crafted: the threat of home-grown terrorism, the threat of man-caused climate change, and the threat of epidemics. Though they all seemed overblown if not outright deception to the thinking man, they kept the masses in a state of constant fear, more than willing to surrender freedom if it offered them hope for survival.

What he didn't understand was how the public had been dumbed down to where they could be duped by such dubious storylines. How could they not see the difference between real terrorism and Rogue-awareness or patriotism? Between pollution and the global-warming hoax? Between real epidemics and bugs that were more dangerous than the seasonal flu but not true epidemics?

For a while, the conservative media had resisted the trend, but one by one they had thrown their towels in the ring. The only outlets now who were outspoken in their challenge to the great reset were the alternative news outlets, despised by both the left and the right.

Woody swung the truck door open and greeted his friend. "Hey, cowpoke! What took you so long? We figured your return trip at two and a half days, and here it is deep into the fourth day."

The weary traveler shook his head. "The past few days have been a nightmare. I got stopped three times at checkpoints in Louisiana and Texas, losing more than an hour each time. I lost another hour when a Homeland Security agent stopped me on the highway after a Texas checkpoint to search the camper. And I burned up four hours at a checkpoint between Colorado Springs and Denver. Not only was it backed up, but they searched the camper pretty thoroughly.

"At that point, after two hair-raising camper searches, I got so nervous that I started routing myself around the checkpoints.

"When I stopped in Loveland, a trucker informed me that the checkpoint north of Fort Collins was backed up even worse than the one south of Denver. He advised me to take 287 to Laramie, then head for Casper.

"At Casper, another trucker told me that both U.S. 25 and U.S. 26 north were slowed down with checkpoints. He suggested that I double back, take Wyoming 220 to Muddy Gap, then take U.S. 287 to Lander. From Lander, I worked my way north through Shoshoni, Worland, Greybull, Lovell, and Bridger to Laurel, avoiding two checkpoints by taking back roads.

"All in all, these reroutings cost me more than twenty-four hours. It would have been quicker to use the checkpoints, but like I said, after the close calls, I started routing around the checkpoints."

Woody set his hand on his shoulder. "At least the ordeal is over, and you guys made it back safe. Come on. Let's go inside." Blake dragged himself out of the truck and lumbered after him.

Inside it was a madhouse. The folks had surrounded Ariele and Sam and were plying them with questions about their adventure. What was it like in the swamp? How big was the cabin? What did the wendigo look like? Does your snake bite still hurt?

Ariele and Joby were standing side by side, enjoying each other's company. When she laughed, the star-of-David earrings that he had given her swirled and danced. They did make a cute couple, especially now that Joby's hair had grown back.

Woody and Blake walked past the commotion to the kitchen. The old soldier returned to his buttermilk-pancake project. The young buck poured himself a cup of coffee, laced it with cream to protect his sour stomach, and took a seat at the table. A few minutes later, Red started dropping bacon into a hot fry pan. The sizzling and popping were mesmerizing music to Blake's ears. He felt his whole body relax. He perked up even further when Red set a plate in front of him with two strips of the meat from heaven still sizzling hot.

After a joyous afternoon breakfast, Sally volunteered to wash the dishes. Ariele seized the opportunity and followed her to the sink with a stack of plates, hoping they could speak in semi-privacy once the others had retreated to the main room. While the sink was filling with hot water, she asked her former boss about her Rogue experience. Sally gave her the whole story in abbreviated form: the original phone call, the trips to Washington, her initial doubts, covering for Woody, her flight, the hitchhiking ride, her arrest, her detainment in 286, the adjustments she had to make, meeting Jack, and the escape.

The account of the breakout and flight stunned Ariele. "How did you ever find the strength to face the sewer? I mean ... you had to crawl a half mile in ice-cold water filled with filth and human waste. By your own testimony, you were a petite woman who didn't work out and didn't have any active hobbies. You once told me that the most exercise you ever got was shopping at the mall in heels."

Sally turned to Ariele and looked her in the eyes. "I rose

to the occasion. Sometimes a woman just has to man up and crawl through a lot of crap to get what she wants."

"I get that. But people don't generally rise to the occasion without motivation. So where did you find the motivation? I mean, that was one ugly ordeal."

"At first I didn't have any motivation. Jack and I talked about escaping, and we made some preparations, but to me, it was more an exercise in escapism than reality. I honestly figured that I was stuck there for life with no realistic hope of getting out and nothing on the outside that I valued enough to risk internment in a 300-series camp, much less death"

"But you went along with the planning?"

"It served a purpose. It kept us occupied."

"But something changed."

Sally laughed. "After Irina escaped, Jack stepped up the tempo in gathering intel, planning, and making preparations. That made me nervous. After his assessment trip in the sewer, which revealed that it actually was a workable plan, I went through some difficult soul searching. Did I really want to try to escape with him? Did I have anything on the outside that made it worth enduring the nasty crawl and risking a 300-series camp? My initial thoughts were *no*, but somewhere along the line, it dawned on me that escaping offered a second chance at a lost opportunity."

Ariele stared blankly at her.

Sally blushed.

"A guy thing? she exclaimed. "You mean, like, Woody?"

"Yeah. I've been interested in him since I arrived at

Caltech. But he didn't make it easy. His mixed signals left me feeling rejected. When he left for his last hiking adventure, I had a gut feeling that our paths would never cross again, so I gave up on him and buried my feelings. But when it became obvious that Jack really was going to attempt to escape, hope sprung anew."

"Are you going to pursue him?"

She shrugged her shoulders.

"Hey ladies!" Jordy called from the main room. "Time for the news!"

As Ariele walked to the great room to join the others, she found herself encouraged by Sally's experience. *If she can brave a sewer for an uncertain hope, I can face anything to follow Joby, even my fear of moving to Israel … even my fear of commitment.*

"Good evening from New York City. I'm Tom Overbright and this is *The World Report* on CVN—your first choice for news from a conservative viewpoint.

"Our headline story tonight is the ESA's announcement earlier today that it has tentatively settled on a replacement mission for the failed ExoMars mission. If you recall, last November the ExoMars probe failed to engage Mars in orbit due to a failed thruster. It hurtled around the planet in slingshot fashion and was flung into an orbit that will bring it fairly close to Jupiter. The technicians working on the thruster glitch think they have fixed it with a software patch, and the flight engineers are confident they can salvage the mission by landing the probe on a Trojan that shares Jupiter's orbit.

"For those unfamiliar with this astronomical term, Trojans are small bodies that share the orbit of a larger body. Neptune has twenty-two, Mars has nine, Uranus has two, and Earth has one. Jupiter, however, has more than seven thousand that are cataloged. They're divided into the Greek camp at L4, which is the Lagrangian point ahead of Jupiter, and the Trojan camp at L5, which is the Lagrangian point behind Jupiter.

"At this time the ESA has not settled on a definite target, but they have selected a dozen potential targets. They plan to announce their selection in the summer of 2023 when the probe is still several months out, and they will attempt a landing that fall."

"Lying scoundrels!" Jack shouted. "They might be able to keep this comet under wraps for now, but they won't be able to maintain the cover-up forever. Their fraud is going to come crashing down on their heads, and then it'll be worse for them than if they had just been straightforward in the first place."

"No doubt about that," Jordy agreed. "But before this country collapses under the weight of ugly reality, the Minoa cover-up is going to get more expansive, more invasive, and more aggressive. We don't have long before we're going to start feeling the heat, maybe only months. We need to start thinking about contingency plans."

"I've been having similar thoughts," Woody replied as he reached for another raspberry scone on the tray on the coffee table. "But I don't want to think about that tonight. Not when Ariele and Sam just arrived."

47

the Compound
Thursday, February 13, 2020

"Here's your refill," Ariele said as she handed Kit another mug of hot chocolate. Then she curled up on the couch close to her friend. The two of them watched the flames flickering in the fireplace for maybe half a minute. Ariele's heart was singing. She was back at the Compound. She was in her favorite room—the great room. She was born-again, a true follower of Yeshua. And she was growing in her understanding. Knowledge was heady stuff.

She turned toward Kit. "So what was the book you were reading earlier today?"

"*The Great Alaskan Dinosaur Adventure.* Jordy recommended it."

"So what's it about?"

"A group of paleontologists and adventures who brave the harsh weather and terrain of Alaska in a search for unfossilized dinosaur bones."

"Sounds like a great read."

"It is."

"I have wished a thousand times," Ariele said longingly, "that I could see a live dinosaur up close."

Kit's face brightened. "I think we'll see them someday."

"What? Unless you're talking about going to Indonesia and seeing a Komodo Dragon, or something like that, how are we going to see a dinosaur?"

"In the coming kingdom of God."

Ariele arched her eyebrows, uncertain whether Kit was serious or punking her. "Are you serious? Dinosaurs walking on Earth again?"

"Serious as a heart attack. The Bible speaks of 'the restitution of all things.' Jordy says that all of the extinct animals and plants will be restored, and after studying it out for myself, I think he's right. When the Lord comes back to establish his kingdom here on Earth, Creation will be brought back into the full glory of its original pristine state."

"Wowzers! I never heard that before. That would be pretty cool if it were true. Can you imagine canoeing down a river, coming around the corner, and passing under a Brontosaurus? That would be sick!"

Kit smiled. "Never really thought of it like that before. But yeah, that would be pretty cool."

Ariele screwed up her mouth, hesitated for a moment, then blurted out the question which had been burning on her soul, "Why did you reject evolution?"

"The evidence just piled up until I was forced to either unplug my brain or submit."

"What kind of evidence?"

"Take intelligent design for example. We would laugh at

the idea that a box of scrap metal could self-assemble into a functioning watch if given enough time, say a million years. A watch can't exist without an intelligent designer. Why don't we laugh at atoms and molecules self-assembling into complex molecules, which self-assembled into simple life forms, which evolved into more complex life forms, which then evolved into all living creatures including man? We ought to be laughing. The simplest living organisms are millions of times more complex than a watch. If we were consistent, we would acknowledge that the complex design we see in nature can't exist without an intelligent designer."

"Been thinking about that argument myself. Pretty hard to miss the voice of God in nature."

"Complex information is another good argument. Computer code, for instance, doesn't just happen. A coder has to write it. Ink and paper sitting in the same room for billions of years won't write one line of code. We all know that. Yet the coding in DNA is millions of times more complex than computer coding, even that used for sophisticated robots. We are forced to conclude that life is the handiwork of the most amazing coder in the universe. We code because we are imitating our amazing Father."

Ariele nodded, soaking the information in.

"Another example is anomalous discoveries in archaeology and paleontology. If you find human footprints and dinosaur footprints together, then they walked on this planet together. If ancient artwork portrays dinosaurs and mammals together, then the artists saw them together. And if you find unfossilized dinosaur bones, then dinosaurs lived in recent history, not millions of years ago."

Ariele raised her eyebrows. "If that kind of evidence is actually laying around, then evolution over hundreds of millions of years is vaporized."

Kit smiled. "It is laying around. Lots of it. It's not merely hearsay and fairytales peddled in questionable books. With my own eyes, I have examined sites where dinosaur and human footprints appear together. I have photographed coal beds where fossilized trees are standing upright through many layers. And I have visited several sites which feature anomalous ancient artwork.

"On top of that, in my digs, I have uncovered unfossilized T-Rex femurs with intact red blood cells and a rib bone from a hadrosaur with nicks that are best explained by a spear point or arrowhead. This kind of geological, archaeological, and paleontological evidence obliterates evolution."

Ariele exhaled long and slow. "I suspect you're right. I want to believe that creation is true. But still, I find it hard when the entire scientific world is convinced of evolution."

Kit set her hand on her friend's arm and nodded reassuringly. "I understand where you're coming from. Been there, done that myself. But there are a few things you have to understand.

"For one thing, not all scientists believe evolution. Many embrace biblical creation. And all of them have paid a price for their stand. Some of them an enormous price.

"For another thing, evolution isn't science. It's a religion—a fanatical religion. If anyone dares to challenge its supremacy, they're railed against as heretics who deny the great god Evolution, and they're hammered with flimsy arguments that are the pseudo-science equivalent of prooftext theology.

"On top of that, there's a mountain of evidence which upholds creation. Men don't reject the evidence on rational grounds. They reject it because they want to believe the lie of evolution. That evil theory sets aside God, trashes the Bible, and trots out the lie of moral relativity. Evolution gives men permission to live and do as they please."

"But are all those scientists intentionally ignoring the facts?"

"Yes. What you have to understand is that this is a spiritual battle, not a mere intellectual debate. The world doesn't want God to be their sovereign. So they walk away and turn to the father of lies. Following his lead, they love and invent lies that defend their rejection of God. Over the centuries this rejection agenda has passed through several permutations from classic idolatry to the rise of atheistic science in Greece, to Rationalism, to sophisticated evolutionary theory. But all of this focus on creation rather than the Creator stems from the same lie—there is no infinite, eternal, almighty Creator God."

"I can see your point. The world has always had its excuses and alternatives."

"That's right. The debate has never been about sincerely weighing the evidence. The movers and shakers of the world have already made their minds up. They ignore the vast majority of the evidence, press a few selectively chosen scraps into service for evolution, brainwash the public with slick marketing, and use the peer-review system to promote evolutionary theory and squelch any evidence or arguments that challenge the status quo."

Ariele sat in silence, biting her lip, struggling with her emotions, trying to absorb and catalog the information. She had counted the cost to follow Yeshua. There was no way she was going to turn back. But she was now more acutely aware than ever how deeply entrenched the world's unbelief was. She wanted to be free of it—every last vestige. But it wasn't going to be easy. Faith was going to take her to places she had never imagined.

48

the Compound
Saturday, February 15, 2020

The UTV skidded around the last corner before Blake's house, spraying snow. Joby, who was squeezed in between Ariele and Sam, kept a firm grip on the grab handle on the dash. Ariele straightened, accelerated out of the curve, and raced for the shoveled parking spot next to the patio roof. At the last second, she braked, cranked the wheel hard, and skidded nearly to a stop, spraying more snow, then goosed it again, nosing the vehicle into an open slot between Jordy's truck and another UTV.

Sam was laughing hysterically as she loosed her hands from the rollbar and the seat. "Girl, I don't know if you're fearless or reckless or both. But you handle this machine like a professional racer. I was holding so tight that my hands are stiff. I can hardly pry them off."

"I do get a bit of a rush from driving this crate fast," Ariele replied.

"There's a bit more to it than that," Joby remarked. "The adrenalin junkie regularly needs to burn up excess energy in edgy endeavors."

"True that," Ariele blushed and confessed. I don't get to push the envelope with snowboarding anymore since I have to lay low on the Compound and avoid the feds. So now the UTV has become one of my favorite outlets."

Sam teased Joby. "I noticed that the laid-back hippie looked like he was actually enjoying the adrenalin rush himself."

He grinned in return. "Before I got to know her, I pretty much avoided adrenalin. Now I think I might be developing a taste for the stuff. She has even gotten me to try her slackline in the barn."

"Emphasis on the *try*," Ariele said, laughing.

The three of them trooped up the path—waist-high snowbanks on each side—and bustled through the garage door into the shop.

"Man, am I glad to be out of the cold," Joby groused as he climbed out of his snowmobile suit and hung it on the rack. "I hate snow. First chance I get, I'm out of here."

"Where would you go?" Sam inquired as she pulled off her snowmobile boots and slipped her feet into her Eddie Bauer mocs.

"I dunno. Somewhere warm."

"But leaving isn't realistic, is it?" she pressed.

"Generally speaking, no. My face is plastered all over the land. And every security camera is looking for my ugly mug. It's probably just wishful thinking."

"But if you really could get away, where would you go?"

"Israel."

"And what would you do there?"

"Eventually, I would like to join a Messianic kibbutz, but first I would have to spend a couple years in the IDF."

"Excuse me," Blake said, interrupting their conversation. "Here you go, Joby. A piping hot mug of hot chocolate. And here's one for you, Sam. And one for you, Ariele." He pointed to the corner of the garage. "The table between the stove and the compressors is loaded with snacks including Baklava and pfeffernusse."

Sam wanted to continue the conversation, but Joby headed for the gaggle of guys hugging the stove, and Ariele followed him.

Jack was filling his mug at the spiced cider bowl when Sam sidled up to him. He turned to face her. "Ariele tells me that you have found the Lord."

"Yes, the Lord was working on me while we were in the swamp. Conversations with Peggy Sue helped me to see that the true meaning of life is found in Jesus. During the drive home, I turned my life over to him. Now the empty spot in my heart that was always begging to be filled with adventure, but never really got filled, is filled with the infinite King and his infinite reward."

"Glad to hear it, Sam. I've been praying for you since the day we met." He raised a hand to make a point—

A shrill whistle pierced the noisy hum of conversation in the shop. Jack and Sam glanced in the direction of the high-pitched summons and noticed Ariele withdrawing her fingers from her mouth.

Blake smiled. "Ladies and gentlemen, the moment you have all been waiting for. Andrius and I have completed the modifications necessary for the larger mirror. So we present to you our motorized telescope platform." He nodded, and Andrius, who was standing on a ladder, pulled a large blue tarp off the unit.

The crowd broke out into applause. The unit was as cutting edge in its appearance and materials as anything NASA could build.

"Dude!" Joby exclaimed. "That's mega awesome."

It was the RUSA signs, however—mounted on all four sides of the cab—that caught everyone's eye.

"Love the NASA-looking signs," Kit said, "but what does RUSA stand for."

Before Blake could respond, Ariele spat out the answer, "Rogue Underground Space Agency."

"How did you know that?" Andrius demanded.

"Didn't," she replied. "Just an educated guess. But I got my own question. How did you make the signs?"

"I cut them out with the plasma table. Had to remake the first one several times until I had a pattern that I liked. Then I made the rest."

Andrius directed their attention to the main features of the unit while Blake narrated. The platform was eight feet wide and sixteen feet long. At the front end and the back end, stabilizing arms rolled out on swivel wheels. The front half featured the telescope cradle, though the telescope was not yet installed. The cab covered the back half. It featured a heated tractor seat, triple-pane windows, a small propane heater, a computer with a full-size keyboard, a four-cup coffee brewer, and a cabinet for storage. The heavy-duty battery packs were stored outside in aluminum cases mounted on the sides of the cab.

After a walk around the exterior, Andrius climbed inside the cab, powered up the unit, and demonstrated its forward, backward, and turning capabilities. It skittered a bit as it turned. He poked a reddened face out the cab door. "Sorry about the jerky movement. The steering algorithms need to be tweaked a bit. I originally wrote the program for a smaller platform with smaller tires. I should have the bugs ironed out in a month or so."

He returned to his chair and demonstrated the stabilization arms, extending and retracting both the fore and the aft pairs. They had an impressive reach of four feet. Then he demonstrated the ability of the cradle to rise six feet on hydraulic arms. After he returned the cradle to the bed, he demonstrated the cradle's ability to swivel 120 degrees. Finally, he demonstrated the ability of the whole unit to rise another eighteen inches.

When he stepped down from the cab, Woody slapped him on the back. "Excellent job, Andrius. I'm sure glad you're on the team."

"Me, too!" Blake agreed, throwing his arm around his sidekick's shoulder. "Without Andrius's help, this thing would have been a heavy clunker that would have been a beast to use."

While everyone gathered around the craftsmen and peppered them with questions, Ariele kept to herself and slowly walked around the unit, marveling. *Can't believe that Irina and I get to use this gem—all the telescope time we want.*

But her hopes were tempered. Though she hated to admit it, she knew that she might not ever get to use the RUSA 72-inch. There were several obstacles in the way. Joby wanted to go to Israel. Federal agents were tightening the noose around the country on the Rogue-aware, preppers, and deucers. And there was no guarantee that the mirror would ever make it to Montana. *But it's sure nice to dream.*

49

Magadan, Russia
Sunday, February 16, 2020

The team reached the outskirts of Magadan in the evening twilight on Sunday, February 16, 2020. A fading "Welcome to Magadan" sign greeted them.

Andy slapped the dashboard. "That's what I'm talking about!"

"Finally!" Irina exclaimed. "I'm so done with Siberia."

"I hear ya," he replied. "Twenty-three days in this drafty cab and nine days riding out storms in the back."

She laughed. "That was nine days too many. Not gonna miss the smell of damp canvas and propane."

Tony sat in silence. Irina elbowed him. "What are you thinking about, bro? You've been gloomy all day."

"Don't get me wrong. I'm glad this stretch is over. But I got a gut feeling that the next stretch is gonna make Siberia look like a Sunday School picnic."

Irina shuddered. His morbid negativity on what lay ahead was starting to get to her. She changed the topic. "First priority is a hotel. I need a hot shower."

"You don't have to convince me," Tony grumbled. "Baby wipes only get you by for a couple days."

"This last stretch from Nizhny Bestyakh is the longest time I have ever gone without a shower."

"I wish my record was only four days," he replied, shaking his head. "It's a couple days north of two weeks."

Andy nodded. "Yeah. We got pretty ripe on those observation and scouting operations in Afghanistan."

Irina dug out her Nebesa Smotret business laptop, activated a local hotspot on her Nebesa Smotret cell phone, and searched for a hotel. "We have several decent options, but I vote for the Magadan Hotel."

"Long as they got showers, hot food, and laundry facilities," Tony replied, "I'll be a happy camper."

***

That evening the boys set up their laptop on the kitchen table and navigated to the Channel One website to catch the noon broadcast live from Moscow. Irina joined them.

The Eurasian news was dominated by familiar stories. The turmoil in eastern Europe from the Baltic states to the Balkans continued with new uprisings in many cities. Russia defended herself before the United Nations, denying that she was meddling in her former Soviet-bloc neighbors. She pointed the finger at American policies and western mercenaries.

The world's oil markets continued their downward spiral. Falling demand in the world and rising exports from the United States and Russia were hammering OPEC. Saudi

Arabia had cut its production another ten percent to maintain oil prices, dropping it to the world's third-largest producer. A pundit observed that this was yet one more indication that we're witnessing the death knell of OPEC, which had long dictated world oil prices. Iran, Qatar, Libya, Algeria, and Venezuela were threatening to leave the organization and join a new petroleum and coal alliance with Russia and China.

The main story was the continuing movement of equipment and troops in Syria, Jordan, and Lebanon in response to Israel's recent attacks on terrorist targets. In the past few days, Syria's air bases had been bustling with activity, receiving many tons of supplies, dozens of aircraft, and a battalion of spetsnaz from Russia.

"Wonder where this is headed?" Andy thought out loud.

"If Dad is right," Tony replied, "it can only be a buildup for the Psalm 83 War or the Russian invasion in Ezekiel 38 and 39."

"Yeah, but how are things going to unfold?"

Irina grabbed the laptop and spun it toward her. "Let's focus on things more immediately related to our mission. We can worry about the future wars in the Middle East later."

Tony laughed. "What do you got in mind, Nikkie?"

"The weather forecast so we can get an idea of what we might face in the Sea of Okhotsk and the North Pacific." She navigated to marine.weather.gov, then weather365.net. There was nothing in the forecast that was cause for alarm. The next few days called for typical late-winter weather with winds from twenty to thirty kilometers per hour and swells from one to three meters. Two early spring storms were brewing out in the Pacific, but neither threatened the Sea of Okhotsk or lower Kamchatka.

"I think we should check SpaceWeather.info," Irina suggested.

"Space!" Tony scorned. "Why should we care about the weather in space? We're taking a fishing vessel to the Bering Sea, not a rocket ship to Mars."

"Because the primary cause of severe weather patterns on Earth is the sun. This website frequently predicts major weather events before the storms develop."

Andy was skeptical. "This I gotta see."

She clicked on the most recent video. "Good morning, listeners. It's 5 a.m. here in Sun Valley, and we have a lot on our plate this morning. To begin with, we have now completed seventeen days in a row with zero sunspots evident on our star. This is unusual itself, but the context is even more so. Normally solar minimums last from six months to a couple years. The current minimum has been going strong for well over three years now, and the sun's magnetic field is showing no signs of strengthening. If anything, it appears to still be decreasing slightly.

"Folks, I have said it before, and I'll say it again. The evidence is mounting that this is not a run-of-the-mill solar minimum like we experience every eleven years or so. This minimum is exceptional. I believe that we're entering a grand minimum. The low sunspot activity could last for decades. If this proves to be the case, then we're not facing the threat of global warming, but the threat of global cooling. The last grand minimum, the Maunder Minimum, which lasted from 1645 to 1715, slammed Europe and America with unusually cold winters.

"Let's move on to coronal holes." He pointed to three dark regions on his photograph of the sun with his laser. "I draw your attention to this unusually massive hole and the two smaller ones associated with it. By my estimation, the large one will be directly over the lower Kamchatka Peninsula on the morning of Saturday, February 22 and will also cover the eastern portion of the Sea of Okhotsk and the northern third of the Kuril Islands. The smaller hole underneath will be centered over Hokkaido and the southern Kuril Islands about a half hour later. The smaller one trailing even farther behind could pose a threat to the state of Washington a few hours after that."

"I give Washington a moderate watch. They won't get any severe activity, but unusual activity is probable. I give Hokkaido and the southern Kuril Islands a severe watch. They can expect quakes that register 7.0 or higher on the Richter scale. And I assign the lower Kamchatka peninsula and the northern Kuril Islands a severe watch. Be advised, the Kamchatka hole is very large and dangerous. It's almost certain to bring an earthquake over 8.0 on the Richter scale. And it will most likely destabilize volcanoes and nurture typhoons in the region."

"Oh my!" Irina gasped. "This could create serious problems for our trip to the Bering Sea."

"Sounds hokey to me," Andy snarked, unimpressed.

"Using sunspots to predict earthquakes was debunked long ago," Tony noted. "It's junk science that belongs in the same category as ancient civilizations on Mars."

"You two weren't paying attention!" Irina retorted. This theory has nothing to do with sunspots. It's based on coronal holes, an entirely different phenomenon."

"So what are coronal holes?" Tony demanded.

"They're not really holes. They're dark regions on the surface of the sun caused by a reduction in the density of the magnetic lines of force, and they allow massive amounts of fast solar winds to escape. When coronal holes directly face Earth, the solar winds interact with Earth's magnetic field and atmosphere and the planet itself. This electrical activity spawns earthquakes, volcanic eruptions, typhoons, and super-cell storms."

Tony rolled his eyes.

"This stuff isn't mythology," Irina insisted. "It's science! Testable and observable science. It makes predictions for large earthquakes with an impressive degree of accuracy. Check out the information on the SpaceWeatherNews.com website for instance."

"So where did you learn about this stuff?"

"Shortly after I arrived at the Compound, Woody enlightened me on the electric universe. One of the tenets of this school is that the stars are not nuclear reactions that will eventually burn out. They're plasma discharges powered by the electricity generated by the galaxy which is spinning in a magnetic field."

"Plasma discharge?"

"Yeah. The sun is a glowing orb of electrified plasma."

"So how does an electric sun cause an earthquake?" Andy asked. "I thought earthquakes were caused when faults slipped."

"That's the old theory. It confuses the cause and the effect. The truth is, earthquakes are not caused when faults slip. Faults slip when earthquakes rock them hard enough."

Andy cocked his head. She had his interest now. "So what causes earthquakes?"

"The solar wind carries an electric charge that interacts with our planet. Some of this energy charges our atmosphere, creating things like electrical storms, lightning, and above-the-clouds lightning (like sprites and jets). And some of it charges Earth's crust and mantle, creating charge imbalances that result in shakings as the imbalances resolve themselves."

"Hold on!" Tony interjected. "Are you saying that earthquakes are electricity passing through the bedrock?"

"Not exactly. Earthquakes are underground thunder caused by underground lightning."

Andy's face lit up. "Now that's a theory that intrigues me. To be honest, when Woody talked to us about electric universe stuff in the past, I tuned him out. I was too busy worrying about geopolitical upheavals and the threat of fundamentalist Islam. I didn't have time for scientific gobbledygook that didn't have any practical application. But if this theory is true, I can see how it offers a predictive edge in the face of threats like earthquakes, volcanoes, and hurricanes."

"And the threat is only going to increase," Irina replied. Earth's magnetic field has been measurably weakening for the past century. This makes the planet more susceptible to the electrical energy from the sun, which means we'll experience more and bigger earthquakes, volcanoes, and storms. On top of that, the big increase in coronal hole activity increases the amount of directed energy we receive from the sun, further increasing these acts of God."

"Does this interaction with the sun have anything to do," Tony asked, "with the climate change we're supposedly experiencing?"

Irina nodded her head. "Absolutely. Climate change is all about solar cycles. Don't get me wrong. Pollution is wrong. But man hurting the environment with poor stewardship is not causing global climate change. And reducing CO_2 emissions will not significantly alter the weather that we experience from the natural cycles. Earth alternates between warming and cooling stretches. Greenland was once so warm that the Vikings planted vineyards and grew wheat there. Then the Little Ice Age hit, and they were forced to largely abandon the land.

"If we look at the pattern of the cycles over the past few thousand years, we're overdue for another cooling cycle."

"So what's the big deal with the global warming message?" Andy asked.

"It's all about control. They're manipulating the world with the fear of man-caused global climate change. The goal is to make the populace desperate enough to fix the problem that they're willing to embrace a solution which takes away their freedom and makes them dependent on the system."

"As Dad often says, if you want to manipulate the masses, you need to manipulate their emotions with manipulated data."

"Exactly. Exploit what you can. Ignore what you can't. Exploit the fact that men focus on the near term and overlook the long term. Capitalize on the short-term warming trend. Ignore long-term weather cycles. Correlate the harsh weather over the past fifteen years with the rise in CO_2 emissions. Ignore the fact that you could just as well correlate it with the rise in video games or social media. Ignore the periods of extreme weather in the past centuries because they can't be correlated with CO_2 emissions. Exploit the fact that men wither in the face of ridicule and scorn. Ridicule all who deny man-caused climate change as ignorant hicks who are opposed to science."

By the time Irina finished her little tirade, the boys were splitting their sides. Her sarcasm could be downright hilarious when she got rolling on some piece of nonsense she disagreed with. And the belly laugh gave them all a much-needed release. They had been on edge for the past few days because they knew that the next stage of their mission still bore significant risk. They needed to hire a fishing boat to take them to the Bering Sea so they could rendezvous with an American trawler. And they needed to do this without drawing the attention of either the local police, known as the militsya, or the Federal Security Service. If either somehow got involved, their cover might not hold up.

50

Magadan, Russia; Sea of Okhotsk
Thursday, February 20, 2020

It was late morning, and Irina was getting discouraged. The team had already spent three frustrating days tracking down captains who fished the waters of the Bering Sea and had gotten nowhere. They had canvassed the docks, diners, boat shops, and taverns asking for names and contact information for captains. Eventually, they had compiled a list with eleven names. But the leads had been hampered by bad addresses and conflicting information.

A half hour earlier, she had crossed number ten off their list. They were down to the last name. Their conversations to that point had been discouraging. Only three of the captains had ever fished outside the Sea of Okhotsk, and none of them were interested in hauling dubious cargo to the Maritime Boundary Line where it would be transferred to another ship. The risk of getting caught by the authorities was simply too high. It meant nothing to them that the trio were Federal Security Service agents and could afford to pay them handsomely. Agents, regardless of which branch, were notorious for demanding bribes and double-crossing those who assisted them.

She pondered the remaining name on her list, Arkady Chugunkin. Rumor had it that he was going back out in a few days on his second Bering Sea trip of the season for pollock. That was what she wanted. Nonetheless, anxiety pummeled her. While five of the captains had suggested him as her best option, noting that he had a reputation for engaging in shady activities, the other five had warned that his ship, the Morskaya Ved'ma (Sea Witch in English), was not seaworthy. The ancient, rusty crate had failed its last three annual inspections and was operating on temporary waivers which, according to rumors, had been purchased with bribes. On top of that, his crew was a bunch of drunks who had all spent time in jail.

Irina sighed. They had to go forward. They had no other options. But where to start? Nobody had a permanent address for him, and his phone had been turned off for over a week. All they had was vague leads. She decided to start with the boatyard. An involuntary cringe coursed through her body. She hated the putrid stench of the place, a noxious mix of diesel, rotting fish, and decaying seaweed.

Their visit to the boatyard, a haphazard conglomeration of aging piers, run-down boat services, and ramshackle sheds, proved to be a dead end. Arkady's ship, tied up on the northernmost pier, was empty. There was no evidence that anyone had been there recently. His rented shed was locked, and there were no footprints in the snow. Moreover, none of the employees or shipmates had seen him for over a week.

Next, they visited the two dilapidated hotels where the captain had been known to rent a room between fishing runs. But neither of the clerks had seen him for a couple months, and he wasn't listed in the guest registries.

They checked with his first mate Pyotr, who was staying at one of the hotels, but he hadn't seen his boss since they had returned from their last trip a few weeks earlier.

After that, they paid a visit to his brother-in-law, Vadim, on the other side of town, who claimed that he hadn't seen the captain since he had stopped in for dinner a couple weeks earlier.

Finally, they checked the taverns that Arkady frequented. At their second stop a cheerful drunk, who claimed to be an occasional crew member, insisted that the captain was staying in one of the rooms over The Three-Legged Dog. He had seen him coming down the stairs yesterday.

By the time they obtained this intel, it was well after lunch, and Irina was unable to fend off the complaints of her companions over their grumbling stomachs any longer. They had noticed a pizzeria and hankered to satisfy their craving for American food. She conceded reluctantly. But their expectations were dashed to the ground. The pepperoni was pathetic, and the cheese was—as Tony had aptly so described it—practically AWOL.

After their dining mishap, the three walked to The Three-Legged Dog to investigate the lead. The bartender informed them that the captain was staying on the third floor in Room 6.

At Arkady's door, Irina raised her hand to knock, but

Andy grabbed it and put his finger to his lips. Two voices could be heard inside, engaged in a passionate discussion. One sounded like Vadim, his brother-in-law, whom they had just talked to.

"Listen to me, Arkady. I'm telling you. A woman and two men with the Federal Security Service are looking for you."

"What did they want?"

"They said that they want to hire you and your boat."

"But you don't trust them?"

"No."

"How do you know that they're not honestly looking to hire a boat for an unusual load?"

"I don't know for sure. All I know is that they made me uneasy."

"What made you uneasy? Was it the fact that they're Federal Security Service agents or was it something they said or did?"

"I just don't trust them. The guys carry themselves in a manner that suggests a military background, likely Spetsnaz. And the gal has a cold professionalism about her that reminds me of the female FSB agents that I met on several occasions when I was young and dumb and working with the Bratva in Moscow."

"So you're worried because FSB agents carry themselves like FSB agents?"

"No. That's not what I'm saying."

"Then what are you saying?"

"I don't know. I guess it just bothers me that FSB agents

are asking about you. Why are they looking for you?"

"I don't know, Vadim. Maybe they want a cut of the vodka that some of my boys were accused of stealing from the warehouse last week. Or maybe they want a cut from the spotty fishing results I've had the past few years?"

"I'm serious, Arkady. Round up your crew and head out to sea as soon as possible. Get out of here before they find you. You don't want to get tangled up with them. If you stay away long enough, maybe they'll get tired of looking for you and go away."

Irina pushed Andy's hand away and pounded on the door. "FSB, open up." The two brothers looked at each other dumbfounded. Tony nodded his head, encouraging his brother to follow her lead. It was all-in or all-nothing at this point.

Inside the apartment, the men had stopped talking. Two chairs scraped across the wood flooring. Presumably, they were standing up. A nervous silence reigned. Those outside listened for the response of those inside. Those on the inside hoped against hope that those on the outside would leave them alone and go on their way. Irina banged the door again.

"Just a minute," bellowed Arkady. His boots lumbered across the floor toward them. A chain safety lock slid out and rattled against the wooden door. The knob turned, and the man cracked the door a few inches. "Who are you looking for?"

"Arkady Chugunkin, the owner and captain of the Morskaya Ved'ma," she replied as she flashed her Federal Security Service badge through the narrow opening.

The man nervously replied, "Look. I know that my crewmembers are a bunch of troublemakers. But they swore to me that they weren't behind last week's liquor store robbery. Nonetheless, if I do happen to find out that any of them were involved, I swear I'll turn them in myself. I've got my ears to the ground."

Irina tried to push the door open, but the man stood his ground and blocked the way.

Tony pushed Irina out of the way and slammed his body against the door, forcing it open. Arkady stumbled backward and fell. Irina burst through the opening, grabbed him by the coat collar, and raised him to his feet. "The FSB has a lot of dirt on you and your crew," she began. "But that's not why we're here today. However, if you don't cooperate, things can rapidly change."

Arkady and Vadim looked at each other nervously. Irina picked up on their unintentional clues. *Must have played the right cards.* She pointed to the table, and the two sat back down. Andy closed the door, then stationed himself in front of it. Tony stood a few feet from the table, arms crossed, staring at the men, looming over the situation like a cat ready to pounce.

Irina sat down, swept the bottle of vodka and two half-full glasses aside, and began. "We need a boat," she began, "and we're interested in hiring you, your ship, and your crew."

"What do you need it for?"

"A classified mission that involves transporting us and a crate to a precise location in the Bering Sea near the

Maritime Boundary Line where we'll rendezvous with another vessel. You'll then transfer us and the crate to the other vessel with your boom."

"That sounds like a smuggling operation."

"Or an operation that looks like smuggling."

"How big is the crate?"

"It measures 2.1 meters per side and is 0.5 meters thick. The total weight is a little over one metric ton."

"What are you offering?"

"Twenty million rubles for yourself and sixty million rubles for your crew. We'll pay the first half upfront once we and the crate are on board. We can pay with Bitcoin or a bank transfer from an account in the Cayman Islands. Once the crate is successfully offloaded onto the transfer vessel, we'll forward the second tranche with the same payment method as soon as we have access to decent high-speed internet where we can make a secure connection."

"Twenty million rubles is a lot of cabbage."

"There's a lot at stake. The threat we're tracking is a danger to the entire world ... not merely Russia."

He closed his eyes to avoid her piercing stare and tried to wrap his brain around the supposed gravity of the mission, the potential upside of a lucrative job with the FSB, and the potential dangers of working with the Russian government. Opening his eyes again and meeting her gaze, he asked, "When do you want to sail?"

"Tonight, if possible."

The answer jolted him. He turned to his brother-in-law, who nodded his head *yes*, then turned back to Irina. "I think

I can make that work, though it would be a late start. But …" He hesitated and bit his lip.

"Speak your mind, captain."

"We got two problems. First, if you really want to leave tonight, I'm gonna need your help loading and storing supplies."

"My two assistants can help with that." Irina eyed him waiting for him to divulge the second problem. "And?" she asked, gesturing with her hands.

He fiddled with his hands, then exhaled heavily. "To put it bluntly, we're cash strapped. Harvest has been down the past few years. I have no cash reserves. Can you advance me five million rubles to buy supplies for the trip? We need groceries, fuel, oil, a new winch, and some new cables and ropes. Actually, can you make that seven and a half million, just in case some of the guys have bills to pay before we sail?"

"That won't be a problem."

"Good. Send it to Vadim's business account."

Irina looked at Vadim, then back to the captain.

"Vadim owns a business that purchases and delivers supplies for the fishing boats. Many of the captains depend on him."

"I see." She logged into her TOR browser on her secure phone, logged into her Buster account, accessed a Cayman Islands account that Red had given her access to, entered Vadim's bank number and routing number, and transferred the requested amount. "Done," she announced.

Vadim checked his account on his phone. Sure enough, a transfer of seven and a half million rubles was pending.

"Looks like we're golden," Arkady said. "I'll give my men a call."

"There's one difficulty," Vadim noted.

"What's that?" Irina asked.

"My truck is in the shop and the needed part won't arrive for a couple weeks. It's getting shipped from Krasnoyarsk on a freight truck that makes a ton of stops on the way."

"We have a solution."

"Oh?"

Irina smiled. "We need to get rid of the Army truck that we used to transport our cargo."

"An Army truck?" he sneered. "That's the problem I have right now. When the Army retires a truck, there isn't much life left in it. I can hardly keep the one I have running."

Tony smiled. "Our truck isn't your typical retired military vehicle. It was owned by a headquarters company and has low miles. It's in great shape: rebuilt engine, lots of new components. We drove it here from Moscow without a hitch except for the water pump. And it comes with several crates of spare parts and supplies."

"Are you authorized to sell it? I don't want to be thrown in jail for the illegal possession of a vehicle owned by the FSB."

"There's nothing to worry about. It isn't registered as government property. We're on a covert mission, and all of our equipment has been purchased under our false identities."

"How much do you want for it?"

"Nothing. If you want it, it's yours. Consider it a gift from your country."

His eyebrows raised. "All right then. I'll take it."

Arkady grinned with anticipation. Even if they never dropped their nets, this trip would be his most lucrative by far. And if the fish cooperated, it would be bigger yet. He could hardly wait to get started. He stood up. "We should unload the crate immediately so I can send Vadim with the truck to get the supplies."

"Sounds good to me," Irina replied.

"I'll call my first mate, Pyotr," he added, "and have him meet us at the boat. Once the crate is on board, I'll have him go round up the crew."

At 4:04 that afternoon, Pyotr lifted the crate out of the back of the truck, swung the boom toward the Sea Witch with one smooth motion, retracting it along the way, and set it down on the upper deck. Andy was impressed. It reminded him of the magic that he had seen special operations chopper pilots work in difficult terrain. Pyotr then bounded down the plank and hopped into his red Hyundai Solaris. As he sped off to round up the crew, Arkady tossed a massive strap over the top of the crate, the first of five that would secure the load.

On the pier below, a shower of ice crystals exploded into the air as Andy and Tony dragged the frosted tarp back over the top of the last hoop on the truck bed. The crystals glittered like diamonds in the light of the low-hanging evening sun. After the tarp was secured, the boys and Vadim drove to Arkady's shed and unloaded most of the crates and equipment, then a giddy Vadim jumped into his new set of wheels, and departed to purchase the supplies for the journey.

While the boys and Irina watched the truck barrel down the road, Arkady hollered to them from the upper deck, "Take your stuff up to the wheel room and get out of the wind. I'll give you a tour and get you settled in your room later."

Glad for an opportunity to get out of the biting cold, they lugged their bags up the gangway, barged into the glass-lined room, and dropped them on the floor underneath the propane heater on the back wall.

"Other than the wind," Irina huffed, "There isn't much difference between outside and inside." She held her mittens near the glass doors of the heater and warmed her hands.

"Gonna contact Woody?" Andy asked.

"Yeah," she replied. "Soon as my fingers thaw out."

A few minutes later, she sat on one of her duffel bags, pulled out her secure phone, logged into the *Rogue Underground* website with her stiff fingers, and sent Woody a text. MIRROR LOADED. TEAM ONBOARD. SHIP DEPARTS TONIGHT. NO CONTACT UNTIL ALASKA. Then she checked her inbox. The only message was from Woody. SKYGAZER CHASSIS DONE. JAILBIRDS IN BIG SKY. SWAMP TEAM BACK. ALL SEND LOVE. PRAYING. This was good news. Especially the update on Ariele and Sally. Woody was probably ecstatic. Well, maybe not. A smile with a twinkle in his eye was about as much excitement as he ever showed.

But the text took her down a melancholy path. Would she ever see Blake again? Montana? Join her friends in laughter in the lodge around the fireplace? How about her family? She shook her head in frustration at herself. She didn't want to sink into a funk with Tony.

The ship shuddered, rousing her from her sullen thoughts. From somewhere deep in its bowels, the massive power unit had coughed, then began to run roughly. Over the next few minutes, the awkward chug slowly morphed into the distinct rumble of a diesel engine.

A half hour later, a fuel truck lumbered up the battered surface of the concrete pier and parked next to the ship. Two men uncoiled a large hose, dragged it up the ramp, connected it to the fill tube, and began filling the ship's diesel tanks. Minutes later, the crew began to arrive, bundled up in parkas to fend off the below zero weather. Some parked their vehicles near the shed and plugged them in. Others were dropped off by girlfriends and wives. One by one, they carried their seabags up the ramp and disappeared into the crew hatchway.

Around six, Arkady burst into the wheel room, where Irina and the guys were hugging the propane heater to ward off the chill of the new cold front which was descending. "Leave your bags here for now. I'll give you a tour." He vanished back down the narrow stairwell. They followed him. At the bottom of the claustrophobic stairs, Irina reached out to steady herself and immediately retracted her hand. Though the diesel engines had been running for an hour and a half, and the vents were emitting a hint of warmth, the walls were still cold to the touch.

Arkady turned to his right down a narrow passageway and pointed to rooms on both sides. "These are the crew quarters. Rooms 1 through 5 have two narrow bunks with a tiny closet between them. Room 6 is reserved for the second and third mates. It has two single beds with drawers underneath". He pointed to Room 5, the far room on the left. "Alex, the three of you will be staying in this room with Sasha, one of the cooks." Irina was mortified. It had never dawned on her that she might have to share a room with a stranger.

She poked her head in the doorway to get a glimpse of their quarters. A pudgy young man in his early twenties smiled at the pretty brunette and jumped up from his bunk. "I'm Sasha. The guys call me Kartoshka."

She resisted the urge to giggle. "I'm Aleksandra Aksakova. You can call me Alex. What's with the nickname?"

"I serve potatoes with most of my meals. They're cheap, filling, and nutritious."

Irina smiled and hurried after the captain who had continued down the passageway. Just past the crew quarters, he pointed to the right. "This is the head." The trio squeezed into the cramped room. Four sinks on one wall. Two tiny shower stalls and two small toilet stalls on the other. There was barely room to stand between the sinks and the stalls. "We have two head rules. The first is, don't use the wrong heads. That's a capital offense. This is the main head. It's the only one with hot water and showers. All share this room equally. The one in the engine room is for engine-room and maintenance personnel only. The one on the bridge is for the captain and mates on watch only. The one on the main deck is for the hands and mates. You three will have the same head privileges as the mates.

"The second is the water ration rule. Crew members are allowed a one-minute shower after their shift on workdays when they've gotten dirty with fish slime. Otherwise, they're limited to a sink bath." Irina rolled her eyes. *Lovely. This is gonna be worse than sponge bathing in the back of the Army truck.*

The next stop was the galley. The diminutive room was barely big enough for four tables that seated six men each and three feet of walkway in front of the serving counter. On either side of the entry, bookshelves filled with books and DVDs rose to a height of three feet. A chalkboard stood over the shelf on the left side of the door and a corkboard over the right. The shift schedule was written on the chalkboard. Several oceanographic maps, a few newspaper clippings, and a dozen photos were pinned to the corkboard. Behind the serving counter, a tiny kitchen could be seen.

"Beyond the galley," he noted, "in the hallway on the left, you'll find the first mate's room and my room. In the hallway on the right, you'll find the dry storage room, cooler, and freezer." He turned and faced them. "The meals aren't fancy around here, but they're nutritious and filling. We eat lots of pork, sausage, beets, cabbage, potatoes, bread, and cheese. And we don't take kindly to complaints about the cooking. If people complain, we chop them up and use them for chum."

Irina fought a smile. *Reminds me of grandpa's tough talk. Used to think it was him. Must be military and sailor talk.*

After the dining facility, he showed them the engine room, the fish freezer, the compressors, the maintenance shop, the fish processing area on the main deck, the crane, and the lifeboats and life jackets.

When the tour was finished, the guys went topside to help the crew load and store supplies. Irina, feeling a tension headache coming on, retreated to the galley, hoping she could ward it off with coffee, sugar, and a chapter of *Anna Karenina*. Sasha kindly provided her with caffeine and chocolate salami, but he dropped a bomb on her Tolstoy plans. "The Captain always serves the crew a special meal after we set sail, and I'm shorthanded in the kitchen. One of the cooks is helping to load supplies and the other hasn't shown up yet. Can you lend me a hand?"

The request struck Irina as odd. Did this imply that the captain hadn't informed his crew that she was an officer with the FSB? Or was Kartoshka simply a little slow? Either way, she liked the cherubic fellow and didn't want him to suffer for an inconvenience that she had caused. "Yeah. I can help. Where do you want me to start?"

He pointed to a pile of groceries. "You can start by putting that stuff away. Some go to the freezer, some to the fridge, and some to dry storage. Try to keep things organized. And you'll have to hustle. They'll be hauling a lot more down over the next few hours.

"When you get all the groceries put away," he added, pointing to the corner, "then you can prep that bag of potatoes for baking."

Irina groaned. *Anna Karenina* was going to have to wait, again.

Ten minutes before midnight, Irina, her back and arms

sore from working in the kitchen, watched from the wheelhouse, which was finally warm, as the last two members of the crew staggered up the gangway. She was steamed. *God help us if they're allowed to drink on the ship.* A few minutes later, the captain began barking orders over the intercom for launch. "Throttle up!" She felt the vibration increase as the engine revved up. "Cast off!" The crew untied and stowed the ropes which held them to the pier, then retracted the gangplank. "Set sail!" At precisely midnight, the Sea Witch pulled away from the pier.

Irina joined the guys at the rail to watch the lights of the city sink below the horizon. Glancing at the crew, huddled in small groups, she felt the angst of their bittersweet moment. They were leaving loved ones behind for a dangerous job. For the first time in her life, she empathized with those who engaged in risky lines of work and those who worried about the risk-takers. Now she knew for herself what it felt like to shoulder the burden of dangerous employment. She was a changed woman. Never again would she take soldiers, or fisherman, or oil workers, or spies, or other any other risky jobs for granted.

When the last light on the distant hills disappeared, Tony nudged her and nodded with his head toward the door. She nodded back and followed him to the galley below.

The three were too hungry and too tired to engage in conversation. They shoveled in the steak and potatoes, chased it down with some chocolate salami, then retired to their room. Within minutes, the guys were snoring away. They had prior experience at sea, so the rolling and pitching hardly fazed them. But this was Irina's first time, and she felt like she was trying to sleep on a carnival ride. Her discomfort was aggravated by the fact that their beds were thin mattresses on sheets of plywood. She forced herself to take her mind off her trials and count her blessings. She had landed her cowboy. Jack and Sally were safe. Sam and Ariele were back. The telescope chassis was finished. The hardest part of the mission—what they had come to call the Russian Run—was over. Now it was just a matter of time. They and the mirror were headed for the Bering Sea and a rendezvous with an American trawler that would take them to Alaska. Then they would make their way to Puget Sound. After that ... *Montana*.

Made in United States
North Haven, CT
29 April 2023